THE
CONDOR
SONG

*The legal expertise of John Grisham meets the
environmental activism of Barbara Kingsolver in
this thriller by veteran author Darryl Nyznyk.*

—Sheila M. Trask, ForeWord Review

THE CONDOR SONG

DARRYL NYZNYK

Cross Dove Publishing, LLC
Redondo Beach, California

First printing 2013

ISBN 978-0-9656513-9-4
LCCN 2012946884

DEDICATION

To my mother, Vera:
thank you for the determination to hold truths dear
and the work ethic to stay the course through the struggle.

To my father, Leo:
thank you for the sense of life's whimsy and
the understanding that "it will all work out" if you
keep moving forward.

To both my parents:
thank you for life's guidance, complete loyalty,
unflagging support, and the joys of a happy family.

ONE

THE JOHN MUIR TRAIL cuts a tortuous track across the rugged peaks of California's southern Sierra Nevada Mountains. Approximately one hundred forty-five miles south of the trail's head sits the Golden Staircase—a treacherous maze of switchbacks carved into sheer cliffs that fall off sharply to the boulders of Palisades Creek. Vegetation is sparse along the staircase as only small groves of foxtail pines occasionally break the monotony of grey granite. It was in one of those groves that the assassin waited.

His job this day would be comparatively easy. The former East German snowman had made a fortune in the years since the fall of the Iron Curtain doing exactly what this assignment demanded. There would be no witnesses along this rugged trail. It was late in the year, and only the hardiest of souls would consider venturing into the Sierra Nevada backcountry when snows threatened. Fortunately, his prey was one such soul. The seventy-four year old intended victim would never know what hit him. The seven-millimeter rifle hanging across the assassin's back would take the old man's head right off.

Buck Anderson stepped gingerly along the steepening track, forty pounds of food and pack equipment weighing heavy on his back. An occasional misstep sent loose rock cascading to the frothing waters of Palisades Creek yet barely interrupted his fevered pace to Mather Pass.

Buck had noticed the charcoal clouds peeking over the ridge at the top of the staircase early that morning as he broke camp in Grouse Meadow. He'd considered staying another night on the meadow's velvet grasses, but blue skies overhead convinced him he could make it through the pass before the weather turned.

He smiled as he labored on, his breath coming in shorter gasps. Icy wind impeded his progress, and he realized he might have miscalculated.

"You've got a helluva sense of humor, Lord," he whispered as he glanced heavenward and smiled. "I should've learned by now not to try to outguess you."

He was confident he could make it through the pass before the storm broke. The problem was that he wouldn't be able to do the sightseeing his treks were all about. He had to focus on getting through the pass to shelter. The sights would wait for another time.

The cold bit at the exposed flesh of his face and hands and pierced his flannel shirt, denim jeans, and thermal underwear. He wouldn't stop to don his parka, however, until he reached Muir Point, a narrow plateau upon which Buck would take his only rest before putting his head down to make the last push through the pass.

The assassin pulled his wool skullcap over his face and tugged at his gloves before he lifted the binoculars to the eyeholes. He had trained himself to withstand the hours of waiting his job entailed. Even in the bitter cold, he could handle the waits by continually changing position to maintain circulation. The air this day promised a cold he hadn't experienced in many years, however, and he knew he'd have to find shelter if his quarry didn't appear soon.

As the assassin's appendages grew numb and he was about to drop the glasses and move to dispel that numbness, he caught sight of movement on the trail two hundred yards below. He waited another instant until his man stepped from behind a large boulder into full view. The assassin placed the binoculars neatly on his pack, removed the glove from his right hand, and lifted the mask from his face. He flexed his fingers against the numbness and swung the seven-millimeter from his back. The biting cold was forgotten as he focused on the narrow plateau upon which his prey would die. He permitted his concentration to waiver only an instant when his victim stopped on that very plateau as if he wished to provide the best possible target. The assassin smiled.

———————

Buck glanced over the edge. Palisades Creek was like a waterfall at this point, the terrain so steep that the water tumbled over itself and the rocks and boulders three hundred feet below.

He stretched to his full height, just over six feet, to suck in a lung full of cold air and marvel at the view. He smiled and nodded at the beauty of this place even as the cold cut him, and he decided to don his parka. Buck made a jerking turn, slightly up the slope, to swing his pack to his right arm, remove it, and extract the jacket.

The crack of the assassin's rifle shattered the brittle air at the instant Buck moved. The weapon's projectile struck a glancing blow that sent Buck's pack hurtling over the edge and spun him around completely. He teetered precariously with his back to the gorge. His left arm reached for balance, his hand clawing air for a hold to prevent his fall, but he found none. He tumbled backwards ... in slow motion, each millisecond lasting an eternity as he struggled to stay upright. His eyes scoured the cliff face in search of anything to grab; but he saw nothing, and for a split second, he knew his end had come. Then he struck the ledge. The shock jarred him; bolts of pain shot through his back and neck. His body bounced and started a new descent, but the fall's slight interruption provided him one last desperate glance, and he spied the root.

Its two-inch diameter snaked out of the cliff face, curled like a half-moon for three feet in open air, and then bit again into the earth at the end of the ledge upon which he'd bounced. He reached desperately until his fingers locked onto the wayward root. His body continued downward, however, and he closed his eyes in concentration as his body pulled his left arm to its full extension before it crashed against the face of the cliff. He twisted in the gusting wind and swirling snow and then smashed against the rock again. His weight tore at his fingers.

Buck was dazed and in excruciating pain, yet somehow he knew he had only seconds to assess his situation. His right shoulder was broken; his arm hung useless at his side. The rest of his body appeared intact, however, and that would have to be enough.

Buck had never taken his physical condition for granted. At seventy-four, his arms and legs were supple and strong from years of rigorous outdoor adventure. His mind, too, had stayed sharp, for oftentimes he'd found himself in trying circumstances that required creative thought and action simply to survive. There was never time to take his physical and mental capabilities for granted. Instead, he thanked God every day for the gifts with which he'd been blessed. As he dangled fingertips from death, Buck struggled to clear his mind. His fingers could not hold much longer.

His mind played with thoughts of letting go, ending the struggle, and going to his maker. He was prepared for that. He'd been prepared for death for years—not in a defeated way, for he loved the world, but rather at peace, accepting the specter of death if it came despite every effort to survive because he knew death was simply a new beginning.

In times past, he'd managed to work up the will to survive impossible situations through prayer and the realization that he still had work to do. On this occasion that realization was stronger than any before. He couldn't die on the rocks of Palisades Creek where his remains would never be found. If this was his time, the world had to know he was murdered, because without that knowledge, people would never search for the reason, and they would never learn what he had discovered.

Buck's booted feet scraped the cliff face in frantic search of a protrusion onto which they could hold and relieve the pressure on his numbing fingers. Without the use of his right arm, he had no idea how he would balance and grip, but he gave it little thought. He had to survive. Finally, his right boot caught the lower lip of a crack that ran horizontally through the rock face at knee level. He glanced up at his red-tipped fingers and willed the aching joints to hold just a few seconds longer. His right foot gripped the lip, and he pushed upward with his numbing right leg. The movement relieved some of the load borne by his fingers, and without thought, he flexed his left arm pulling his body up and forward, then released his finger grip and re-caught the root with a full hand.

In an instant he was standing erect, the ledge upon which he'd bounced at chin level. His left foot continued its own search of the rock wall and soon found a hold that carried him higher still until finally he was waist high and able to lean on the three-foot-wide shelf. With his teeth, he locked onto another smaller root for balance, quickly repositioned his good hand to another firm hold, and threw a leg onto the ledge. Only when he was safely atop the shelf, breathing heavily and leaning back against a stone wall did he begin to understand his predicament.

It was a gunshot that destroyed his right shoulder and sent him over the edge. He was sure of that. He resisted thoughts of "why" because it didn't matter now. He had to survive.

As far as Buck could tell, except for his right arm, his body, though throbbing with pain and cold, was sound. He reached down to the outside of his left boot, lifted the pant leg, and withdrew a large hunting knife from its leather sheath. Whoever had been up there waiting for him in this wilderness would soon be at the plateau's edge to view his handiwork. If that weren't enough to convince Buck he'd have to move quickly, the fact he would freeze to death in the growing cold did. His pack and its contents bobbed down-stream in the roiling waters of the creek, beyond rescue. His only hope of survival was to confront the killer.

Buck scanned the cliff face above him. The Muir Point plateau was a good eight feet above his head. Although several hand and footholds presented themselves, his clear thinking told him it would not work with only one good arm. Even the tree roots from the plateau's lone Foxtail offered little aid. As his eyes moved beyond the roots, however, he saw the ramp-like path that provided a narrow way to the top.

"Shit!" whispered the assassin, for once letting his emotions escape his taciturn veneer.

The old man moved at the exact instant he squeezed the trigger. It wasn't a clean shot … but he went over. Either his body lay broken amid the churning waters of the creek, or he was hanging precariously to the last threads of a life that would be taken from him shortly.

Snow fell with greater force, powered by black clouds and a wind that whined angrily. The assassin leaned into the wind and picked his way cautiously down the slope. It was several minutes before he finally stood at the edge of Muir Point, peering over the side. Far below, evidence of the old man's fallen pack was visible as the rushing waters surged over rocks groping for articles they hadn't already claimed. Yet there was no sign of the body. Maybe it was already washed away, although somehow, as his eyes followed the creek's path, he knew that wasn't the case.

He leaned out a little further, holding his weapon behind him for balance. He immediately saw the ledge. It was about ten feet below and clearly bore the imprint of a person's buttocks and legs in the snow. Then, just to the right, he could make out subtle footprints moving up a narrow ramp, and he understood.

He turned sharply, his weapon poised at his side. With his free hand, he unzipped the top of his snowsuit and withdrew a revolver for the close quarter combat he now anticipated. Before moving toward the rocks lining the plateau, he repositioned the rifle across his back and cinched the strap tight over his chest to keep the clumsy weapon out of the way as he searched for the old man.

It was quickly clear his prey had lost everything except the clothes on his back. It was also clear, from the elongated prints of a shambling step he noted at the flat just above the ramp, that the old man was hurt badly or was so cold he could barely move. It was possible he lay dead, frozen in the numbing cold, but the assassin didn't believe that. He knew the old man was still alive. He knew his prey awaited him.

———

Buck pressed deep into the fissure of a boulder, first to protect his body from the increasing wrath of the storm, and second to hide from his pursuer in a place from which he could launch a surprise attack. The fissure was in a large boulder at a level approximately four feet above the ground. It was tucked in behind another boulder, thus creating a darkened cave-like opening with access directly onto the path his pursuer would have to take if he were to find him. Buck's hope was that the dark would prove impenetrable to his pursuer's eyes long enough to enable him to attack. His fear was that his mind and body would be too numb to carry it out.

He recognized the signs of the death-sleep brought on by freezing temperatures and over-exposure. The warm, soothing desire to close his eyes and sleep was overpowering, and it was only his belief that he had to be found that strengthened him to fight a little longer.

The old man's shuffling gait left clear signs in the deepening snow. The assassin moved quickly for, despite his caution, there was need of urgency. He needed to complete the kill, dispose of the body, and return to shelter to ride out the storm before he too became a victim.

The assassin considered the possibility of an attack. It would come from one of the dark places between the large boulders. He adjusted his goggles against the now heavy snow, pressed his right arm to the outside of the nearest boulder and sidestepped warily around it. At the junction of two enormous rocks, he hesitated. *This would be the place*, he thought. He peered around the corner and into the dark, cave-like opening. He smiled smugly, pushed away from the nearest rock with his weapon in front of him, and stepped across the mouth of the opening. He squinted to adjust to the darkness when suddenly he heard a whistling sound as of some object falling from the sky. He glanced up in time only to glimpse the body that hurtled at him and struck in a rush of feathers and overpowering force. In reflex he squeezed the trigger. The explosion pierced the wind as he stumbled backwards and fell, striking his head.

Then came the old man. Out of the blackness he flew and fell atop the assassin, who struggled feebly with consciousness. The old man was weak; the assassin could feel it. Yet the blow to his head caused him a moment's paralysis; a moment he knew would be his last.

Buck dragged his blade across the assassin's throat, cutting deep with his diminishing strength as the killer struggled frantically under his weight to cast off the effects of the paralysis. The assassin's face was a mask of rage as with gritted teeth and bulging eyes he gave up his last breath in a gurgling gust of blood from his throat. His body convulsed once and then lay still.

Buck pushed himself to a sitting position atop the dead man. His left hand and fingers were numb, almost beyond feeling, but he struggled to remove the assassin's clothing.

With one hand, the work was agonizingly slow, but soon he had donned the assassin's snowsuit and gloves, pulled the stocking cap, face mask, and goggles over his head, and leaned against a boulder rubbing the suit's warmth into his body. Life returned to his limbs slowly with excruciating pain, but he didn't mind. It meant he was alive, if only for a short time longer.

Snow pelted Buck. He peered around a boulder to the path of the Golden Staircase. The raging wind and driving snow obliterated visibility beyond his shelter, and Buck knew the storm was becoming a blizzard. He sank slowly back behind the rock and glanced at the freezing body of the dead man. He was tired and sure that various parts of his own body were frozen. If he did live, he would lose these parts, but that was thought for a later time. Now he needed to get back between the boulders and generate enough heat to survive.

With his last strength he dragged the body of his assailant to the darkened shelter, and pulled it atop him between the rocks. His eyelids were heavy, his mind exhausted. After several minutes of struggling to stay awake, he knew he would not be able to do so. He smiled and leaned back, casting his eyes skyward into the swirling snow. For an instant, clarity returned and the storm seemed to abate. A line of sight heavenward opened, and he could see the dark shape circling higher on massive wings spread to catch the gusts of savage winds.

Buck's smile broadened. He whispered, "Thanks old man," before the creature disappeared and Buck drifted off to sleep.

TWO

IT WAS AN OBNOXIOUS sound, dissonant, awkward, and shrill. It mocked him, over and over, in discordant, tinny tones that played at Led Zeppelin a million miles away yet so close he could no longer ignore it. Slowly, painfully, the fog of his mind lifted and consciousness came to him. It was his Razr, the ancient, pocket-thin cell phone he despised. With eyes closed to manage the pain, he reached for the nightstand, his fingers searching as his brain demanded that he throw the device far away. But that would do no good. He couldn't throw it far enough that the sound would disappear. When his hand finally found it, it vibrated urgently, and the ring tone started again. He flipped it open, dragged it to his ear.

"Yes," he slurred, barely audibly.

"Mr. Donovan?" The frantic, high-pitched voice on the other end hesitated. "Mr. Donovan, this is Patty ... from the office. You asked me to make sure you were awake?"

"Patty?" he grunted, turned over, and finally opened his eyes to the debilitating glare of the morning sun.

"Mr. Donovan, you're supposed to be in court at 9:00," she said anxiously. "It's 8:30, sir."

Sean Michael Donovan's eyes shot open. The pain pierced his brain. It pulsed and pounded and tried to force the eyes shut again but he couldn't permit it. He struggled to sit up, placed his left hand to his forehead, applied pressure, and moaned softly.

"Mr. Donovan? Are you okay?"

"Yeah ... Patty ... thanks ... for calling," he mumbled.

"I've been calling every five minutes since 8:00—just like you asked. I was getting worried. Are you okay? Should I ask Mr. Nelson to go down to the courthouse?"

"Mr. Nelson? Jim? No ... thanks ... I'm fine Patty. I'll be there. Thanks for the call."

Donovan flipped the phone shut as Patty started to say something else. He threw his legs over the edge of his bed and hung his head to dispel the dizziness ... to catch himself ... to get right.

"Dammit!" he thought and struggled to his feet and the bathroom.

Sean liked to remember that Mondays had always been bad for him. He told himself he had always avoided setting hearings or client meetings or anything else on Monday mornings because he liked to forget the office on weekends, and it usually took Monday mornings to get back into it. But it was a lie. It hadn't always been so. Weekends used to be extensions of the week, and whatever energy and passion he'd mustered for his work during the week stayed with him through the weekend and into Monday. He never forgot. He never overslept.

He hated to admit it might be age catching up to him. How could it be? There were plenty of early-fifties attorneys at the top of their game. They weren't forgetting or oversleeping or having to have their secretaries call every five minutes to make sure they were where they were supposed to be. No ... it wasn't age, but the reality that was even more disheartening than age was that he just didn't give a shit. He couldn't bring himself to admit it fully because the few clients he had really cared about their cases. Yet that was it; he knew it. His clients cared, but he couldn't find it anymore.

Sean made it to the courthouse on time for his hearing. Had Judge Kinnesaw been timely in taking the bench, he would have been late for the first calendar call. But she'd been delayed herself. She didn't come out of her chambers to face the fidgeting, time anxious attorneys strewn about her courtroom until 9:15. By then, Sean had downed four aspirin, splashed cold water on his face, brushed his teeth, run out the door with his electric shaver in hand, and made the fifteen minute drive to the courthouse from his Torrance apartment. He negotiated the security checkpoint at the courthouse doors and took the elevator to the third floor, where he jogged to Department J, looked into the courtroom, and found that the judge had not yet come out.

Five minutes later, Sean was sitting uncomfortably in the gallery between two young attorneys he didn't know from any of the other young attorneys in the courtroom. He was sweating from the exertion, and his frayed tweed sport coat, the only relatively clean garment hanging in his closet, smelled of that sweat and other odors that emanated from his unshowered body. His hair was askew because when he tried to brush it quickly before running out the door, it hadn't worked. The sleep-kinked hair and natural cowlicks that still worked their way through his thinning mane simply found their places and wouldn't budge. He looked bad; he knew it, because he felt worse. Although the aspirin had taken effect, it had only dulled the pain; his mind was mush. His battered briefcase lay flat on his lap, his elbows propped atop it, and he cradled his face in his cupped hands. He closed his eyes to rest until the judge appeared.

———

"Remain seated and come to order," the rotund bailiff grunted mechanically. The judge entered the courtroom as the murmur of discussion abated, and the bailiff continued. "Department J of the Superior Court of Los Angeles County, Southwest Division, is now in session; the Honorable Myra Kinnesaw, Judge, presiding."

Judge Kinnesaw glanced over the assemblage before she took her seat. She grabbed a stack of files from the right corner of the bench and said, "Good morning, everyone."

"Morning Judge," was the mumbled response.

"We have a full calendar this morning, ladies and gentlemen, so let's get started." She glanced at her audience and continued. "As always, I'll read the case names first. When I read your case's name counsel or parties in pro per, please stand and give me an estimate of how long you anticipate your argument to be."

The judge leaned forward and glared hard at the bleary-eyed, dark-suited officers of the court and a few motley-garbed clients.

"We are hearing motions today, counselors. You are not speaking to a jury. You are not in front of cameras. You are in the courtroom of Myra Kinnesaw ... Judge of this Superior Court. Your estimates will therefore be reasonable, and they will be accurate." She paused for a moment so her final words would hold their greatest impact. "Note carefully ... I will hold you to your estimates. You will not speak one second longer than your estimate, and if your estimate is too long, in my sole and arbitrary opinion, I will give you an estimate that I can live with."

The judge sat back and stared again for impact. She had developed her opening speech out of necessity. Her experience was that attorneys usually chose to be overly verbose precisely because the calendar was swamped. It seemed everyone needed to make sure her case was the one matter on the calendar about which the most words were expended. The judge would not tolerate such "eloquence" in her courtroom.

Judge Kinnesaw's ruddy face, creased from years of intense reading and analysis, dropped back to the stack before her. Her steel gray hair fell forward as it hung straight in a bob, cut above her thick brows and just below her ears. She was not an ugly woman. In fact, she might have been comely in her younger years. It just seemed at sixty-two years of age, her looks meant little to her or anyone else. She wore no makeup and did nothing to disguise her large, red proboscis, which seemed to have grown over the years while her head and face shrunk around it. The judge had lost interest in her physical appearance and had turned more and more to her work, something for which she was widely recognized.

"Do we have any requests for preference?" the judge asked. She looked up before opening the first file.

Sean Donovan hadn't intended to ask for preference. The thought didn't come to him until after he was seated, waiting for the judge. The nausea came in sporadic waves. The dull pounding was there continuously, but the dizziness is what convinced him. He couldn't sit through the entire calendar call. The dizziness led to greater perspiration and ultimately the anxiety of claustrophobia. He was in a courtroom, a place he'd been hundreds of times, yet he felt closed in. He couldn't understand it; it made him angry, but he couldn't control it. The younger attorneys on either side of him fidgeted, tried to turn away from him. Sean had to request the preference. He stood up, stumbled out of his row, stepping on and over feet and briefcases muttering "excuse me" as he went.

"Is that you, Mr. Donovan?" The judge leaned forward.

"Yes, Your Honor." He glanced up before again looking down to clear the last hurdle and step into the aisle.

"It might be a good idea, Mr. Donovan, to sit on the end next time you wish to have a preference."

"Yes, Your Honor, thank you," he said and moved toward the swinging doors at the bar.

"What case is yours?"

"Number twelve, Your Honor," Sean answered, hoping he remembered correctly from the calendar he'd read outside the courtroom. He approached the counsel table on the side nearest the jury box.

"Is anyone else here on number twelve?" asked the judge.

One of the young, fidgeting attorneys stood up slowly and stammered, "Yes, Your Honor."

"Well, come forward young man. Let's get this over with."

The young attorney was resplendent in his charcoal pinstriped suit, starched white shirt, and charcoal-with-red-splashed tie. He provided a sharp contrast to Sean, whose tattered tweed coat bore badly scuffed suede elbow patches and rested atop wrinkled blue slacks and a matching wrinkled white shirt. His tie was multi-colored and, on close inspection, probably bore stains from some recent meal.

Judge Kinnesaw wondered at Donovan's appearance. He was a good looking man, once quite handsome with piercing green eyes and light brown hair, streaked slightly with gray amidst the reddish highlights. But he was now so disheveled and shaggy, very different from the man she'd first seen years before.

"Did you have a rough weekend, Mr. Donovan?" the judge asked when she noticed the red streaks in his eyes and the puffiness of his face.

"It was okay, Judge," he tried to smile and nod his reassurance. "I'm fine."

"I suppose that's why you'll be asking me for a continuance?"

"Well, Your Honor, that and the fact that I have another hearing downtown in a half hour." The statement was not completely a lie. He did indeed have a minor hearing scheduled in downtown L.A. in a half hour. The lie was in the implication that he would make the appearance. He'd made arrangements with another attorney in his suite to step in for him while the attorney appeared on one of his own matters.

The judge smiled at Donovan. "State your appearances please."

"I'm Sean Donovan appearing for the plaintiff and responding party, John Mapleton."

The judge waited for several seconds for the young attorney to speak. He simply stared at Donovan, however, as if he expected more from him.

"Your appearance please, counsel," the judge finally prompted.

"Oh, I'm sorry, Your Honor. My name is James D. Phelson ... I'm with Gill, Johnson & Shou. I represent," he hesitated and glanced down at the manila file in front of him, "I represent the defendants and moving parties."

"Now Mr. Donovan, you were about to ask me for that continuance, is that correct?"

"Yes, Your Honor," he smiled respectfully though his head and eyes ached with the exertion.

"Well, Mr. Donovan, I'm sure your reasons are very good. Unfortunately, we don't have time to listen to them. You will not get your continuance," the judge smiled. She hated continuances; they meant lack of preparation, and she hated lack of preparation. "You've both read my tentative ruling?" She referred to her intended ruling posted with the calendar.

Both counsel nodded. Sean opened his thin, barely used file to review the notes he'd taken after reading the tentative in hopes of changing the judge's mind.

"Mr. Donovan, I see no responsive pleadings in the file from your office."

"Yes, Your Honor, that's one of the problems. We weren't able to get them filed on time. I do have them here, however," he held up the three pages he'd typed after realizing late Friday that the office's law clerk had not filed a response. "I am prepared to argue."

"Well, Mr. Donovan, I'll save us all the trouble. We have time deadlines for one purpose ... so that the judge can take the time to clearly understand the argument and reach an informed decision." Judge Kinnesaw leaned forward, again adopting her harsh veneer. Her smile disappeared. "I am granting the moving party's demurrer and giving you ten days to amend your complaint, Mr. Donovan."

"Ten days, Your Honor?" he grimaced. The normal grant was thirty days. "Could you make it twenty, Judge? I'm really bogged."

"Ten days, Mr. Donovan; and I suggest you hire assistants if your work load is too heavy."

This last statement was made with a hint of sarcasm mixed with sadness at the knowledge that Donovan's practice was almost nonexistent. The chance he actually had a hearing in L.A. this morning was slim. What bothered Judge Kinnesaw most about Sean Michael Donovan was that he had once been very good, even brilliant at times. She'd seen him in his early years as opposing counsel before she ascended the bench, and she'd seen him since then from the bench. He'd cared for the little guy while in a firm not known for such care. He even tilted with the occasional windmill and felled some mighty dragons, but all that was in the distant past. Perhaps it was the suspension that did it, or maybe the loss of his family, something Judge Kinnesaw heard about through the attorney grapevine some years ago. Whatever it was, the Sean Donovan she'd known didn't exist anymore. His will had been broken by some great weight, and he appeared to have fallen into the abyss of apathy. It made her sick. Incompetence borne of lack of interest was unacceptable of any attorney, especially one who once had so much to give.

Sean wasn't happy with the ten days. The judge was sticking it to him, but he knew better than to argue further. It was his fault the response wasn't filed. He could blame his clerk, a part- time attorney, but he knew the fault lay with him. It was his responsibility to follow-up and make sure the work was done and the papers filed. He failed, and he knew it.

"Yes, Your Honor. Thank you for your time," he said meekly and closed his file. He tried to smile to cover his embarrassment as he turned from the bench, but the smile did no such thing.

Sean's young opponent's head bobbed back and forth. He wasn't sure what to do.

"You've won counsel," said the judge impatiently. "Will you give notice?"

"Yes Your ..." he started.

"I'll waive notice judge," said Sean as he glanced back from the swinging doors.

"Thank you, Mr. Donovan," said the judge caustically. "Notice is waived."

"Thank you, Your Honor," said the young attorney. He closed his file and, without putting it into his new cordovan leather case, followed Sean out.

THREE

AN UNUSUALLY SAVAGE WINTER raged through spring and into summer in the Sierras. One storm after another forced the Forest Service to shut down the John Muir Trail for the entire season. No one in his right mind would have thought to traverse the higher reaches anyway, and certainly no one even considered attempting passage over the Golden Staircase. It wasn't until one morning in late August that two hikers decided to brave its rigors. They hadn't intended to go further south than the stone-shack ranger station at Le Conte Canyon, but a casual sighting of something they never imagined drew them on.

For two days they watched a monstrous bird glide effortlessly on updrafts of warm winds crashing into the sides of mountains ringing the Sierra valleys. Only occasionally did the creature's mighty wings move out of their glide position to provide a slight lift. It simply circled on a southward trajectory, as if directing the hikers to some pastoral trap.

By the end of that second day, if it was indeed a trap to which they were being led, Cameron Fontes and Derek Young were hooked. Never, despite years of hiking, camping, and outdoor adventure had the two recent graduates seen a wild version of the monstrous creature. During their studies, they'd grown to love the nearly extinct California condor. An ugly bird by most accounts, it was magnificent in its element, as had become clear over the last days. The creature they'd been tracking had given them both just enough of a glimpse to draw them on with the knowledge they were seeing the largest bird in modern history.

Their first glimpse was of a dark speck in the distant sky. In fact, so inconsequential and unexpected was that glimpse that neither hiker recognized the momentous nature of the sighting.

Every year during their graduate studies at UCLA, the two friends trekked into the Los Padres National Forest in hopes of catching such a glimpse of the majestic condor in its natural habitat. The nearly two million acres of ruggedly wild land along California's central coast was home to the last of the wild condors for years, until suddenly they simply disappeared. Even in the Sisquoc and Sespe Sanctuaries, large acreages within the forest that were set aside as condor habitats, no wild versions of the bird had been seen in years. The only real hope for those wishing to see the bird was in the government's captive breeding program. But even in that program, less than two hundred condors existed, none of which had bred in the wild. The birds in the program were born and raised in human captivity and then released into the wild with numbered wing tags and transmitters attached for close monitoring. Even the monitored birds were rarely seen by hikers, campers or the general public in their natural habitat. Cameron and Derek had been lucky enough to see the bird in its captive environment during their studies. It was that sighting that started their love affair with the bird, an affair they had only recently abandoned amid the realization that the feral, natural life for their creature was gone. Despite efforts by the mighty creature's benefactors, the world had shut them off. There was nowhere large enough to withstand human "progress" and enable the creature to breed and thrive in the wild.

That's why the initial sighting caused so little interest. It was unexpected. As a result, its significance didn't strike them until later that morning when Derek looked up again and saw the clear outline of the massive wingspan and the triangular white-feather under-cover against the black body as the bird glided in circles, ever lower. While Cameron pushed on, muttering incessantly about the rich colors of the meadows and hills, Derek stopped in his tracks and stared heavenward.

"It's a condor, Cam!" he stammered.

"What?" asked his friend, dazed by the beauty of his surroundings.

Derek pointed, "Look at 'im."

Cameron's eyes followed his friend's gaze until he too stared at the creature hurtling with incredible speed toward them, its ancient, remote eyes peering at them, beckoning as the mighty bird suddenly leveled out only fifty feet above and started its re-ascent.

Cameron fumbled for his camera while Derek watched it disappear into the tiny black spot they'd first seen early in the morning.

They berated themselves that their cameras were not at the ready. This was certainly the largest bird ever seen, and they had missed a chance of a lifetime to capture its image. Although ancient literature described condor wingspans ranging from eleven to fourteen feet, the largest wingspan recorded in modern times was slightly less than ten feet with a body weight of thirty-one pounds, similar to that of a small child. The creature the two hikers saw surely exceeded even the estimates from ancient times. This one approached prehistoric magnitude, and there were no tags or other human markings anywhere in evidence.

Neither of them saw the bird as they broke camp on the morning of the third day. They'd taken a few long-range photos the previous two days but they knew they'd be lucky, even with enlargements, if anyone would be able to discern the features of the dark speck in the sky. While Derek lay on his back that third morning, the sweet smell of the meadow's grasses soothing him as he patiently scoured the sky for the creature, Cameron crouched at the ice cold waters of the nearby creek, rinsing their tins.

Cameron's mind played with the notion of fame and fortune their photos would bring if they were ever able to get a clear shot. As he crouched, lost in such thoughts, he suddenly spied the reflection of an errant sunray upon some shiny surface to his left. He stood slowly, peered into the tall grass and brush along the creek bank. He cocked his head at different angles and elevations to recapture the reflection. When he stepped up the shallow slope he finally caught it again just a few feet away.

Within seconds Cameron held a dark brown leather case slightly larger than a hardcover book. It was zipped closed and dry. It appeared well tended except for the dirt that spotted it and the signs of natural wear at its corners. As he gingerly unzipped the case, he found a thick stack of spiral bound pages that appeared to be of a journal.

The pages were wrinkled and stiff, many of them stuck together from the wet and subsequent drying. In a few places the ink had run, thus smudging words, but all in all, the journal appeared to be in good condition. Even the drawings of great peaks, tall pines, and curious creatures were clear and undamaged for the most part.

Cameron closed the pages and looked at the inside of the front cover of the leather case. There he noticed the engraved name of "J. Bucklin Anderson." The gold leaf had worn away; all that remained were the indentations of the name itself and an inscription in quotes which read, "God has to nearly kill us sometimes, to teach us lessons," then below the words was the name "John Muir," and then below again were the final words, "Learn your lessons while you live, and pass them on to those who follow."

Cameron knew Buck Anderson. They'd never met, but he knew him. He'd heard the famous environmentalist speak on numerous occasions. He'd read his books, studied from his video programs, and knew the man by his work. He recalled the shock and despair he shared with the environmental community only months before when word leaked through the media that Buck hadn't returned from his Labor Day hike into the Sierras. Many feared the old man dead beneath the weight of the worst snowstorms in decades. Cameron, like many others, held hopes Buck would come wandering, tired and bedraggled, out of the mountains during the spring thaw; but he never did.

When winter wore on through spring and into early summer with no word of Buck, most people gave up hope of ever seeing him alive again. Yet, with the loss of that hope came the realization that if he truly was gone, he had died in the very place he would have chosen: his beloved Sierras.

Now, as Cameron held Buck Anderson's last journal, the enormity of his hiking trip hit him. What luck, first to see the condor and now to find the last words of the most renowned environmentalist the world had known since John Muir himself?

Before starting back up the slope to camp, he searched the banks for more signs of Buck. Deep down he hoped he might even find the body, which had to have been somewhere upstream. As he turned slowly from the creek his eyes fell upon the path leading onto the Golden Staircase, and he knew suddenly that if the body was to be found, it would be there, for that was the trek the old man had planned according to media reports that covered his disappearance.

When Cameron returned to camp, he found Derek standing, smiling. The black speck had returned and was now circling lower, beckoning them again.

"He's back, man. Let's go," said Derek as he bent to grab his pack and camera.

"We can't follow him. We've got to climb the Staircase," said Cam softly.

"What are you talking about?"

"I found this by the creek." He proffered the leather bound journal. "It's Buck Anderson's. I think he's up there somewhere."

The friends stared at the lower portions of the Golden Staircase before it disappeared into the granite walls. Each wrestled with his thoughts, clearly understanding the significance of the decision he was about to make when they suddenly knew the answer. Whether by luck, or some strange cosmic will, the decision was made for them.

As Derek's eyes drifted skyward, the mighty bird's speck had grown significantly. Its features were clearly visible and, once again, Derek was convinced it was the largest bird alive. It disappeared beyond an outcrop of rock high up on the Staircase. He smiled and turned back to his friend.

"Looks like he's going our way."

Cameron followed his friend's gaze. The bird emerged from behind the outcrop on widespread wings only to circle back and disappear again. "He wants us to follow him, Cam," Derek continued.

They stared at each other, neither understanding what was happening, but each realizing they had no choice but to follow.

For the next three hours, they trudged along the steepening track, stopping only occasionally for a sip from their canteens or a snapshot of the magnificent bird which suddenly seemed willing to permit close-ups. So consumed were the hikers with the enormous bird that they spent virtually no time viewing the wonders of the Staircase itself … until they rounded yet another bend and saw the family.

They stopped dead and stared at the sight among the boulders on the near side of the small plateau at Muir Point. Perched atop the tallest boulder was their guide. The condor stood regally, facing them, head cocked to the right, black eyes watching. Its wings were spread to their full sixteen-foot span as the bird basked in the warmth of the sun's rays. The hikers' quick assessment was that its body weighed in excess of forty pounds. Beneath the king, huddled in the shadows of his wings and the rocks were three other birds, each much smaller than the first.

When Cam and Derek were finally able to overcome their shock, they began to snap photos while absentmindedly inching closer to the group.

From his perch, the king suddenly crouched, dropped his wings and head and pushed off, falling at first like a heavy weight until his wings again caught the updraft and he began to glide far out over the chasm above Palisades Creek.

The hikers moved closer to the other birds as one and then another in turn lifted its head and stared with one dead eye at them. After each quick look the head dropped again to whatever was occupying the three and another head lifted. Derek continued shooting photos but Cameron dropped his hands to his side, letting the camera hang. He stared intently at the bobbing heads. It was the color that caught his attention, that and the ragged chunks that hung from their beaks.

The heads of the birds were various shades of the standard orange, one a little more yellow and another a little redder. Yet it was the extra red he saw that struck him. It was so much darker, and each face, on closer scrutiny, was mottled with it. But it wasn't until he realized what the ragged chunks were that Cam's stomach lurched. The birds were feeding; he could only imagine the human remains upon which they feasted. Surely Buck Anderson never dreamed he'd end up on the table of some carnivorous beast, and Cameron was suddenly enraged. He shouted and ran to the rocks, arms rotating furiously like some maniac. In unison the three feeding heads came up and spied the onrushing threat. As one, they leapt away from their meal, and one after another ran to the edge of the plateau, whence they launched themselves into the chasm and joined their patriarch, gliding effortlessly above Muir Point.

"What the hell are you doing?" shouted Derek incredulously. "Cam! What's wrong?" he shouted again when his friend continued his insane charge without answering, and then finally stopped to view the carnage.

"It's human, Derek. They were eating a human being."

Cameron's stomach continued to churn as he viewed the bloody remains of what he believed was the body of Buck Anderson. The body's entrails lay torn from the stomach, and the face and rest of the head were picked clean, beyond recognition. The fact the body was naked didn't strike him until his friend stood next to him and pointed to the obvious drag marks tracing a path in the dirt between the boulders to yet another boulder, the one upon which the king had previously perched. At the foot of the boulder, two boots protruded from a cave-like opening.

"There's another body," Derek pointed and fought his own queasiness. He pushed past his friend and around the half eaten corpse to the two boots while Cameron continued to stare at the gruesome remains.

Derek peered into the darkness of the cave and satisfied himself that there was at least some bulk attached to the boots. He could only guess as to its level of decay or consumption by rodents or other creatures. Certainly, however, it could be no worse than the naked body lying behind him.

He tugged once at the boots and felt little movement. The legs were stiff and easy to apply leverage, yet his first pull was weak as hideous thoughts of what might come with the pull almost overwhelmed him. He struggled to keep his composure and fight off his rising revulsion. He closed his eyes, breathed deeply of the cool, thin air and pulled again, this time with all his strength.

After only a second's resistance, the body popped loose and slid out of the opening. Derek fell backwards, landing hard on his posterior only inches from the other ravaged body. He opened his eyes upon impact and found himself staring into the frozen visage of J. Bucklin Anderson. The body was bent, still frozen in a sitting position. The facial expression was one of calm passivity, even contentment.

"It's him, Cam," Derek whispered.

They stared at Buck's body in silence for several minutes, each reflecting on the events that might have transpired during the great man's final hours. What had brought about the eminent environmentalist's death, and what of the other body, unclothed and ravaged while Anderson's body lay partially frozen but untouched?

From above them suddenly came a stifled cough, and then the sound of wind rushing through wings. They looked skyward as the massive body of the king hurtled past and back out over the chasm to join his circling subjects. Derek focused his camera and began firing. Cam simply stared. He understood. Whether they had the mental capacity to understand who Buck Anderson was, was of little consequence. The fact is that the king led the hikers to this place to find the old man. And the other three had left him alone, feeding only on the other body as if they knew Buck was one of them and that he was to be preserved.

The birds circled higher until they were specks again in the sky's blue expanse, and then they disappeared completely.

FOUR

TUESDAY MORNING, SEAN DONOVAN amended the complaint himself, not because he didn't trust his clerk, but because he had to do it. His embarrassment in court led him to again commit to take control of himself. He knew better than anyone else that he wasn't performing the way he could. He knew it because he'd been better once. He couldn't waste time thinking of why he had fallen so far, because such thoughts angered and ultimately depressed him. He didn't need anger or depression. He needed to move on. He was a good attorney who didn't want sympathy and certainly didn't want to embarrass himself again.

Sean was not a heavy drinker. One might think because of his Irish heritage and the fact his father died at 52 of a heart attack attributed to his own predilection for alcohol that he might be. And although he'd done his share of drinking through school and his early professional years, he had never felt the need to drink. It had always been a choice. The fact he was suffering from a hangover in Judge Kinnesaw's courtroom was more a testament to a bad choice than to a drinking problem.

He was celebrating some good news for a change. He'd put the finishing touches on the settlement of the *Clarkson vs. Herndon* case, his one good-sized case, and one for which he had not been paid for almost two years. Trial was scheduled to begin at the end of the week, and although Sean didn't know if his finances could survive two weeks in court without progress pay, he didn't let on to his opponent. He'd maintained a strong countenance, as if he was ready to go "all the way" and relished the thought of it. His ultimatum that "if it isn't settled by the end of the weekend there would be no more talking" had worked. His opponent appeared even more concerned than Sean about trial, and the call came Saturday morning to the same Razr that woke him Monday morning. He spent the weekend typing and revising the agreement. By early Sunday evening, it was signed, faxed, and delivered to all parties. Sean celebrated at Hennessey's Tavern in Redondo Beach, where he ate, drank, and joined some locals to watch the Dodgers. He ended up drinking too long and too much and, unfortunately, using his maxed-out credit card to pay more than his share of the cost. Luckily, the settlement would get him paid before the bill came due.

As he completed the amendments, he thought about James D. Phelson, his opponent in the demurrer hearing. The young man had literally bounced out of the courtroom after his victory, undoubtedly his first after probably just graduating from law school. Sean knew the feeling. He'd been there himself once.

The top law firms in the country had recruited Sean Donovan as a result of his "high honors" class standing at USC's law school. He ultimately accepted a position with the august Los Angeles firm of McCormack & Stein and was making more money than he dreamed possible immediately after graduation. That was back when he was known as S. Michael Donovan, back when everyone went by a first initial and a middle name. He worked long hours then, along with everyone else at the firm, but he loved it. He loved the challenge and he loved the responsibility. He even remembered his first courtroom triumph in a meaningless hearing similar to the one in which James D. Phelson obtained his. Sean knew the feeling of euphoria that came from having a judge rule in his favor after all the work that went into preparing the motion that brought him into the courtroom, especially the first time. He couldn't begrudge Phelson his day in the glow of his first victory. In fact, he silently congratulated the young man even as he whispered caution for the times to come.

The complaint was covered with red ink interlineations and deletions when Sean approached Patty at her secretarial bay. Her plump, normally jolly face grimaced as she placed the telephone receiver back into its cradle.

"Why so glum, Patty?" Sean asked. He actually felt somewhat upbeat with the work he'd done on the complaint. He knew this one would pass muster with the judge, and it felt good to focus interest and energy on a case for a change.

"Oh, nothing, Mr. Donovan," she said, and forced a smile that might have seemed real to a casual observer.

"Patty, what is it?" Sean asked again.

She dropped her head and shook it slowly.

"That was the manager from Trifoil Properties, Mr. Donovan. I was trying to put him off until the settlement money came in, you know, from the *Clarkson* case?" Sean nodded slowly. "I'm sorry, Mr. Donovan, he said they won't wait any longer. He said they want their rent money now. We're three months behind, and if he doesn't hear from you personally today, he'll be serving eviction papers tomorrow morning. I'm so sorry, Mr. Donovan."

Sean dropped his head. Couldn't he feel good just for a short time? Did the other shoe always have to drop?

"Patty, this isn't your fault," he finally said. "Don't worry about it. Give me his phone number; I'll get it straightened out."

Patty handed him a post-it note with the manager's name and number on it.

"He said even if you paid today, he would demand that rent be paid three months in advance from now on," Patty muttered sadly.

Sean nodded, forced his own smile, and said, "I'll take care of it. Can you type up the amendments for me? I'd like to get this in before I leave on Thursday."

Patty took the complaint, nodded slowly, and returned Sean's smile as he walked away.

Sean spent the rest of the morning and early afternoon trying to convince Trifoil's manager, a man named Irmak Ahbout, who spoke only broken English, to be patient for just ten more days. Sean told him he'd bring the rent current and pay six month's advance rent if he'd only give him the time to collect the *Clarkson* settlement money.

Sean hated this part of the law. He hated what he referred to as the business of law. When he was at McCormack & Stein, he never had to worry about rent, bills, expenses, or collections. That firm had entire departments dedicated to such matters. All he had to do was work a case and get his time sheets in. That was it: practice law and be a billing machine. If a client didn't pay, no worries, someone else would chase him down. If rent wasn't paid … well, that never happened; but he never even gave such matters a thought. That all changed years ago, though, back when he lost the last of it and was forced to start doing the "business of law" or die.

He breathed a sigh of relief when Mr. Ahbout and his supervisor finally agreed to ten more days, and he hung up the phone. The $175,000 *Clarkson* settlement would provide him $45,000 plus the costs of the litigation, and his client was ecstatic, an emotion he hadn't elicited from a client in some time. His portion of the settlement would bring him current on all his bills and buy him another four months of life during which he hoped to find, bill, and collect from other clients, a thought that didn't exactly excite him.

As Sean leaned back in his chair and closed his eyes, his intercom buzzed. He glanced absently at the telephone.

"Yes?" he finally said.

"Mr. Donovan," Patty responded, "it's your mother on the line. Should I tell her you'll call back?"

Sean leaned forward to grab the receiver. "No, it's okay, Patty. I'll take it. Thanks."

"Hey, Mom," Sean said, trying to sound upbeat.

"Sean Michael," his mother responded in her still thick Irish brogue. "You sound sad son. Are you well?"

"I'm good, Mom," he said and couldn't help smiling. Always a mother, he thought, always concerned about her children. "How are you doing?"

"Lord be praised, Sean. I'm alive, a bit sore in the morning, but happy to still be breathing the good Lord's air. Did you settle the case?"

"I did, Mom. Thanks for remembering. Settled it Sunday," he concluded and then realized he'd made a mistake.

"Did you work on Sunday then? The Lord's day?" She was silent for a second awaiting a response that didn't come. "I pray for you every day son. I pray that you come back. It'll turn your life around for you Sean."

"I know," he said softly. "Someday, Mom, someday." He didn't want to continue this discussion. "So, are you looking forward to your birthday party this weekend? The big seven five, is it?"

"Oh, don't remind me. I think it best not to remember the age, Sean. The party is fine, something I always enjoy with me kids around. But, it's best not to discuss the age, I think."

Sean smiled.

"I'll be up Thursday night," he said.

"Good … good. There's somethin' I need you to do first though, Sean. You remember Mrs. Jackson, the wonderful woman who'd make such scrumptious peach pies?"

"Sure, Mom." He remembered the tiny black woman and her brood of four massive football-playing sons. Sean had gone to high school at Mt. Whitney High and played ball with three of the boys, Sean as a mediocre defensive back and the Jackson brothers as the county's best offensive and defensive linemen, depending upon which of the brothers one was discussing.

"I'd like you to call her before you head up this way. She's involved in some legal matter that I think she may need some help with."

"Why don't you have her call me, Mom? Attorneys don't normally go calling people to see if they need help." Although attorneys used every conceivable means to solicit clients, Sean's real reason for his comment was that he didn't want to get involved in some neighbor skirmish all the way up in Visalia. "Besides, Mom, I think it would be better if she got an attorney up there."

"Sean Michael," she switched to using both names when she wanted to make a firm point. "Mrs. Jackson would never call you because she wouldn't want to bother an important Los Angeles lawyer or take advantage; you know that. As for hiring someone up here, I doubt she has the money for something like that."

Just as Sean suspected, his mother was volunteering his services. Her voice lowered to a whisper as if Mrs. Jackson were in the same room overhearing her, a tactic she often used to indicate the significance of her next statement.

"I'm concerned about Mrs. Jackson, son. I think a big city lawyer has sued her over the property she owns near the Silver Lode. She mentioned somethin' about a summation of judge or claim or somethin' like that."

"Summary judgment?" asked Sean, his interest slightly piqued.

"That's it, isn't it?" his mother replied excitedly. "I'm afraid she believes some nice men are asking to buy her property and I think there's much more to it, don't you?"

"If it's a motion for summary judgment, it's much more than that. I'll give her a call," he said and asked for Mrs. Jackson's number.

They spoke a few more minutes about Sean's sisters and what was happening in Visalia until Sean finally interrupted his mother.

"Mom, I've got to get back to it here. I'll see you in a couple days, okay? We can talk then."

His mother signed off with an "I love you" and reminded him to please call Mrs. Jackson right away. When he did so, he got no answer. Mrs. Jackson had no answering service or machine. He promised himself he'd try again tomorrow. He made a note in red ink in his calendar as a reminder.

FIVE

EARLY THE PREVIOUS SATURDAY, before Sean had gotten the call that started the *Clarkson* settlement negotiation, Derek Young and Cameron Fontes emerged from a copse of pines near the Bench Lake Ranger Station west of the Golden Staircase. They dragged two bodies with them. They had wrapped the bodies in sleeping bags and crafted litters to lug them out of the wilderness. The trek was long and arduous, taking them two days over rushing streams, across jagged rock, and finally through still soggy meadows. They decided to keep word of the condor sightings quiet for the time being. They needed time to implement the grand plan that would make them famous in environmental circles around the world. They decided to sell the Buck Anderson story first and then, after sufficient time elapsed and the excitement surrounding the return of the environmentalist's remains had passed, they would deliver their photos of the birds. The double exposure was sure to bring them the notoriety they sought.

The two friends considered holding back Anderson's journal but decided their story was more dramatic with the find of the book preceding the find of the body. Their only real concern was whether the county coroner would be able to decipher the kind of scavenger that had opened up the second body. However, they quickly decided it was unlikely someone would guess "condor," since, to the world's knowledge, none existed in the Sierras. Everything seemed just right for Derek and Cameron. Their futures were set, or so it seemed until Tuesday evening. Suffused with the glow of fame from numerous interviews and bookings for talk shows, and imbued with the languor of drink, they emerged from the Black Crow Inn, a biker bar in the foothills of the western Sierras, and boarded Cameron's Jeep.

"Who was that guy, Derek?" asked Cameron as he turned the ignition and the vehicle roared to life.

Derek stared at his friend, a stupid smile covering his round features. "Who?"

"The guy you were just talking to. Isn't he the same one we saw yesterday?" Cameron looked ahead, shifted into first, and the Jeep rolled toward the exit apron.

"Yeah," Derek giggled. "He's a good guy. Tell's a helluva joke."

"I think I saw him at the news conference last night, too. Do you remember seeing him?" asked Cameron.

"No ... but so what? We're celebrities. Everyone wants to get close to us." The young man was clearly enjoying his fame.

"What were you guys talking about for so long?" Cameron pressed his friend.

"What else? He wanted to know all about it, like everyone else."

"About what?"

"Anderson, Cam. C'mon, what's the problem? He wanted me to tell him how we found the bodies." Derek was getting irritated at the grilling. He stared hard at his friend and then turned back to face the road, hoping he had shut Cameron up. He didn't feel like a serious talk.

Cameron watched the road in the funnel of his high beams. He picked his next words carefully hoping Derek hadn't blown it but hesitant to ask directly for fear of the answer.

The grade steepened downward. Cameron pumped his breaks and then had to ask.

"Did you talk about the birds?"

Derek didn't answer. After several seconds Cameron glanced at him.

"Derek, did you mention the birds?"

"No ... he did," Derek mumbled.

"Derek!" Cameron shouted. "What do you mean?"

"He asked me about 'em, okay? He brought them up."

"How could he? How would he know?"

Derek glared out his side window.

"Derek, talk to me. How did he know?"

"Yesterday," whispered Derek. "We talked yesterday for awhile, and," he shook his head slowly, "I told him about the birds."

"God dammit, Derek! Can't you hold your fucking liquor?" Cameron glared out the windshield but lost focus of the fact the Jeep's speed was increasing. "You blew it. You fucking blew it."

"He doesn't know they were condors," Derek whispered, ashamed.

"What? What the hell are you talking about?"

"I didn't tell him they were condors," Derek rejoined, suddenly feeling a little stronger. Maybe he really hadn't screwed up so badly.

"Oh," snapped Cameron. "You told him we saw some birds feeding on the bodies and he believed they were sparrows right?"

"I slipped, man. I'm sorry. I slipped yesterday, and he just kept asking more and more questions today."

"Derek, listen to me," Cameron tried to calm himself. He had to do a damage assessment in order to plan their next move. "Did anyone mention condor?"

"He did. He asked me today if they were condors." Derek whispered, his head low.

The Jeep was moving very fast.

"I told him yesterday that I didn't know ... that we had pictures we were going to develop and take to the environmental studies labs back at school." Derek turned to his friend, "But he knew somehow. He came right at me tonight, Cam. He knew they were condors."

Derek stopped short when he realized his friend was no longer listening to him. Through the haze of his drunkenness, he could see Cameron's sudden anxiety.

Cameron depressed the brake slowly at first, but when it hit the floor and nothing happened he lifted his foot and slammed hard.

Again, nothing.

The vehicle continued to pick up speed down hill as shadows flashed in and out of the glow of his halogen beams. His knuckles turned white with his grip on the steering wheel.

"Cam!" Derek shouted when his quiet entreaties went unanswered.

"Brakes are gone!" Cameron shouted. "We gotta stop it."

He reached for the handbrake and pulled, but there was no response. The Jeep's speed was nearly beyond his control. He swerved through bends and around curves, grateful only that there was no traffic on the dark mountain road.

"Shift down!" Cameron shouted. He slammed down the clutch while gripping the wheel with both hands.

Derek grabbed the stick, jammed it into first, and Cameron lifted his left foot off the clutch. The vehicle lurched forward with the initial shift and immediately slowed, but the grade steepened, and the initial sharp deceleration was followed by the transmission's heavy whine. He had to act quickly or the transmission would go before they'd be able to slow the vehicle enough to scrape to a halt along the rock wall.

"Put it in reverse!" he shouted. He again stepped on the clutch to relieve the transmission whine and tried desperately to control the hurtling vehicle.

Derek, his drunken languor gone, reacted quickly. He drove the stick into "R," and when Cameron lifted his foot, the vehicle jerked and lurched in spasms of grinding gears that destroyed the transmission and slowed the vehicle sharply.

Cameron turned the wheel into the oncoming traffic lane, maneuvering the Jeep toward the rock walls towering into the darkness above. He could feel loose gravel beneath the wheels and then the scraping and tearing of rock through metal as he sidled up to the rock. The vehicle began to slow. Cameron let out a breath. But another bend approached, and a massive boulder loomed before them. He swerved sharply away from the rock wall, around the boulder, and back into the oncoming lane only to be struck by the high beams and blaring horn of a one ton pickup and camper heading directly toward them. He was blinded, shocked. He jerked the wheel to the right. The Jeep shot past the oncoming truck into its own lane, but its speed was still too much for Cameron to right their course. The Jeep skidded onto the narrow shoulder and fishtailed sideways for an instant before continuing its headlong course into the concrete barricade, a barricade that was never intended to withstand the force of a head on impact. It gave without resistance, and the Jeep hurtled off the shoulder, over the cliff.

Derek stared wide-eyed over the dashboard as the Jeep's nose tilted downward. He turned pleadingly to his friend whose own eyes bore into the empty space before them. An instant later, Derek turned back to the windshield, which burst in on him as the Jeep struck the ravine floor two hundred feet below the roadway. The vehicle exploded in a fireball that consumed their dreams of riches and fame together with all evidence that they or anyone else had ever seen the king and his wild subjects.

SIX

VISALIA IS A SMALL town between Fresno and Bakersfield, about one hundred sixty miles north, along State Highway 99, from Los Angeles. Founded in 1852 by a bear hunter named Nathaniel Vise, who combined his surname with his wife's given name, Sallie, to name the town, it has lost the rebelliousness that marked it during the railroad/cattle wars of the 1870s and 1880s. Since Visalia was a ranching community in those years, inhabitants, dependent on wide open grazing lands, encouraged revolt against the U.S. Congress and its support of railroad construction. Many residents gave refuge to hunted rebels and saboteurs. But that was all in the past. Visalia became a sleepy community, still somewhat dependent on farming and ranching as it inched ever closer to the look of a modern day urban metropolis.

The Donovan family moved to Visalia from Massachusetts shortly before Sean was born. "The streets of California are paved with gold," Billy Donovan heard from his father time and again. "There are wide open spaces where a man can get rich by pickin' up some land cheap and workin' it the way we Irish know how to work land. I only wish your dear ma, God rest her soul, was still around and I was healthy enough to join you out west. We'd have a helluva time, you and me, making the Donovan name in that land where opportunity don't only knock, she comes right up and grabs a man."

It broke Billy's heart to watch his father fade away with a disabling war wound and a heart that broke when his wife died of polio before they could even celebrate the end of the war. Rather than wait around for the man's last breath, twenty-two year old Billy joined the massive 1950s migration to California. He packed up his new Irish bride, Mary, and their baby daughter, and he hauled them west in a battered truck he bought from his dad for $200 and a promise that he'd send for him as soon as he got settled. Unfortunately, his father died shortly after their departure, and Billy didn't even learn about it till nearly a month later—too late to see him buried.

Billy's truck took the family as far as Visalia before it died, and that's where he and Mary chose to make their home. He sweated through years of back breaking farm labor to mine the "gold" with which the streets of California were paved and ultimately ended up owning a five hundred acre spread upon which his family grew and made their living.

It was a good life for the Donovans in Visalia even though it wasn't exactly what Billy had envisioned. The Donovans did indeed make a name for themselves in the small town from which their three children moved as soon as they could find a way out.

Sean left his apartment later than he'd intended. He had to make some last minute changes to the *Clarkson* agreement and confirm that one of his suite mates would be in court for him Friday morning to read the settlement into the record. He didn't reach his mother's house until about 9:30 p.m., three and a half hours after he'd set out and after one stop along the way for a burger and fries at a Carl's Jr. along the Grapevine.

Sean called Mrs. Jackson's number two times Wednesday and once again on Thursday to no avail—no answer and no machine. Finally, he phoned his mother to suggest she let Mrs. Jackson know Sean would stop by her place on Friday to see what she'd gotten herself into.

"Are you sure I can't get you anything to eat, Sean?" Mary Donovan asked for the fifth time since her son arrived ten minutes earlier.

"Mom, I'm good," he said with another headshake and a smile. "Let's just have a drink and talk a bit before we go to bed. It was a long drive. I'm a bit tired."

Mary still had the flaming red hair, streaked liberally now with gray, and bright green eyes set in the ruddy, cherubic face Sean remembered so well. Hers was a face that couldn't stop smiling no matter how serious she tried to be, and it was that characteristic that Sean remembered most whenever he thought of her. Strangely enough, it was that constant smile and the sense of hope it carried that helped him make it through his most trying times.

Mary sold the Donovan family farm shortly after her husband's death. She never had the attachment to the land that Billy did, but she'd always gone along with him because she loved him so much. Her decision to sell turned out to be very timely, a good move in the late 1980s when Southern California real estate was skyrocketing just prior to the crash of the 90s. The sale provided Mary enough to purchase a small three-bedroom house in town and live comfortably while she worked on charitable causes for her church and community.

"You look good, Mom," said Sean as he nursed a Myer's Rum and orange juice. "You're taking good care of yourself."

"Ah," she smiled, "I'm an old woman with arthritis just livin' out me days, son. You know that. But, how about you, Sean? Are you well?"

"I'm good, Mom." He smiled and didn't elaborate.

"Have you spoken to Marie or Johnny?" Mary asked about Sean's children.

He shook his head and dropped his eyes to his glass. He'd been through this so many times before with his mother. His children didn't call him, and his former wife would never allow the kids to the phone to talk to him whenever he called after the divorce. It was as if he never existed in their lives. He sent letters and cards in the first few years but never heard back and surmised his missives never reached the kids. He would have loved to fly to New York to force his way back into their lives, but he was dealing with a battle that consumed him.

"No," he said simply. "You?"

Mary shook her head and the corners of her lips curled down sadly for one of her rare frowns. "Such beautiful children," she whispered.

Sean wanted to move away from a topic that made them both sad.

"I heard about Buck Anderson. That was a shock," he said.

Mary looked up sharply and stared at Sean for a moment. She nodded slowly, and the frown that covered her features in the discussion about Sean's children seemed to worsen. She dropped her head again.

Mary and Billy Donovan were long time friends of Buck's brother Tom and his wife and children. Sean had known the oldest Anderson boy, and Sean's younger sister Shannon had been very close to Carla, the Andersons' daughter. Through that family, the Donovans occasionally met Buck during breaks in his travels for the environmental causes that made his name and put his home community of Visalia on the map. But those meetings had never resulted in any great friendship, so Sean was surprised at his mother's reaction to the comment about Buck's death.

"You okay, Mom?"

She nodded and lifted her eyes to him. Even in the semi darkness of the room Sean could see the glint of moisture in them.

"I'm fine. It's just a shame is all, to have a good man die the way he did. Murdered, they say, although there's no official word yet."

Sean nodded his understanding and decided to move on yet again rather than investigate further his mother's reaction. That discussion would have to hold until Sean was wide awake and hadn't just consumed a Myer's and O.J.

"So when will Katie and Shannon be home?" he finally asked.

Mary brightened at the mention of her daughters.

"Tomorrow. Shannon is flying to Sacramento to meet Katie early, and they'll be driving down together."

"Will they be bringing their families?"

"No, not this time. They're busy with one thing or another. It'll be a Donovan weekend for your old ma's seventy-fifth." She smiled broadly, apparently liking the idea of spending the days with her children without the distraction of husbands and grown grandchildren.

Sean smiled too—happy he would not have to discuss business with his brothers-in-law. He liked them well enough. They were good to Sean's sisters and seemed to be good fathers. He simply had no interest in the looks and comments he'd get from men who'd at one time felt inferior to the successful "lawyer son" and now were clearly more successful as accountants than Sean would ever be again.

"That'll be good, Mom. I'm looking forward to it," Sean said.

Friday morning Sean pulled up in front of Mrs. Jackson's ramshackle house at 10:30. He woke up much earlier and went for a short jog before returning for a shower and joining his mother for an orange juice and poached egg. It was nice getting into running shorts and shoes again and working up a sweat—things he now did all too rarely at his apartment.

Mrs. Jackson's was a small clapboard house badly in need of repairs and paint. It was in a neighborhood that hadn't seen much growth over the years and, for that matter, not much maintenance either. Most of the homes bore similar marks of age and disrepair with landscaping that looked more like the arid sands of the Mojave than a once middle-class neighborhood. Somehow, though, Sean was able to look past the decrepit appearance and remember the times he shared after football practice with the middle son, Horace. Even now, his mouth watered at the memory of Mrs. Jackson's fresh peach pies, or maybe it was the scent that emanated from the porch window as he walked up the steps and knocked.

The door opened slowly and a little black woman stood behind the torn screen squinting through coke-bottle thick glasses at Sean.

"Mrs. Jackson?" he asked. He didn't remember her being so tiny and frail.

"Is that you, Sean?" she asked with her still strong, high-pitched voice as she pushed open the screen. "Lord, Sean, you a grown man with gray hair comin' in already." Her mouth was spread in a wide grin that exhibited a staggered set of still white teeth. "Come on in."

Sean stepped into the front room he remembered so well. It carried the same cozy warmth, albeit more worn and somewhat smaller than he recalled. And he did indeed smell Mrs. Jackson's familiar baking.

"Is that peach pie?" he asked, his own smile wide with the memory.

"Heh," she chuckled. "It shore is. You set down here." She pointed to a plastic-cushioned chair next to the Formica-topped, metal-rimmed table in her kitchen. "It just needs to cool a bit and then it'll be ready to eat."

Sean stared after the woman as she busied herself reaching for pie plates, silverware, napkins, and glasses for milk. He didn't really want to eat pie at this time of day but figured that was a discussion he couldn't possibly win with this woman, so he let her go about her business. When she placed a setting in front of him, she asked, "How's your mama?"

"She's great, Mrs. Jackson. Complains a little about the arthritis and all, but she's okay."

"Arthritis," she frowned. "Your mama's too young to be suffering through that, Sean. God shoulda only give that to old folks like me, not young'ns like your mama."

Sean smiled. Mrs. Jackson was only five years older than his mother.

The old woman placed a steaming chunk of pie on Sean's plate, smiled at eye level with him until he cut off a piece and put it into his mouth, and smiled more broadly as he closed his eyes involuntarily to savor the sweet wonder of its taste.

"Amazing as always, Mrs. Jackson. Thank you," he mumbled out of a full mouth.

When Mrs. Jackson continued to stare with the excitement she exhibited anytime someone enjoyed one of her pies, Sean had to finally get to the point of his visit.

"Do you have some papers you want to show me, Mrs. Jackson?"

"Oh, it's nothing important, Sean. I was tellin' your mama 'bout those ol' papers an' how I was goin' to go to court an' talk to the judge an' she kinda got worried. I tol' her they's nothing to worry 'bout but she said she'd have you call. They don't mean nothing Sean. I don't need to bother you with 'em."

Sean nodded slowly as he finished the last bite and pushed his plate aside.

"Why don't you get me the papers and let me take a look, okay?"

Mrs. Jackson frowned and turned slowly to a straw purse that hung on the back of another one of the chairs. She extracted crumpled sheets of paper and handed them to Sean.

"They say I gotta go to court an' all, don't they?"

Sean took the stack and started to organize it in page order. He had about ten sheets in front of him but realized several pages were missing when he saw that the last page, which was not the signature page, bore page number 22. On the first page, the case caption read *Flow Corporation vs. Beverly Cora Jackson*. To the right of the caption, he read the words "Notice of Motion, Motion For Summary Judgment and Points and Authorities in Support Thereof." He leafed through the remaining pages, not wanting to read them without having the entire package. Nevertheless, he was concerned. A motion for summary judgment, if granted, would end Mrs. Jackson's case, whatever it might be, against her interests.

"What's this all about, Mrs. Jackson?"

Recognizing his concern, Mrs. Jackson smiled. "Oh, it ain't nothing. These folks have been trying to buy my land for years. But I ain't sellin'. It's been in the family too long, since way back when Black Jack's son, my husband's great gran'daddy, first owned it. I guess they just want some judge to ask me if I'll sell it; but I won't, and I'll jest tell the judge that, and that'll be the end of it. Would you like some more pie?"

"Mrs. Jackson, this is a very important paper." He held it up in front of her. "It's part of a law suit where these nice people who keep trying to buy your property are actually going to try to take it away from you. Why didn't you call me?"

"Oh, I didn't want to bother you. Besides, you know I ain't got much money."

Sean was exasperated. He could use the money, no doubt about that. But that wasn't the issue. There was an injustice about to be perpetrated here upon someone Sean knew and loved.

"Mrs. Jackson, you don't need money for me. You know that. I'm sure my mother told you that, even if you don't know it yourself."

"I can't take advantage, Sean. That wouldn't be right, you being a busy man like you are."

He shook his head slowly and stared again at the papers.

"Look, Mrs. Jackson," he finally said, "you just make me some of your peach pie occasionally and we'll be even, okay?" She smiled, and he continued. "Do you have the rest of the papers?"

She turned and looked around the tiny kitchen. "I think I have more papers somewhere."

She ambled away from the table and began poking into cupboards and closets. Sean took the opportunity to read what he could of the papers in his hand, and his concern grew. The motion against Mrs. Jackson was one not traditionally favored by the courts of California. If granted, it would preclude a trial on the merits of the case because it would have been determined that there were no disputes between the parties on the relevant material factual issues. In such case, Mrs. Jackson's opponent, a California corporation by the name of Flow Corp., would win without a trial.

The claim by Flow Corp. appeared to be for adverse possession—another name for the legalized theft of another person's land in American jurisprudence. This could be accomplished in California by simply using another person's property openly and hostilely to their ownership, and by paying property taxes on it for a period of five or more consecutive years.

The problem in Beverly Jackson's case was that even though such motions to decide the case without a trial were not favored, the undisputed facts as presented in what Sean had of the moving papers not only gave adequate support for a ruling in Flow Corp.'s favor, they were compelling for any judge with basic legal acumen and competence. Sean could not be sure the facts were truly compelling until he reviewed the entire file, but if it turned out the way it appeared, Mrs. Jackson was going to lose a valuable piece of property without a fight.

As Sean placed the papers down on the table, he stared at the name of the law firm in the upper left hand corner and the three attorneys listed at the signature line for the Notice of Motion. McCormack, Stein & Wolf was representing Flow Corporation, and Richard Wolf, Sean's one time friend and now a name partner in his old firm, was the lead attorney. Sean's stomach tightened. He stared in numb surprise at names from his troubled past, unable to conjure any thought for several seconds.

Mrs. Jackson finally returned to the kitchen with another stack of disheveled papers. It measured more than four inches thick and included what appeared to be a bound document of some kind.

"I found this in the front closet. Does it help?" she asked hopefully.

"I'll take it all with me and read it next week, Mrs. Jackson. If you find anything else, please let me know," he said as he handed her a card. "My phone number is right here." He pointed. She squinted through her thick glasses. "Call me if you get anything else from the lawyers or court, or if you find anything else here in the house."

"Okay," she said. "Is it bad, Sean?"

"We'll see. I'll read the file and we'll talk next week, okay?"

She nodded as Sean stood up and walked with her to the front door.

"Thank you for visitin' me, Sean. My boys'll be happy to hear you came by."

Sean turned and stared down at her. He then bent over and hugged her.

"You just keep making me the best peach pie in the world, and we'll figure out a way to make this go away."

She waved as Sean drove off. He would have waved back, but the stomach tightening he'd felt in the house turned to churning, and his mind grew heavy. What was he getting himself into? Did he really want to do battle with Richard Wolf and his former firm? How in the world was he going to pay his rent once the *Clarkson* money ran out?

SEVEN

SATURDAY MORNING VISALIA WAS still abuzz with the news of the death of one of its favorite sons. Buck Anderson's body and that of the "John Doe" lay on tables in the coroner's lab. The cause of death for the environmentalist seemed obvious from the outset: over-exposure to the elements. But the mutilated remains and unusual throat wound of John Doe together with Buck's shattered right shoulder spoke of foul play, and the final verdict was delayed.

Most people in the community had long since given up hope of ever seeing Buck alive again, but no one imagined the gentle man could meet death at the hands of another human being. Although there was no official word, rumors spread quickly, and people followed the stories closely for any substantiation.

The county coroner, a small pudgy man named Orson Hoffman, although never considered anything more than an efficient coroner, would have surprised some people with his quick grasp of his situation, dealing with the body of the world's most famous environmentalist. The rumors of foul play had reached his ear and not gone unnoticed. In fact, if the truth were known, some of those rumors originated from his office. He, by God, would make the most of this unfortunate event by holding the bodies for as long as he reasonably could and then coming up with a plausible murder story. That would get him noticed, and if there were any chance it was true, his name would be on everyone's mind when the next big county coroner needed replacement.

Hoffman figured he knew how to milk a situation. He kept quiet officially, pending completion of his autopsies, while subtly fueling the rumor mill through the ears and mouths of his sieve-like staff.

Saturday's other news was the seventy-fifth birthday party for Mary Donovan. Although rightfully overshadowed by Buck's death, the party was an event for the many in the community touched by Mary's work and friendship. The party turned out to be much bigger than either Sean or Mary thought it would be. Shannon and Katie weren't surprised, though, because they helped plan it from afar with the help of Mary's friends at the church.

More than one hundred people showed up for dinner, drinks, and birthday wishes for Mary Donovan at the Mountain View Grill, an ages-old family establishment with magnificent uninterrupted views of the Sierra Nevada Mountains from its back deck. Shannon and Katie shared the cost of the affair and told Sean not to worry about it; after all, "you always picked up the tab back when none of us could afford it. You can get it next time, when things are better for you," they said.

Sean nodded and accepted the hugs of his sisters. They'd shown their support for him through his ordeals. He loved them for it, and it was clear they still viewed Sean with a respect and love for a brother they knew would die for them if it ever came to that. Still, it hurt. That he couldn't help financially bothered him beyond simple pride. It created a kind of distance, as if he really wasn't a part; he wasn't a contributor to the family's event. He was more a visitor, an invitee, if you will, despite the love he felt from his mother and sisters. He wished it could be different, but for the life of him he really didn't see any way it ever would be again.

At the party Sean talked with people he'd known since he was a child. They asked him how things were going, none knowing the totality of what had happened over the past sixteen years. To a person, these family friends begged him to leave the big city riches and come on home to help them through the changes that were coming to their community. Sean smiled and nodded with the knowledge that dreams of sudden growth and the riches that would follow were commonplace in Visalia. Ever since Walt Disney's ill-fated attempt to build a ski resort in the Mineral King Valley, some 50 miles east in the 1960s and '70s, there had been rumors about other developers. Now those rumors swirled around the other family entertainment giant, Golden World Resorts. Apparently, Atticus Golden was planning a world-class ski resort in the Silver Lode Valley, less than one hour's drive northeast of Visalia. By all estimates, the development was all but approved. Speculators were already buying up land that would skyrocket in value once the approval was complete. The good folks of Visalia needed someone they could trust to help them through the process, and those at Mary's party knew they could trust Sean Donovan.

When Sean finally broke away from the discussions, he wandered outside and found himself standing on the restaurant's back deck, leaning against the rail, and staring into the moonlit darkness of the mountains. It was a balmy night, suffused with the smell of late blooming honeysuckle. Although the year had been unusually cool, the heat of the central valley had come on strong in recent weeks. This night was perfect as he clutched a tumbler of VO and seven and took in the lazy evening.

"So, have they convinced you to come back?"

Sean turned sharply, sloshing his drink. Behind him stood a beautiful woman he didn't recognize. He'd seen her from afar at the party several times. He'd even caught her looking his way and quickly averting her eyes when he caught her gaze. But he didn't know her; or, at least, he thought he didn't. He smiled and turned to face her. She held a glass of wine as she stepped toward him.

"You don't recognize me, do you, Sean?"

His mind struggled. He suspected his look was pained for the effort. He tried to smile even as he tried to remember. The woman grinned impishly at him, her crystal blue eyes sparkling in the deck's torch light beneath a shock of thick Nordic blond hair tied in a loose pony tail that dropped at the sides over her ears and fell softly below her shoulders in back.

"I'm Carla ... Carla Anderson," she said as she came to the rail and leaned down on her elbows next to Sean.

"Carla?" he stammered, recognition coming immediately. "You look ... different ... you've grown up." He couldn't think of anything else to say.

She smiled and glanced sidelong at him.

"I hope so. It's been ... what ... twenty-five years since we've really seen each other? Your wedding, I think," she said and turned back to the saw-toothed silhouette of the Sierras.

"I saw you inside but," he stumbled for something to say. "You look great," he finally offered.

Carla turned to face him. "It's been a long time, Sean," she said and stepped toward him with a hug.

Sean immediately reciprocated, and his grasp of her lingered longer than the scores of other hugs he'd endured this evening. The pressure of her full breasts against his chest sent a shiver of excitement through him. "Carla Anderson," he thought as images of the little girl raced through his mind.

Finally Carla's arms loosened. It took him a few seconds, but Sean finally got the hint. Carla pushed away slowly and looked up into his eyes, eyes she'd dreamed about since they were kids when he was the older brother of her friend, Shannon Donovan.

At arm's length, Sean held her shoulders loosely for another second. He stared into her eyes, which danced above high cheekbones and a whimsical smile.

"Can we sit and talk awhile?" he asked and waved toward two cushioned Adirondack chairs and a lounge table. She nodded and followed him.

Sean's surprise at Carla's beauty was complete. He'd always thought of her as a cute girl, but she'd been his little sister's best friend, more of a pest than anything else when they were young, though she and Shannon were only three years younger than he. Even when he saw her at his wedding and then, as he now recalled, in tears at her brother's funeral as a result of a wound in the Gulf War, he hadn't paid attention other than to thank her at the wedding and give his condolences at the funeral. Both times, Sean was with Susan, his bride and wife. Now, as he sat next to her, the scent of spring from her hair intoxicated him, and he could feel the warmth from her body only inches away.

"You didn't answer my question," Carla tried to break the awkward silence.

"What's that?" he asked.

"Did they convince you to come back from the big city?"

Sean smiled and shook his head.

"No," he dragged out the statement and turned pensively to stare out past the deck. "They're still dreaming of growth here, aren't they? I guess they don't understand what it means. Does anyone really want a big city here?"

"I don't know about a big city. But they sure would like the money they think will come with it," Carla said.

"Are you living in town?" Sean asked and turned to her again.

She nodded. "I left San Francisco three years ago. Uncle Buck needed some help in his office. I'd pretty much had it with the craziness up there anyway. It turned out to be a good move for me. I did some real interesting work with my uncle."

Sean knew he had to say something about Buck, offer condolences, but his mind raced with wonder at her beauty, and that, combined with the evening's warmth, prevented him from forming coherent thoughts. Thankfully, they were interrupted.

"So sorry to hear about your uncle, Carla," said Mrs. Connor, who walked arm in arm with her husband, Sid, a man known even when Sean and Carla were younger as "Old Man Connor."

"We're going to miss him," Mrs. Connor finished with a sympathetic smile that wasn't mirrored by Old Man Connor. He leered at Carla in one of those lost moments where his private, lecherous thoughts were written all over his face.

"Thank you, Mrs. Connor," Carla said, and she chose not to look at Mr. Connor. "It's difficult for all of us."

Mrs. Connor nodded slowly, had nothing else to say, tugged at her husband's arm.

"Well, have a wonderful evening you two. Come Sidney, let's leave the young ones their conversation."

Reluctantly, Sidney permitted himself to be led away by his wife.

"Well, it's nice to know some things don't change," Sean laughed. Carla joined the laughter as her eyes opened wide in mock shock at the looks from Old Man Connor.

"Sorry about Buck, Carla," Sean finally said as the laughter died. "We heard about it in L.A. A real shock."

"For us, too," Carla responded. She shook her head sadly. "He made that hike dozens of times and knew every part of the Staircase. It's hard to believe he would get caught unawares in that storm."

"What do you think happened?"

"I don't know. The coroner's still looking into it. I don't know why it's taking so long, except that he's dragging his feet for the publicity."

"You think there's something to the rumors?"

"Might be," Carla shrugged. "He made some enemies because of his work, but it just doesn't seem possible someone would want to kill him."

They sat quietly for several seconds staring absently toward the mountains.

"Buck and your mother were sweet on each other, Sean. Did you know that?" Carla asked.

Sean turned sharply and stared at Carla, whose eyes continued their focus on the darkness beyond the deck. His immediate reaction was doubt, and even denial, but in a flash of sudden awareness, he remembered his mother's reaction when he mentioned Buck's death Thursday evening, and Sean knew it was possible. And why not, he wondered. Billy Donovan had been gone for more than twenty years. Mary was an attractive woman who still had the passion and lust for life he took for granted growing up with her.

"What makes you think so?" he asked.

She turned to him and smiled.

"I don't think so, Sean. Buck told me he was in love with your mother. He wanted to marry her. He asked her a few times over the years, but your mother wouldn't consider it. She told him one happy marriage was all the good Lord provided a person, and she had hers with your father. I don't think it stopped her from loving Buck, though. They were cute together."

Sean wondered why he hadn't noticed anything about the relationship. He never even thought to ask his mother if she had anyone in her life. It never seemed important. He was steeped in his own issues; he never considered what was going on in his mother's life. He assumed she was okay, and his sisters were there for her if she needed it. It never occurred to him she might be carrying on a relationship. Sean leaned back and smiled.

"What's funny?" Carla asked, her own smile widening.

"I just think it's great, that's all. My mom and Buck; good people who were able to share some happy times together. I'm sorry I didn't know … never bothered to find out," his smile faded.

Carla caught the change and the sudden pensiveness.

"How about you, Sean. Any new loves in your life?" She got right to the point.

"Naw … not really," he inadvertently made it sound like there were some casual relationships even though there had been no one in years. "How about you? Married?"

"No. That ended a few years ago. That's one of the reasons I left San Francisco. I needed to get as far away from that relationship as I could. Things have been good here, though," she finished hopefully.

Sean nodded.

"How are things going for you?" Carla asked softly.

Sean didn't want to get into that on this beautiful evening, but he also didn't want to end the conversation. He wrestled with possible responses that wouldn't destroy the comfortable mood. That was when Shannon stepped onto the deck and spotted them.

"There you are," Sean's sister said as she glanced from Sean to Carla. "It's about time you guys said hello to each other." Carla smiled, and Sean nodded. He could feel his color reddening. Luckily the dark covered it.

"Mom wants us for some pictures, Sean." She took his hand and tugged for him to rise. "It'll only take a minute. I'll send him right back out, Carla."

But she didn't.

After pictures, other guests again invaded their time. Sean found himself glancing at Carla and was surprised to see her glancing back with the occasional smile. He wasn't sure what was going on because it had been so long since he could remember feeling anything but melancholy at the turns in his life. Yet, now he was excited—unsure what it meant, but excited nevertheless that this beautiful woman appeared to be interested in him. He tried to maneuver into conversations in which Carla was involved, but before long the evening was ending. As the Donovans stood at the Mountain View's front door saying their goodbyes and thanks, Carla walked past with her father, Buck's brother Tom, on her arm. As Tom commiserated softly with Mary about Buck's death, Carla turned to Sean.

"Will you be able to make it back for Uncle Buck's funeral next week?" she asked.

Shannon, standing next to Sean, glanced at him and smiled expectantly. Sean wanted to say yes, but he wasn't sure. Did she really want him to come, or was she just being polite—looking for something to say? He wondered if there was more in the question before he came back to his senses. It was a funeral, for God's sake. What did he have to think about? Either he could make it or not; it was that simple. But it wasn't; he knew it. He had to figure it out.

"I don't know, Carla." Shannon frowned next to him, and he continued. "I'd like to."

Carla nodded and dropped her head for a second.

"It would be good to have another Donovan here with your mom, Sean. I think she'd appreciate it since Shannon and Katie can't make it." Carla sounded noncommittal. "We'd like to have you come, if you can; but I understand if you're busy."

Sean smiled. "I'll try to make it."

The goodbye hugs were awkward, and Sean wondered if he'd made yet another mistake as Carla turned away. He watched her still tightly rounded hips sway her calf-length skirt, and he ached over his insecurity.

"Damn," he said under his breath. He closed his eyes in frustration before taking his mother's arm to escort her to their car while his sister's eyes bored into him.

EIGHT

ORSON HOFFMAN WADDLED ABOUT his lab, a smug smile lifting the corners of his mouth. Hoffman was a man who usually didn't smile. He never gave smiling or frowning much thought. It was just that his heavily jowled face was turned down in a perpetual kind of absentminded scowl. This Sunday evening, however, he was very excited, and even those heavy jowls couldn't keep him from smiling.

The county coroner's ship had come in. He completed the autopsies Saturday evening and spent all day Sunday working on the press conference presentation scheduled for Monday morning. It was very clear to him what had happened.

Hoffman straightened the white lab coat that hung on the back of the door. He fussed about the lab making sure everything was just right for the onslaught the next morning.

The two bodies lay on adjacent tables in the middle of the stark room. Although he'd completed his work the previous evening and stored the bodies for the night in the refrigerated drawers on the far wall, he'd replaced them on their respective tables when he arrived Sunday morning. Hoffman did his best thinking in the presence of the bodies upon which he was working. Even the stench of decay didn't bother him anymore. It was all part of his wondrous profession. And, truth be told, he actually liked the dead. He liked the company, particularly when that company was the bodies that would make him famous.

"Well Mr. Doe, you bad man," he sighed, the smile still playing across his face. "It's time for you and the eminent Mr. Anderson to go to sleep for the night."

The pudgy man covered the assassin's skeletal face and slid the pallet upon which he lay onto the gurney to roll the body back to its nightly quarters. The coroner's mind ran with the details he'd finally accepted.

Shell fragments mixed with Buck Anderson's shattered shoulder told the story. It was obvious that the gaping exit wound spoke of a large caliber shell, which had entered from the rear. How Anderson had been able to get the drop on the other man was unclear. Hoffman was only sure the second man was the aggressor and that Buck had somehow hidden himself and struck unexpectedly. While one might have argued the environmentalist cut the other man's throat first and then was shot as he tried to make his escape, that scenario was most unlikely. Orson Hoffman discerned the telltale sign of the other man's head wound. And the blade that cut the path across the man's throat had entered with a deep straight-on puncture at the left side of his neck and had then been dragged with pressure from above to the right side. The Doe was surely the one who had started this. It was while he lay on his back dazed from the head wound that the throat cut was made from above. That much was clear.

What wasn't clear in the beginning was why. It had taken Orson Hoffman quite some time to figure that out. If he'd been pressed, he'd have had to admit it was the marks of the scavengers that were in the process of devouring the body that solved it for him.

While Hoffman never paid much attention to news beyond his own field of interest, he had sufficient general knowledge to know that birds the size of the creatures that must have been feasting on the man simply didn't exist in the wild. That's certainly what the rest of the world believed. How shocked they would be when he revealed the truth: that wild condors had ravaged the body.

"Condors," he smiled broadly. "You bad man," he said again to the dead Doe. "You were trying to prevent ol' Buck from telling the world, and it's your own body that gives up the secret. Serves you right." He actually giggled.

Behind Orson Hoffman a dark figure stood in the shadows of the now open doorway. He listened intently to the coroner's last words and knew that the destruction would have to be complete. He stepped into the light of the lab, the rubber soles of his shoes squeaking on the shiny white tile floor.

The coroner whirled around, his body jiggling with the motion. Hoffman's smile disappeared immediately, gravity, his heavy jowls and the shock of the intruder finally overwhelming his previously buoyant mood.

"What are you ... you aren't supposed to be here. Who ... who are you?" he sputtered.

The man, clad in black from head to foot, held both hands behind his back and stared, smiling at the coroner.

"You're a smart man, Mr. Hoffman."

Hoffman recognized the face. It was a pleasant face—calm, smiling, and encouraging, yet somehow rugged and strong. He'd seen the man among the reporters who'd been pestering him since the arrival of the two bodies. But he'd been different than the others. He didn't force himself upon the coroner with inane questions. He stayed in the background and listened, always with a pleasant smile. Hoffman remembered thinking if he were to say anything to any of the reporters, it would be to this one because he seemed such a pleasant, smiling man. But the coroner wasn't quite ready to talk this moment, and there was something about the man's dress and stance that unnerved him.

"You'll have to leave," he stammered as he tried to smile. He leaned heavily against the table of the Doe. "The press conference is tomorrow morning. I'll tell you everything then."

Hoffman's voice grew shaky and cracked at the end of his statement. He didn't know why he felt it, but he knew this man had no interest in knowing what really happened. In fact, he probably already knew it all and was here because he didn't want anyone else to know.

"That won't be necessary, Mr. Hoffman." The man's voice was smooth, flat, and calm, with an accent Hoffman should have recognized—hard and guttural, yet pleasant, even elegant.

The man stepped toward the coroner and brought his hands from behind his back. The right one held a weapon, which, under calmer circumstances, Orson Hoffman would most assuredly have been able to identify. But this time his mind froze the second he saw the reflection of the room's light off the silenced barrel.

"Unfortunately your brilliance will cause my friends some terrible problems," the man purred. He raised the weapon slowly and placed it lightly against Orson Hoffman's forehead. "You do good work, sir."

The coroner's mind raced crazily. The compliments were what he'd always deserved and never received. He knew he was good ... brilliant? ... yes ... brilliant ... but ... he was going to die. Could he save himself? Tomorrow was very important. He had a lot of work ... please don't kill me ... I won't talk ... This is my chance ... It can't end ... His mind suddenly went blank and he fainted at the feet of his killer.

The man stood over the coroner's crumpled body. This made his job much easier. He wouldn't have to hide a bullet.

Shortly after midnight, Visalia was awakened by the explosion that destroyed the county building that housed the coroner's lab. As sleepy residents watched clouds of acrid black smoke billow across the moonlit sky, the bodies of Orson Hoffman, Buck Anderson, and his assassin burned to ash.

NINE

"I'M GETTING TIRED OF this, Richard. It's almost ten years, and we're back at square one." The old man's voice cracked, but his authority was unequivocal.

Richard Wolf, partner at McCormack, Stein & Wolf, leaned forward at his desk and looked at the phone. "We're almost there, Atticus." He screwed up his face, angry they had to contend with yet another injunction. "This one's a formality. The judge had to grant it pending the final hearing. We're three months away."

"Then what?" the old man asked. "What else can this damn Sierra Club come up with?"

Wolf glared around the spacious office at the faces of the two junior partners and four senior associates with whom he'd been meeting when Atticus Golden returned his call and he'd had to relay the bad news.

"That's it," he finally said. "They've shot their wad, Atticus. The EIR is clean ... the Supreme Court said so. They're finished. We'll all have a great Thanksgiving."

"This new judge was supposed to be developer friendly," rejoined the old man, ignoring Wolf's attempt to lighten the mood. "Hell, the whole state wants the jobs and taxes this project will bring. I don't like it, Richard."

"Bear with it, Atticus, just a little longer. I told you we know this guy. Besides, the Supreme Court has already directed his hand. Singleton is long gone. It'll all be over soon." Richard Wolf referred to Judge John Singleton, the maverick environmentalist judge who had given the Sierra Club its original order ... the one that had recently been overturned, after years of battle, by the United States Supreme Court. Singleton had accepted a new position in the California State Appellate Court's Third District. A pro-California president bent on keeping the state in his reelection camp had appointed his successor, Tom Marks. Marks was a conservative, pro-development jurist who had graduated from USC twenty-five years earlier along with his classmate Richard Wolf.

"It's been a long haul, Atticus, but we're almost there," continued Wolf.

"I want this during my lifetime, Richard. I won't be here forever."

Wolf smiled for the first time during the conversation. "You've got a long way to go yet, my friend. This world needs Uncle Atti for a few more years."

"Maybe so..." Atticus hesitated pensively. "You take care of it this time, Richard," he finally said. "Don't let this go any longer."

"My crew's ready for the last push. I'll keep you posted," Wolf said and pushed the button to end the call.

Richard Wolf stood behind a brilliantly polished, black onyx table with brushed steel frame and legs. It was a piece of priceless handmade art that served as his desk. The man's stance in front of his black leather chair was spread, balanced, and ready for battle. His left hand rested on his hip while the right held his chin as he stared pensively at the telephone. Finally, he turned slowly, walked out from behind the table, and looked up at the group of expectant lawyers.

While they still wore business suits early in the morning, Richard Wolf had done away with his coat. He wore a perfectly knotted tie at the collar of an unwrinkled white shirt with cuffs down and clasped with gold. Beneath the shirt were the lines of a muscle-toned body to which he paid considerable attention. His mass of thick black hair was combed straight back to reveal swatches of grey at the temples. The hawk nose, black eyes, and sharp, powerful jaw completed the look of a man not to be trifled with. Richard Wolf was the center of this group. He was clearly in control.

"Liz, I want you to get in touch with that prick at Forest," he pointed at Liz Harris, a thirty-eight year old junior partner at the firm. She was severe in every aspect, from the dark charcoal, form-hugging suit to the tightly pulled hair and sharp featured face. She was one of Wolf's clutch of highly proficient young litigators, part of his team within the firm. "You tell him we'll get him ready for the hearing, and I'll be there with him in front of Judge Marks."

Harris nodded and jotted a note. Wolf turned his attention to the others.

"Anything new on the *Jackson* case, Matt?" He looked at Matthew Dunne, thirty-year old senior associate, and, from Wolf's perspective, the best of the lot. He was tough, unemotional, and highly organized. He viewed his duties to the firm and his mentor, Richard Wolf, as his highest priority in life. He nodded.

"It looks like Beverly Jackson might have found an attorney." Before Wolf could get the next question out of his mouth, Dunne continued. "A guy from Torrance. He called yesterday. I talked to him briefly. No substitution yet, but he said he'd have it for us by next Monday. His name is Sean Donovan."

Wolf was taken aback. It wasn't often he was surprised by information from one of his associates. He was usually far ahead of them, but this information shocked him.

"Sean Michael Donovan?" he asked.

Dunne nodded as he turned back to the first page of the biography he had put together the night before.

"Sean Michael Donovan … that's right. He apparently worked for us back in the '80s and early '90s. I checked firm records. He became a partner for a short time before he left in '94 I think it was. Do you know him, Richard?" He looked up expectantly.

Wolf nodded slowly and smiled.

"Yes, I know him. He was one of us. He was fired in '94—didn't leave," he said.

"It looks like he's fallen on hard times since. He was suspended from the practice of law back in 1997, divorced a year earlier, reinstated to the

Bar in 2000, doesn't have much of a practice—small matters, neighbor disputes, the occasional divorce, and some minor business and real estate matters. I don't know how Jackson happened to get hold of him."

"I think he grew up in Visalia," Wolf said. "She's probably a family friend. Does he have any associates or partners?"

"Doesn't look like it. Looks like he's a sole practitioner in one of those shared suite arrangements in Torrance. He's not doing much. Is he any good?"

"He was," Wolf said before turning slowly and walking back to his table. He wondered what the hell S. Michael Donovan was thinking taking on a case against his old firm, the very firm he shamed and from which he was unceremoniously booted so many years before.

"That's all for now," Wolf said as he fingered a stack of papers on the desk. "Let's get to it. We've got a lot of work to do. Matt, stick around for a few minutes."

As the others got up to leave, Wolf's intercom buzzed. He pushed the button and answered absently, "Yes?"

"Mr. Perez is on the line for you, Richard. He says it's urgent."

Wolf thought for a moment before responding. "I'll take it," and he pushed the hands-free button on the phone.

"Hi, Carlos."

"What the fuck is going..." started the caller before Wolf lifted the receiver.

———————

Sean made the call the previous afternoon. He'd called to let them know he was subbing in as counsel for Mrs. Jackson. He asked for the second attorney listed at the signature line, someone named Matthew Dunne. Dunne was cordial and professional, but he was clearly surprised Beverly Jackson had an attorney.

"I'm sorry, you said your office is in Torrance?" Dunne asked. "How did you..." He paused, as if looking for words but apparently found none. Sean smiled at his discomfort and chose not to relieve it. He knew they'd figure it out quickly enough.

"I'll get you the substitution sometime next week," Sean said. "I wanted to let you know she is represented. I'll send over a confirming letter."

Sean didn't want to speak to Richard Wolf. The truth was that he wasn't sure he even wanted to be involved in a case against his old firm. He knew what the firm's capacity was. Los Angeles based McCormack, Stein & Wolf had become one of the best-known firms in the country. Although not the biggest, it was growing and already ran offices in New York, Chicago, London, and Beijing. The fact the firm had three attorneys listed as contacts on the *Jackson* case was good evidence they had more attorneys than were necessary, and now that there was an attorney on the other side, it would free them to work the case to its finest detail. They would throw a gaggle of clerks and young lawyers at it with orders to churn out discovery and motions that would overwhelm a sole practitioner opponent and earn the firm some big fees.

Sean had followed the firm's growth since his departure. The big shock in the Los Angeles legal community came when the old time firm added Richard Wolf's name to the letterhead. It happened during the unprecedented real estate boom of the early 2000s, when Wolf's real estate department was suddenly generating more than half the firm's gross billings. It was, in fact, the success of his department that prompted expansion of the New York and Chicago offices and the opening of the London and Beijing offices. Unsubstantiated rumor had it that Wolf threatened to leave the firm and take his team and clients with him unless he got top billing equal to the long deceased founders of the firm. Over the objection of the older attorneys—the ones who believed one hundred twenty-five years of McCormack & Stein reputation was sacred and inviolate—Richard Wolf got what he wanted, just as Sean Michael Donovan suspected he eventually would.

Sean was concerned about taking on McCormack, Stein & Wolf. He didn't have the guns to contend with a costly litigation. His hope was to find a way to defeat the motion brought by the firm and then associate a larger firm that had the staff to assist with the litigation if Wolf and his people decided to take the case further. Sean's initial analysis was that Wolf would not have his associates generating any significant new billings before the hearing because they had already done all the research and preparation they needed when they created the motion. Therefore, he surmised, they couldn't bury him until later, provided he even got to later. Beating them on their motion was a prospect that was looking unlikely.

Sean completed his review of the materials he picked up from Mrs. Jackson by Wednesday, the day he called McCormack, Stein & Wolf. The materials were sparse and disjointed with the only complete document being the deposition of Beverly Jackson. That was the bound document in which Mrs. Jackson's oral testimony under oath in response to questions artfully posed by Matthew Dunne was transcribed by a court reporter. It contained one hundred twenty pages, far less than even the most basic deposition, but it was damaging.

To say Matthew Dunne had gotten the "most out of the least" was an understatement. He went for the major points of his motion right from the start. Every point he needed to establish that his client had obtained the right to title to Mrs. Jackson's property by adverse possession was made succinctly and without equivocation. He appeared on paper to be a gentleman who asked simple questions and received simple answers that supported his position even while he was being overly polite to the old woman. Had it not been for one final question the case might have been a lost cause for Sean. As is often the case when things appear to be going too smoothly, however, the young attorney, perhaps caught up with his own brilliance and congratulating himself a little too soon, asked that final question.

After establishing each element of his case, the last question appeared in the following sequence:

> "Q. I have only one or two more minor questions, Mrs. Jackson, and then we can all go home. Is that okay?
>
> A. (Witness nods)
>
> Q. I want to confirm that no one received permission to use your property for grazing or any other purpose. Is that correct?
>
> A. No.

Q. No? Mrs. Jackson, you said earlier that you never gave permission to anyone to use your property, didn't you?

A. Yes, that's right. I never give no permission.

Q. So your answer to the previous question should have been yes, correct?

A. No.

Q. Well, you just …

A. I can explain. You see, you asked me if someone received permission to use my property. I never give no permission but my husband's gran'daddy done it.

Q. What was that? Your what?

A. My husband's gran'daddy and his daddy before him give permission for them folks to do sheep grazing and such.

Q. Thank you, Mrs. Jackson. That'll be all for today."

Dunne proceeded to provide the usual deposition closing information, but the "cat was out of the bag." If permission was indeed granted, and it could somehow be proved, Dunne's motion was lost. The reality, however, was that proving permission would be all but impossible because anyone who might have any direct knowledge of the granting of such permission and any agreement associated with it was dead. Still, a crack had appeared. Sean needed to find a way to break it open.

"Your boy may have blown it, Richard," he whispered as he read the words again.

TEN

AT 4:31 A.M. ON JANUARY 17, 1994, *a magnitude 6.7 earthquake struck the Northridge area of Los Angeles. Although the quake's magnitude was strong by any measure, it was the ground acceleration associated with it, the highest ever recorded in an urban area in North America, that wrought the death and devastation that brought L.A. to its knees. Freeways buckled, apartments crumbled, people died, and the economy of Southern California took yet another blow. The decade started with the end of the Cold War and the immediate reduction in military spending that was the lifeblood of the economy at the time. Then came the Japanese economic collapse that sent billions of dollars in buying power back home followed quickly by the triple whammies of the Rodney King riots, the devastating fires that dropped ash over and engulfed the entire region, and finally the quake. Property values plummeted as much as 30% by mid-decade as hordes of people chose to move to more hospitable environs, thus creating the first net negative migration from the state in decades.*

For many speculators, visionaries, and well-healed investors this was the best of times. The fear that "Southern California is cursed" stigmatized the region. But those who knew it would recover were undaunted. They bought properties at prices not seen in years. It was a buyer's market, but for sellers, it was terrible.

Salvatore Leone owned hundreds of apartment units in buildings spread throughout Los Angeles, Riverside, and San Bernardino counties. His units were in what was referred to as "B" areas: neither the best nor worst areas, but areas that were not bad under normal circumstances. He had two major problems, however. The first was that none of his buildings was impacted by the quake, so he couldn't take advantage of insurance payouts to bolster his bottom line. But it was the second problem that made the first one even bigger. Because of the economic hits to the economy he couldn't keep his buildings occupied. The people who normally rented his units were the very ones who were emigrating to more prosperous locales. Leone's operation was losing large sums of money, and those losses would ultimately bring down his entire real estate empire if they were not stopped. He sought guidance from his attorneys at McCormack & Stein for whom he was a major client to the tune of over one million dollars in billings per year.

S. Michael Donovan and A. Richard Wolf, USC law school acquaintances and top 10% graduates, joined the firm right out of law school. During their ten-year association with the firm, a friendship that didn't exist in school developed between them. Although Donovan was the more personable with better client management and legal and financial analysis skills, Wolf was tougher, more calculating, and better able to deal with what some referred to as the "slimy underbelly" of business. The firm used their unique skills as part of the business and real estate team in which they were considered that department's most gifted players. During the summer of that fateful year, they were each enthusiastically accepted as junior partners in the firm.

The two became the firm's lead counsel in matters relating to Salvatore Leone, each one taking the lead position on different matters with the other offering backup where needed. They met often with Leone, his accountants, and property managers to discuss his apartment holdings. They analyzed his financials and ultimately helped determine the major cause of his problems. Eight buildings were losing a total in excess of $250,000 per month. All the other buildings combined were slightly positive, but the losers were killing him. By late 1994, as luck would have it, a market was developing for buildings that could be run by small owner/operators who could find cost efficiencies in their personal management of buildings as opposed to the corporate owners like Leone who had to manage large overheads. Leone's attorneys and accountants advised him to sell the losing buildings. Donovan was lead counsel for the matter.

Leone hated the idea of selling in such a tough market, but when confronted with the real facts by Donovan when his own employees wouldn't do it for fear of his volcanic personality, he realized he had no choice. Once he set the course for sale, there was nothing that would get in the way of Salvatore Leone's plans to offload the losers. The properties were listed, and the marketing began. Almost immediately, potential buyers poked their heads up, and offers were made for the buildings. It was during the review of the financials requested by potential buyers that Donovan noticed a problem.

"Something's wrong here," he said. He stood in Richard Wolf's office holding a stack of papers. The top sheet was a profit and loss statement for the Countryside Apartments, a one hundred fifty unit complex in Riverside. "This is one of the losers, Richard. This report shows a profit."

Donovan placed the stack down on Wolf's desk so they could view it together. In front of Wolf already was another stack for the Riverview Terrace Apartments, a similar sized complex in East Los Angeles, also owned by Leone and on the block for sale. Donovan's quick glance at the P&L revealed the same discrepancy.

"These were both losers. Sal wouldn't be selling them otherwise. Did we get it wrong?" Donovan asked.

"I don't know Michael. It looks like they were profitable after all," Wolf said.

Donovan shook his head.

"No, I don't think so. I compared the reports we used when we were reviewing this for the past several months. These numbers are wrong. I'm going to Sal's office to meet with Dave Rohr." He referred to Leone's head of property management. "I called. He's ready to meet us now. We should get going," Donovan concluded and began to collect his papers.

"You go, Michael. I'll finish the review of the purchase agreement and be available on the phone if you need me."

Donovan nodded and without further discussion left Wolf's office.

"*Those numbers are wrong, Dave,*" *Donovan said to the pudgy property manager.*

Dave Rohr glanced at the papers Donovan had placed in front of him. His lazy brown eyes came up slowly. He said nothing.

"*You left out some cost items.*" *Donovan was looking down at papers clasped in his manila file. He ran his fingers down a column and continued. "You're missing office overhead costs, on-site management costs, and the maintenance and repair costs are a lot lower.*"

Dave Rohr didn't hesitate in his response.

"*We had to do that, Michael. The building wouldn't sell if we put all the costs in there.*" *He tried to speak with authority, matter-of-factly, as if he was in command and knew exactly what he was doing.*

Donovan stared at him, stunned. He shook his head quickly to make sure he was hearing Rohr's actual words.

"*Did you hear what you just said, Dave? You said we have to commit fraud to sell the buildings. You can't do that.*"

"*C'mon, Michael, everyone does it. It's the way these things are sold. They all work the numbers.*"

"*We don't. We don't work numbers, Dave.*" *When Dave didn't respond, Donovan continued. "You're better than this, man. You know you can't lie. Even putting aside the morality of the whole thing, the reality is that it'll come back and get you. It'll get Sal, and frankly he can't afford the fallout, either civil or criminal.*"

Rohr dropped his head and said, "Sal'll be pissed, Michael. He's the one who wants it done this way. He saw the numbers after the buyer asked for them. He wants it to look better."

Donovan was stunned yet again. Salvatore Leone, one of his firm's major clients was telling one of his employees to commit fraud using the age-old excuse "everybody does it." He shook his head slowly, steeling himself for a reply.

"*You can't be a part of this, Dave. I know I can't. None of us can.*" *He hesitated, knowing full well it would not be pudgy, malleable Dave Rohr who would say anything to Salvatore Leone. "I'll talk to Sal tomorrow. I'll think of something.*"

And he did; or, at least he thought he did.

Donovan spent the rest of the afternoon and the early evening hours making sure he fully understood the numbers, real and fabricated. He clearly understood the needs of his client and analyzed potential roads to travel to meet those needs. He discussed it with Richard Wolf and ultimately read his solution to Wolff who was enthusiastically supportive. While he completed his preparation for tomorrow's meeting with Leone, Donovan asked Wolf to contact their real estate department senior partner, John Denton, at home, brief him on what was happening, and request that he join Donovan and Wolf at Leone's office the next morning. He agreed to do so.

———————

By the time S. Michael Donovan pulled into the driveway of his Manhattan Beach home his head was heavy with strategy on how best to handle the volatile Salvatore Leone the next day. He was grateful Richard Wolf and John Denton would be there to back him up.

Before sitting down to a Chinese chicken salad Susan had picked up for him, he went into the kids' rooms to wish them good night. Unfortunately, six-year-old Marie was already asleep and eight-year-old Johnny was fading fast.

"I missed you today, Daddy," his son mumbled, half asleep.

"I missed you too, buddy," Donovan said as he sat on the edge of his son's bed and caressed his cheek lightly. "Sorry I'm so late. I had a lot of work to do today."

Johnny yawned and spoke through it. "That's okay, Daddy. Can you come home early tomorrow so we can play baseball?"

Donovan smiled at the simplicity of the little boy's love, how the tribulations and drama of the adult world hadn't yet tainted him. He wished it could always be that way for his kids.

"You bet, buddy," he said as he tousled the boy's hair and kissed him goodnight.

A few minutes later, Donovan sat alone at the kitchen nook table, sipping a glass of Chardonnay and picking at his salad. Susan sat before the T.V. in the family room. She was already in her robe and starting to drift off to sleep when Donovan left his salad and stepped into the family room to sit with her.

"Hey," he said. "Can we talk for a few minutes?"

Susan glanced up at him, shook herself awake, and smiled. "Sure. What's up?"

Her eyes were moist from sleep. The room's dim light sparkled off their deep brown radiance. After more than ten years of marriage, she was still the beautiful co-ed for whom he'd fallen even before law school. Her hair hung long, black, and curly, and the figure that had labored through two pregnancies was as firm and shapely as it had been before the children. Her commitment to her health and appearance was obvious, and the smoldering sexuality that had always attracted Donovan was still there.

He stared at his wife for several seconds, lost first in her beauty and then in his own reflections of idealism and right and wrong.

"What's the problem, Michael?" Susan finally asked, exasperation tingeing her tone.

He shook his head slowly and told her about the Leone number discrepancies, how Dave Rohr was so willing to commit fraud in order to avoid his boss's rebuke, and of how he, Michael Donovan, was going to have to be the one to confront Leone the next day.

"Richard and John will be there to back me up," he said. "Still, it shouldn't have to come to this. It's hard to believe anyone would object to my... our firm's position, but it looks like Sal is the kind of guy who could end up firing the firm over this. I don't get it. The right and wrong of it seems so obvious. You'd think he'd want to thank us for bringing it to his attention."

Susan nodded slowly, seemingly deep in thought. She had let Donovan get it all out without a word. Finally, she made her point.

"I don't think you should do it, Michael."

He stared at her in disbelief. She couldn't possibly mean he should say nothing, that he should let his client commit fraud. But the conviction of his wife's words and the pointed stare made it clear she meant what she said.

Donovan's immediate thought was to question her about what had happened to the college idealism they had shared; the belief you didn't cheat; you did right even if no one knew about it, and you didn't do wrong, even if no one would ever find out. But discussions like that had ended between them over years of high living, child rearing, and mundane responsibility.

"What? I shouldn't tell him not to lie? Susan, it's fraud," he said. "I can't be a part of that."

"Well, you're not are you? You're the attorney, not the guy who signs the statement or even transmits it. Maybe you should let them deal with it. Anyway, it might mean more fees in the future if this client is sued."

"He's my client. I can't look the other way while he buries himself. I can't let him damage someone else with his fraud."

Susan nodded slowly and eyed her husband. "You're not letting him do anything. He's doing it; you've told his manager what the problem is; they can make their own decisions. You've done your duty, haven't you?" She dropped her head and spoke softly, deliberately. "Look, Michael, you just made partner. They like you there, and we have a good life. Why do this and anger such an important client? How will it help us?"

"That isn't the point. What he's doing is wrong. I can't stand by and let it happen. If nothing else, I need to let him know what's happening and the potential consequences. That's my duty as his attorney."

Susan pushed herself up off the couch. "You've obviously made your decision, Michael. I don't think there's any point in discussing it further. I'm going to check on the kids and go to bed."

She walked away, angry it seemed, and Donovan couldn't understand it.

The next morning, as he traveled up the 405 Freeway to the Century City office of Salvatore Leone, he wondered what had happened to Susan, or maybe it was him. Maybe he was just too stubborn, too idealistic and self-righteous.

Her parting words were, "Don't do it Michael. It'll only get you fired, and we can't handle that."

He wasn't sure what she meant. Of course they could handle it if he was fired. He was a damn good attorney, and he could get a job in any of a hundred firms. Hell, he could hang out his own shingle and build up a practice in no time. But that wouldn't happen anyway. They wouldn't fire him. His firm would stand with him.

Richard Wolf and John Denton met Donovan at Leone's office. They were ushered into Leone's palatial conference room where Dave Rohr was already seated. Donovan tried to reassure Rohr with friendly small talk and nods of understanding. Everything would be alright. After all, Donovan had come up with an alternative that would make the fraud unnecessary.

Salvatore Leone lumbered into the room a short time later. He was an imposing man, big in every aspect, over six feet tall and at least two hundred fifty pounds. His hands were thick and powerful when he greeted a man, and his voice was deep, guttural, commanding.

"So, what's the problem, gentlemen?" He got right to the point.

Donovan glanced at Denton before he stood, papers in hand. He had previously distributed folders containing copies of the original financial statements for the two apartment buildings they were discussing. These were stapled together in separate packets. In addition, the folder contained separately stapled statements containing the false numbers. He explained the problem succinctly but noticed immediately the red rising in Salvatore Leone's massive face.

"I believe I've got a solution to this, however. I've drafted language that should take care of it. Please refer to the single sheet in your packet." They found their copies and read the paragraph typed on it.

The paragraph stated in clear, concise language that some information had been omitted from the financial statements. It specifically identified the expense categories that were omitted and stated the seller's opinion that these were corporate costs in an operation that didn't properly allocate overhead and maintenance on a per building basis but rather prorated them on a companywide basis. Therefore, including those numbers would not create an accurate picture of any individual building's performance. The wording concluded with a statement in bold print: "IF THE BUYER WISHES TO SEE THE EXPENSES THAT HAVE BEEN OMITTED, THEY ARE AVAILABLE UPON WRITTEN REQUEST BY BUYER." It closed with an acknowledgment and signature line for the buyer. Each page of the financials was to include such a statement.

"What if they ask for the information?" asked Leone.

"You give it to them," Donovan replied.

Leone laughed—a booming, dangerous laugh.

"We give it to them?" He leaned forward and glared at Donovan. "We lose the sale if we give it to them."

Donovan was not intimidated. "Maybe we do, Sal, but maybe we don't. It's probable that most buyers will substitute their own numbers based on their own experience and won't even ask. If one does, we have to give it to them and deal with the consequences." When Leone looked around the room and then came back to him, Donovan continued. "You can't afford this, Sal. With the Justice Department's investigation heating up on the bank fraud allegations in the residential housing sector, we don't want any attention brought to you or your company. The publicity, even though not true, would be devastating. We can avoid it by being honest here."

Leone's eyes narrowed, and the muscles in his jaw clenched.

Donovan looked at Richard Wolf, and then at John Denton, for support. Neither one returned his look. Each occupied himself thumbing through his own file while Leone's eyes moved around the room.

Finally Leone turned back to Donovan.

"Thank you, Mr. Donovan," he said despite the fact it had always been "Michael." "That'll be all for today, gentlemen. I'll discuss the matter with Mr. Rohr and get back to you." Then, as they stood to leave, he turned to Denton. "John, stick around for a minute."

Two weeks later, the Los Angeles law firm of McCormack & Stein fired S. Michael Donovan.

ELEVEN

ATTICUS GOLDEN LEANED BACK into his worn leather chair. The lumbar support pillow was uncomfortable, but it had been so for years, and he knew he had to endure that discomfort to avoid the pain he'd suffer if he didn't use it.

The old man considered his most recent conversations with his attorney, Richard Wolf. He wondered again if he was on the proper course. He swiveled his chair away from the ancient mahogany desk to his left so he could look out onto his creation.

Atticus had never wanted a credenza behind his desk. Instead he'd built floor to ceiling windows through which he could view the growth of his dream from the discomfort of his lumbar supported leather chair. Now, as he looked to the horizon he could see it all. The thriving wonder of Golden World was resplendent before him: from the ancient castles and creature-filled moats of Medieval Land to Norman Rockwell's America, to Fantaworld, where wizards and dragons roamed, to the skyways and space stations of the distant galaxies of Spaceworld. Atticus could see it all. He'd spent more than fifty years dreaming, planning, and building by many accounts the most spectacular themed lands the world had ever known. Millions of people from around the globe visited the southern part of Ventura County annually just to visit Atticus Golden's world. For many, the creatures, stories, and worlds of Atticus Golden rivaled those of Walt Disney himself.

When Walt Disney died unexpectedly on December 15, 1966, Atticus Golden was still a young man. At the age of thirty-seven he and his company were on the threshold of unprecedented growth. While Disney's death was mourned the world over, Atticus Golden viewed it, quietly, as his opportunity to make his move.

In his early days, Atticus worked for Walt as a cartoonist, but only for a short time. Atticus had bigger dreams. He saw what the possibilities were for the youthful, vibrant American society of the early 1950s. Children would proliferate, and he knew what families would need to keep them happy. They'd need to dream ... to live dreams ... to make dreams.

His idea was to build a dreamland, followed by dream books, dream movies, and dream music. Atticus Golden had the creativity and drive to make it happen. His only problem was that Walt Disney beat him to the punch with the opening of Disneyland in 1955.

Atticus's initial reaction was disappointment. He'd only started to piece together the two hundred acres in Ventura County that would ultimately become his dream. Walt was way ahead of him. But Atticus was a smart man. Because of his youth, he knew he could go more slowly, learn from Walt's mistakes, and build a kingdom beyond anything Walt ever imagined.

So Atticus made his name in cartoon and film production in the fifties. He watched the growth of Disneyland closely, and, in 1962, with his cheap Ventura land paid for, he broke ground on Golden World. The park opened for business two years later.

By the time of Walt's death, Golden World was approaching its rival in annual visitors. What Atticus hadn't anticipated was Walt's move to Florida, where he intended to build an even bigger park. Despite Atticus's good fortune, Disney was ready to jump completely out of his league. Atticus chastised himself for missing the signs of Disney's move, and he angrily set a new course for his company. Every morning he demanded new creations, new thoughts, and new ideas, and, as a result, his studios nurtured and developed some of the most creative imaginations in the world. But pursuing the constant enemy started to change Atticus. He found himself becoming more interested in surpassing Walt Disney than in creating dreams.

After Walt's death, the Disney Empire fell into lethargy. Its movies were boring, its cartoons lost their edge, and park attendance was flat. It was Atticus's chance, and he took advantage.

During the 1970s and early '80s, Golden World's war cry changed. It was no longer "Beat Walt Disney." It again became "Create the Dream." As a result, Golden World's growth was extraordinary. Even through troubled economic times, Atticus Golden prospered. During these years, Atticus, with his wife, Joan, and four sons in tow, traveled the country delivering aid to troubled America from the back of Uncle Atti's Aid Train. At every suburban and inner city stop, the characters of Golden World disembarked, gathered hundreds of needy around the train, and Atticus Golden handed them their dreams. They loved Uncle Atti.

By the late 1980s, Golden World had grown to include one hundred hotels worldwide, scores of hit movies and cartoons, and park attendance second to none. Uncle Atti's fame equaled Walt at the top, and he might have become bigger if the world hadn't changed.

The change came so quickly that no one realized it until it was too late.

By 1988, Disney shareholders had grown tired of the dismal performance of their stock. They watched the growth of privately owned Golden World and wondered why their older and once better-known company wasn't growing comparably. As a result they replaced Walt's son-in-law at the helm of the sleeping giant with a young movie mogul, and Disney again took off, this time to become the most powerful entertainment company in the world. By the end of the millennium, the names of Disney's characters were again on everyone's lips, and family-run Golden World was losing its appeal and back where it should be ... in second place.

In 1993 at the age of 64, as his empire struggled to find balance, Atticus began work on the plan that would once and for all push him past his old nemesis. But it wasn't until three years later and the sudden death of his beloved wife that he finally turned the day-to-day operations of the company over to his two eldest sons and focused full-time on the new plan.

He told himself he was doing it in Joan's loving memory, but he also viewed the effort as his final battle with the ghost of Walt Disney.

Now, as Atticus stared out his window to a world of which any man would be proud, he didn't see fifty-five years of sweat, struggle, planning, and hard work that had made him famous. All he saw was that he was not complete.

John and Sanford Golden were capable businessmen. They were never the dreamers their father and youngest brother, Will, were, but they were good businessmen. In the first years in charge of operations, they reduced expenses, cut fat from the company's budget, and stabilized income so that the financial statement began to show a small but consistent pattern of growth. After another few years, the company's growth was strong and steady, and the Golden brothers were preparing to take it public and move to the next level. But John and Sandy were troubled. Despite the growth, they needed Uncle Atti for the next push. He, after all, was the dream maker, but at 83 years of age, he'd lost track. They were concerned their father's obsession might kill him before he could ever appreciate all he'd done.

The old man closed his eyes, reminding himself again that although he was tired, he couldn't stop. He was almost there; he had to press on. Lost in these thoughts, Atticus didn't hear the knock at his door.

It wasn't unusual that he didn't hear a knock at his door. Even when he wasn't remembering the struggle or immersed in some other deep thought, it would not be hard to miss the sound that would lose most of its force by the time it reached him anyway.

In front of Atticus's desk was a twenty-five foot long mahogany conference table. On either side of the table's length sat eight burgundy leather rollaway chairs, and at the far end sat another. The office itself was filled with Golden World knickknacks, photographs, paintings, stuffed creatures, and other paraphernalia strategically placed to remind visitors of the dreams. The office was a veritable museum of Golden World, and sound had a difficult time wending its way through to the ears of Atticus Golden. That's one of the reasons each station at the table was equipped with a microphone. It was little wonder then that he didn't hear the knock.

He didn't even know someone had entered the room until John stood in front of him, at his desk's side.

"Dad, are you okay?" John asked when he saw Atticus leaning back with his eyes closed.

Atticus was startled as he rocked forward in his chair and then recognized his oldest son.

"Good morning, John." He smiled, turned to the desk, dropped his eyes, and began to organize papers. "Just daydreaming again, I guess. That's what it's all about, huh?"

Daydreaming had always been encouraged of everyone at Golden World. It was therefore not unusual to catch Atticus in such a state. But it was different today. John could see his father was brooding.

"Can we talk, Dad?" he asked.

Atticus looked up and for the first time noticed that his other three sons were standing near the end of the conference table.

"Sure," he said, trying to be matter of fact. "Good morning, boys. C'mon over. Let's talk."

"Over here?" John motioned to a blue denim couch and three chairs bearing the faces of several Golden World cartoon characters.

Atticus smiled and nodded. "The think tank?" He pushed himself up slowly. John moved to assist him, but Atticus shooed him away. "I can move these old bones myself, son."

Atticus surveyed his progeny. Fifty-four year old John was smart looking in his white shirt, conservative tie, and navy slacks. He was not a handsome man by most accounts because he looked like Atticus, square faced with thick black hair streaked plentifully with grey. He hadn't been blessed with any of his mother's fine looks, but he'd gotten much of her drive and business sense. John was the most capable businessman in the family. His undergraduate degree was in economics from UCLA, and he'd gotten an MBA from the same school. John was the backbone of the "business" part of Golden World. He made sure money was made.

Sandy, too, had a business head. Where John wore a white shirt and tie because it was professional, Sandy wore tailored suits because that was Sandy. He, too, had a mind for business, but his specialty was promotions.

Sandy had been fortunate enough to garner some of his mother's good looks to surround his father's dark brown eyes. Because his light brown hair was thinning at the age of fifty, he wore it short and always held his head high in the knowledge that he was a Golden, and the world knew what that meant. Sandy spent every waking moment selling the company to bankers, promoters, and the world. He was hard driving and loved success.

As John and Sandy sat stoically, prepared to discuss momentous things, the third son, Curtis, fidgeted nervously, and the youngest, Will, smiled impishly.

As much as Atticus loved the older two, it was to the younger boys that his heart was lost.

Curtis was the outdoorsman. He had no interest in books, accounts, or the pursuit of money. He was unmarried and completely unattached save for what he felt for the outdoors. He sat forward on the couch, his knees bouncing through the holes in his denims. He placed his elbows atop those knees, clasped his hands in front, and fixed his grey-blue eyes on his father. Despite his forty-two years, he wore his blonde hair long, tied back in a loose ponytail. By far the most handsome of the boys, it was clear Curtis wanted to get this over with and get back outside.

Will was the dreamer. He, too, wore jeans, but his were not worn to holes. He, too, wore his hair long, but it was not tied back. It fell haphazardly in streams of yellow white on either side of his oval face. His features were soft and childlike, and, like Curtis, he was impossibly handsome. But unlike Curtis, whose looks were those of a rugged outdoorsman, Will's, even at the age of thirty-five, were the unlined looks of a child who lived in a world of dreams. It was Will who had found his father's ability to dream.

Atticus watched the boys with a pride he rarely let himself admit these days. He had to stay focused for the final push, and he couldn't let his mind wander. But he was proud, and with all four of them in front of him, he acknowledged it internally.

John spoke first.

"We heard about the injunction, Dad."

Atticus nodded. "I just spoke to Richard yesterday. He says we're only a few months away."

"That's been his constant story, Dad," intoned Sandy. "I don't think Richard has a clue."

"It's under control, Sandy," Atticus said, perturbed. "Richard Wolf is the best connected attorney in the state. The judge had to grant the injunction in order to make the final hearing mean something. The hearing is in less than ninety days."

John was about to speak, but Sandy cut him off.

"We've been getting the same story from Wolf for years. 'It's only another three months. Hang with it guys.' Jesus, Dad, we've got to put an end to it. Golden World is ready for the next big move. We can't be held back by this litigation."

Atticus stared hard at Sandy. His jaw muscles twitched as he bit down hard and tried to hold back the anger. They just didn't understand.

"Look, Dad," John stepped in again, "we're getting close to the public offering. Golden World is firing on all cylinders. We're ready for the big cash infusion that will help us make all our dreams a reality. Our underwriters are concerned about the Silver Lode."

"Fuck the underwriters," Atticus erupted. "They don't know shit about the Silver Lode," he spewed. "This is huge, and they have no clue. Can't you see what a world-class ski resort in Southern California means?" He glared at his sons and slowly calmed himself.

"Look," he continued, "Southern Californians have no choice but Mammoth, which is a six to eight hour drive, Tahoe, which is eight to ten hours, or out of state. Big Bear is small potatoes to real skiers. Silver Lode is the mother lode."

Atticus pushed himself to his feet and walked gingerly to a map on the wall to the right of the couch. He flipped a switch, and a pattern of direction lights was illuminated to show the proximity of the proposed Silver Lode development to all Southern California starting points.

John and Sandy bit down hard, restraining their own frustration and anger. They'd seen it a hundred times before. They'd memorized the plan. All the boys had visited the pristine valley thirty-five miles east of Visalia numerous times on winter ski and summer fishing trips, and each would admit that the Silver Lode Valley was one of the most magnificent of nature's wonders. It was home to wild creatures of every imaginable kind and flora of scented buds and rainbow hue that made dreams come true. For skiing, the untamed valley provided courses that, when properly groomed, would become the world's most magnificent and challenging. Atticus Golden and his brilliant planners had worked for years with environmentalists to create a plan that would make the wonders of the valley available to outdoor enthusiasts and skiers without destroying its natural beauty.

Every structure had been meticulously planned to blend into the natural landscape. Every roofline was planned to be hidden from every vantage beneath and behind the valley's native foliage, and all development was designed to enhance the feeding and living conditions of the valley's animal life.

Years of planning since the Golden family's first visit to the valley on a helicopter ski trip had come full circle, and the final plan was in place. There was just one more hurdle, and it was a mere ninety days away.

"The Sierra Club will never stop, Atticus," said John resignedly. John and Sandy used their father's name only in business meetings with outsiders or when they felt there was no other way to get through to him. "You've said it yourself," he continued. "The Club is like a pit bull. They never let go once they've grabbed hold. They ruined Disney. Don't let them ruin us."

John referred to Walt Disney's ill-fated attempt to develop the Mineral King Valley of the Sierra Nevada Mountains into a ski resort in the 1960s and '70s. Walt's dream was similar to Atticus's. He wanted to build the ultimate Southern California ski resort, and he had tremendous political support. Even environmental groups favored the Disney plan. What Walt hadn't counted on was the Sierra Club's spirited opposition. He was, after all, an honorary member of the Club because of his wildlife films; but the Sierra Club fought it ... and after years of battle the Sierra Club won. As a result, Mineral King became part of Sequoia National Park and remained undeveloped.

Atticus turned from the wall map and walked back to his sons. He grabbed the back of the chair upon which he previously sat, dropped his head, and spoke softly.

"I understand your concerns, John." He looked up with a reassuring smile. "I won't let it go on forever, son. But we're close. I can see it, boys. It will be one of our best investments. The underwriters will love it soon enough." He looked each one in the face and then stopped at Curtis. "You see it don't you, boys?"

Curtis nodded and smiled. "It's a beautiful place, Dad. You know me. I love the valley, and our plan will make it accessible without destroying it. If we can do it, let's go."

Atticus smiled broadly despite the frowns on John and Sandy's faces. His eyes moved to Will, who leaned forward and smiled.

"Look, Dad, we all love the plan." He raised his hands and stared at the ceiling. "God, it's creative and wonderful, and it's our dream." He looked again at his father. His smile faded. "But we're concerned about you, Pop. You gotta get this behind you so you can enjoy it."

Atticus nodded. He realized yet again that he could never make them truly understand.

He was on the verge of attaining the goal he had pursued his entire adult life. He would soon accomplish something his old nemesis had never accomplished. Though Disney wanted it ... dreamed of it ... pursued it, and expended time, energy, and creativity in such pursuit, he never built Southern California's premier ski resort. That task was left to Uncle Atti, and he, by God, would complete it.

Will's final words, "We want you around to help us get to the next level, Pop," were lost on Atticus.

"We're almost there, boys," he said before dismissing his sons and turning back to his plans for the Silver Lode.

TWELVE

SEAN DROVE UP TO Visalia again Thursday afternoon. He could have mailed the Substitution of Attorney to Mrs. Jackson with a self addressed stamped envelope for her to return the signed form, but he decided a face to face discussion with the old lady was necessary to learn more about the "permission" door opened during her deposition. Besides, his mother would probably appreciate his arm to lean on at Buck Anderson's memorial service on Friday, and he wouldn't mind seeing Carla again, even under the circumstances.

Sean again sat at Mrs. Jackson's kitchen table as the gloaming descended upon Visalia. This evening, the food aromas included the rich spiced scent of pot roast mixed with the sweetness of peach pie that together made Sean's mouth water. Mrs. Jackson was making dinner for herself and Ronald, her eldest son, four years Sean's senior. Ronald was expected late from a meeting in Bakersfield. Mrs. Jackson told Sean it would be wonderful if he would join them. Although tempted, Sean had plans with his mother for dinner, adding that she would be thrilled if he came home with a large slice of Mrs. Jackson's peach pie. Mrs. Jackson broke into another one of her toothy grins, of course, and was more than happy to accommodate Sean.

When Sean was finally able to get Mrs. Jackson to sit and sign the Substitution, he moved immediately to the issue that was so important to her case.

"You remember when that young attorney asked you questions in front of a pretty young lady, and she had a little machine in front of her that she was typing on?" he asked.

The old woman nodded slowly and said, "I remember, but that young lady who done the typing, she was nice and all, but she wasn't pretty a-tall."

Sean couldn't help but smile. The woman might be naïve to the machinations of business and those who played at it, but she didn't miss a beat in terms of honesty. She heard statements and questions clearly, and thankfully she responded not only to the point of the question or statement but to the subtle untruths that could change the context of any answer she gave. That's the reason Matthew Dunne's deposition hadn't gone perfectly for him.

"When you answered Mr. Dunne's last question—he was the attorney who asked you questions," Sean explained in response to Mrs. Jackson's puzzled look. She nodded and smiled her thanks. "You said your husband's great-grandfather gave someone permission to use the land Mr. Dunne's client wants to take from you. Do you remember that?"

She nodded again. "Sure, I remember. I said it, Sean, not too long ago. My memory ain't failing me jest yet."

"How do you know that, Mrs. Jackson? How do you know he gave that permission?"

"Willie tol' me so," she answered firmly. "He always used to say how his great-gran'daddy and his daddy befo' him was really smart; smarter than ol' Willie, he'd say, 'cause they knowed good land when they saw it and they knowed how to get and work that land 'til they got too ol' to do it no more."

She smiled at Sean. He wondered what that had to do with anything. They sat in silence for several seconds before Mrs. Jackson started again.

"Before Willie Jackson, my good husband, was born, when his own daddy was jest a little one, Willie's gran'daddy decide he don't want to work the land no more. He want to come down to the city and make lots a money. Heh… heh… he never done too much a'making lots a money but he done his best, educatin' Willie's daddy and all. The land was too big for

Willie's great gran'daddy to work it alone when he got older, so he rent it to some folks wantin' to do some sheep grazin."

"Did he receive rent payments from these folks?" Sean was excited at the mention of rent.

Mrs. Jackson nodded. "Sure. I'm pretty sure."

"Mrs. Jackson, have you been receiving any rent for the property?"

She shook her head. "No. I never got no rent money."

"Did you ever meet the folks who used your property?"

"Oh, sure. They was nice folks who owned the property next door. They was the Finnertys," something Sean had determined through a title search. "They done ranchin' an' farmin' and such," Mrs. Jackson continued, "an' they'd give us peaches from they orchard, an' sometimes we'd get beef an' lamb from they ranchin'. They give that stuff as gifts 'cause they was good folks. Haven't had much in the las' ten years or so though," Mrs. Jackson concluded.

"Mrs. Jackson, this is very important," Sean leaned forward with his elbows on his knees and looked closely into the old woman's eyes. "Did you ever have a written agreement that said these folks could use your property for grazing or any other purpose?"

"Well, Sean, I wouldn't a done nothing like that. Willie took care of business matters."

"Do you know if Willie ever had such an agreement?" he asked hopefully.

Mrs. Jackson shook her head as she looked to the ceiling in thought.

"No … I wouldn't know that."

Sean's hopes had risen at the mention of gifts of peaches and meats. It could certainly be argued those gifts were rent for the use of the land. The problem was that they had ended more than five years ago, which, if true, would play right back into Flow Corp's hands. It might even suggest a more hostile claim of ownership, since payments were once made and then stopped.

"Is there any chance you might have papers somewhere like you did with the legal papers? Is it possible you might have an agreement that Willie might have made?"

"Might be, Sean," she said even as she shook her head no. "But Willie, as smart as he was, wasn't much for writin' stuff. I don't even think I'd know where to look."

Sean dropped his head, and Mrs. Jackson frowned.

"I'm sorry, Sean. We're jest simple folks. Willie was a good man, a man another could trust with his life. I guess we jest done things by word and left it that way."

Sean raised his head slowly. He had to try one more path.

"Do you know who your husband dealt with from the Finnerty family?"

She smiled.

"Sure, that was Boner Finnerty." She chuckled. "He was a funny fella, and it was a sad day for all of us when he died some years back. His sons weren't never as friendly as Boner."

Sean was frustrated that nothing seemed to be opening up for him.

"Was one of the sons named Morgan?" he asked about the name he found in the title search as the signatory on the deed of the Finnerty property to Flow Corp.

Mrs. Jackson brightened at the mention of the name. She shook her head no, however.

"No, Morgan is a gran'son. He took over the family business and run it until he sol' a few years back, I guess. He's a good boy," she said.

"You wouldn't happen to know where Morgan Finnerty lives would you, Mrs. Jackson?"

She nodded. "He sends Christmas cards ever' year. I believe he lives in Sacramento, up where my Melvin lives."

"I'd like to talk to Morgan, Mrs. Jackson. Is there any chance you have his address somewhere? It would make it a lot easier for me to contact him."

Mrs. Jackson smiled broadly. That was something she did have.

Buck Anderson's memorial service was at St. Mary's Catholic Church on the Friday after the explosion. Fire and bomb experts from Los Angeles

THE CONDOR SONG

were invited up to assist in the separation of the ashes, but the flame had
burned so hot, fast, and complete that it was impossible to make much
distinction. Remains of the victims simply didn't exist. It appeared they
had all been astride the flash point, and every part of each body had either
disintegrated or been dispersed to a distance beyond reasonable search.

As disturbing as the fact of the blast and the complete destruction of
the bodies was the fact that investigators were unable to determine the
exact cause of the explosion. To be sure, the coroner's lab housed numerous
highly volatile chemicals, which in sufficient quantities and proper
conditions could create a blast the magnitude of the Visalia government
buildings. What was difficult to understand is why Orson Hoffman would
be using such large quantities under exactly the worst possible conditions
near the two most famous corpses the city had ever seen.

While authorities spent their days interviewing witnesses and trying
to unravel the mystery, Carla Anderson and her father, Tom, dealt with
the media crush surrounding the last mystery of the life of Buck Anderson
and the onslaught of dignitaries from around the world who descended on
Visalia to pay their last respects.

Friday afternoon, at 1:00, Monsignor Paul Fisher entered the church
of St. Mary's through his chambers behind the altar. Already seated
were several U.S. and state representatives and senators from around the
country. Officials of every environmental group in the United States and
others from around the world were expected, and Monsignor Paul knew
the church's thousand seats would not be enough. He made sure speakers
were strategically placed about the church grounds so those who couldn't
find seats inside would be able to hear the final send off.

Over two thousand people attended the service and applauded
Monsignor Paul's wonderful words. They applauded all the eulogists, and
for three solid hours afterwards, a line of mourners of every ilk filed past
the front of St. Mary's altar. Buck was memorialized in a large photograph
in which he was dressed in ragged denims with an arm around a grizzled
old cowboy against Yosemite's Half Dome as a backdrop, and he sported
his patented mischievous grin.

92

By seven o'clock with the sun still hot above the western horizon, the crowd and commotion had dissipated enough for townsfolk and Buck's closest friends to gather with Carla and Tom at the local Elk's Lodge. There they shared a buffet dinner and memories of Buck.

Sean made several attempts to talk to Carla, but the continuous crowd of mourners and well-wishers made any real conversation impossible. So, he sat and talked with his mother.

"Did you love him, Mom?" he asked.

"I did, Sean. He was a wonderful man. Not like my Billy, mind you, but wonderful just the same." She dabbed her eyes and continued. "Buck wanted to marry your old mother, son, but I told him no, time and again. I suppose your dad wouldn't have minded since he, himself, was fond of Buck. They had their times together, those two." She looked off wistfully for a moment, laughed through a tear, and continued. "But there's only one marriage for me, and that was to your dear father."

"Buck was a good man, Mom," Sean said and placed a comforting hand on her shoulder. "Did he make you happy?"

"Oh, that he did. He was fun, lively you might say. Loved the outdoors, but not just the sportin' part of the outdoors like some men, you know, the huntin' and fishin'? He loved just walkin' and enjoyin' the beauty of it even more. He was fun."

Sean encouraged his mother to reminisce about her days with Buck. He asked questions and learned much about the passion for life his mother still carried. It was a wonder to him, particularly since he had all but given up on his own life of passion and purpose. To him life had become simple survival, although it was often difficult for him to understand why he should even worry about that. Passion? What for? Purpose? He doubted there was any. Cynicism set in long ago, and with it a sadness that he couldn't shed. Yet, on those occasions when his eyes wandered to Carla, his thoughts changed. He didn't suddenly realize a purpose and passion. There was no sudden revelation, no sudden understanding of the importance of a life lived fully. It was more that for the brief moments his eyes rested upon her he forgot the sadness. Even in her sorrow at the loss of her uncle, there was a spark in her—a spark she occasionally directed his way.

"You should go and talk to her, son," Mary said. "Carla's a wonderful girl. She helped Buck with his work. He was very fond of her. It's a big loss to her, Sean. She could use a strong arm to lean on."

Sean nodded slowly, smiled at his mother. He glanced toward Carla and noticed that Senator Walker Krebs, the senior senator from California and an avowed environmentalist who was one of Buck's biggest supporters in the U.S. Congress, had sidled up to her offering his heartfelt condolences and quiet conversation.

"She's got enough to handle now, Mom. I'll talk to her later when there aren't so many people around."

But that time never seemed to come.

Toward the end of the evening, as the crowd thinned and Carla sat alone with her father for the first time, Sean took his mother's arm and escorted her to their table. But just before they arrived two men stepped up to her. Sean veered wide and directed his mother to the seat next to Tom as he listened in on the conversation the two men were having with Carla.

"Ms. Anderson," the tall thin one with a thick reddish beard and long hair pulled back in a ponytail said. He was the younger of the two men, in his early to mid-twenties.

"My name is Pete Luckman, and this," pointing to his partner, "is Andrew Harper. We're with the Sierra Club's Legal Defense Fund. We wanted to offer our condolences to you and your father for Buck's death."

Carla shook hands slowly but remained seated. She was exhausted and had no interest in formality.

"Thank you," she said for the millionth time. "This is really for friends and family tonight," she said, almost too tired to complete her sentence.

"We understand that, Ms. Anderson, and we apologize for intruding on your sorrow." This was from Andrew Harper, who stepped forward and flashed a radiant smile. Carla was taken aback by the brilliance of his blue eyes set against the tanned face beneath the mid-ear length white blond hair. He was in his early forties but looked a good ten years younger. "We only need a few minutes, and then we'll leave you in peace."

"You see, Ms. Anderson," rejoined the red haired Luckman, "We believe we know why your uncle was murdered."

THIRTEEN

CARLA WANTED TO SPEND time with Sean at the wake. She was happy to see he made the effort to come and wanted to thank him while continuing the process of getting to know him again. But it wasn't happening. By the time the Sierra Club lawyers left her, Sean was helping his mother to her feet to escort her home.

"Sorry we didn't get to talk, Carla," Sean said. "I wanted you to know how sorry I am about your uncle. Buck was a good guy." He took her quickly in his arms and hugged her. As he pulled away, his hand slipped down to hers, and her heart skipped when he smiled and said conspiratorially, "You were right by the way," he nodded toward his mother, "... about my mom and Buck." He shook his head as he watched Mary's retreating figure. "Good for them, huh?"

"Yeah," Carla said. "Do you have to leave now?"

Sean nodded again to his mother, who had reached the door. "I think I do. This was pretty difficult for her. I need to get her home."

There was an awkward silence as Sean released her hand. Finally, she grinned up at him.

"So, are we ever going to see you again up here in Visalia?" she asked.

"Sure. I've got family here," he nodded again toward his mother. "And it looks like I've got a real live client. I'm helping Beverly Jackson with a lawsuit she's gotten into."

"I heard," she said and then hesitated, but only for a second. There's no reason to be coy, she thought. "Don't forget to look me up when you're in town, Sean. I could use a cup of coffee with an old friend now and then."

He nodded awkwardly. He didn't know how to respond to something so obvious yet so innocent. As he glanced beyond her once again, he saw the Sierra Club guys approaching the door where his mother awaited him in conversation with another friend.

"It looks like you might need some help yourself with those two."

She turned quickly and nodded. "Yeah ... I don't know."

"Let me know if I can give you a hand with anything," Sean said.

"I'll be sure to do that," she said with another smile.

"I'll see you soon," he said, and turned toward the door.

"I hope so," she whispered when he was beyond hearing.

———————

By 8:55 the next morning, Carla was wondering why she agreed to meet with Luckman and Harper instead of just sending them on their way the night before. No one had any evidence that Buck was murdered. As far as Carla and her father were concerned, it was all rumors created by society's hunger for anything sensational. Who would want to murder Buck? Discussion on the subject was academic anyway. Because both bodies were destroyed, no one would ever know the real truth. Yet the Sierra Club representatives were persistent.

When Carla made one last effort to put them off by suggesting they take their story to the police, they informed her it would do no good. They had no concrete evidence. In fact, their theory was largely conjecture, but if she would please hear them out, she and they together might be able to learn the truth.

Carla loved her uncle. Her decision to do environmental work was due to his stories of still existing wild lands during her youth. If she hadn't been so damn obstinate after high school, she might have stuck around, spent time with Buck, and really learned about the wonders of the world. Thankfully, she smartened up in time to spend the last three years working with him.

Now that Buck was gone and nine o'clock was approaching she wondered if it was really worth it. Buck died in the only place in which he would have chosen to die. Even though his body was gone, his spirit was still up there, at peace, she believed. Why should she disturb him now when he was where he wanted to be? On the other hand, of course, common sense told her that if Buck was murdered, someone had to pay, although it appeared someone already had if Buck's companion in death was any indication. In any event, she was beyond the point of canceling the meeting as the front door of the Anderson Environmental office creaked open.

She'd chosen the office for the Saturday morning meeting because she wanted to keep it as formal as possible. She doubted Luckman and Harper would have anything meaningful to show her. That they were committed to whatever position they were taking was clear. However, she expected nothing more than the typical hysteria many environmentalists often accepted as gospel. It was that hysteria, after all, that kept the movement strong. It was rare to find environmentalists like her Uncle Buck who could really see and understand both sides of an issue and then discuss it in a way that would make even the staunchest anti-environmentalists listen and respond intelligently. She doubted that Luckman and Harper were in her uncle's mold. She wondered again why she had accepted the meeting.

Carla showed her visitors to the conference room, a well-worn room that was more a library of chaos than conference room. It was crowded with books, boxes of files, and faded photographs, some framed and others not, of nature's wonders. An ancient oak table bearing the inscriptions of hundreds of visitors from years past was centered in the room surrounded by five castered chairs, only one of which actually had rollers intact and working. The other four were in various states of disrepair but still served their basic purpose. Carla offered the men coffee, which she poured from a thermos she'd brought from home into ancient mugs her uncle kept around the office.

"Sorry about the mess, guys," Carla quipped, "we're still doing spring cleaning."

"It's no problem, Ms. Anderson," said Luckman.

"Carla," she said. "My name is Carla."

Pete Luckman nodded firmly, and Andrew Harper got right to the point. He withdrew a stack of papers from a worn shoulder pack and flipped them onto the table in front of Carla. The caption read that the papers formed a complaint filed by the Sierra Club against the U.S. Forest Service in the United States District Court for the Northern District of California in San Francisco. Carla glanced at it and then looked up expectantly.

"This is the lawsuit we filed to prevent the development of the Silver Lode Valley," explained Harper.

Carla glanced down at the paper again, and then up at the two men again.

"So what's this got to do with Buck?" she asked.

Harper shook his head slowly and smiled his broad, white-toothed smile. "Sorry, Carla, we'll start at the beginning."

"Back in 1995 the U.S. Forest Service published a prospectus and request for proposals for the development of the Silver Lode Valley as a major Southern California ski resort. The Forest Service had been on a kick for such a development since the late forties. Their first attempt was to have an area known as Mineral King developed by Disney. You may recall that good ol' Uncle Walt, an honorary member of our organization," Harper said sarcastically, "spent his last couple of years developing the concept that the company tried to carry on after his death."

"Actually, Andy," Carla responded, "you and I weren't old enough to have a clue what 'good ol' Uncle Walt' was involved in. So, I don't recall. I don't think Pete was even born yet," she smiled and pointed at Luckman.

Again Harper nodded and smiled at the obvious truth of the statement. Luckman looked up from papers he was scanning intently with a quizzical look on his face.

"Right," said Harper, "of course." He was derailed and looked for the way back to his story. "In any event, Disney failed because of work done by the Sierra Club, and Mineral King was made part of Sequoia National Forest.

"As you might expect, many people in the Forest Service were upset over the whole thing, so they started looking for another location. To assist them, they went through the nearly thirty years of records of the Mineral

King project and found that we, the Sierra Club, had suggested alternatives to Mineral King. One of those alternatives was the Silver Lode Valley. Our predecessors in the Club viewed the valley as more accessible and less sensitive than Mineral King. The Forest Service thought it had a location that no one could argue with."

"But they were wrong?" Carla asked with feigned interest as she wondered again what all this had to do with her uncle.

"You bet they were wrong," blurted Luckman with an intensity that threw Carla back in her chair.

"Wait, Pete," Harper interjected, "let me finish." He turned to Carla. "Please hear me out; you'll see the relevance shortly."

"Forest Service representatives went to Disney hoping the company would simply convert its Mineral King plans to fit the Silver Lode. But Disney wasn't going to have anything to do with it, so Forest looked elsewhere. That's when Atticus Golden stepped to the plate."

"Golden World Atticus Golden?" Carla interrupted.

Harper nodded.

"Atticus and his family had spent winters helicopter skiing in the valley. He fell in love with it and started, even before Forest's prospectus, sending engineers, topographers, and other experts into the valley. While there wasn't any invasive or destructive testing they could do, they apparently brought Atticus back some wonderful reports. The valley is ... magnificent."

"I suspected that," Carla said with just enough acerbity to alert him to move on.

"The bottom line," Harper continued, "is that Golden World presented a preliminary plan and official bid almost as soon as the prospectus was made available by the Forest Service. Things happened so quickly that before we at the Sierra Club knew what was going on, the Golden World bid was accepted, and Atticus's engineers were busy doing formal testing.

"The Sierra Club jumped on the project as quickly as it could, and within weeks after acceptance of Golden's bid, we had our own engineers and environmental experts testing alongside Uncle Atti's."

"Wait," Carla interrupted. "Hadn't the Sierra Club already given its imprimatur? Didn't you say that the Sierra Club suggested the Silver Lode as an alternative to Mineral King?"

"Yes," Harper said and then hesitated lest he give Carla the impression the Sierra Club was indeed the obstructionist organization many people believed it to be.

"Things had changed, Carla," he finally continued. "Please understand ... by the time Mineral King was added to the protected part of the National Park system in 1978, about twelve or thirteen years had elapsed since that report. Within that time, continuing studies revealed that the Silver Lode Valley was sensitive as well. Although it was not added to Sequoia National Park with Mineral King, it did become part of the Sequoia National Game Refuge to be managed in a manner that would protect wildlife and habitat in the valley.

"As a result, when we got involved in the project proposed by Atticus Golden, our primary concern was that the environmental impact report address every potential impact to flora and fauna in the valley and that the development provide adequate mitigation measures for each impact. The task was an enormous one when you consider the hundreds of different species of animal and plant life in the valley. Thanks to advances in our field between the time of the Sierra Club's original report and our efforts with Silver Lode, we were able to address concerns that had never before even been considered."

"It looks to me like you were working hand in hand with Golden," said Carla. "Where's the problem?"

Harper took a deep breath and put a hand on Luckman's arm, as Luckman was about to respond indignantly. If they were to enlist Carla's aid, they couldn't come off as the fanatical environmentalists Luckman epitomized. The rest of the presentation was delicate. He would not permit Luckman's obdurate approach to his environmentalism jeopardize their plan.

"Through Atticus's son Curtis, the Golden Company was doing a marvelous job addressing and offering mitigation for all the environmental concerns. They even offered to set aside monitored habitat preserves for certain endangered species of snails and rodents found in the valley. The problem was it became clear that the effects on the valley as a whole were beyond mitigation.

"The Golden Company had taken each individual impact and suggested individual mitigation measures for each. What we have argued is that the effect on the valley as a whole was immitigable. We have taken the position that there is no set of circumstances under which the valley should be developed as a ski resort or anything else."

Harper could see he had reached the point where he was going to lose Carla. Here the Golden Company had done everything they could possibly do, and the pain in the ass Sierra Club was simply engaging in its standard anti-development rhetoric.

"This is where your uncle comes into the picture," Harper said as he eyed Carla closely.

She leaned forward, interested again.

"Buck had been following the whole thing closely by the time he approached us in the spring of 2005. Apparently the whole of Tulare County was interested in the outcome of our battle, which was beginning to heat up as a result of this lawsuit," he pointed to the complaint on the table before them, "which we filed in December of 1999."

Carla nodded and flashed a knowing smile.

"Visalia's been waiting for that development for decades. Everyone's been talking about a ski resort outside town for as long as I can remember," she said. "I suppose if it ever got built, townsfolk would have nothing to talk about."

"Buck understood that," Harper said. "He knew the tremendous impact such a development would have on Visalia. He knew the city would mushroom and all the dreams of wealth from tourism would come true. Despite that, he offered to help us because he knew what the Golden development would do to the Silver Lode.

"It's hard to verbalize, Carla, and that's probably the reason the Supreme Court finally turned our argument aside."

Carla looked surprised.

"Well, if the Supreme Court rejected your argument, why are you here and what makes you think Buck was murdered?" Carla was frustrated and angry. "C'mon, guys, if you're trying to link Buck's death to this Silver Lode development, you've just blown your case."

"It is linked, Carla. We know that!" exclaimed an equally frustrated Pete Luckman.

"Wait, please. Both of you wait for another minute," Harper interrupted. "We weren't finished, Carla, and the other side knew it."

Carla shrugged as if to say, "no kidding." Harper raised his hands in supplication, begging her to wait just a moment longer.

"Buck visited the valley for extended periods every spring and winter for the past several years. He wrote essays of the wonders of the valley. He wrote of how five thousand rooms, ski lift capacity for fifteen thousand people per hour, water ski, and camping facilities that would bring millions more visitors each summer would destroy the natural balance of the last of the southern Sierras' magnificent valleys. You may have been part of that while working with him."

Carla nodded slowly. She did remember Buck's letters, op-ed pieces, and essays on the subject. It had become a pet project for him. He hadn't gotten Carla involved to any great extent because he knew how the project was favored in his home city, and he preferred not to get her embroiled in the middle of it until he knew for sure his position was provable.

"Buck joined us in our belief that despite Atticus Golden's efforts to provide an environment friendly development plan, he couldn't possibly prevent the spread of ancillary development and destruction that would follow on the heels of a Golden World project.

"So, while the Sierra Club legal arm litigated, the Sierra Club political arm, with Buck's help, lobbied our federal government to take a final step and designate the Silver Lode as a wilderness under the Omnibus Wilderness Act. Hearings were scheduled for last fall, continued till spring, and again till November when Buck didn't return. But you must know that?"

"I knew he was pushing a position, but I really didn't learn all that much about it. He had me working on other projects. What was the hearing for?" asked Carla. "Do you have anything more now than you've had and presented to Congress over the years? Do you have anything more than you presented to the Supreme Court?"

"We didn't and still don't," Luckman interjected. "But Buck did." He glared at Carla with an intensity that almost made her laugh.

"What do you mean 'Buck did'?" she asked acidly.

"Last spring Buck found something, Carla," Harper rejoined. "He went back to the valley and spent the whole summer there. He told us before the summer that he'd found something, but he wasn't sure. He didn't want to say anything before he was sure. We were to meet with him after his Labor Day hike to plan our presentation to Congress. Buck never made it back."

Harper dropped his head and leaned back while Luckman stared expectantly at Carla.

Carla stared back expecting more, and then she shook her head sharply as if to clear a fog.

"I'm sorry, guys. I don't see what this has to do with Buck's death. On the one hand you're saying you believe he found something that would have stopped this Silver Lode development, but on the other hand, you have no idea what it was. Are you saying Buck didn't tell you what he had yet he told the other side? And that's what got him killed?"

"We don't know," said Harper.

"What we do know," said Luckman "is that Curtis Golden was up there in the spring and part of the summer. We also know he and Buck hiked and camped together in the valley."

"Wait," said Carla, "are you suggesting Buck turned to the other side?"

"No!" Harper exclaimed. He turned to Luckman, who was about to jump out of his seat. "Wait, Pete, let me finish this." He turned back to Carla.

"We have no idea what Buck and Curtis talked about. All we know is that Buck had something important. He told us as much. We also know what the world knows ... that Buck died on the Golden Staircase with a crushed right shoulder, wearing clothes that weren't his, with another naked, half-eaten body next to him. We believe the rumors we heard. They came from the coroner's staff. They were clearly seeded to keep interest high in anticipation of his press conference. Buck had something Carla ... something that could save the Silver Lode Valley, and there were people who didn't like that."

Carla nodded slowly. She rose from her chair and stretched, as her eyes fixed above the heads of her guests on a grime-smeared window behind them.

"It's possible, I guess," she said. "But Atticus Golden ... Uncle Atti...? Could he have ordered Buck's death?" she asked dubiously. "How could Uncle Atti kill anyone?"

Harper shrugged.

"We don't know. We've heard he's obsessed with the Silver Lode project. But, we don't know. That's why we can't go to the police. We do know Buck's dead and his death opens the door for destruction of the Silver Lode because we don't have whatever information he discovered that could save the valley."

Despite the melodrama of his last statement, Harper's words had their intended effect.

"Why do you tell me all this?" asked Carla. "What can I do?"

"We need access to your uncle's papers. We know he carried a journal with him and that it's gone. But he had other papers, Carla. Older journals, files, and other papers that might help us piece together what he learned before it's too late."

FOURTEEN

AT TEN O'CLOCK MONDAY morning, Sean stood in Richard Wolf's private waiting room. He gripped the handle of his battered briefcase tightly as he followed the receptionist assistant through the doorway of Wolf's suite and introduced him to Wolf's personal assistant.

"Good morning, Mr. Donovan," said Vanessa Jones, an attractive black woman. "Mr. Wolf's just finishing a conference call. He'll be with you shortly. Why don't you sit over there?" She pointed to a leather couch.

"Thanks, I'll stand if it's okay," Sean said.

Vanessa smiled and turned back to her computer. She adjusted the headphones and picked up typing where she had left off as Sean's escort smiled prettily and left the suite.

Sean's first thought was that this room was an antechamber to some grand ballroom, which waited in all its splendor beyond the massive carved, dark-wood entry door that provided ultimate access. He ambled about the chamber. It was richly appointed with dark wood and leather. Original paintings of subtle sunsets and moonlit evenings adorned the few open wall spaces, and on the others were dark wood shelves crammed with volumes of legal text and literature. The whole look was the soothing one of a rich man's library with the only sound being the clack of computer keys beneath Vanessa's racing fingers.

When Sean stopped circling the room, he turned slowly in place and took it all in. Its richness was astounding. He'd been in many law offices over the years; never had he seen anything like this. Attorneys often adorned their offices to show their position in the hierarchy of the firm. Art pieces of incomparable value had been in vogue for years, and those with the most sublime pieces were clearly at the top of the pecking order. Sean had seen offices with odd artifacts commemorating distant travels, awards given by adoring civic minded leaders, letters from politicians, pictures of entertainment and sports personalities bearing words of undying support and thanks for jobs well done, and other such symbols of high success, but never had Sean seen an attorney's office that was a suite unto itself, as if the occupant were a separate firm within the firm and the most important one at that. Clearly Richard Wolf was someone special at McCormack, Stein & Wolf.

The firm itself was centrally located to be a significant part of the again burgeoning Pacific Rim business while also positioning itself as a leading boutique representative of the growing number of biotech companies sprouting from Ventura County south to Orange and San Diego Counties. What Sean hadn't known before checking on-line was just how big the real estate department of the firm had become. Richard Wolf's department was the backbone of the entire firm, and it was apparently that backbone upon which the firm relied for the phenomenal wealth experienced by all the partners as reported by Los Angeles's legal journals in their annual reviews of such matters. Wolf was recognized as the top "rainmaker" among law firms in Southern California for five straight years. His clients included many of the top local, national, and international real estate developers, financiers, and players, and his name was always mentioned among the most influential people in the country. Richard Wolf had come a long way since his early days at McCormack & Stein.

Sean's thoughts drifted back as he found himself staring at Vanessa Jones. She was intent on whatever matter occupied her at the keyboard, at which she seemed so proficient. What struck him most, however, was that she was beautiful. The ebony skin of her face was milky smooth beneath the loose weave of her dreadlocks. Her low-cut sweater exposed the swell of her ample breast, and out of its short sleeves the same milk brown arms extended to thin hands and beautifully manicured fingers that danced effortlessly across the keyboard. She was the perfect accessory for Richard Wolf's antechamber.

Sean stared even after the buzzer on Vanessa's intercom alerted her that she could send him in to see Wolf.

"Mr. Donovan," she said again when Sean did not respond the first time.

"Oh, I'm sorry," he finally stammered, embarrassed that he'd been caught.

Vanessa smiled. "Go on in, Mr. Donovan. Mr. Wolf is waiting for you."

Wolf's office was the exact opposite of his waiting room. As expected, it was large and spacious with enormous west-facing plate glass windows that overlooked the expanse of Los Angeles's Westside to the Pacific Ocean in the distance. The north-facing windows of the corner suite looked down upon the slowly developing Mulholland Hills. While the waiting room was of dark woods, soft leathers, and autumn colors, clearly calculated to put a visitor at ease, Wolf's inner sanctum was bright with modern decor of granite, glass, and steel, all colored severe blacks and grays. The intent was clear: to maintain an edge and to intimidate. Sean had stepped into another world.

Wolf stood behind his onyx table. His legs were spread and his hands rested on his hips as if he was in the midst of some oration when he was interrupted by Sean's intrusion. One chair in front of his desk was occupied while the other was empty, presumably intended for Sean.

Sean's first glimpse of Richard Wolf in nearly thirteen years was a surprise, no less perhaps than the surprise on Wolf's face at his sight of Sean. Wolf looked as if he had come straight from a GQ cover shoot. The perfectly pressed white shirt was stark against Wolf's deep tanned skin and pitch black hair combed straight back to reveal the strategic streaks of gray at his temples. The build that worked beneath the shirt, a tribute to undoubtedly long hours in the gym, combined with the powerful bearing of a man of confidence made the first sight imposing. By comparison, Sean's slumped, haggard frame and threadbare garb was out of place, both in Wolf's magnificent office as well as in Wolf's very presence.

Yet just as Sean wondered for the hundredth time what he was doing in this case against Wolf and his firm, he dropped his head and smiled as something else suddenly struck him.

Richard Wolf seemed taller.

It wasn't so in their early years. In fact, as he recalled, Sean was a good two inches taller than his former classmate and partner. Yet, now, somehow, Wolf seemed taller. Sean knew his own posture had suffered over the years, and he knew he'd lost some of his height as he'd moved into his fifties, but surely not that much. He wondered if Wolf wore platform shoes or perhaps he had the floor behind his desk raised an inch or two. Whatever the reason, Sean's smile broadened, and for the first time this day he felt at ease.

"Michael," Wolf said. He smiled and continued with a deep and practiced interest, "so good to see you. Come in and sit down." He pointed to the empty steel-framed chair padded in rich black leather in front of his desk. He did not step out from behind his desk.

"Richard," Sean nodded and walked to the chair without extending his hand.

"This is Matthew Dunne." Wolf pointed to the young attorney seated in the other chair scribbling notes. Dunne looked up, took Sean's extended hand in a quick, firm handshake. "He's second chair in the Jackson case," Wolf concluded.

"Yes," said Sean, "I saw his name on the pleadings. I think you took Mrs. Jackson's deposition, didn't you?"

Dunne stared at Sean for a second and then nodded. "I did."

"So, sit Michael. It's good to see you again," Wolf repeated himself and then bit down hard on his back teeth. The muscles in his jaw twitched with the exertion.

"I've got Mrs. Jackson's substitution," Sean said.

He reached across Wolf's table to hand him a certified copy of the document executed by Mrs. Jackson.

"I'll take it," said Dunne, who stood and took the document from Sean. The three men sat in awkward silence for several seconds.

"Matt's made copies of the pleadings, discovery, and correspondence for you, Michael," Richard finally said. Dunne handed Sean an accordion pouch loosely stuffed with manila files.

Sean quickly fanned the folders and then looked up at Wolf.

"Well, thanks, Richard. I've got to get back to the office and start going through this. I'll get in touch with you regarding any additional discovery." He started to push up out of his chair.

"Michael, hold on. Let's talk a bit. You have some time, don't you?" Wolf asked.

Dunne looked quizzically at his mentor. He'd never seen Wolf show such deference to another attorney, particularly one of the apparent low caliber of Sean Michael Donovan.

"I've got nothing but time, Richard," Sean said and sat back clutching the accordion folder tightly on his lap.

Wolf eyed Sean for a second and then smiled confidently.

"Look, Michael, there's no need for us to get into something crazy here. We both know how this is going to turn out for the old la …" he hesitated, "Mrs. Jackson. It's a loser for her if you fight it. You know that."

Sean didn't want to reveal the one potential opening he had in the case. He knew before he entered Wolf's lair the approach his former partner would take. He knew Wolf would try to make it sound as if there was absolutely no chance Mrs. Jackson could win the motion. He promised himself he would not slip. But he did. Against his better judgment he made his first mistake of the meeting.

"Don't be so sure of yourself, Richard. You never know what might come up—like a final question by your associate here that opened a pretty interesting door."

Wolf's glance at Dunne was almost imperceptible, but it was there. He was immediately back to Sean, however, and he smiled smugly.

"You're probably talking about her husband's daddy's daddy's possible oral agreement made while he stood on the back forty with a pint of rum in his hand. If that's all you've got, my friend, you and I both know it won't hold water. There's no proof, and even if her husband's great granddaddy were still alive, who would believe a self-serving statement like that? We know damn well there's nothing in writing and no one alive who can testify to any agreement."

Sean gritted his teeth. He glared daggers at Wolf, knowing full well he'd made the same rookie mistake Wolf's associate had made during the deposition. He should have followed his instinct: don't tell anyone what he had; try to make a case for it on his own. He could have played the part of an attorney who had nothing and tried to lull the arrogant assholes into complacency, but he didn't. He'd shown his only card, and it was clear Wolf would be prepared for it. Sean tried to regain his composure, but Wolf had the upper hand.

"Look, Michael, there's no need for us to argue the point here. There'll be plenty of time for that in court," Wolf patronized Sean. "My client isn't interested in dragging Mrs. Jackson through the cost and aggravation of this litigation. They understand this property is special to her, and they're willing to pay for it."

Sean didn't want to talk anymore. He berated himself for his stupidity but knew he had to regain control. He stared as Wolf spoke, and when he finished, Sean responded.

"It looks like they're interested in her welfare, Richard," he said as he lifted the accordion file slightly. "Why the lawsuit if they're so willing to pay?"

"She wouldn't talk to us," interjected Dunne in exasperation.

Wolf glared at Dunne. Sean saw his opening back into the conversation.

"I doubt Mrs. Jackson didn't want to talk, Matt. She's a very talkative woman. I suspect she doesn't want to sell the property. That's all."

Dunne glared sharply at Sean. "That's the point, Mr. Donovan." He used Sean's name with sarcastic emphasis. "Our client has rights. She wouldn't listen to reason. She ..."

"Matt," Wolf interrupted firmly. He turned back to Sean.

"I think Michael gets the picture. I think we all do. Look, Michael, my client isn't interested in taking advantage of the lady. They're willing to pay her a substantial sum of money. It's more than she could ever realize for the property on the open market, more than it's worth in all probability."

Sean smiled and shook his head slowly. He could deal with this. He could remain calm and get in his own little dig.

"You still don't get it, do you, Richard? Money isn't the issue here. She doesn't give one whit about the money. This property has value beyond money. She's not going to give it up."

Dunne started to go to the attack but was restrained by one look from Wolf, who then leaned back and turned his penetrating black eyes to Sean again.

"I'm trying my best to be fair with you here, Michael, help get a victory for you and your client before I sic the dogs loose on you."

Red anger surged into Sean's face, and his green eyes blazed.

"Are you threatening me, Richard?"

Wolf shook his head and looked matter-of-factly at Sean.

"Not at all. I know you've had a tough go, that's all. Just trying to save an old friend some embarrassment; trying to help you, that's all."

"Don't do me any favors you sonuvabitch," Sean suddenly shouted. "You don't do favors, Richard. I know you!"

Wolf smiled.

"You know, Michael, I was hoping we might find a way to put the past behind us. I was hoping I could help you get a leg up in your practice, what there is of it. That's not going to happen though, is it?" He stood up then, before Sean could do so.

"My client is willing to be reasonable. But I warn you, Michael. If this goes any further, their largesse will disappear. If you let your hatred for me color your judgment, this will go badly for you and Mrs. Beverly Cora Jackson."

Before Sean could say anything else, Wolf turned to Dunne. "Matt, show Mr. Donovan out, will you?"

Sean stood, grabbed his briefcase, and turned to the door.

"I know my way," Sean said firmly in a meaningless show of pride.

Sean breathed deeply as he took the long slow walk to the door. He had promised himself he wouldn't let it get out of control, and the first opportunity he had, he did just that. He couldn't just walk out again, naïve and beaten again, but he had no choice. In his anger and frustration, he almost missed the signs of Wolf's own frustration, apparent in his demeanor and carriage as he ordered Sean out of the office. Fortunately, Sean had one more opportunity presented to him. Just as Sean reached the door, Wolf's intercom buzzed.

"Yes! What?" Wolf responded sharply.

From far back in his mind, Sean sensed irritation in Wolf's voice, something he wasn't expecting. He stopped, his back to Wolf and Dunne, and dropped his head to listen carefully.

"Mr. Wolf? ... I'm sorry to interrupt," said Vanessa Jones hesitantly. "Mr. Perez is here to see you, sir," she finished meekly.

Sean turned slowly. Wolf was staring at the telephone. He nodded as if he was trying to resolve some internal argument, perhaps trying to strengthen himself for what was coming.

"Tell Mr. ... tell Carlos I'll be right there," he finally said tersely.

Sean smiled. Wolf was concerned. Despite the cavalier approach with Sean, he was concerned. He'd seen it before, in the way Wolf held himself. He had always tried to stand tall, strong, confident, and in control, but his initial reactions to problems in the early days would often give him away to more seasoned opponents. Clearly, he had overcome his weakness over the years, but to someone who knew him well, the telltale signs of concern were there.

Wolf looked up from the phone and stepped out from behind his desk. Sean had turned back toward Wolf and was standing at the door smiling.

"Are you still here, Michael?" he asked.

Sean shook his head slowly.

"No, Richard, I'm not. Haven't been for a long time."

He turned, pulled open the door, and stepped back into the antechamber, happy that he could at least leave Wolf with a smile and perhaps some concerns after the fool he'd made of himself.

As he made his way past Vanessa Jones, two Hispanic men were standing in front of her desk. One who stood about three inches shorter than Sean had the bearing of a man considerably larger. He stood with legs slightly spread and hands clasped loosely in front of him. His face carried an aloofness, not of financial superiority but of power and control, as if a single word from him could mean the difference between life and death in a man. He and the mountain that stood behind him watched Sean closely as he walked past them.

The second man's enormous height and girth dwarfed the room. A long red scar cut a path across his right cheek and provided ample proof, if any was needed, of the position he held with the first man.

"Carlos," said Richard Wolf. "Come in." He waved them to his door. "It didn't take you long to get here. Traffic light?" Richard asked.

"I want good news, Richard." He turned back to the mountain that accompanied him. The big man continued to stare at Sean. "Esteban! Let's go." He motioned sharply with his head, and the man's focus on Sean was broken. He followed his boss into Wolf's office as Sean left the antechamber.

FIFTEEN

IN THE TWO WEEKS *between his meeting with Salvatore Leone and his firing, S. Michael Donovan wrestled with his dilemma.*

"I don't understand you, Richard. Sal's committing fraud. Isn't it our duty to tell him we have to withdraw from the representation if he doesn't back down? Shouldn't I, at least, do that? I'm lead counsel."

Donovan sat in Wolf's office. Wolf leaned forward, propped his elbows on his desk, arms in front of him, his hands wringing nervously. His eyes were fixed on his hands.

"Then what? What if he decides to do it anyway, Michael? What do you do then?"

Donovan stared at his partner.

"We'd have to withdraw," he said, as if the answer was obvious and correct.

Wolf shook his head.

"We've got to let this go, Michael. Sal will pull his whole account. We can't blow off such a big client."

Donovan nodded.

"He probably would pull his account, but isn't our responsibility greater than earning money from Salvatore Leone for God's sake? We're supposed to be protectors of the law, officers of the court. We can't let him commit fraud."

"We're not letting him do anything. He'll be doing what he wants." Wolf shook his head again. "It'll be as if we don't even know." His words sounded strangely familiar, as if Wolf and Sean's wife had discussed the matter.

Wolf looked up at Donovan. "I don't think you should do anything unless you talk to Denton and get his take on it."

Donovan nodded slowly. "Will you stand with me, when I talk to Denton?" he asked, although he felt he already knew the answer.

"I ... I don't know, Michael. I'm not sure I agree with you."

They stared at each other for several seconds until Donovan finally stood to leave. He started to say something but thought better of it.

John Denton, the firm's senior real estate partner, was approaching retirement in the next year with a sense of anticipation that detached him from most of the matters in the office. He was overweight, some might say sloppy, and if the truth were known, his coming retirement was as much a desire on the firm's part to burnish it's image in its fastest growing department as it was for him to spend the rest of his life on the golf course and at the nineteenth hole. The department had highly capable members to handle most matters. Denton's involvement wasn't really needed for guidance of junior partners and senior associates. Although his replacement as head of the department would not be determined for another year, Denton had already made a recommendation to replace him. S. Michael Donovan was, in the minds of many in the firm, including Denton, the best-qualified lawyer and rainmaker. Yet there was something Denton was a stickler about. The client was number one, and a lawyer should never do anything to piss off a client, particularly one as important as Salvatore Leone. Good lawyers looked for ways to resolve issues. Never, under any circumstances, did they throw the client out.

"You know we can't do that, Michael. Sal is a good friend. We can't abandon him, especially now, when things are so tough. We must stand by him, help him out as best we can."

Donovan viewed Denton as an insipid character. He was a senior partner, of course, and he had an imagination, that, in his best days, was beneficial to the firm's growing list of real estate clients. But Donovan also knew Denton's best days were behind him. The growth of the department over the past few years was largely attributable to the work he and the rest of the attorneys below Denton were doing. The major problem with respect to Leone, however, was that he was Denton's client—a client he'd cultivated and nurtured for years and a client who was the only major one who still viewed Denton as his main contact at the firm.

"I understand all of that, John. Sal's important to us, and we're important to him. But isn't that another reason we can't let him do what he's planning? With the Department of Justice's investigation heating up, won't any hint of wrongdoing shine the light on him? We have to make him understand how significant this is."

Denton liked Donovan. He liked that he never shied away from even the most menial tasks. It had made Denton's last several years at the firm a whole lot easier, helped him to reduce his handicap to single digits. But something was definitely wrong with his protégé, as he often referred to Donovan, although no one else in the firm felt Donovan owed any of his talents to Denton. The fact of the matter was that Denton had no real response to Donovan's position. Of course it was an attorney's responsibility to alert a client to problems that might arise from actions he might take. But, once alerted, the attorney couldn't prevent a client from doing whatever he pleased.

"Michael, we've alerted Sal to the potential problems. That's all we're responsible for. You, of all people, know that. I'm proud of you for raising the issue, but that's where it has to end. We can't force Sal to do anything other than what he wants. We can only be there for him if he falls and needs help afterward."

Donovan's look was quizzical. This wasn't right. It couldn't be.

"We have an obligation to tell him in writing what he's doing is wrong and that we will withdraw if he chooses to proceed. You know our obligations, John. I certainly do. I'm lead counsel in Sal's sale of his properties. As such, I have to do what's right or I'll have violated my oath to the State Bar and this profession." Donovan was frustrated. He didn't care if he wasn't showing *a senior partner proper respect. This was too damn important to simply let it be.*

Denton's already ruddy complexion reddened considerably as he leaned forward. The patronizing smile with which he'd conducted the entire meeting was gone. The heavy folds of his face sagged in anger as he glared at Donovan.

"Don't you do anything you'll be sorry for, Donovan. I'm telling you right now that there is nothing more for you to do in this matter. Lead attorney or not, this is not your call. This is the firm's call."

"I'd gladly take it to the firm's committee, John, but I can't. Sal is moving on this as we speak. We don't have the time to wait around for a discussion and decision. We need to act." Sean's tone was as strong and compelling as Denton's. Although he respected any attorney who had been a successful practitioner for almost forty years, he would not compromise his morals and the ethical duties he saw so clearly no matter what decision the firm made. He stood up abruptly and turned away from Denton.

"Donovan!" shouted Denton.

Donovan turned, anger and frustration on his face.

"You walk out that door and do anything that jeopardizes this firm's relationship with Sal Leone, and I promise you your career will be over."

Donovan stared at Denton's florid face and had a vision of a sudden heart attack. He shook his head slightly, inadvertently, dropped his head, and walked away.

The next day, Donovan sent Salvatore Leone the letter.

It was a simple letter that clearly defined the fraud he believed was being perpetrated. He stated the possible consequences of any action Sal might take in sending out false information, and he could have left it at that according to Richard Wolf. But that wasn't enough. Donovan wrote that, as lead attorney, he could not associate with Salvatore Leone in the building sales if he chose to send out the false information. He then said that in such event, the firm would have to withdraw from the representation of Leone on those matters.

Salvatore Leone was enraged. His call to John Denton was profane and threatening. Denton assured him Donovan's letter did not state the firm's position. He had taken a rogue position and would pay for his stupidity.

Denton, enraged now himself, presented the issue to the very same committee that, only months before, had unanimously agreed that Donovan should be admitted as a partner to share in the financial success of the firm. The decision this day was also unanimous. The decision this day was to fire S. Michael Donovan for his insubordination in the face of a direct instruction of his superior and for his rogue action taken without consulting the committee when he disagreed with his superior's decision.

But that wasn't the end of the matter.

California Business and Professions Code Section 6068(e) read that "[i]t is the duty of an attorney … to maintain inviolate the confidence, and at every peril to himself or herself to preserve the secrets, of his or her client." There were no exceptions to that rule.

So strict were the California requirements in this regard in 1994 that even if an attorney learned a client intended to do extreme bodily harm to or even kill another person, the attorney could not warn the potential victim or do anything else that would violate the confidence of his client by revealing his or her intent. And, although that strict interpretation was fodder for much argument over the years, the potential for economic harm to another resulting from fraud was never considered a basis for compromising a client's confidence.

Donovan was most intimately aware of his obligations in this regard, but he was also aware of his additional duty as an officer of the court in the state of California. If he knew a fraud was being perpetrated, he had a duty to do something. He could have asked the State Bar to give him a formal opinion, or he could have consulted other attorneys expert in such matters, but he didn't have time. The deals were proceeding. He couldn't call the buyers and tell them what Salvatore Leone was doing, but he felt he knew what he could do, and he did so.

The Los Angeles Law Journal, *the daily legal newspaper that covered law and law firm news reported the termination by McCormack & Stein of S. Michael Donovan, an attorney who had only the previous summer been made a partner in the firm. The story was relegated to an interior page, and not much more was printed. The reality was that such news should have been bigger. To have a newly minted partner fired from a highly visible law firm only months after becoming partner should have been big news, but it wasn't. Undoubtedly the newspaper, an occasional firm client, was influenced to be discreet lest it hurt another of the firm's clients.*

Donovan made copies of the newspaper snippet and mailed it to each of the attorneys for the potential buyers of Salvatore Leone's apartment buildings. The cover letter stated that he, S. Michael Donovan, was no longer the attorney for Salvatore Leone because of differences between himself and the former client. All correspondence relating to the purchase of the respective apartment building was therefore to be directed to someone else at the firm.

Shortly thereafter, a complaint for violation of his ethical responsibilities to his client was filed with the State Bar of California against S. Michael Donovan, formerly of the law firm of McCormack & Stein.

SIXTEEN

THE MIGRAINE STRUCK ON the drive back to the office. The hole in the screen of Sean's left eye was the start. It created a blind spot everywhere he looked on the road. He had to close that eye, drive at a snail's pace in the slow lane and exit the freeway to take surface roads back. He knew it was going to be a migraine. He'd had them before, not so much in recent times, but back when things were real bad for him. He remembered the hole in his vision as the first sign, always followed quickly by blurriness and the headache. The headache came as anticipated, and his struggle to get back to the office intensified. He didn't know how he made it back. He stumbled past Patty, right hand glued with white-knuckle ferocity to his forehead, into his office where he slammed the door and quickly downed four extra-strength Tylenol with a few quick gulps of the warm, bottled water he'd left on his desk the previous week.

Now, nearly three hours later, he leaned forward in his chair cradling his head gently between his hands. He'd slept, he thought, for part of the time, leaning back in his chair and doing the best he could to calm himself. When he finally opened his eyes, the blind spot and blurriness were gone. The headache was considerably less acute now, but the heaviness of his head remained. He knew the cause, of course. He still remembered the first one he'd ever had back when he'd been fighting for the life he'd built for his family, only to lose it all in an avalanche of anxiety, anger, and hatred.

Sean lifted his eyes and surveyed the cramped interior of his tiny office furnished with second hand desk, chairs, and bookcases with little room for anything other than the chaos of papers that festooned it. He shook his head sadly. Why was he still killing himself; practicing at law; living? What was the purpose of it all? And what the hell was he doing in the *Jackson* case? Put aside the realities that his puny practice couldn't possibly contend with the deluge of work that would be created by McCormack, Stein & Wolf, the fact he wasn't being paid a penny for all the time he would have to expend, and the fact that even now, just two weeks after the *Clarkson* settlement, most of those funds were spoken for, so that the four months cushion he thought he had, had been slashed in half. The thing that most troubled him was that maybe he wasn't even up to the task of representing Mrs. Jackson.

Sean knew before he entered Richard Wolf's office that he would have to control himself. The personal animosity he carried for his former partner was evident whenever he thought of Wolf and the firm, but even with that knowledge he believed he could handle it. He was a grown man, for God's sake, a good lawyer who was surely strong enough to put personal feelings aside and represent his client to the best of his skill and ability, especially when the client was such a close friend. But he'd failed, just like he'd failed in so many other ways during his career. He couldn't control himself. He let Wolf get to him even though he knew it was coming. How could he take care of his client, protect her interests, fight for her when he had such deep seated and lingering personal issues after so many years? And how could he do anything of any substance if the tension and anxiety of doing so would lead to the debilitating headaches—conditions he thought he'd mastered with his calming exercises but now found he had not?

Maybe he should help Mrs. Jackson find competent counsel big enough to deal with the big firm so he could move on and find clients who would actually pay him for his services; or, perhaps do something else all together. He had to survive, didn't he? Yet, even as he thought it, he knew none of it would work. Law was what he knew. There was nothing else he could do. And, as far as Mrs. Jackson's case was concerned, what attorney in his right mind would take on a major battle against McCormack, Stein & Wolf, particularly if he wasn't getting paid? Sean could refer Mrs. Jackson to one of the county's legal aid groups that represented the indigent, but he knew that wasn't right. They were competent attorneys as far as Sean knew, but how could he turn Mrs. Jackson over to people she didn't know?

He had no choice. He knew when he took the case it would be this way. He saw Wolf's name. He knew what was coming, and he knew then he had no choice. Now it was up to him to find a way to overcome the irrational anxieties that caused the migraines and the fears that brought the doubts.

Mrs. Jackson needed him. It was rare these days that anyone did. He couldn't let her down as he had let so many others down—as he had let himself down. He needed to buck up. So he moved to thoughts of the case to again try to convince himself that if he could only find a way to win the motion, Wolf and his cohorts would see the weakness of their case and back away from the big fight. Even though he knew deep down that would not happen, that was his only hope. He had to press on for Mrs. Jackson, and he had to do it competently. He needed to put aside his personal issues and the anxieties they caused and be the attorney he once aspired to be. He needed to get to work.

Sean pushed aside the clutter of papers on his desk and made room for the yellow legal pad upon which he'd previously written his list of things to do. First on the list was the simple statement: "Get paying clients." He chuckled through the heaviness in his head, knowing the truth of the statement. He glanced at his phone and decided he should start with Patty and any messages she might be holding for him. She'd had the good sense not to bother him after she saw him enter the office.

"Yes, Mr. Donovan?" she responded tentatively.

"Any calls, Patty?" he asked in as cheery a voice as he could muster.

"A couple sir. Should I bring them in?"

"Sure. Please."

She pushed the door open seconds later and strode slowly to his desk. Sean tried to smile as she handed him a thin stack of messages. He glanced quickly at the first, which was from his landlord, and decided this stack could wait till tomorrow. He laid them aside.

"Thanks, Patty."

"Are you okay, Mr. Donovan? I could see your head was really hurting. I was worried, but I didn't want to disturb you."

Sean smiled. He appreciated her concern.

"I'm okay. Thanks. I appreciate that you didn't interrupt me. I just needed to rest for a while. I think I'll head home and get it all out of me. I can get to these tomorrow. Thanks," he said again, anticipating she would nod and leave. But she continued to stand in front of him, her eyes flitting furtively back to the stack of messages.

"Is there anything else, Patty?" he asked.

"Well, yes, actually. I think there might be a couple of those calls you might want to return today, Mr. Donovan. I wasn't sure which order to put them in so I put them in the order I received them."

Sean glanced at the stack.

"Anyway, Mr. Donovan, there's a call in there from the Sierra Club. They said it's urgent. And then Melvin Jackson from the Sacramento police department said he was returning your call and that he'd be waiting for you until about mid-afternoon … about now, Mr. Donovan. I think it's on the *Jackson* case."

Sean lifted the stack and flipped through. He saw the message from Melvin and nodded.

"Thanks, Patty. I'll take care of these now."

Patty's face screwed up with concern.

"I don't mean to push you when you're hurting, Mr. Donovan. I just thought some of them might be important."

Sean smiled again.

"It's okay, Patty. I appreciate it—honestly. You did the right thing to bring them to my attention. I'll make the calls right away."

She smiled for the first time since entering the office. She nodded quickly, turned, and left. Sean smiled after her and was grateful for the one bit of good luck he'd had in recent years: the efficient and compassionate Patty as his assistant.

"Sean Donovan," Melvin's deep baritone laughed into the phone. "It's been a long time. I was surprised to hear you were representing Mom. Hell, it was a surprise to me she'd been sued."

"She didn't tell you about the suit?" Sean asked.

"You know my mother as well as anyone, Sean. You spent enough time with us," he chuckled. "She wouldn't tell any of us anything that might worry us."

He paused for several seconds and then laughed again.

"Damn, you and Horace drove me crazy. I coulda killed you guys a few times."

Sean chuckled on his own end at the memory.

"Younger brothers and their buddies are supposed to bother older brothers aren't they?"

"Yeah, I suppose," Melvin mused. "Listen, Sean, I was going to call you as soon as I heard last week. I just never got around to it. I want to thank you for helping Mom out—actually, for helping us all out. When my mom told me what she was into, I started to get angry, but I want to tell you, I felt better about it when she said you were on the case."

Sean was surprised at Melvin's confidence in him. He remembered the older brother well: big, strong and mean as hell on the football field, not much nicer to his younger brother and his friends either. He'd become a policeman in Sacramento, and from what Sean could glean from what information he'd been able to pull off the Net, a pretty good one.

"Thanks, Melvin, I appreciate that. It's going to be a tough case. Unfortunately your mom's already had her deposition taken, and the opposition got most of what it needed."

"Yeah," Melvin drew out the acknowledgement and was pensive in his tone. "Sean, I want you to know that me and my brothers are prepared to cover your fees and all," he hesitated a moment, "provided they aren't outrageous. I know what some of these attorneys charge."

Sean was flabbergasted. It wasn't that he thought so little of Melvin and his brothers that they wouldn't cover his fees. It was more that he never thought to suggest that they do so.

"Thanks, Melvin. I appreciate that." There was an awkward silence for a few seconds.

"You just go on and send the bills to me."

"I will, Melvin. Thanks." He wanted to move on, somehow feeling dirty talking about money yet acknowledging his relief to himself. "Listen, Melvin, the reason I called in the first place was because I needed some help from you on the case."

"You mean you didn't call to talk about money? Well, man, I guess I better take back my offer," Melvin said. Dead silence followed and he laughed. "I'm kiddin'. How can I help?"

"I've got to talk to a guy named Morgan Finnerty. Apparently he's the grandson of …"

"Yeah, I know him. He's the grandson of ol' Boner. He's the one who took over after Boner died. The old man's sons were worthless. You remember any of them?"

Sean shook his head into the phone. "No."

"Yeah, I guess not. They were older. The youngest was a year older than me. So what can I do?"

"I need to contact Morgan about the property the family owned next to your mother's. I don't know how receptive he'd be to taking a call from an L.A. attorney. Do you know him?"

"Not well. I know he sends my mother Christmas cards every year, the way his grandfather did. We always thought the old man was kinda sweet on Mom after Dad died. We ribbed her a lot about that, him being a crusty old white guy and all. I only met Morgan once or twice, but Mom spoke well of him because of the Christmas cards."

"Yeah, I heard. I was wondering if you could maybe talk to him, pave the way for a call from me?" Sean asked.

"Sure. He lives outside town, up the hill a bit. Auburn, I think. I can look him up and give him a call, let him know you'll be calling him."

"That'll be great. There is some urgency here, Melvin," Sean finished, needing Melvin to understand the significance without turning him off with some ridiculous attorney demand.

"I understand, Sean. I'll get on it and get back to you after I talk to him."

The second call Sean returned that day was to the Sierra Club's Legal Defense Fund. His first reaction upon hearing that the Sierra Club had called was to throw the message out; it was probably a solicitation for funds, and frankly Sean wasn't in a position to be sending money to charities these days despite the revelation he was going to be paid for the Jackson case. Even the fact it was marked urgent didn't move Sean. It was the name of the caller in the message that struck him: Andrew Harper. He remembered the name as that of the older of the two men who spoke to Carla Anderson after Buck's memorial service.

"What we're interested in ... at this point in time ... Mr. Donovan," Harper seemed to be dragging out getting to the point. They'd already been through all the introductory matters and the fact that Harper was coordinating the Sierra Club's long battle to prevent the development of the Silver Lode by Golden World. "... is for you to join our team," he finally concluded.

"Join your team? What do you mean?"

"Well," he started hesitantly again. "We'd like you to assist us in the fight."

Sean sat quietly for several seconds.

"Are you still there, Mr. Donovan?" Harper asked.

"Yeah, I'm trying to figure out what you're talking about. I mean, I understand your question, but I don't understand why you're calling me. What do you think I can add?"

Now it was Harper's turn for silence, and just as Sean was about to call his name, he spoke.

"Well, we'd like to talk to you about that, Mr. Donovan. Our information is that you were once part of the firm McCormack, Stein & Wolf ..."

"McCormack & Stein. It was McCormack & Stein back then. What does that have to do with this?"

"Although our suit is against the U.S. Forest Service, the real party in interest is, as I believe you know, Golden World. They are represented by McCormack, Stein & Wolf."

"Who's their lead counsel?" Sean asked even as he mouthed the name with Harper.

"Richard Wolf."

Sean closed his eyes, leaned his still heavy forehead against his free palm, and spoke softly.

"Look, Mr. Harper, I can't do any pro bono work. I've got to earn a living here. I'm really sorry I ca ..."

"This isn't pro bono, Mr. Donovan. The Sierra Club will pay. It won't be at the hourly rates you Los Angeles attorneys are used to, but we will pay."

Sean was silent. Harper spoke again.

"Look, Mr. Donovan. Your time on this matter could be minimal. We don't see it as any kind of disruption to your practice. We need you simply to join the team."

Sean smelled a rat.

"What's this all about, Mr. Harper? You don't need some old, one time litigator in a case dealing with environmental issues he knows nothing about. You guys are bright. You know all about me. Why don't you cut the crap and tell me what's going on here?"

This time Harper didn't hesitate. It was as if he was waiting for an opening because he too was sick of beating around the bush.

"We need immediate access to Buck Anderson's notes, journals, and private materials, sir. His brother referred us to his daughter, Buck's niece. Her name is Carla Anderson. When we spoke to her, she agreed to help us on one condition: that you participate in this case. She said she would need the assurance of your involvement so we don't take advantage of her and her father. We don't understand her concern, but there is the real answer."

Sean started to smile and then began to wonder. What was she concerned about? The Sierra Club was an ally of her uncle and everything he stood for, perhaps his greatest friend. What would they have to take advantage of? And then it struck him, and he was suddenly embarrassed and angry. Is she feeling sorry for me? Trying to get me some work? As if I can't do it on my own?

"Look, Mr. Harper, you tell Ms. Anderson I've got plenty to do and I don't need to get involved in some case I know nothing about."

"We've tried that tact, believe me, Mr. Donovan. It didn't work. She won't help us unless you're on board. We could try to subpoena the materials, of course, but we don't have the time for that battle, and, frankly, we need the Anderson family on our side. Can you help us?"

Dammit, Sean said to himself. Why the hell should he get involved?

"I don't know, Mr. Harper," he finally said. "What would you want me to do?"

"My associate and I have set up a base of operations in Visalia. It's close to Buck's office and all his records. Buck also had a lot of friends here. It's possible he talked to people and said something that could help us. We've got limited time to put our case together. Visalia is also the closest city to the Silver Lode. What we'd like is if you could come up here one day this week and meet with us at Buck's old office. We could discuss the case with you then."

Sean didn't want it. He didn't want anything to do with a case intended to once and for all destroy the dreams of many of the citizens of his hometown. That's all he needed, to have even his hometown supporters turn against him. To compound matters, the opposition would again be Richard Wolf. What the hell was going on? Was this to be more punishment for his stupidity just when he was starting to get a life going again? Then, almost as soon as that thought crossed his mind, he laughed to himself. What life?

"Look, Mr. Harper, I've got to be up that way soon. I'll have my secretary call you and let you know when that will be. We can get together then."

"Please, Mr. Donovan, this is vital to our success. Is it at all possible for you to make it this week? We will pay you for your trouble."

Vital to their success, Sean wondered. What did he care? He could use the money, though, and he needed to talk to Carla anyway—to straighten her out.

"I'll try to set it up for Thursday or Friday. I'll have my secretary call you by tomorrow afternoon."

"Thank you, Mr. Donovan."

The formal appellation struck Sean for the first time despite the fact he and Harper had used the "Mr.'s" throughout the entire conversation. His first thought was to tell Harper to dispense with the "Mr." but his second was to let it be. His second thought won out.

SEVENTEEN

RICHARD WOLF WASN'T HAPPY. Ordinarily the concept of happiness was irrelevant to him. It was a child's game to reflect on one's happiness. Happiness was simply a state of mind over which strong, intelligent people had complete control. Today, however, he felt he didn't have that control, and it bothered him.

That Wolf was angry with Matthew Dunne for his deposition mistake was unimportant to his happiness. Anger was a tool he often used to manage and control his world. Strategically accessed, anger could work wonders in negotiation both in and out of court. And in dealing with his minions, anger was most effective. He used anger when he dealt with the firm's partners, its associates, and everyone else who looked to him for the firm's high standing and the vast wealth to which they all aspired. It was Richard Wolf's real estate department that was the largest contributor to the firm's collections, and it was Richard Wolf himself who managed the investment of those collections for the benefit of the entire firm. If he got angry occasionally, it was okay; he had that right. And his anger never made him unhappy. If anything, it invigorated him, motivated him, and drove him. But this day, he was unhappy.

Wolf stared out his west-facing window at the brown haze of smog that hung over the Pacific, blown there from the baking desert communities of Riverside and San Bernardino by the Santa Ana winds. His hands gripped each other tightly behind his back as he finally began to understand the reason for his unhappiness, and it unnerved him. He'd long since forgotten the days when he'd envied Michael Donovan—back when Michael was the firm's shining light, the up and coming rainmaker, the one the clients loved, the one everyone trusted. Wolf admitted, even then, that it wasn't all smoke and mirrors with Michael either; he was a damn good attorney. But Michael had blown it for himself. In the process, he'd almost brought down the firm. Michael was arrogant, self-righteous, caring only about himself. Wolf and the rest of the firm were forced by Michael's stupidity to take the action they took, and that action was proper. It saved a good law firm, it saved jobs, and it, by God, upheld the integrity of an entire profession. There was never anything to be ashamed of. In fact, there was much of which to be proud. And, as it turned out, if success and failure were the measuring sticks, Michael had been wrong, and Richard and the firm had been right.

Richard Wolf never agreed to take Michael Donovan's side in the meeting with Salvatore Leone. He supposed, in the strictest sense of the word, what Leone was planning was wrong. He was intending to commit fraud, which could ultimately have dire consequences for him and his companies as well as the buyers who would rely on the information. But, to turn his back on a good client because of some "high and mighty" moral stand wasn't right. Hell, if he and the rest of the firm did that, not only would they lose Leone and his million a year in fees, they'd lose every major client who learned of the firm's abandonment of a client in need. No, Wolf knew he never agreed to stand with Donovan and bring the firm down.

Wolf remembered clearly that he had warned his friend and partner, Michael Donovan, not to take the action he was proposing. He recalled stating that the firm had no power to control what its client did. All they could do was alert the client to the potential dangers of his actions, and if the client took the actions anyway, without the direct assistance of the firm, of course, then they would be there to help the client if the consequences were realized. Wolf remembered telling Donovan that and begging him not to do what he was planning. But Donovan wouldn't listen. It was as if Donovan had something against Leone. It was as if his moral compass was the only one giving a true reading. But he was wrong, just as Wolf told him he was.

That's how Wolf saw the entire affair—in hindsight, of course, no matter what his thoughts may have been at the time—and that's exactly how he testified against his friend in the State Bar Court's disciplinary proceedings.

When Donovan's letter stating he was no longer representing Salvatore Leone because of differences of opinion between himself and the client reached legal counsel for the potential buyers of Leone's apartments, most of the counsel and their clients heard Donovan's message loud and clear: that there was something wrong with the information given them by Leone. Rather than investigate further to get to the correct information, those buyers simply withdrew their offers and walked away from the transactions. Those who didn't terminate ended up discarding Donovan's letter and completing their purchases without further investigation.

The complaint against Donovan was filed by Salvatore Leone and supported by Donovan's firm. The basic argument was that Donovan's actions were in blatant disregard of the confidentiality to which communications with his client were entitled. His revelations of confidential information resulted in the loss of deals that would have closed but for the ethical breach. Donovan, of course, argued that he revealed nothing. He simply withdrew "loudly" from the representation of the client, as was his duty to his profession and to himself. He was not permitted by the State Bar Court to spend any significant time discussing the nature of the information that prompted his action, but only the fact that he took the action Mr. Leone claimed breached the obligation of confidentiality.

It took more than three years of conferences, negotiations, hearings, and testimony before the California Supreme Court confirmed the Bar Court's ruling on Donovan's right to continue practicing law. The final decision was based in large part upon the eloquent oration of Richard Wolf, who closed with what was one of the best summations he had ever given.

"Mr. Donovan took it upon himself, Your Honors, to prosecute, judge, and decide the propriety of his client's actions. He had every conceivable resource available to him to handle the matter differently, and instead of calling upon *those resources, even those of myself, a friend and colleague, he took his own course and violated the ethical principle that we lawyers hold most dear: that of the confidentiality of a client's information. Even though he didn't come right out and reveal specific information, his actions did just that, and ultimately the result he sought was the very one that came out of his actions. That result was in direct contravention of his former client's best interests. I respectfully submit that it is this august body's obligation to punish Mr. Donovan. He is not above the law. He is not above the duties of every lawyer. He can never replace his own moral code for that of the wonderful profession of which we are all a part. To permit him to do so would be to besmirch this profession in the eyes of the world. That, gentlemen, is something I cannot countenance and something I implore you to prevent."*

The California Supreme Court upheld the decision of the State Bar Court to suspend S. Michael Donovan for a period of three years. Since he was not on temporary suspension during the three years of hearings, the suspension was to start thirty days after the Supreme Court's ruling and run consecutively. Donovan was prohibited from engaging in any activity that could be considered a part of the practice of law. The order further read that at the end of the three year suspension, Mr. Donovan could seek reinstatement to the Bar, provided he showed satisfactory remorse for his actions, completed a State Bar sponsored legal ethics course, and passed an exam testing him on the very same principles of ethics.

Richard Wolf watched S. Michael Donovan leave the final hearing a beaten man. He was slumped under the arm of his attorney who supported him as they walked out of the courtroom. His face was ashen, his eyes fixed on the ground. Wolf might have felt sorry for him if he had at least acknowledged his wrongdoing. But he hadn't and probably never would. That his career was over meant nothing to Wolf because it was what he deserved. You let your ego control you and take your own path in a brotherhood that is supposed to stick together, and you ultimately get what's coming to you. S. Michael Donovan got just that from Richard Wolf's perspective.

Donovan was reinstated in the middle of 2000, slightly less than three years after the order for his suspension. Richard Wolf had intended to contact the State Bar in protest of Donovan's application, but his partners at the firm thought it best to let the matter rest. Unlike Donovan, Richard Wolf followed the advice of those partners.

Since Donovan's reinstatement, Wolf heard little of him. In fact, until the meeting in which Matthew Dunne mentioned his name on the *Jackson* case, he hadn't given Donovan a thought in years. In truth, once he heard of Donovan's involvement, Wolf wanted to see him, to see what the years had done to him while he, Wolf, was becoming one of the most celebrated attorneys in California.

The first sight was a surprise. He looked older, much older, in fact. Wolf was proud of his own appearance, of course, that he looked much the same as he did sixteen years earlier, albeit in much better physical condition due to his strict nutrition and exercise regimens. But the change in Donovan was dramatic. Gone was the confident swagger Wolf remembered in his carriage. Gone, too, was the spark of passion even the most casual observer could see in his eye. He was still a beaten man, and for a fleeting instant, pity for the man he once struggled to compete with came to Wolf's mind. But that thought was gone even before it was fully formed, for there was something else that made what should have been a time to gloat a time for reflection.

Even as Wolf smiled with the knowledge that he was better than Donovan, that he was the one who had succeeded in the profession they both pursued, Wolf was ill at ease in his presence. He couldn't put his finger on it at first. Even when Donovan mentioned Matthew Dunne's deposition mistake, and it was clear Donovan was following the only path that gave him even the slightest chance of success in the *Jackson* case, Wolf didn't understand, because his immediate and cutting response clearly unnerved Donovan. Then, when Wolf riled his former friend with the patronizing tone and offer of reason, Donovan again stumbled into the weakness of a passionate response completely unrelated to the matter at hand. All in all, it would seem the meeting had gone well for Wolf—that he'd met the opponent, gotten the measure of him, and beaten him. It wasn't until Donovan walked away that Wolf finally understood.

He hadn't beaten him. He never had. Though he couldn't admit it, whatever insecurity he'd always felt in Donovan's presence lingered. They'd always believed Donovan was the better attorney, even after the suspension. As Wolf watched him walk out the door just before Carlos Perez entered, he realized that the insecurity he still harbored was one borne of fear, a fear that he would not measure up, that Donovan might in fact be better than him.

Richard Wolf stared out the window and understood whence his unhappiness came. He was the head partner in one of the most prestigious law firms in the country. He was one of Los Angeles County's most powerful men. Yet S. Michael Donovan was still there. Somehow, after all these years, he was still there.

Wolf turned away from the window, surveyed his sanctum. There was no room in his life for any of this, for fear or insecurity of any kind. He was Richard Wolf, and what he needed was to take care of business once and for all. He needed to complete the task he started some sixteen years before. He needed to bring S. Michael Donovan down, and he had the resources at his disposal to do just that.

EIGHTEEN

AUBURN IS A TINY hamlet nestled in the western foothills of the Sierra Nevada Mountains, thirty-five miles northeast of Sacramento along Highway 80. It's a picturesque burg straight out of old west lore with a quaint downtown sparsely sprinkled with small shops and eateries that cater to the locals as well as visitors making their way to Truckee and Lake Tahoe or the gambling dens of Reno beyond. It's close enough to Sacramento to give its residents "the City" and its pleasures, yet far enough away to be considered "away from it all." Morgan Finnerty and his family made their home at the northernmost edge of Auburn. It was there that he was to meet with Sean Donovan.

After Melvin Jackson cleared the way, Finnerty readily agreed to the meeting with Sean with an "I'd be happy to help Mrs. Jackson, if I can. When can you get up here?"

Sean left early Saturday morning to make the Finnertys' by 1:30. He took Interstate 5 over the Grapevine and stuck with it at its "Y" junction with the 99. The drive up 5 is monotonous as it parallels the California Aqueduct past barren foothills, the occasional fast food/gas stop, and the even more occasional small town. The scenery is typically brown and arid with the only break being the ribbon of water that runs through the open concrete trench of the aqueduct to the thirsty households of the parched southland. The monotony of the surroundings provides a driver ample opportunity for life reflection, music, mind games, or simple daydreaming to occupy his time. Sean didn't care much for daydreaming. The dreams had long since been squeezed out of his life. As for life reflections, his were too painful. That left music and mind games.

There weren't that many vehicles heading north on Highway 5 Saturday morning, mostly trucks carrying cargo from the ports of Los Angeles, some local pickups, and occasional passenger vehicles taking the same route as Sean. There were enough vehicles, however, to occupy Sean with his mind games.

He began noticing vehicles he passed or that passed him more than once after a rest stop or a period in which he found himself absently pushing his car past all reasonable speeds only to see a "Speed Monitored by Radar" sign and pull off the accelerator. He began to view his fellow travelers as part of a caravan traveling together for protection as they journeyed to some northern outpost. He smiled at his silliness, especially after the caravan broke apart completely by the time he reached the southern edge of Sacramento.

As he transitioned from the 5 to the 80, he was surprised to see one of the cars from his caravan still with him—at least he thought it was from the caravan. The car was a non-descript white Chevy Malibu, like hundreds of others on the road, but the driver seemed to have the same square, bulky shape of the man he'd noticed in the Malibu that was part of his caravan. When Sean finally exited the freeway in Auburn, the Malibu followed. At the traffic light, they stopped at red, and Sean glanced into his rear-view mirror. He could make out what appeared to be a heavy dark mustache, and the build he indeed recalled from the caravan. Sean smiled into the mirror, shrugged as if to say "what a coincidence," and gave a quick wave into his mirror before feeling silly again and dropping his hand. To his surprise, the man in the Malibu lifted his hand and held it steady, palm facing Sean, in a wave of his own.

Sean turned left at the light; the Malibu went right. Sean wondered where the driver was heading and at the coincidence of the long drive together. But, as the Malibu disappeared around a bend behind him, Sean smiled again and gave it no more thought.

———————

Morgan Finnerty was a man of medium build. He looked to be in his late twenties with long dark hair that swept back wildly from his face. The scraggly facial hair, tattered jeans, and faded green t-shirt put Sean in mind of the typical beer swilling, pot smoking hillbilly wastrel, but that impression could not have been farther from the truth. The young man's bright eyes, firm handshake, and engaging smile were the first signs the impression was wrong, and his rich-toned, articulate, and refined speech confirmed the misimpression.

Morgan's wife, Emily, was a beautiful young woman who wore her blond hair long in a loose ponytail. She was of slight build, surprising given the twin four-year-old blond bruisers who ran frantically into everything in their way. Her bright green eyes sparkled above a genuine smile that welcomed Sean readily into her home.

Sean and Morgan sat on the sun-bleached redwood deck that extended from the back door of the Finnertys' log built home. The view was remarkable of the innumerable pines, firs, oaks, and birches that stretched uninterrupted up the slopes behind the home, but it was the air that most struck Sean. He'd never experienced anything like it. The oppressive heat of the Sacramento Valley seemed to have hit a wall at Auburn and turned back. In its place was the clean, balmy summer air of the mountains, borne on lazy gusts, suffused with the scents of pine and the ever-present hillside blooms.

"This is beautiful, Morgan," Sean mused and sipped a glass of freshly brewed iced tea.

"Yeah, we kind of got lucky finding it. Emily wouldn't buy just anything with our share of the proceeds from the sale of Grandpa's land. She wanted to be in Auburn. I guess she knew just what she was looking for." He smiled and looked off into the sun spackled growth.

"Your grandfather had an interesting name," Sean smiled, leaned forward, and tried to get into the conversation as he adjusted his note pad in front of him.

Morgan nodded and returned a broad smile.

"Ol' Boner, that's what they all called him. He was a crude old cuss, I'll tell you that. He liked to let folks think the name had something to do with his sexual appetites, particularly the ladies. He'd wink at 'em when they'd ask him how he came by the name, and then he'd just walk away tall and proud, like he was something special. The truth was different though. I got it out of 'im one day when we were sitting out back of his place sharing a bottle. His own grandpa gave him the name when he was a teenager. He wrapped a few cars around poles and trees and such, kinda "T-boned" 'em if you know what I mean. Well, his grandpa started calling him T-Bone Finnerty to make fun of him, hoping to shame him into settling down. It didn't work, though. When his buddies got hold of the name, they just took it the next step. He ended up liking the new version because it always resulted in funny conversation, and it stuck with him to his grave."

"I saw what looked like an old roadster or something under a cover in your driveway," Sean said and cocked his head over his right shoulder. "Is that one of Boner's T-bones?"

"Naw, that's his, but he never wrecked that one to my knowledge. It's a '48 Pontiac Silver Streak. She was in his garage when he passed on; a real mess. I got it as part of my share of the estate. I had it hauled up here. Been restoring it ever since. It runs pretty good now. You interested in seeing it?" Morgan asked with a hopeful smile.

Sean nodded, "Sure, after we finish here if that's okay?"

Morgan nodded and smiled.

"Your grandfather sounds like a character. Did he work the property next to the Jackson property for a long time?" Sean asked.

"Sure. His whole life, I guess, just like his own father and his granddad before him. That was the family livelihood for a lotta years. They ranched and farmed the land, sold lamb and wool for a time, then beef, and, of course, their crops. It was a good living."

"Do you have any idea when your family started working the Jackson property?"

Morgan looked off pensively.

"I don't know exactly, but I think it was almost from the beginning. You see, Willy Jackson's great, great granddaddy, Black…" He hesitated when he saw Sean's reaction to the unusual name. "They called him Black Jack's son on the plantation," he said and shrugged matter-of-factly. Sean nodded.

"Black Jackson came out West right after the Civil War. He joined the migration of folks looking for a new start. I suppose it had to be real tough for a black man then, but he managed to lay claim to five hundred of the flattest, finest acres this side of the mountains. Boner's relative, a Southern son named Grant Finnerty, lost everything in the war. He came west, too, and ended up getting our one hundred acres, which, by the way, was never as good as the Jackson property.

"Anyway, Black and Grant somehow became good friends. The way I heard it, they worked both properties together and shared a fair living."

"That makes sense," interjected Sean, "but how did it happen that the Finnerty clan ended up working the entire property?"

Morgan nodded.

"Yeah, you'd think it would be the other way around if anything. Apparently Black's son didn't want anything to do with working the land. It reminded him too much of the plantation where he was born. He wanted to educate himself and make his fortune in the city. So, he left.

"When Black got too old to work and realized his son would never come back, he made a deal with Grant. We Finnertys could keep on working both properties and keep all the profits except that as long as Black or his wife lived, we were to pay them what they needed."

"That was it?" asked Sean. "He didn't provide for any of his heirs? Didn't require your family to pay or do anything once he and his wife were gone?"

"No," Morgan shook his head. "Black wasn't real happy that all his kids left the land he'd worked so hard on. He felt if you didn't work the land, you weren't entitled to its benefits." He shrugged. "Black passed the property down to the kids, but, the way I heard it, he figured the only way his kids should benefit from it is if they worked it."

"So what happened after Black and Grant died?"

"I don't know much except that we just kept right on working the land and none of the Jacksons ever came back to work it. They'd come out to picnic by the stream that runs along the north half, and sometimes some of the Jacksons would come out just to walk the property. But none ever came to work it again."

"Didn't any of the Jacksons ever ask for payment or anything like that?"

"Not to my knowledge," Morgan answered slowly. "But, I know when I was a kid hanging out on the property, our family would send them meat and fruits from the land. Our families were friends over the years, some years better than others, but we usually would send off wagons and then truckloads of goods a couple times a year. Willy and Beverly ... Mrs. Jackson ... had a pretty big clan they had to feed."

"Yeah, I grew up with that big clan," Sean laughed. "Mrs. Jackson said the meats and fruits stopped coming about ten years ago or so."

Morgan shook his head as a frown spread across it.

"You know, that's possible. In Boner's later years, he was real forgetful. His sons, one of which is my own father, didn't much care for ranching and farming because it was too much work for so little money. So, they weren't paying attention to anything. By the time I started to help Boner, most of the ranching and farming was shutting down. I guess I just never checked to see whether anything was still being sent to Mrs. Jackson."

Sean dropped his head in frustration. That there had been cooperation and even friendship, at times, between the families was potentially beneficial to the case. The problem was that as the story wore on, it began to look like the Jacksons took little interest in the property. If they never bothered to exercise ownership by demanding lease payments or anything else, maybe they really did forsake it. The wagonloads of goods would have been helpful had they continued to the present day, but it was clear they hadn't. Sean had only one hope.

"Look, Morgan, what about property taxes? Did the Finnerty family pay the property taxes for the Jackson property?"

"Oh, yes," he nodded even as Sean frowned. "I forgot to mention that, didn't I? That was part of the deal," Sean perked up at the mention of a deal. "When I started helping Boner, he reminded me about property taxes during one of his lucid moments. He said we should check with the assessor before the tax bill is sent out and we should just pay it. He didn't want Mrs. Jackson to be bothered with it. He had promised Willy he would handle it."

"There was a promise? Is it possible it was in writing?" Sean asked hopefully.

"I wouldn't think so, Sean. Boner wasn't much for writing anything down. Did you check with Mrs. Jackson? From what I understand, Willy was a pretty smart guy. He might have written something."

"She's not aware of anything," Sean answered.

The fact Morgan could testify to his uncle's statement was good. It wasn't great because it was hearsay from a witness who wasn't around to be cross-examined. It was possible that a declaration from Morgan might be enough to defeat Flow Corp.'s motion, but it was unlikely it would win the lawsuit. Any good attorney would have a field day with such testimony, and Richard Wolf certainly fit into that category. Something in writing would be much better.

"Morgan," Sean started again. "I'm going to have a declaration prepared for your signature if that's okay. It'll relate some of what we've discussed with particular emphasis on the promise to pay property taxes. I'd like to send that to you sometime next week for your signature and have you send it back. I need to submit it to court with my papers for Mrs. Jackson. Would that be okay?"

"Sure," he said.

"I have to tell you, Morgan, your declaration will be good, but it would sure be great if you could find a writing of some kind signed by Willy and Boner. Is it possible there are records somewhere that you haven't looked through?"

Morgan smiled and nodded.

"We've got a whole slew of boxes of Boner's stuff in storage. I've meant to go through them but just haven't gotten around to it. I'd be happy to take a look over the next few days."

Sean nodded. "Thanks."

"I really don't think I'll find anything, though. Like I said, Boner didn't like to write. He was really a shake-of-the-hand type guy. He was tough and crusty and all, but he was honest, and if he shook a man's hand on something, he lived by it."

Sean nodded appreciatively before he looked down and ran his finger down his notes as he flipped through the pages of his pad.

"Is there anything else you can think of regarding the property and any permission that may have been granted for your family's use of it?" he asked.

"Nothing about permission, Sean, but if you've never seen it, you really should take a drive out to it. It's beautiful," Morgan said as he looked off wistfully into the distance. "I remember wandering out toward the stream and sometimes just sitting for hours. I'd see deer, bear, and sometimes even a cougar. The most beautiful things though were the birds, the way they just seemed to glide, rarely even moving their wings. I saw hawks and eagles and," he turned to Sean suddenly, "I even saw a condor."

Sean looked up quickly, surprise written on his face.

"A condor? I thought they were extinct. When did you see it?"

"A few times, but the last time was just before we closed escrow, about two years ago. It was unbelievable—an ugly head and face through my binoculars, but gorgeous in flight. The biggest bird I've ever seen."

"So why'd you sell the property if you loved it so much?"

Morgan looked quizzically at Sean.

"Ten million dollars," Morgan said slowly and deliberately, and Sean's eyes opened wide. "They paid us ten million dollars for those hundred acres. I wanted to wait because I'd heard about the Golden World ski resort, but the rest of the family just wanted out. They figured talk of the resort was cheap and there'd be no better time to sell than when everyone was so excited about the talk. The family started talking about selling even before the offer. My dad and his brothers heard some people were buying up properties from Visalia to the Silver Lode. They wanted in on the rush. Then, out of nowhere, some real estate broker comes to our door saying he has a client who's interested in our property. When we first discussed price, his client, this Flow Corp., negotiated pretty hard. That all changed, though, when I mentioned we'd been working the adjacent property for years and that they'd probably be able to do the same. They asked me if we had any written agreement to work the property. When I told them I didn't know of any but that we had paid the property taxes for years, they stopped negotiating price. The deal moved smoothly after that. My family was pretty happy about the whole thing."

"I guess so," said Sean. "Did you ever meet anyone from Flow Corp.?"

"Yes," Morgan nodded. "Midway through the escrow, I met a couple well dressed Mexican fellas and their attorneys. They came out to see it but spent most of the time trying to get a handle on the Jackson piece. I thought they would make Mrs. Jackson an offer."

"They did, even before they offered to buy yours, I think. Do you recall the names of any of the people who came out?"

"I don't remember the attorneys, a man and a woman in their early thirties. They kind of stayed in the background. One of the Mexicans was the biggest guy I'd ever seen up close—mean looking. The other, the smaller guy looked to be the boss. I'm pretty sure his name was Perez, Carlos Perez."

A half block up the street from the home of Morgan and Emily Finnerty, a non-descript white Chevy Malibu was parked under the shade of a massive old oak. It had been there since early afternoon, about the time its occupant called his contact and confirmed that Sean Donovan had indeed come to Auburn to meet with Morgan Finnerty.

NINETEEN

CARLA WAS HAPPILY SURPRISED when Sean called. It was around one o'clock Sunday afternoon. Sean had spent the night at a Motel 6 and then went back to the Finnertys' in the morning to clarify a few items for the declaration. He ended up having lunch with the family. He asked Carla if she would be available to join him for dinner; he had something he wanted to talk to her about. She was delighted to join him and postponed tentative plans with an old high school boyfriend, a recent divorcee named Gunther "Gunny" Daar. Daar was an environmental engineer with a Los Angeles firm heading north for a business meeting in Sacramento. He stopped in town for a weekend with his parents and heard Carla had moved back. He was hoping they could reconnect. Carla put him off with an offer of a rain check, which he graciously accepted.

The next call didn't come until shortly before seven o'clock. Sunday traffic had been heavy all the way down, and Sean was just getting close to Visalia, probably twenty minutes away. He felt it might be best if they met at the restaurant to save time. Carla offered to bring in some Italian and open a bottle of wine at her place. Sean seemed distracted, however, and felt a restaurant would be better.

Sean had a lot of time to think on the road. He was happy about the declaration he was getting from Morgan Finnerty. It would at least give him a fighting chance of defeating the motion. It wasn't a case winner by any stretch of the imagination, and even if it won the motion, it wouldn't have the effect of derailing his opponent. The evidence was so weak and probably easily overcome in a full blown litigation with an artful cross examination of Morgan Finnerty that there would be no way Richard Wolf would concede. Thus, in the event Sean won the motion the deluge would start immediately upon the judge's ruling, and Sean would have more to contend with than any one man could handle. A writing would have been helpful. All of that occupied at least a part of Sean's thoughts, but what weighed heavy on him, particularly as he got closer to Visalia, was not Morgan Finnerty, nor was it the *Jackson* case. It was the Sierra Club phone call and Carla Anderson's involvement in it that bothered him.

Sean had brooded over the call since his discussion with Andrew Harper. Carla was treating him like a charity case, like a man who needed her help to get his life back on track, as if he didn't have his own mind and his own abilities. She'd no doubt heard of his struggles. She was his sister's best friend, after all. Although he didn't begin to understand her interest in him until the drive from Auburn, he had to admit the interest had been blatant. Although he didn't mind that, he did mind that she was acting like all the other women he tended to meet—seemingly more interested in molding a man into their ideal rather than taking him as he was. She figured if she could force the Defense Fund's hand to hire him, he'd start to make money again and start to fit the mold she was creating. He'd seen it before—women who liked the look and figured they could create the man they wanted beneath the look. He'd had a wife like that once. He didn't realize it until it was too late in Susan's case, but he sure saw it now, and he didn't appreciate it. He didn't need Carla Anderson's help. He'd been on his own for a long time, dammit, and he'd survived without it. He'd survive without it in the future.

The problem for Sean was that he liked Carla. He didn't want to believe she was like Susan and the others he'd met since the divorce. He wanted her to be the earthy beauty he pictured, not the conniving woman on the make for the man of her creation. In short, he wanted her to fit his mold, and he couldn't see the irony of his position.

He tried to work up a sustained anger for his meeting with her. But his mind wandered. On the one hand, he tried to give Carla the benefit of the doubt, arguing she really believed he could help the case and simply recommended him as a good attorney. On the other hand, he didn't do environmental work. Wouldn't they be crazy to hire him? Then the argument would shift again. He was a good litigator, one who had once been able to argue a point persuasively without antagonizing the decision maker. Certainly those skills would be beneficial to any case. *Besides*, he thought, *Carla was beautiful.*

Then his mind would regroup and his thoughts would flip. That was all in the past; he didn't have the edge anymore; he couldn't get it back. And wasn't that all beside the point anyway? He didn't need her help.

It wasn't until just before he called Carla the second time to suggest they meet at the restaurant that he was finally able to maintain a legitimate focus, to formulate the position he had to take with her. By the time he reached the quiet Italian restaurant, Sean was ready.

The first sight of Carla was as stunning as the night he'd spoken to her at his mother's party. She had a warm, welcoming smile as if she was genuinely happy to see him. She wore a black dress and simple diamond pendant, both of which set off her white blond hair and sparkling eyes. "This is going to be difficult," was Sean's immediate thought.

Once the non-committal hug and discussion of traffic were out of the way, they were seated in a candle-lit corner of the cozy restaurant.

"I'm glad you called," Carla offered.

He smiled stiffly and nodded.

"I'm glad you were able to make it."

An awkward silence followed until the waiter approached and asked if they were interested in wine. Sean glanced up from the wine menu and ordered the Coppola Claret after a quick look at Carla and a smile and nod of agreement from her.

"Did the meeting go well up in Sacramento?" Carla asked as the waiter turned away. She sensed tension and tried to find a path to a discussion.

"Yeah, it went okay," Sean said, nodding slowly. "I don't know if you ever met the Finnertys." She shook her head no. "I met with the grandson of the guy who ranched the land next to Mrs. Jackson's. I was hoping he'd be able to help our case."

Carla waited expectantly, but Sean ended there.

"Can he help?" she asked.

Sean nodded, his eyes darting furtively around the room.

"A little, I think," he said. "I don't know if it'll help over the long haul. I guess I'll find out soon enough."

He glanced down at his menu, and Carla looked quizzically at him. The waiter returned, opened the bottle, and poured a taste of the rich red liquid into the bottom of Sean's glass. He lifted the glass quickly and took a sip without the usual swirling of the liquid and smell of the wine's bouquet.

"It's fine," he said. "Thanks."

The waiter poured and asked if they were ready to order.

"We'll need a few minutes," Sean said.

The waiter nodded and walked away.

"Sean, is something wrong?" Carla finally asked.

He didn't know where to start. He'd had it all planned, and now it seemed so childish. His mind was a jumble of cross-thoughts and arguments. He looked at Carla with an expression that showed deep pain—something he wanted to say and couldn't or didn't want to say but felt he needed to. Carla's brow creased with concern, but her eyes remained soft, warm, and compassionate.

"What is it, Sean?" she asked and reached across the table for his hand.

Sean pulled away involuntarily before she touched him. He pushed back in his chair, rocked his head back and shook it slowly, steeling himself.

"I'm upset with you Carla," he finally said more harshly than he'd intended.

Her look changed to surprise and then sadness, and Sean was sorry he said it.

"Why?" she whispered.

And he couldn't stop.

"This Sierra Club thing. What made you think I needed that? I don't. I've got plenty of work. I don't need help getting work. I've been clawing my way back for a long time, and I've done it alone; all of it; without your help or anyone else's. I don't need anyone feeling sorry for me, trying to get me work, particularly in something I know nothing about." His words came in a torrent. Carla shook her head and tried to explain, but Sean was on a roll that he couldn't stop.

"I don't need this now. I've got enough to do, and I don't need anyone's charity. I can get my own clients as I've done for years. I can handle it on my own."

"Sean, I didn't mean anything by it," Carla finally interjected. "I'm not looking at you as a charity case. That never even entered my mind. You said at Buck's wake that if we needed any help, I could call on you. My father and I wanted someone we could trust, someone we could go to and get the answer from if we needed it."

Sean was taken aback. He did offer, didn't he? He'd forgotten that. He dropped his head and then realized he didn't believe her. At least that's what he told himself. He remembered offering his assistance, but he didn't believe that's why she recommended him to the Club. Most of him wanted to believe her, but his defense posture wouldn't let him. She again reached across the table.

"No, Carla, I can't do this. I don't need it. I don't need the work or you or anything. I don't," he hesitated, dropped his head knowing he'd blown it yet again. "I can do this on my own," he closed softly and glanced back up at her.

Carla stared at him. Tears glistened off candlelight in her eyes. She shook her head slowly.

"You know, Sean," Carla started, "when we were kids, I had a terrible crush on you. I guess I thought I still did. I was excited that maybe you could work on this thing with us. I'll admit that part of the excitement might have come from that crush, but the truth is that I believed you were the one person we could trust in this mess. They think Buck was murdered and proof lies somewhere in Buck's papers. We didn't want them making a circus out of Buck."

Carla dropped her head to hide the tears that were again coming to her eyes. The tiny café seemed to close in around Sean. He stared at her, tried to think of something to say. He wanted to reach across the table and say he was sorry, but he couldn't. He didn't know how. The "sorry" had been torn out of him. He'd used it for years with everyone who was important in his life, and it hadn't helped. He'd lost it all, and "sorry" had done nothing to bring it back. It had done nothing but harden his heart with the knowledge that it meant nothing. He wondered now why he had been so cold and so committed to being that way, how on the entire drive from Auburn he'd tried to convince himself that it was the way he had to be. He had no answer.

Carla looked up at him again. A stain of mascara marred the corner of one eye.

"You *have* done it on your own, Sean, whatever that means," Carla started, trying not to look frustrated and then realizing it made no difference. "Maybe that's how you want to keep it."

She hesitated a moment, her eyes fixed on him, her sadness clouding them.

"I'm sorry, Sean. I didn't mean to hurt you or force anything," she finally said.

These were the words he should have spoken. Instead he heard them from Carla, and he knew she meant them.

Carla stood up and slung her purse over her shoulder. She looked at him with moist eyes.

"You're right. Don't bother to show up at the meeting tomorrow," she said with a hint of anger growing in her voice. "I'll tell them you aren't interested."

She stormed past him, and he couldn't call out her name. He couldn't formulate a thought. Emotion was drained out of him completely. All he could do was what he had become so adept at: he could hate himself.

TWENTY

SOUTHERN CALIFORNIA'S ECONOMIC MELTDOWN *was still in full swing in the summer of 1995. Although emigration was slowing, people were still moving away. Business, while turning around in much of the rest of the country, was still slow in Southern California, particularly any associated with real estate. Property values reached their nadir toward the end of that year.*

The Donovan household was living on savings sufficient to last them another six to nine months.

Immediately after his firing, S. Michael Donovan landed a position with a small but growing firm in Torrance. The firm's two partners were thrilled to take on an attorney of Donovan's caliber, not to mention his potential book of business. Their hope was to create a regional boutique centered on their business practice and Donovan's real estate expertise. That ended with the filing of the State Bar complaint by Salvatore Leone. Normally it would not have mattered, but Donovan intended to inform potential clients that he was dealing with the complaint, and both he and the local firm's partners felt it would affect their plans for growth. Donovan gave up the position with the promise he'd be back as soon as he resolved the State Bar complaint. He expected it to blow over with a settlement in a few short months.

Donovan stood at the curb waving at Susan and the kids as the Super Shuttle van carted them off to LAX. Middle of June cloud cover, known to the denizens of the Southern California beach cities as June Gloom, cast a grey pall over Donovan. He forced a smile for the kids but couldn't help feeling the wave meant something more than the "see you soon" he intended.

"Why aren't you coming with us, Daddy?" Johnny asked just before he stepped into the van.

Donovan bent down to hug him.

"I'll be along in two weeks, buddy," he said as he tousled his son's hair.

He turned to Marie, who stared at him with sad, moist eyes. He held his arms open. She ran into them and hugged him tight.

"You be good for Mommy, okay? Say hi to Grandma for me," he said and squeezed his little girl.

"Okay, Daddy," Marie nodded into his shoulder.

He helped them into the van and turned to Susan to assist her. Her touch on his hand was cool. After she sat, he leaned in to kiss her. She turned slightly and gave him her cheek.

"I'll see you in a couple weeks, okay?" he said.

Susan nodded. "Okay. Take care of yourself, Michael," she mumbled, and he slid the door shut.

Susan was angry with him. He had put the family in jeopardy. Because of his stubbornness, he'd lost his job and was now fighting for his professional life all at the expense of Susan and the kids. At least that's how Susan viewed it. She felt he should have listened to her and kept quiet. He was a top attorney at a top law firm earning a tremendous amount of money. Why would he jeopardize that on some meaningless moral stand? He had other options, and just like all the other times, he wouldn't listen to her. He had to choose his own path. He never listened to her. At least that's how she saw it.

"Don't you see I had to do it? I didn't ignore you. I heard what you had to say. I understood. But I wouldn't have been able to live with myself if I'd stayed quiet in the face of an obvious wrong. I needed to do something. It was the right thing," Donovan explained.

"Spare me, Michael. You've always done what you thought was right regardless of what anyone said and regardless of the effect it would have on me and the kids."

Donovan stared at her, stunned. He believed he'd spent his entire married life focused on his family's welfare. He'd been home to coach the kids and have dinner with them and Susan most nights, even at the risk of losing out on the eventual partnership because he simply wouldn't work the fourteen-hour days all the other partner-track attorneys worked. He'd stood on principle regarding time spent at work for the sole reason that he had a wife and family, and he wasn't going to lose them to any job. He was a good dad, and he was an attentive, loving husband, he thought. But that wasn't what Susan was talking about, was it?

She'd been angry from the beginning. The proud, independent co-ed with the exotic look of a Middle Eastern beauty brought doubt into the marriage. She, her mother, and younger brother had been all but abandoned by a father who ran off to start businesses in Europe, promising all along that he would return a rich man and they would all have the life they dreamed of. And he did return... occasionally. He'd come home periodically bearing gifts and hugs and more promises, and then he'd go off again before anyone could get too attached.

Donovan thought his love would overcome the demon in Susan's closet. He thought he could show her he was a different type of man, one who would always be there for her and the kids, one she could rely upon forever. But she never seemed to believe it.

There were subtle instances of distrust for a time. Then the smallest things became large and were never forgotten and definitely never forgiven. Simple mistakes that occur in any relationship were blown into justification for greater doubts and further distrust, and Donovan began immersing himself in his work. And for a time, that brought a change. It seemed to satisfy Susan. He was making enormous sums of money, and the prestige of his success opened doors to a world she longed for, a world of wealth and station. Although Donovan was happy to see Susan smiling, he wondered if it was real.

As the Super Shuttle's blue van turned the corner and moved out of his sight, he reflected on the conversation of the night before.

"You're consumed by this, Michael. It's best for me to take the kids to New York to visit my mother for the month. We haven't been back in a few years, and it'll give you the time you need to fight this State Bar thing," Susan said. "You can join us in a couple weeks."

"This is going to work out, Sue. I know in my heart I did the right thing. Just hang in there, and before we know it, it'll all be over."

She nodded and dropped her head. "I hope so. I just wish you'd listened to me, Michael. Just this once, I wish you'd listened."

Donovan stared at her. He tried to understand why she couldn't let go of the recriminations, why she couldn't give him a smile and support him with a positive word. Maybe he really did understand. Maybe it was all borne of the fear she had because of her father. Sean stood up and put a caressing hand on her shoulder.

"I'll take care of this. I promise you. Everything will be alright."

She'd looked at him then, and there was a tear in her eye. She wiped it away quickly and walked away to finish packing.

One week after he waved goodbye to his family, as events in the State Bar matter were heating up, S. Michael Donovan was served with a complaint for divorce by the Beverly Hills attorney hired by Susan Donovan.

Donovan's immediate reaction was shock. He needed to call his wife, tell her it had to be a mistake, that he was sorry, and that whatever the problem was, they could work it out. But when he called, Susan wouldn't talk to him. Her mother, Myra, suggested that it would be best for him to handle it through the attorneys. When he asked to speak to his kids, she said they weren't in. Donovan told Myra he'd be there to see them in a week. He didn't give a damn how Myra thought it should be handled. She, of course, hung up on him, and when he arrived at the airport with the boarding pass Susan had gotten him before she left, he learned it had been cancelled and his seat resold.

When Donovan tried to make reservations for another flight, he found the only credit card in his pocket had been cancelled only days before. To compound matters the bank accounts he held with Susan had been emptied. The only money S. Michael Donovan could get his hands on was a small savings fund he kept so Susan wouldn't see from credit card bills or bank statements when he was planning something special for her.

When Donovan finally reached New York and appeared at Myra's door, no one was home. A neighbor informed him that Myra had left for a trip the day before with her daughter and grandchildren.

"Do you know where they went?" he asked.

"She didn't say," the neighbor responded.

———

Donovan hired two attorneys, one for the divorce and the other for the State Bar complaint. The costs were exorbitant in both matters as his opponents peppered him with discovery and other documentation. Time began to stretch out. Six months to negotiate a settlement in the State Bar matter extended to a year and then more. The divorce became vindictive. Donovan was forced to take contract work for firms in town to earn some cash. He made minor appearances and did research for minimal fees. He had to fund the litigations as well as his own living expenses, which included the suddenly overwhelming expense of his home, an asset he couldn't sell in the weak market even if he'd had Susan's consent.

Donovan had not seen his kids since the Super Shuttle turned out of sight one year earlier. It had taken a court order forcing Susan to make the children available on the phone before she would permit even that contact. Once he could speak to them on the phone, he did everything he could to convince them they would one day soon be together again.

It was about a year after the service of the divorce complaint, another June Gloom day in 1996, that Susan appeared at the front door of the house she and Donovan had shared for ten years. The home's postage stamp sized lawn was dead, and all the shrubbery was overgrown. The place was becoming an eyesore in the neighborhood. When Donovan appeared at the door, he looked haggard and beat. His eyes were puffy and bloodshot. Scraggly stubble covered his face. The odor of stale liquor wafted in waves off his sallow skin and from the interior of the house.

Sean's immediate reaction when he opened the door to Susan was to strangle the life out of her right there. But the passion for such an act seemed to have been sucked right out of him. He could only stare, dumbfounded that *she stood on the stoop. He didn't invite her in, an invitation she would not have accepted even if he had.*

"I know how difficult things are for you, Michael," she said without preamble as she looked past him to the chaos and filth of the house's interior. She was dressed immaculately like a businesswoman of considerable means. Donovan was dazed, as if this weren't real: he with his world crashing around him and she with the sympathetic smile of the bourgeoisie looking down upon her subject.

"I have papers here I'd like you to consider, Michael. I know they should go through your attorney, but I thought I might be able to save you some money and end the pain of this whole thing."

He stared at her.

"Where are my kids?" he mumbled without emotion as he craned to look past her to the car on the street.

"They're with my mother. I didn't bring them with me. I thought it would be best."

He chuckled with angry sarcasm.

"You thought it would be best for me not to see my kids? What the hell do you know?"

"Michael, let's not argue. I didn't come here to get into a fight with you," Susan said.

"Why the hell did you come? What's wrong with a fight anyway?" Donovan asked and took a step toward her, smiling malevolently.

Susan stepped back to maintain the three-foot separation. Fear crept into her eyes.

"I think it would be best for all of us, the kids in particular, if we could end this as soon as possible."

Sean gave her a quizzical look.

"I've had my attorneys draft an agreement that I think is fair, Michael," Susan continued. "It will allow you to focus on the State Bar case and get your life going again. It calls for an immediate decree of divorce; we will pay the house payments for you and the cost of fixing the house up for sale when it's time. I won't demand any alimony nor will I demand any child support. In fact, we'll pay you fifteen hundred dollars per month until this State Bar

thing is over. *The only conditions, Michael, are that we sign this agreement now and that you relinquish custody of the kids and allow them to be adopted by my new husband."*

"Your new husband?" Donovan stammered.

"As soon as the divorce is final, Walter Abrams and I are going to be married."

Donovan recognized the name. Wasn't he one of the McCormack & Stein partners in New York? How could she be marrying him? Hadn't she just met him a few times at firm parties once or twice a year? How could she be marrying him?

"Walter loves the kids, Michael. He'll take good care of them, send them to the best universities. He'll give them the life they deserve."

"Get out of here," Donovan growled and stepped menacingly toward her. "Do you think I'm crazy? You come here telling me to give my kids up? Get out of here before I do something we'll both regret."

Susan jumped backwards, fear etched in her eyes. She bent down without taking her eyes off Donovan and placed the agreement on the ground.

"Think about it, Michael, for the kids."

"Get out of here!" he shouted and lunged at her, stepping on the agreement and kicking it aside as Susan scurried away.

TWENTY-ONE

CARLA ARRIVED AT THE office early Monday morning. The day promised to be a scorcher just like every day of the past week. Since the office hadn't been open for a while, she opened windows and doors to circulate the stale, dead air. She was going to proceed with the meeting with Harper and Luckman of the Sierra Club Legal Defense Fund even though Sean wasn't going to attend.

As soon as she woke that morning, she made the decision to assist them without Sean. Buck wouldn't have minded. He would have wanted her to do just that. There wasn't any reason to be concerned about the Sierra Club, which happened to be her uncle's greatest fan. She convinced herself that the whole "Sean Donovan thing" was a silly flight of whimsy, and she had to get back to reality. If there was any way of determining how Buck died and bringing the killers to justice if he was murdered, she had to help.

Carla was upset when she left Sean the previous evening. He'd said he didn't need her, but she knew he meant he didn't want her. Whatever fairy tale hopes she might have had of a relationship were crushed. She tried to convince herself it wasn't Sean's rebuke that upset her, however. She was embarrassed because she had made such a fool of herself.

Carla actually had it in mind that she could turn her childhood crush into the dream she'd harbored off-and-on for years. When she'd first seen Sean again, a rush of giddy emotion almost overcame her. She was surprised at her own reaction. It took all her strength to control the excitement that surged through her when she approached him on the deck of the Mountain View Grill. She felt like a young girl again, particularly when it was clear he was interested in her as well. How stupid, she thought, to believe that Sean Donovan was anything other than any man in his early fifties. By the time a man got to his fifties and was unmarried, by divorce or otherwise, he would have so much real world cynicism and baggage that there could be no room for fairy tales and flights of whimsy. Those passions would have long since been forgotten. Sean Donovan was no different from the rest, and the baggage he carried was too heavy even to consider the silly hopes of Carla Anderson. By the time Carla stormed away from him, she was embarrassed and angry. It wasn't until she was almost home that she focused on the hurt.

She cried for the last few minutes of the drive, and then before she went to bed she cried again. Despite her best efforts to convince herself she was angry more than sad, she couldn't do it. The truth is she felt sorry for herself, for how the uncompromising reality of life always seemed to destroy the dreams. She mourned the death of passion in her for another human being. She wept for a lost love that never was. And as she finally started to doze off into a fitful sleep, she tried to resolve once and for all to forget about him, to let go the dream and find real purpose in life. But... even then she couldn't. There was still something there; something she couldn't simply dismiss; something she couldn't release.

Andrew Harper pushed the door open shortly after nine o'clock.

"Where's your buddy?" Carla asked as she peeked around the conference room's doorjamb and saw Harper standing alone in the tiny lobby.

Harper smiled and thumbed over his shoulder.

"Pete's collecting a few things from the trunk. It'll help us with the presentation to Donovan. Is he here yet?" he asked and pointed to the conference room.

"No," Carla shook her head. "He won't be joining us. You can tell Pete he doesn't need to bring anything in for Sean—just what we need for our purposes."

Harper smiled. Carla shook her head.

"I'll bring the coffee into the conference room," she said.

Carla turned into the kitchenette as Harper stepped back out of the office to inform his partner of the good news.

———————

Sean pulled into the strip center's parking lot just before nine o'clock. He drove slowly past the Anderson office, saw the door slightly ajar and discerned movement inside. Several parking spaces were available directly in front of the office, but Sean cruised past. He found a space across from Starbucks, four doors to the left, and backed into it amidst the vehicles of Starbucks junkies. He shut off his engine and sat in silent contemplation for several seconds, wondering if he was doing the right thing. Finally, he noticed the approach of a light blue Toyota Prius. It rolled soundlessly past him to a slot in front of Anderson's. Sean watched nervously, knowing that if the passengers were the Sierra Club representatives, his time for a final decision was near.

The Prius's driver door opened, and Sean could see the man he remembered as Andrew Harper exit the vehicle. From the other side of the vehicle, the bushy red head of Harper's partner, whose name Sean could not recall, stuck up above the Prius's roofline. Sean watched Harper exit the vehicle and stride purposefully through the Anderson office door as his associate began gathering rolled maps or plans, together with manila folders and files from the back of the Prius. Several seconds later, Harper reappeared with a broad smile on his face. He said something to the other man who returned a smile, replaced some of the materials, and followed Harper into the office.

Sean leaned his head back, closed his eyes. He tried to steel himself for the meeting he still wasn't sure he should attend. He'd felt so strongly the day before regarding Carla's interference in his life. Sean didn't blame Carla for walking away from him. He'd handled the whole thing poorly. He knew that. But she understood, didn't she? Once she gave it thought, she would have understood that he had to state his position. She had to know he wasn't a charity case; that he didn't need anyone's help; that he was a man who could stand on his own.

He shook his head, eyes still closed, and wondered whom he was trying to kid? He'd sure done a good job on his own, hadn't he? He'd been trying for more than thirteen years to get his career back on track. It had been a monumental struggle and abject failure all the way. The truth was that his "stand on his own" posture hadn't gotten him close to a stable career. Who would care anyway if he did it on his own or someone sent clients his way? Isn't that the way professional practices work: by referrals? He should be thrilled to use whatever help someone was willing to give.

Though Sean wrestled with these thoughts, there was a more dangerous thought that kept creeping into his consciousness. The thought was one he didn't want to contemplate, one that scared him. Yet there it was. Since the moment she walked away from him, it preyed on him, forced him to consider it.

Sean Donovan liked Carla Anderson. That she was beautiful was apparent the moment he first saw her, but it wasn't her beauty that caused him such anxiety. He wished it were the beauty alone, for that was something with which any man could contend. But Carla had something more. Sean saw an earthy sincerity in her wondrous eyes. He felt a compassion and softness in her demeanor, not borne of pity but of interest in the welfare of someone for whom she had real feelings. She wasn't out to mold him, as he had feared, but rather to be part of him—something he hadn't seen in any woman since his days of college idealism. He'd only seen Carla a couple times, yet he could sense the passion in her; not just the passion one might have in a new relationship, but rather the eternal passion for life and love to share with the world. Yet he'd done everything he could to ignore it, to keep her at arms length and engage with her only at the superficial level of a man attracted by physical beauty alone.

Sean had hurt Carla. He'd acted selfishly the day before, just as he'd done with others his entire life. Now he had to apologize; not to resurrect a relationship with her, for he knew that wouldn't happen. Apologies didn't work that way in the real world. No, he had to apologize just to let her know that he understood he was wrong, that her passion was good, and that she should not let it slip away because of the insecurities of one has-been attorney. Yet he was afraid—afraid of the commitment that such an act entailed.

He opened his eyes slowly and wiped away the moisture that had gathered in their corners. He leaned forward, one hand gripping the wheel, the other holding the keys in the ignition. It would be easy to turn the key and drive away. Who would blame him if he did? Who would really care anyway? But as soon as he asked the questions he knew the answers. He would blame himself and he would care, as he always had.

TWENTY-TWO

CARLA GLANCED UP FROM the conference table as soon as she heard the door open. She stood slowly and stepped to the conference room door. Sean was standing in the lobby. His look was grim, uncertain. Should he stay or turn and walk back out the door?

Carla stepped out of the conference room and stared at Sean for several seconds until the surprise with which she first greeted him turned into a smile.

"I'm glad you could make it," she said and waived him forward. "We're just getting started."

He nodded, approached her slowly, his eyes fixed on hers.

"I'm sorry about last night," he said as he drew near. "I ..."

She held her hand out directing him toward the conference room.

"I know," she said softly and nodded. "C'mon in."

As Carla introduced Sean to Harper and Luckman, their disappointment was apparent. An awkward silence hung heavy when Sean took his seat in front of a yellow legal pad until Carla finally chuckled.

"Well, it looks like we've got the whole family together finally," she said and elicited a smile from everyone at the table. "Why don't we get started, okay? I think you'd better start from the beginning, guys. Tell Sean what you told me so we're all on the same page."

Sean appreciated Carla's light tone, but he had trouble concentrating on Harper's presentation. His focus was on how to act and react in her presence. She'd been immediately gracious, as if yesterday had never happened. He hadn't been able to fully express his sorrow for his actions and words, but it didn't seem to bother her. How could he be natural in this setting where all he really wanted to do was talk to Carla? Maybe he'd made a mistake by joining this group. Maybe he should just leave and try to catch up with her later. Luckman and Harper would love that. He couldn't walk away, however. He knew he'd never have the courage to do it again. So he sat and listened as Harper and Luckman told their story.

They meandered over the same facts Carla had already heard; yet she asked new questions to try to pique Sean's interest. Luckman spread out aerial and topographic maps of the Silver Lode and pointed to various locations that corresponded with the issues Harper was discussing. When the narration finally turned to the reasons for their suspicions about Buck's death, the discussion opened up fully as Sean began to engage. He actually began to consider legal issues at which he was most adept.

"What court is the matter in again?" Sean asked.

"U.S. District Court in San Francisco. Judge Marks is the presiding judge," Harper responded.

Sean was surprised at the mention of the name. He smiled.

"That wouldn't be Tom Marks, would it?" Sean asked.

Harper looked down quickly, ran a finger over his notes.

"I think that's his name. He was recently appointed by the President to replace Judge Singleton. I haven't actually ..."

"Yes, it's Tom Marks. Do you know him?" asked Luckman, looking up from his notes.

"I know a Tom Marks. If he's the one who graduated from SC in '85, I know him."

Both Harper and Luckman went back to perusing their notes, flipping through the pages, looking for information on the judge. Harper spoke as he searched.

"I know Richard Wolf was pretty excited when he heard Marks was the judge. I think he graduated with the judge and was pretty good friends with him. We were concerned because of that and the fact he appears to be a pro-development judge."

"This Judge Marks did graduate from USC in 1985," said Luckman. "You know him?"

Sean was pensive for a moment, not really recognizing Luckman's sudden interest in him. Finally he smiled and nodded slowly.

"I know him. We were classmates and on the same intramural football team." He gave a short laugh. "Won the law school championship our last year. He was one of our linemen. Beefy guy. He could drink any of us under the table," he said and then paused for a moment. "So, Tom Marks is the judge. Good for him. That was his goal from the beginning."

"You went to school with Richard Wolf then?" Harper asked.

Sean eyed Harper and nodded.

"I did. I also worked with him at McCormack & Stein. I know him."

Harper was impressed. One of the biggest concerns his recent analysis of the case raised was the removal of the environment friendly Judge Singleton and his replacement by Tom Marks, a good friend of Wolf's from what Harper understood. Although he didn't suspect the judge would take the side of a friend simply because of that friendship, the fact of the matter was that human nature might encourage him to give Wolf's position some leeway in the numerous minor decisions that typically led to the final decision. Harper was congratulating himself on getting Sean on the team to offset Wolf's relationship with the judge.

"It's great you know them, Mr. Donovan. It'll help."

"I haven't seen Tom in over fifteen years. I doubt my involvement will influence him in any way."

Harper frowned for an instant and then picked up the thought again.

"My thought was that it might assist in neutralizing Wolf's influence over him if you were also his friend," Harper said hopefully.

Sean shook his head.

"I don't think you have much to worry about on that front unless things have changed dramatically since I last knew Tom. He and Richard were never good friends. I recollect that he didn't like him in school, and things hadn't changed by the time of our ten-year reunion in '95. Are you aware of any work they may have done together over the years?"

Harper shook his head. Sean glanced at Luckman, who also shook his head.

"I suggest you guys do a little homework and see if they've worked on any matters together. What I can tell you is that Marks thought Richard was an arrogant prick when we were in law school and that his opinion hadn't changed by the time I saw him last."

They both nodded and jotted their notes. Sean began to feel a sense of involvement that he didn't expect.

The conversation continued for the rest of the morning and ultimately turned into a planning session. Sean could feel himself becoming interested in the case, the way he always did when he focused on one. From the standpoint of both Harper and Luckman, it became apparent that Sean was not just some small town attorney who chased ambulances and handled minor family disputes. It was clear his experience and analytical skills could be beneficial as they proceeded toward Congressional and court hearings.

"You mentioned earlier that you believed Curtis Golden hiked with Buck?" Sean said.

"That's what we recall. After Buck's death was confirmed, our entire defense team was in shock. We fully expected him to deliver the 'smoking gun,' if you will. When he didn't, our boss," he pointed at Luckman and himself, "seemed to give up. He decided, over our objections, to move resources to other cases. He figured we'd given it a good run, but without information we were expecting from Buck, there was no chance to win. Pete and I felt differently.

"We went through the entire file again and came across a note of a meeting one of our predecessors on the case had with Buck. That was the note that mentioned Curtis Golden."

"Do we have any idea what they discussed?" Carla asked.

Harper shook his head. "No."

"Has anyone spoken to Curtis Golden?" asked Sean.

"Not to our knowledge. We have no indication anyone did," said Harper. "I wouldn't think he'd talk to us voluntarily with his family's greatest dream weighing in the balance."

"Why don't you depose him? It's not too late to get an ex parte order. You can probably even offer to limit the testimony to a few issues."

Luckman nodded skeptically.

"I don't see that he'd be very forthcoming with any information we'd be interested in. We have no clue what we're looking for and wouldn't even know what to ask," Luckman said.

"It might be worth a try. Hell, if you just asked him what he and Buck talked about on their hike, he might give you something," said Sean. "I knew Curtis. I found him to be a good guy, honest anyway. That was a lot of years ago, but there's no harm in trying. This is assuming you don't find what you're looking for in Buck's files."

Both Harper and Luckman nodded before Luckman glanced at his watch. He motioned to Harper and pointed at his wrist.

"Yeah, eleven forty-five; you're right, Pete. Look, we've got to get back and check in with our main office. We have Monday lunch conferences," he raised his brow and chuckled lightly. "That's what our bureaucracy is all about. We can get back here this afternoon and start the search if that's okay with you, Carla."

All except Sean agreed to gather again at 1:30. He had to get back to his office to take care of the Finnerty declaration and work on the Jackson response to Richard Wolf's motion. He promised he'd stay in touch through Carla and said he could get back up toward the end of the week or early the following week.

Harper and Luckman stood and made their way around the table where they shook hands with Carla and Sean.

"Thanks for your help, Mr. Donovan," Harper said. "It looks like this might work out."

Sean nodded as Carla escorted them out. When she returned, Sean was sitting again, staring into space.

"Thanks for coming, Sean," she said with genuine warmth in her voice.

He turned to her. The grim look with which he entered the office was gone. In its place was a look of calm resolve. He nodded to her.

"Carla, I'm really sorry for the way I came at you yesterday," he said. Carla raised a hand to stop him. Her look was of forgiveness. She didn't need to hear more. But Sean shook his head. "Please, Carla, let me get this out. I was wrong yesterday, and I'm sorry for it. I'm happy to help you and your father in this, and I'm glad to get another case," he frowned slightly and shook his head again. "I've got to get past the distrust, I guess. So, again, I'm sorry … and … thank you for thinking of me." He shrugged slightly as he finished.

Damn, he thought. That didn't come out right. I want to say more…

"Thanks, Sean. I appreciate that," Carla interrupted his thoughts. Her smile began to fade as she was hoping for more from him and realized nothing more was coming. "Would you care to get some lunch before you go?"

"I can't. I've got to get back," he said and at the same instant wished he'd been able to say yes. "I'll stay in touch, though. I'll clear whatever else I have on my calendar and try to be back up here by Friday."

He stood and extended his hand awkwardly. She took it and followed him out.

"See you," he said.

As he walked away she stared after him, hoping he would turn around so they could start the whole thing over again.

TWENTY-THREE

"THEY WANT TO TAKE Curtis's deposition," Richard Wolf's voice said through Atticus Golden's telephone. It was late in the afternoon, just minutes after Wolf had ended a testy exchange with Andrew Harper.

"Can they do that?" asked Atticus. He was taken aback. He and every person on his development team had gone through the deposition ordeal years before. "Dammit, Richard. Haven't we been through all the depositions? They can't keep doing this, can they?"

"I told them we wouldn't agree to make Curtis available again. They already had their shot at him three years ago and we wouldn't permit another."

"So what's the problem?" asked Atticus.

"That's not going to stop them. Harper's making an ex parte motion Friday morning in San Francisco."

"Don't give me legal crap, Richard. What is that?"

"It's an emergency motion. They can get in to see the judge on a day's notice arguing they don't have the time to go through the regular process since we're so close to the trial. The problem for them is that discovery in the case is closed. It has been for a long time."

"And that means what?"

"It should mean they can't take any more depositions. They would need some very strong argument about how they missed something during discovery or they just discovered something that requires further investigation," Wolf said and then was quiet for a few seconds. Finally, he began again in a hushed, resigned tone.

"Unfortunately, I could see Judge Marks granting this so as to avoid any argument for further appeals, particularly if the Club makes a compelling argument of need and relevance supporting their position and Forest is unable to refute it."

"Can't you do something? I thought you were friends with the judge."

Atticus could hear the creak of Wolf's shift of position in his leather chair.

"Atticus, this may turn out to be a matter of form over substance," he said deliberately. "I'm sending Matt up there today to help Forest's attorneys, but I don't want him to make an official appearance. The judge can give the Sierra Club the right to depose Curtis, but Harper will still have to find and serve him with a subpoena. Marks won't order us to make him available, and Matt won't put us under his jurisdiction by making an official appearance. All we have to do is make sure Curtis makes himself scarce for a while. If they don't find him quickly, they might give up and go down some other road."

Atticus's door opened and Curtis Golden walked in. The son motioned silently as if to acknowledge that he was responding to a summons from Atticus.

"Come in, son," Atticus said. "Curtis just arrived, Richard. I'll put you on the squawk box." Atticus pushed the "hands free" button and gently placed the receiver back into its cradle as if he still wasn't quite sure how to do it after all these years. A second later he asked, "Can you hear us, Richard?"

"Yes, fine," Richard replied.

Atticus motioned for Curtis to sit in the chair closest to his desk.

"The Sierra Club wants to take your deposition again, son," he said.

Curtis shrugged. "I'm okay with that; let's do it," he said.

"No," said Atticus, irritated. "Look, son, they want to take it, but we're not going to let them. Richard is fighting to prevent it."

Curtis frowned at his father.

"Why, Dad? We've got nothing to hide."

"I know, son, but it's just a tactic to delay this thing further, and we don't need that. I want this thing to end now without any more of their games," Atticus finished.

"Wait, guys," his eyes flitted back and forth between his father and the telephone. "Wouldn't it be better to be forthcoming and let them have their deposition? Won't it make us look better? I have no problem with it."

Atticus shook his head, exasperated. He started to respond, but Wolf's voice interrupted.

"It may seem that way, Curtis, but it's just a fishing expedition. They're doing nothing but abusing the system and trying to harass us. We can't let that happen. In fact, we're suggesting to Forest that they request sanctions against the Sierra Club for making this ridiculous request at this late stage."

"If it's a harassment ploy, won't the judge deny their request?" Curtis asked.

Curtis and Atticus looked at the phone for a response.

"It's possible; in fact, that's our hope. But, as I was just explaining to Atticus, I could see the judge granting because he doesn't want to give them any argument that might support another appeal. If he does grant the request, it would be good for you to lay low for a couple of weeks so they won't be able to serve you."

Curtis looked troubled. His eyes moved from the telephone to his father for help. It was apparent to him that Wolf was trying to hide something. The thought of being duplicitous at this late stage of the proceedings was so out of character for the entire Golden image that he half expected his father to jump in and stop Wolf. Instead, Atticus stared at him as if in full accord with the attorney. Curtis shook his head.

"What are we worried about? We've covered everything haven't we? We've addressed every single environmental issue and come up with reasonable mitigation measures. The Supreme Court agreed with us on the EIR. What ...?"

"Curtis!" shouted his father. "Don't you understand? You can't go under oath again?"

Curtis stared at his father. Atticus dropped his head to control his anger, but Curtis could see the reddening of his father's pallor. He shook his head in surprise.

"What are they searching for?" he asked softly.

"I wasn't able to get that information from the Sierra Club attorney," Wolf started.

Atticus cut him off sharply and answered his son.

"We know what they're after, dammit. They want to know about that hiking trip you took with the environmentalist. What's his name? The one whose body they found?"

"Buck Anderson," Wolf responded.

Atticus nodded and stared at his son. His eyes were red and his entire bearing was fatigued, old.

"Look, Curtis," continued Wolf, "we don't know exactly what they're after. If the judge grants their request, we're hoping he limits their questioning to areas they specifically identify in court. I suspect Atticus is right, however. The best thing would be for you not to have to talk about it, to stay out of sight. But if by chance you are served, I need to know immediately so we can prepare you."

Curtis glanced again at his father, who was sitting forward in his chair glaring at him. He was stunned at Atticus's attitude. It was almost as if his father had lost his wits completely, that he was in the thrall of some evil spell. Yet he was concerned for his father's health, and he understood it would do no good to discuss the matter any further. He nodded to Atticus and painted a reassuring smile on his face.

"Okay, Dad. I'll make myself scarce."

Atticus nodded, and the intense glare softened as his entire frame seemed to relax.

"Thank you, son," he said and breathed evenly again.

———————

Richard Wolf knew what they were after even before he heard it from Matthew Dunne. They all understood why the Defense Fund wanted to depose Curtis again. Hell, Atticus had come right out and said it. They wanted to question him about the hiking trip he'd taken with Buck Anderson. That was no surprise then when Matt told him the focus of the intended discovery late Friday morning.

"Who was there from Forest?" Wolf asked.

"Some new guy named Jeff Wuller. He was good. I thought Marks was going to rule against Harper for awhile," Dunne said.

Wolf nodded pensively. Just as he expected, Judge Marks had given the Sierra Club what they wanted but hadn't made it easy for them. They would have to locate and serve Curtis.

"Marks was good about limiting the scope of the deposition. He didn't need much prompting from Wuller on that. It was pretty clear Harper didn't want to reveal too much, but Marks kept pushing him," Dunne continued.

"What does he have, Matt?" Wolf asked impatiently.

"He's fishing, Richard, just like you thought. He's definitely interested in the hiking trip that Curtis took with Buck. It didn't look like he had any specific information, though, and he wasn't able to identify anything specific. There's no doubt they're hoping for something they can use, but it's pretty clear they don't know what that is."

Wolf nodded, said nothing.

"Marks limited the scope of questioning to the specifics of the trip and what was discussed and done on that trip. I think we'll be okay even if they track Curtis down. The judge said he wanted the depo completed by the end of the first week of October so nobody can claim a need for any further delays of the trial. He wants this thing off his desk by Thanksgiving," Dunne concluded.

Wolf would have preferred not to have this issue to deal with. He would have preferred to go before Marks with the Supreme Court's ruling that the EIR had properly identified all potential environmental impacts of the proposed Golden World development in the Silver Lode and that adequate mitigation measures had been proposed and adopted. That ruling was compelling to any trial judge. It would result in a final ruling in favor of the Forest Service, which, in turn, would give the last approval needed by Atticus Golden to proceed. The problem the deposition posed was that they might stumble onto some new evidence that would give the

Sierra Club new life before Congress or new evidence that the EIR had not considered.

Richard Wolf was not overly concerned about Curtis's deposition. His team would take whatever time was necessary to prepare Curtis for Harper's questions assuming, of course, they served Curtis. Although he didn't care for the "hiding" strategy any more than Curtis did, Wolf agreed with Atticus on that point because it had the potential effect of limiting the issues at trial to the existing EIR without any chance of stumbling onto difficult evidence. Although the whole deposition issue was an irritant at this late stage of the case, there was something much more troubling to Wolf about the fact that the Sierra Club was requesting it.

Why now? Why hadn't they requested the deposition before this? If they were so interested in the hiking trip, why did they wait so long? They could have made their request as soon as they realized Buck wasn't coming back. Obviously, the thought that there might be value in such a deposition didn't strike anyone until recently. He wondered what had brought it to their attention. He didn't learn the reason until the end of the conversation with Dunne.

"When's your return flight?" Wolf asked.

"I'm at the airport now. My plane leaves in an hour. I'll be in about mid-afternoon," Dunne replied.

"Alright, see me when you get in," Wolf instructed. "Anything else?" he asked as he prepared to hang up.

Dunne chuckled.

"Yeah, one more thing. I don't get it, Richard, but it looks like your old friend from the *Jackson* case has joined the Sierra Club."

"What do you mean?" Wolf asked and knew the answer immediately.

"Harper handed me an Association of Counsel. Donovan has joined their team," he said.

Richard Wolf understood why the deposition request was made so suddenly.

TWENTY-FOUR

SALVATORE LEONE SUED McCORMACK & Stein *for malpractice shortly after those who purchased his buildings sued him.*

By the time of Michael Donovan's suspension from the Bar, the California real estate economy was making a comeback. Values had hit bottom and were finally showing year over year increases—small by historical standards, but increases nevertheless. People could actually feel home values make their turn and start inching up as sales activity picked up along with confidence that the worst of the more than six-year downturn was past. There remained pockets of weakness to be sure, but things were looking up in Southern California.

Among the pockets of continued weakness were some of the inland areas around Riverside, San Bernardino, and East Los Angeles Counties, areas in which Salvatore Leone had sold his apartments less than three years earlier. Unfortunately, even in the stronger areas apartment buildings weren't doing all that well as new California residents were tending to buy the cheaper homes rather than rent. The surplus of homes due to foreclosures earlier in the decade was still large and prices were low enough to attract those who began to trickle back into the state. Had apartment occupancy increased at anywhere near the rate houses began to sell, there might never have been a problem, but they didn't. The "minor" omissions in the financial information Leone presented the ultimate buyers of his buildings ended up being significant enough to put some of the buyers and the properties into bankruptcy. As a result, they filed suits for fraud against Leone. Even those who had been able to survive the misinformation jumped on the bandwagon and filed their own suits when they read that others were suing Leone.

Although the compensatory damages sought in the lawsuits were not of great concern in view of the fact that Leone's real estate development business was picking up nicely, the claims for punitive damages, intended to punish him for his fraud, were troubling. If proved, the damages that could be awarded would put him out of business.

To compound matters, the federal investigation into the frauds allegedly perpetrated by Southern California real estate developers, brokers, and bankers during the heady days of the late 1980s was finally beginning to result in indictments. Although evidence against Leone's development business was not strong, the Justice Department heard about the civil fraud suits filed by his buyers. The U.S. Attorney heading up the investigation believed Leone was as complicit in the banking fraud as he was in the civil fraud claimed in the suits. She figured it was only a matter of time before she would be able to prove it. Leone was quickly indicted, and his battle to stay out of prison and avoid bankruptcy began.

Leone's main defense to the civil claims and the criminal charges was that if there was something wrong, it was someone else's doing. He blamed overzealous employees like Dave Rohr, his chubby director of property management, or outside brokers who sold his properties, or his accountants for not giving him proper information. But Leone's best defense, according to his new attorneys, was the one that implicated McCormack & Stein.

Relying on "advice of counsel" is a recognized defense and basis for cross-complaint in civil actions and is permissible evidence on issues of criminal intent, not necessarily to obtain acquittal, but certainly to shift the focus of an investigation to a "bigger fish" in the eyes of a prosecutor intent on furthering her career.

Salvatore Leone's new attorneys claimed he acted upon the advice of his old attorneys in completing and distributing the financial information his buyers supposedly relied upon in purchasing their buildings. To support his position, he was able to pull up copies of three financial statements bearing the initials of Richard Wolf in the lower right corners. He told his new attorneys that when Wolf approved the form and substance of those two statements by affixing his initials thereto, it caused Leone's employees to believe they were acceptable, and they used the same for all the sales. Fortunately for McCormack & Stein, Leone conveniently forgot a couple very important pieces of evidence, pieces that might have changed his attorneys' entire defense posture. Leone neglected to show his counsel the letters from S. Michael Donovan.

Donovan's first letter clearly stated that what Leone was doing was wrong, that the firm of McCormack & Stein would have nothing to do with the transactions, and that the firm would withdraw from representing him in those transactions if he chose to disseminate false information. Donovan's second letter, the withdrawal letter, was the icing on the cake for McCormack & Stein. Although the evidence would have shown that Donovan's supervisor, John Denton, fell over himself apologizing to Leone over Donovan's withdrawal letter, that evidence was never presented in any court because of Leone's own actions in firing McCormack & Stein shortly after the filing of the State Bar complaint against Donovan.

The ultimate effect of the submission of the Donovan letters as part of McCormack & Stein's defense was that clear evidence of Leone's fraud was suddenly available to the plaintiffs. They would never have seen those letters had Leone not cross-complained against the firm in the main case. The letters would otherwise have been protected under the attorney/client privilege. Once they were delivered to all counsel in response to a mass discovery request, however, the cat was out of the bag, and Leone's fraud was clear.

The punitive damages awarded against Leone were devastating, but it was ultimately his conviction on the bank fraud charges in the federal criminal proceedings that brought about his bankruptcy and his life behind bars.

Richard Wolf wanted to respond to the State Bar's request for comments after S. Michael Donovan filed for reinstatement before his three-year suspension was complete. He felt strongly that there was no reason Donovan should be reinstated early given the gravity of his wrong. Wolf's partners argued, however, that it would not be a good idea. Even before a friend on the State Bar disciplinary board suggested the firm lay low on the issue of reinstatement, Wolf's partners advised him to back down.

McCormack & Stein had just dodged a bullet thanks to Donovan's letters to Salvatore Leone. Not only did the letters win the civil suit against them, it also ended the Justice Department's investigation before it even started. They saved the firm the embarrassment that would have resulted from any press indicating the firm might be under investigation.

"The reality is that Donovan's suspension is suspect in view of recent thinking on the confidentiality rules," said the friend. "Withdrawing 'loudly' is the subject of considerable debate and in fact is being looked upon with favor. How can the Bar demand that an attorney stay silent when he knows a fraud is about to be perpetrated?"

Wolf prided himself on his ability to think quickly and pick up on the subtleties of issues. For some reason, however, he was having difficulty on the issue of Donovan's reinstatement. He kept telling himself he was right and Donovan was wrong in the way he had handled Salvatore Leone. Donovan should have gone to the State Bar for an opinion or to the firm's management rather than take action on his own. Even in the face of Donovan's firm-saving letters, Wolf couldn't seem to let the matter rest.

"You've got to let it go," said George Mahler, the firm's senior practicing partner. "You're not seeing things clearly because of your feelings about Donovan. If the press gets wind of the fact we're fighting the reinstatement of a guy who saved our asses with his unilateral morality, the damage would be devastating. Don't you see that, Richard?"

Wolf clenched his teeth and glared through hooded eyes at his partners gathered around the conference room. Of course he saw it. He wasn't an idiot. He knew what it could look like if it wasn't handled properly. But he'd handle it properly and he'd handle the press too. The firm had great contacts in the press. He knew what he was doing. He couldn't understand their fear. Didn't any of them see that Donovan was dangerous, that he shouldn't be practicing law at all? Donovan had always put himself and his beliefs above the law, above his duty to the law and the fraternity of brothers and sisters who were the profession. He didn't belong. What they should do is fight his reinstatement to the end. But Wolf could see he would get nowhere with his argument. So, he agreed to back down. He accepted his partners' position but vowed never again to be forced to accept a position contrary to one about which he felt so strongly.

TWENTY-FIVE

SEAN E-MAILED MORGAN FINNERTY'S declaration to him late Tuesday morning. He'd called earlier to alert him to expect it.

"Were you able to go through Boner's files to see if there's anything in writing?" Sean asked.

"No, Sean ... not yet. I'm sorry," Morgan said sheepishly. He wanted to help but wasn't able to get to it on Monday. "I will though. I promise you. I'll get over there this afternoon and take a look. I know how important it is to you."

"Thanks, Morgan. I'd appreciate it. After you sign the original, can you fax or e-mail me a copy and then drop the original in the mail?"

"It'll be fax," Morgan chuckled. "I don't have a clue how to get the signature back into the computer yet. I'm learning, but I'm not there yet. I'll fax it to you today or tomorrow, and I'll let you know if I find anything written."

Sean was fine with that. So long as he had a copy of the signed declaration before Friday, he was okay. The opposition had to be filed with a copy served by mail on Wolf's firm by Friday evening. As long as everything was in the mail, postmarked by then, it would be fine.

Morgan Finnerty downloaded and printed the declaration as soon as he received it. It was pretty basic with the operative statements being that his family had given meats, crops, and wool produced on the land to the Jacksons over the years, that, to his knowledge, none of the Finnertys ever claimed they owned the Jackson property, and that the Finnertys paid property taxes for the property for years pursuant to an agreement between Boner Finnerty and Willy Jackson. What was missing from the declaration was any reference to an attached exhibit, which would have been a certified copy of a written agreement. Sean reminded Morgan in his cover letter how important such a writing would be if he could locate one. Morgan felt so badly about not following through on his promise to search for a writing, he immediately addressed a large manila envelope to Sean, placed too many stamps in the upper right corner, slipped the signed declaration inside and placed the unsealed envelope in his backpack. If he were lucky enough to find anything in storage, he'd include it in the envelope and get it mailed this evening.

Morgan drove Boner's '48 Pontiac Silver Streak, a bright red convertible with polished chrome bumpers, grill, and detail around the lights, at the windows, and lengthwise over the hood. It was shaped like a torpedo from behind and tapered larger as one looked forward from the sleek trunk lid to rounded fenders and hood until it reached a front end that spoke of a large engine and sturdy countenance. Morgan loved the old car. He'd spent long hours since the sale of the Finnerty property restoring it. It had new paint, new or refinished chrome, a restored original soft-top, and brand new leather upholstery over the original spring built seats. The body rested on the original chassis and carried an original 248.9 cubic inch engine that Morgan rebuilt himself. He could get her up to an easy cruising speed of seventy miles per hour. With the top down, he loved the excitement of the open road. There was no question the car still had some kinks, one of which he was feeling as he motored down Highway 80 toward Sacramento. It was a slight wobble in the front end on the right side. It was something he hadn't noticed before. He'd take a look under the front end at the storage yard. For now, all he could think of was the road splayed open before him, the wind that blew his hair, and the looks from envious drivers he passed along the way.

The storage facility was a small one right off the freeway on the eastern edge of Sacramento, thirty-five miles from Morgan's front door. He punched in his code, and the metal security gate slid open, giving him access to several rows of concrete boxes with aluminum roofs and roll-up doors. He turned down aisle C and rolled to a stop in front of space number 147.

The cheap, rusted lock responded grudgingly to its key but finally slid open so he could remove it and roll up the door. Morgan was met immediately by tattered cobwebs torn by the raising of the door and swirls of dust from the suddenly disturbed interior of the garage. He turned his head and waved his hands to clear the dust and push away the last faint tendrils of web. He coughed, brought his hand to his mouth to prevent another but coughed again, and just managed to hold back the sneeze. After a few more seconds of watery eyes he was able to step into the clutter of the cramped box.

Six four-drawer high filing cabinets, now chipped and rusted, stood against the wall on the left. They were stacked high with dust covered, dilapidated cardboard boxes torn and misshapen by their bursting contents and the weight of other boxes on top. The same was true in front of the cabinets and throughout the rest of the garage. Boxes were stacked from floor to ceiling from one foot inside the opening all the way to the back of the ten-foot deep enclosure. Morgan's immediate impulse was to turn around, pull the door down again, hop into Boner's Silver Streak, and drive home. He had no interest in diving into the dust and grime in search of a document he doubted existed. He didn't even know where to start.

He stood with his hands propped on his hips, his head shaking. His mind wrestled with whether he should walk away or proceed with what he had promised; and it was that thought that ultimately determined his course of action. He had promised to look. He had promised to help if he could. When he thought about what Carlos Perez and his attorneys—people he found hard to like from the moment he met them—were trying to do to Mrs. Jackson, he realized he had no choice. Now, all he had to do was figure out some way to organize the search so he didn't have to look through every single cabinet and box.

When Morgan packed up the family archives after the sale, he'd lumped materials from different locations around the ranch house, the barn, and the storage shed in separate boxes and labeled them with a general reference to contents and their locations. He'd had some help from family members but not enough to spend time distinguishing between important materials and garbage. Since the packing didn't occur until the "eleventh hour," he told himself he'd just pack everything and then look at it more closely later to determine what was really important. Almost three years later, he still hadn't gotten around to sifting through it.

Morgan began moving boxes onto the roadway outside the garage to clear a path in front of the cabinets all the way to the back. He organized the removed boxes according to buildings and rooms reflected in black felt marker on their sides and then made his way to the filing cabinets where he intended to start his search, anticipating that the most recent and operative documents relating to the ranch and its business would be filed there. He sat on a stump of boxes and started his review.

When Morgan finally stopped to stretch sore muscles, he was surprised to see that two hours had passed and he still hadn't made it through the filing cabinets. He hadn't maintained even a semblance of the pace he promised himself, mainly because of the history he found in the files. He tried, in the beginning, to be analytical and quick, to take no personal interest in any of the materials. When he'd see the tab of a file that most likely had no relationship to the Jackson property or the Finnerty rights to use it, he'd fan through the pages quickly and move on to the next file. Occasionally, while fanning the pages, however, he'd come upon some ancient document, and he'd stop to read the unusual text and reflect on the colorful history of his family. He found tax returns dating back fifty years. He reviewed supply and sales contracts, some from as far back as the turn to the twentieth century. The sales figures were so low back then—in pennies in many cases instead of dollars—and it fascinated him. But time passed quickly, and before Morgan knew it, the day was drifting away.

He dusted dirt and grime from his hands and clothes, stretched his back, and turned in place to survey the mountain of materials he still had to peruse if he was going to complete the task. It was just when he was thinking how onerous the job was that a thought came to him.

Morgan recalled the time, six months before Boner died, when the old man was lying in bed, frail and infirm, and asked Morgan to read a note that had just arrived. His failing eyesight and headaches weren't permitting him to read it on his own. The note was attached to a boxed fresh homemade peach pie delivered to the ranch on behalf of Mrs. Jackson. She had heard Boner was feeling poorly, so she baked him a pie and sent it up with a note to brighten his day. As Morgan remembered it, the note's contents were nothing special, mostly greetings and wishes for a prompt return to good health, but it was signed with the words "Yours Truly, Beverly." Boner asked him to reread the note several times, and every time Morgan finished and looked up at his grandfather, Boner was staring off wistfully into the distance. Finally, after the last reading, Boner instructed Morgan to place the "letter" as Boner referred to it, in a wooden box in the corner of his room.

"Just open the lid, boy, and place it on top," Boner said. Morgan did just that.

The box was constructed of finely crafted redwood and was approximately one cubic foot in size. It looked more like a large keepsake chest than a box from the outside. Inside, however, was a row of letter-sized files separated by tabs and neatly lined up from one side of the chest to the other. Morgan placed the note atop the files and gave no thought to the box's other contents until this very moment as he stood eyeing the enormity of the task that lay before him.

Morgan had no idea what was in the keepsake chest. For all he knew it was filled with love letters from the women who looked fondly upon Boner because of his name. There was no question now, however, as Morgan reflected upon Boner's wistful looks and the place of significance the contents obviously had in his life, that the chest was important. Since he had no other plan for shortening his search, he decided his next step should be to find the redwood chest.

He glanced again at the writing on the boxes he'd lifted out of the garage onto the roadway. He recognized his writing on most of them since he had done most of the packing. He didn't recall seeing the chest during his packing efforts.

The natural outdoor light that had previously cast its glow into the garage was beginning to fade as the day wore toward early evening. The sun drifted quickly toward the horizon behind the garage. Morgan wished he'd brought a flashlight but spent no time thinking about it as the natural light continued to dissipate. He moved quickly to the back of the garage and began squinting at the writing on the boxes he could see. He was looking for handwriting other than his own on the few boxes actually packed by other family members. When he located three stacks of such boxes, he immediately rejected those that bore locations in the kitchen, bathrooms, and other rooms. He was looking for things from Boner's bedroom and soon found three boxes buried at the bottom of a stack. It took Morgan two minutes and a slight tweak to his back to remove the boxes that sat atop the "Boner's Bedroom" boxes. He dragged the stack of three into the light of the roadway and removed the lid from the top box.

No redwood chest inside—just papers and files haphazardly thrown in by the packer. Perhaps someone had emptied the contents of the chest into the packing box and taken the redwood for her own use. He decided he'd check the other two boxes first before considering that possibility.

Fortunately, the second box in the stack revealed what he sought. He extracted the chest, replaced the lid of the cardboard box, and placed the chest on top. It was much heavier than he had expected it to be, as if it were lined with some protective material of some kind.

Morgan lifted the lid hopefully. He could feel his heart beating faster and actually imagined a drum roll. He laughed as the lid sat fully open. He immediately found the note from Mrs. Jackson sitting in exactly the same spot he had placed it. The interior of the chest was lined with soft red velvet beneath which Morgan could indeed feel a metal protective lining. He put the note aside gently and went immediately to the file tabs. They told the story of the chest's contents. Inside was every letter, card, note, and piece of writing of any and every kind received by Boner and his Finnerty ancestors from the Jacksons. The documents were arranged between tabs reflecting decade intervals dating from the late 1800s through the time of Boner's death.

Morgan quickly moved to the tab for the "1960s," riffled through the pages, and found nothing close to what he sought. He did the same for the "1970s" and "1980s," and although he found notes and letters between Willy and Boner that might, if properly presented, be useful to Beverly Jackson's case, he found no agreement. Finally, as he gingerly opened the file bearing the date "1990s" the very first document he came across bore the signatures of Tecumseh "Boner" Finnerty and William "Willy" Jackson. The writing above their signatures was in a clear and legible hand—not Boner's as the comparison with his signature made clear—that read:

"On this 5th day of June, 1991, we lay down the agreement that our families have lived by since 1890 or thereabouts (the exact date unknown) and will continue to live by as long as the Finnertys ranch or farm the Jackson 500 acre property adjacent to the Finnerty 100 acre property east of Visalia. The Finnertys and all their family can continue using the Jackson property for farming and ranching and other related things, provided the Finnertys pay all property taxes for the Jackson property and provided the Finnertys send down to the Jacksons in Visalia whatever portion of their crops, meat, and wool that the head of the Finnerty family determines is reasonable and economical."

Morgan's mouth stood agape as he read. His shock could not have been greater. This was exactly the document for which Sean Donovan was searching. He brought the paper close to his face and stared at the signatures to confirm they were original. He felt the back of the sheet and realized from the pen's indentations that they were. He breathed deeply of the smell of the old paper. He closed his eyes and smiled broadly. This is great, he thought.

Morgan handled the precious agreement gingerly as he opened his backpack and gently slid it into the manila envelope with the signed declaration for Sean Donovan. He would get it home as quickly as possible, make a hundred copies, fax one to Sean, and then drop the declaration with a copy of the original letter into the mail.

Morgan repacked the storage garage much faster than he'd emptied it. He rolled down the door, jammed the rusty lock back into place, and sat behind the wheel of Boner's 1948 Silver Streak, a massive grin covering his face before he turned the key and headed home.

———

The slight wobble on the right side of the old car's front end wasn't so slight anymore. To make matters worse, the wobble wasn't just on the right side. It felt like it had spread to the left side of the vehicle.

Morgan's mood had been so buoyant when he left the storage garage and made his way back onto Highway 80 that he paid little attention to the unusual tremors that seemed to intensify the farther he drove. As he maneuvered through moderate traffic at upwards of sixty-five miles per hour, his mood began to change. He should have slid under the vehicle and checked out the problem before he left the garage, but in his excitement he had completely forgotten. Now, the intensifying vibrations were starting to scare him. He thought it might have something to do with the front tires possibly needing rebalancing, but as the tremors and vibrations increased, he knew it couldn't be the tires. He had no idea what else it might be, however.

Morgan glanced into his rear view mirror and lifted his foot off the accelerator. He rotated the steering wheel slightly to the right, hoping to maneuver the car to the safety of the shoulder, just one lane away. There he would get under the front end and determine what the hell the problem was. But the steering wheel wouldn't respond to his soft, careful touch. It suddenly jerked violently in his grasp and pulled sharply to the left. He gripped tighter, the wheel pounding a heavy vibration into his palm. The wobbling was suddenly uncontrollable, as if the front end had separated from the rest of vehicle and was bouncing wildly to its own rhythm oblivious to Morgan's efforts at the controls. He slammed on the brakes and felt something catch. It was in the rear, and it caused an immediate swerve into which he turned, but there was no response. Instead, the front end of the old car leaped up like a wild stallion still racing on its hind legs. It rose high, he lifted his foot off the brake, leaned forward in a vain attempt to find balance, and the car came crashing down. It bounced up wildly, immediately came down and crashed to the ground as if its right front support was gone completely. Sparks shot skyward as the right front dug into the pavement and the rest of the vehicle pinwheeled around as it skidded forward. Morgan clenched his teeth and his eyes bugged out in anticipation of the coming collision. Then, suddenly, he was airborne. He could feel the car flipping beneath him. He was weightless at the top of a rollercoaster's highest point, and then he was thrown sideways toward the passenger seat. He thought about the seat belts he'd never installed, but only for an instant, for before another thought could come he felt himself flying out of the vehicle headlong with the car crashing and rolling beneath him. His hands and arms, tangled in something, came up to cover his head the instant before he struck the ground. As Boner's 1948 Pontiac Silver Streak tumbled in a frenzy of crunching metal and castoff parts, Morgan Finnerty lay with his arms and head tangled in the straps of a backpack as a growing pool of blood mixed with the dirt and gravel of the shoulder beneath him.

Not more than four car lengths behind the Silver Streak, the driver of a white Malibu could see Morgan struggling with the steering. His first thought was why it had taken so long. He expected the troubles to begin on the way down the hill, before he got to the storage yard. Damn, those old cars were built, he thought. What a shame to have to mess this one up.

The dark skinned man with the thick black mustache maneuvered the Malibu as far to the right as he could when he noticed the sudden awkward bouncing of the old car. An instant later as the Malibu was pulling abreast and to the right, the old car's front end jumped into the air and the entire right wheel broke free from the car. It bounced crazily away from the descending hulk and continued up the highway. The unsupported right front end of the Silver Streak hung for an instant and then dropped, bounced wildly and finally dug into the pavement sending a geyser of sparks into the air just as the Malibu shot past. The mustached man glanced into his rear-view mirror, saw the red beauty starting to pinwheel, catch suddenly, and then flip high into the air. He pressed his accelerator, as the old car loomed large, seemingly on top of him. He peered forward to find escape and was forced to swerve to avoid the rolling front wheel. Another quick glance showed cars swerving and screeching brakes to avoid the now tumbling Silver Streak until it finally slid to a stop on its crushed topside, its remaining wheels spinning up at the sky.

The mustached man pulled the Malibu off to the right shoulder about a half-mile ahead of the overturned vehicle. He jumped out of his car and started toward the disabled car at a run. The plan had been to be the first one on the scene to offer aid. He would grab the backpack, which he knew held the declaration and something else he'd seen Finnerty place inside it. But as he drew closer, he saw flames coming from the engine compartment, shooting through openings around the hood and up through the vehicle's chassis.

Cars careened around the flames, speeding to the left and right, out of the way. Those, coming up on the other side, whose drivers chose not to brave the flames pulled onto the shoulder or stopped far back of the flame and debris. The occupants jumped frantically from their vehicles and ran from the spreading inferno.

The mustached man stopped, wide eyed. The flames prevented him from getting closer. This was something he hadn't intended. The car was cherry. It was bad enough it flipped over, but now it was burning.

The next instant, an explosion ripped through the sudden congestion of westbound lookiloos and sent a geyser of flame and acrid black smoke together with pieces of the old Pontiac shooting lethally into the sky. The mustached man dove away from the explosion, covered his head, and didn't lift it again for several minutes until the ticks, pops, and thuds of raining metal ceased. He looked at his hands, felt his head and body, and scanned himself for reassurance he had not been struck. He thanked his god for his good fortune before he stood to survey the wreckage. The sight that accosted him was of Armageddon. The flaming hulk of spear-like protrusions that were once the Silver Streak billowed black smoke that caught the breeze and rolled toward him, reaching, it seemed, for the evil that had done this. The mustached man stepped back, shocked at the breadth of the devastation and caught now in his own superstition. He stood open-mouthed, staring trancelike at the surging black cloud until the trance was broken by the high-pitched blare of approaching sirens. He shook himself, looked again at the rolling cloud of smoke and at the shadowed figures stumbling awkwardly through it on the shoulder, and he turned away. It was over. Better to leave before the questions started.

TWENTY-SIX

SEAN SPENT THE WEEK completing his opposition to the motion for summary judgment. The crux of Flow Corp.'s claims was that they and their predecessors had used the Jackson property openly, hostilely, and continuously for at least five years and paid the property taxes for the property the entire time. The single most important question was whether the Jacksons granted "permission" for the use of the property. If permission was granted there could be no "hostile" possession and therefore no adverse possession. Although Sean's evidence of that permission was hearsay testimony of an agreement related to Morgan Finnerty by his dead grandfather, Sean was confident Morgan's declaration would be sufficient to defeat the motion. Then the real work would begin: to find stronger evidence for trial.

In the breaks between his legal research and his drafts of the opposition, Sean spent time looking into Flow Corp. The name of the company jarred him from the first moment he read the caption in Beverly Jackson's kitchen. It wasn't something that rolled off the tongue, and it gave no hint as to the type of business in which the company engaged. There was no obvious connection, so he Googled the company. He found Visalia newspaper references to the company and its activities. Early references were innocuous, on interior pages and dated as far back as five years ago. But, in more recent times, the company had become front-page news.

Apparently, its real estate purchases in and around the community weren't limited to the Finnerty property.

Flow Corp. had been the primary buyer of large commercial and retail parcels sold in and around Visalia over the past five years. The purchases were sporadic in the beginning, and little attention was paid to them. During the last two and a half years, however, starting around the time the company was completing the purchase of the Finnerty property and beginning its use of the Jackson property, the purchases were bolder, faster, and noticeable. It was those purchases that started the mini-land rush that pushed values in Visalia higher as people began to realize the Golden World development would be a reality. Unfortunately for many seeking to take the plunge into real estate whose value would skyrocket upon issuance of the final court decision, there wasn't much property left. Flow Corp. had acquired most of the choice pieces.

As Sean followed the stories and title records through his search, he began to do some rough math and determined that Flow Corp. had already spent more than two hundred fifty million dollars for property. The actual number wasn't clear because it came from calculations he backed into from property tax records. If anything, his estimate was probably low.

Sean's immediate reaction was that Flow Corp., being a client of McCormack, Stein & Wolf, had benefited from information gleaned by its attorneys from dealings with another major client: Golden World Corporation. It was pretty obvious to even a casual observer that Flow Corp. had probably made the purchases with some special information. However, since the fact of Golden World's interest in the Silver Lode Valley was public knowledge for years, it was unlikely any argument of illegality or other wrong could be made. There was no question that if Flow Corp. did obtain special information from the firm, it created a potential conflict for the firm in that McCormick, Stein & Wolf's interest in making sure the Golden World development proceeded for the benefit of Flow Corp. might taint its advice to Golden World on whether it should continue with its plans. It was probable that the firm obtained a waiver of the conflict from both clients, however, as that was customary in such situations.

The real surprise for Sean didn't come until he dug deeper into Flow's corporate information filed with the California Secretary of State. Morgan Finnerty had already informed him that the commanding little Hispanic man he'd seen outside Richard Wolf's office was part of Flow Corp. It was no surprise then that Esteban Ruiz, presumably the mountain of a man who stood with Perez in Wolf's antechamber, was identified as the corporation's President and Secretary, and another Hispanic name that Sean did not recognize was identified as Chief Financial Officer. The surprise came when Sean looked into the shareholders of the company. Two other corporations owned all the shares of Flow: the first of those was owned outright by Carlos Perez and the second by more corporations, which in their turn were owned by yet other corporations and limited liability companies—a classic attempt by owners to bury their ownership so deep that people would give up the search. That got Sean thinking.

He recalled a story from early in his career at McCormack & Stein. It told of a group of lawyers who got rich purchasing properties in close proximity to proposed shopping center developments of its major client. Once the client set its sights on a large piece of property, the lawyers representing it would begin to tie up surrounding properties at ridiculously low prices, which would surge in value once news of the client's intended purchase and development broke. To Sean, being fresh out of law school and the ethics courses he'd taken, there was no clearer potential conflict for an attorney. Over the next several years Sean recalled that Richard Wolf often came back to that story in conversation and argued that it was a way to make money outside the box of hourly billing. He even suggested it might be wise to set up an investment program where some of the firm's annual profits would be placed into an account from which such investments could be made. Although the idea didn't gain much traction while Sean was at the firm, he now wondered if Richard Wolf had instituted such a program since he'd become the firm's lead attorney. It was out of that thought that it finally struck him.

The name of the company suing Beverly Jackson was a play on Wolf's last name. It was his name spelled backwards. Was it possible that Richard Wolf and the firm were participants in the corporation that was buying up

Visalia? Sean didn't see Wolf's name in any of the corporate records he had checked so far. Nor did he know if any of the identified officers or directors of the corporations that were distant owners of Flow Corp. were members of Wolf's firm. But, he wondered if it was possible that Wolf had indeed taken the ultimate plunge. Was it possible that neither he nor his partners understood the conflict inherent in such action, or had they understood it and simply ignored it the same way the society in which they all lived seemed to be ignoring any kind of wrongdoing so long as you "didn't get caught"?

———————

Sean's second surprise that week was Morgan Finnerty's unreliability. He didn't give the matter much thought at first because he believed Morgan would follow through. When Thursday's mail didn't contain the signed declaration, however, Sean began to worry. He called Morgan's number but received no response. He continued to call well into Thursday evening and the next morning with the same result. By Friday afternoon, he was beside himself with worry. He instructed Patty to call Morgan's number every fifteen minutes, but by 3:30 it was clear she wasn't going to talk to him. The problem was that if the opposition wasn't postmarked for filing that evening, the court would not accept it and Flow Corp.'s case would be won without argument. Sean had to make a decision.

He didn't have time to rewrite his opposition, not that it would have made much difference even if he had the time. He knew well his only chance of defeating Flow Corp.'s motion was Morgan Finnerty's declaration. Without it, he didn't have even a hint of credible evidence that permission for the use of the Jackson property had been given. The way he looked at it, he had no choice in the matter.

Sean attached an unsigned copy of Morgan's declaration to his opposition papers with the hope that he would be able to get the original executed in the next week and send that to the court with supplemental documentation. Sean had no intent of making the court believe it was a clerical error that the signed declaration was not attached, so he attached another declaration, this one signed by himself. He declared under penalty of perjury the facts presented in the Finnerty declaration were the facts related to him by Morgan Finnerty and that the reason Morgan's declaration hadn't been signed was because he and Sean hadn't been able to coordinate the signing prior to the due date. Sean begged the court's indulgence and closed his declaration with an apology and an assertion he would obtain the original and file it with the court forthwith.

The package was completed by 4:15. Patty ran it, together with the copy for McCormack, Stein & Wolf, to the post office and had them both postmarked before 5:00 p.m.

Sean prayed the court would accept his assertions and apology.

Upon Patty's return from the post office, Sean asked her to stay alert for calls or mail from Morgan Finnerty through the weekend and Monday. He would continue to try to contact Morgan on his way up to Visalia and, he assured Patty, if he didn't hear anything by Monday afternoon, he would drive to Morgan's house and get to the bottom of this.

Sean wasn't sure he should even be going to Visalia given his concerns about Morgan's declaration. He'd planned to be up there by noon on Friday. He had said as much to Carla. But as things became critical on the declaration, he couldn't leave. He called and explained his problem. Carla, of course, understood. She told him there wasn't much being done on Friday anyway since the Sierra Club duo was in San Francisco for their ex parte motion on the Curtis Golden deposition. She closed the conversation with a light comment about seeing him at his mother's place for dinner Sunday night. Apparently Mary Donovan had invited Carla and her father over for a home-cooked Sunday Irish dinner. Sean was surprised he hadn't heard anything but stated absently that he'd see her then.

As the day wore on with no word from Morgan, Sean thought about canceling the trip north. Maybe it would be better to wait for word himself. He realized, however, it would do no good. He had committed to assist Carla and the Sierra Club in their case. They were also his clients now, and he carried the same responsibility to them as he did to Mrs. Jackson. Besides, there was nothing he could do in Torrance that he couldn't also do in Visalia. At least he'd be working on something in Visalia instead of simply worrying as he would if he stayed home.

By Sunday morning, Sean's attitude toward Morgan had moved from frustration and anger to doubts about whether any of what Morgan said was true and ultimately to fear that maybe something had happened to him. When he still hadn't been able to contact Morgan, Sean realized he had another decision to make: whether to head up to Auburn himself or call on an old friend again. He called Melvin Jackson's home several times throughout the day and finally reached him about mid-afternoon.

"Sean, nice to hear from you again," Melvin's deep voice was cheery on the other end of the line.

Sean felt it was a better use of everyone's time to have his client's son check up on Morgan. That Melvin was a cop was an added benefit; he could locate Morgan, and if something were wrong, he'd be able to get to the bottom of it.

"I'm sorry to bother you on a Sunday afternoon, Melvin," Sean started.

"No problem. I was just getting ready to brush off the barbeque. We're having some folks over later. What can I do for you?"

"It's about Morgan Finnerty," Sean said and paused. He was met with silence on the other end of the line.

"He was going to sign a declaration and send it back to me before Friday. We need it for your mother's case. I haven't gotten it or heard a word from him or anyone else in the family. I've been calling conti…"

"Sean," Melvin interrupted for the third time, this time a little louder before Sean stopped talking. He hesitated before speaking again in a hushed, deliberate voice. "Morgan was in an accident earlier this week."

Sean was silent, shocked by the statement.

"I'm sorry I didn't call you. I know how important he is to you … it didn't strike me to give you a call," Melvin continued.

"Is he okay?" Sean whispered distantly, as if he wasn't really in this conversation.

"He's hurt real bad. Still in a coma as of yesterday."

"What happened?"

"It looks like he was heading home on Highway 80, Tuesday evening. The right front wheel of the old car just came right off, caused it to flip over. The engine compartment caught fire and the whole thing exploded. Luckily Morgan was thrown out during the first flip, before the explosion. He landed on the soft shoulder. He'd be dead if he hadn't."

Sean was too stunned to speak. He held his Razr to his ear but said nothing.

"You still there?" Melvin asked.

Sean shook his head dazedly but did not respond.

"Sean? Are we cut off?"

"No ... I'm here," Sean stammered.

"They think it was intentional," Melvin said softly.

"What?" Sean's voice was cracked, barely audible. "Did you say intentional?"

"Yeah. Our lab boys took one look at the wheel and said it was cut. The axel was cut part way through so it would break off like it did. It doesn't look to be an accident at all."

Intentional? Someone tried to kill Morgan Finnerty? The thought couldn't gain traction in Sean's mind. Why? Why would someone want to do that? What could Morgan have done?

"Who did it?" Sean asked, knowing Melvin had no idea but also knowing he had no other question to ask.

"We don't know, Sean. It's not even certain it was intentional until the lab boys complete their work, but our office is looking into it along with the CHP." Melvin hesitated for a moment as if he was deep in thought. Then he asked, "Do you have any thoughts?"

"Thoughts?" Sean asked absently. "What do you mean?"

"I don't know ... could it have anything to do with our case?"

"No," Sean answered too quickly. "How ... I mean, I don't know Mel. Could it?"

There was silence on both ends of the line. Each was lost in his own thoughts until Melvin finally spoke again.

"Look, Sean ... I've got to get going here. The wife's getting testy. I'll ... keep you posted, okay?"

Sean nodded.

"Thanks," he mumbled before he closed his phone.

TWENTY-SEVEN

SEAN'S APOLOGY TO CARLA the previous Monday hadn't gone as planned. He'd wanted to say more—that he was happy to be helping her with the case, that he was glad they'd seen each other at his mother's birthday, and that he hoped they could start over again as if his stupidity of Sunday night had never occurred. He sensed Carla wanted something more as well, but he didn't know. How could he? He'd been so steeped in his own self-flagellation for so long he'd lost touch. He'd forgotten how to read people, particularly women. He had no clue whether she wanted more or if last Sunday night's performance had soured her completely.

During the week, as Sean began to believe his opposition papers in the *Jackson* case were good enough to win the motion, his thoughts drifted to Carla, and his hopes of pursuing a relationship with her were heightened. He convinced himself he still had a shot, that he hadn't blown it completely, and that if he could just be the sensitive, understanding, and, above all, upbeat guy he used to be, things would work out. He looked forward to getting back to see her.

The news about Morgan changed all that. It wasn't that Sean no longer wanted to see Carla; it was more that his mind was in a fog. It was happening again. Just when he thought his world was turning around, that his luck might finally be changing, it crashed again.

He brooded after the phone call with Melvin Jackson. Morgan was essential to his ... to Mrs. Jackson's ... case. Without Morgan's testimony, Sean ... Mrs. Jackson ... had no case. *He* had no evidence, no witnesses, and no chance. *He* would lose yet another case because every path he tried to traverse closed him out before he even had a chance. When was it going to change?

He spent the rest of the afternoon absently assisting Mary with her preparations for the dinner visit from Carla and her father. They were scheduled to arrive about five o'clock. Sean moved about the house mechanically, deep in thought about his ill fortune. Mary tried to talk to her son but couldn't break through the brooding that had descended upon him. She'd seen the focus and intensity from the moment he'd arrived Friday night. When she'd asked what the problem was, he told her his witness in Beverly Jackson's case was turning out to be a flake and it was weighing heavy on him. He apologized to her and said it would be okay once he was able to touch base with the witness. Then suddenly, about mid-afternoon, his mood took a turn and the limited conversation they were having before the call turned off completely.

By the time Mary greeted Carla at the front door, Sean's mood was morose. His face was creased with concentration, his eyes hooded and unfocused. He tried to smile when Carla greeted him with a hug, but he could see on her face that his attempt failed. The light demeanor with which she entered the Donovan kitchen darkened the moment she looked at him. The evening started with Carla's apology that her father was fighting a cold and wouldn't be joining them. He asked for a rain check, and Mary assured Carla he'd get one.

Mary's Irish stew was thick with beef, potatoes, and vegetables. The broth was spicy and rich for dipping of the fresh out-of-the-oven Irish bread Mary baked. The entire meal was complemented perfectly by the two bottles of Jarvis Vineyards' fine 2002 Cabernet Sauvignon. The meal couldn't have been better with a single exception. Although Carla and Mary kept up a lively conversation, Sean's contributions were minimal despite both women's extraordinary attempts to involve him. By eight o'clock the meal was complete, the table cleared, and Sean was sitting alone on the back patio. Mary and Carla were finishing the clean up.

"I'm so sorry about Sean today, Carla," Mary said sadly.

"What's going on?" Carla asked. "What's happened to him, Mrs. Donovan?"

"He's had a setback in Mrs. Jackson's case, I think. But there's something more, I'm afraid. His heart's still broken, dear," Mary said and turned away to wipe off the counter.

"It's got to be fifteen or sixteen years since the divorce, isn't it?" Carla asked. She was exasperated and not sympathetic.

"Oh," Mary dragged the word out softly and turned back to Carla. "It's not the divorce at all. That's behind him for sure. It's something else, dear," Mary said sadly as her eyes glistened with the moisture slowly forming tears.

Carla nodded and then turned slowly to stare at Sean's back on the patio. Is this it, she wondered? Is he done? One part of her told her she should go to him and help him. He was a good man. She knew that. She remembered the fire and passion with which he'd always seemed to attack life. She remembered it was that Sean Donovan for whom she'd held a yearning most of her life. She now wondered if he was gone for good.

She wanted to ease his pain but didn't know how, and she wondered yet again if his was a pain that could ever be healed. She'd always wanted Sean, but never like this. She'd had enough of moody, brooding men so caught up in their own lives that they had no room for anyone else. That's how her former husband had been. He'd been motivated and aggressive, and she'd mistaken those traits for passion and love. Only after they were married did she learn they were nothing more than his selfish quest for wealth and status.

Carla turned back to Mary. She smiled warmly.

"I think I should be going, Mrs. Donovan. It was a wonderful di ..."

Mary's eyes opened wide. She held up a hand to stop Carla.

"Don't go just yet Carla ... please," she said. "Go out and talk to him. He needs that from someone other than his old mother." Mary's green eyes fixed on Carla, pleading. "Take some pie and go to him, dear." Mary reached toward Carla with two saucers, each with a warm slice of Beverly Jackson's peach pie atop it. She nodded her head toward Sean.

Carla hesitated as Mary again proffered the dessert. "What about you … aren't you going to go out there?" Carla asked

Mary shook her head, "No, dear … I think I need to step away from this right now."

Carla stared at the still attractive old woman made more so in her sadness by the constant upturn at the ends of her mouth. She could see the mother's pain and wished she could help; yet her own thoughts were a scramble. She had no idea what she could possibly say or do for Sean. She wasn't even sure she wanted to say anything at this point. Although she felt Sean was interested in her, she wasn't sure. How could she be when most of her observations were tainted by hopes borne of a childhood crush? Sean hadn't expressed any interest, yet he'd come to the meeting with the Sierra Club. He hadn't expressed any meaningful feelings, yet he'd apologized, and she could clearly see that he'd meant it, that perhaps he'd wanted to say more but was unable. Even tonight, he'd done nothing to make her feel wanted, yet she could see that through his gloom he was struggling to do so. She didn't know if she should, but she turned back to Mary, smiled again, and took the pie plates. She took a deep breath and started toward the sliding doors that opened to the patio.

Sean slouched in the deck chair sideways to the head of the patio table, one leg crossed over the other with his back to the house and a finger of his left hand curled loosely around the stem of the nearly empty wine glass atop the table. The night air was warm, a carryover from the blistering day, but, strangely for this time of year, he could feel a chill. It came on cool drafts, as if the previous year's winter had lingered far to the north where it regained its strength and was now sending its first envoys to warn of things to come. A faint shiver ran up Sean's spine and disappeared again into the evening's still controlling warmth.

The wine had calmed him, but only slightly. The tension of another failure played in his brain and invariably led to his deeper remorse, the one for which there could never be any release, no matter how much wine he consumed. It always happened that way it seemed. He couldn't forget it, of course, and he never really tried to. To a psychologist, his inability to forget would undoubtedly be viewed as a conscious thing, something he simply wouldn't let go of because he had to be punished. He was wrong, and he had to suffer for that wrong because there was no way it could ever be made right. There would never be forgiveness, so how could he ever forget? Thus, despite the wine induced languor that softened the edges of his desperation over the *Jackson* case, the harsh reality of Sean Donovan's real failure stood like a beacon before him at all times.

"Sean," Carla said softly as she stepped through the open slider, "your mother asked me to bring out some pie." She placed a plate on the table next to him

Sean sat up out of his slouch abruptly and turned. His face reddened, although no one other than he could have known since the only light at the distant edge of the patio was dim and pale from the half-moon, which hung low in the eastern sky. His embarrassment came from his treatment of Carla yet again this evening. He nodded his thanks and looked past her to see if his mother was joining them. He wondered why Carla was still here after the way he'd been.

"May I join you?" she asked, hesitation and perhaps some anger tingeing her tone.

"Yes," Sean stumbled, trying to convey in one word that his surliness had nothing to do with her. It was all him, and she should not take anything personally.

As Carla maneuvered around the table to sit on the side adjacent to Sean, he thought about apologizing to her but knew well enough such a gesture would be meaningless. He'd done it before, with good intent, but nothing had changed in him. He'd gone right back to the uncaring cad who couldn't deal with his misery without involving everyone else who came within his orbit, particularly if the one who came within that orbit was someone for whom he cared.

"Mrs. Jackson makes a great peach pie," Sean mumbled nonsensically. "Sorry your dad couldn't join us tonight. Maybe you should take some home fo…"

"Sean," Carla interrupted. She shook her head slowly and stared at him until his eyes met hers. She couldn't help thinking he was still such a handsome man with a strong yet boyish face and passionate albeit sad eyes. "What's going on?"

Sean hesitated, taken aback for a moment. He was about to ask her what she meant but thought better of it immediately. He shook his head and dropped his eyes.

"I received some terrible news today," he started and looked at her again. "My witness in the Jackson case is in a coma."

Carla wasn't expecting that. Her eyes widened.

"What happened?" she whispered.

"Car accident," Sean said and then caught himself with a sarcastic, humorless chuckle. "Well, actually they don't think it was an accident. The police think it was intentional, that someone tried to kill Morgan Finnerty." He hesitated and looked past Carla into the darkness. "Melvin Jackson asked me if I had any thoughts about what happened."

"What did he mean?" Carla asked.

Sean looked at her again.

"I don't know. I was with Morgan … maybe I caused it. Hell, maybe that black cloud that follows me around got him," he mumbled awkwardly and regretted it immediately.

Carla looked at him quizzically. How did he get there? One minute he's talking about the tragedy surrounding his witness and the next he's falling back to feeling sorry for himself, blaming himself again.

"What are you talking about? Did Melvin suggest you had something to do with it?" she asked.

"No … I don't know. He asked me if I had any thoughts about what might have happened. How would I know?"

"I guess he was thinking the same way Harper and Luckman are thinking about Buck, Sean. Maybe someone knew he was going to help you and they didn't want him to. Maybe someone tried to shut him up."

"Well they did a good job of that," he said with a hint of sarcasm. "My case is shot without ol' Morgan Finnerty. I've got nothing." He glanced down at the pie plate resting untouched between his cupped hands.

Carla was put off by the sarcastic tone, frustrated that he would again direct his mood at her. She stared at his bowed head until he finally glanced up.

"So you get other evidence," she said firmly. "From what I understand, they shouldn't win. Mrs. Jackson is on the right side. All you have to do is find the evidence. If Morgan had it, it's got to be out there somewhere," Carla said with hopeful encouragement.

Sean shook his head and smiled patronizingly.

"You don't understand, Carla. There is no other evidence," he said deliberately. "Morgan's information was something within his personal knowledge. It's gone. My case is done."

He dropped his head again. He could feel Carla's glare boring into him.

"What happened to you, Sean?" she finally asked.

He looked up. "What do you mean?"

"Where did you lose it?" she continued without hesitation. She was sick of the negativism and the self-pity. "What happened to the fire you used to have? The fire for life and a challenge? You never used to back away from anything."

"That was a long time ago, Carla, when we were kids. That was before the world got hold of me. Before the shit I guess."

He stared at her as she now sat inches away, fuming again. He could see the frustration and anger, and he knew it was over. Something that had never started was suddenly over, and he dropped his head to ward off the wave of sadness that surged over him in the knowledge that he was chasing someone away yet again had no way to change it. A tear filled his eye.

"Dammit, Sean. Do you think you're the only one who's had to deal with shit? We've all had it. That's part of life. It's the dealing with it and moving on that makes it worth living. You don't wallow in it. You fight it off and move on. You *move* on," she stretched out the phrase.

Sean clenched his teeth, raised his head slowly, and glared at her.

"You have no idea what I've done, Carla. No idea," his voice was low, deliberate, and unemotional. "You can't possibly understand what I'm feeling, what torment I go through every day, how I've tried to move on but can't. It can't be done." He dropped his head and stared at his hands.

"What?" she asked. "What have you done that's so bad? I know about the suspension, and I know you didn't deserve it, that your former firm stabbed you in the back. I know about the divorce and the difficulty you've had. But I also know you've come back. You told me so when you said you didn't need help from anyone. You said you've been able to fend for yourself. So, what is it?"

Carla sat straight-backed on the front edge of her chair. She was worked up and was not going to let this go.

"What have you done, Sean?" she demanded.

He sat silently for several seconds, lost in his misery but trying to control himself.

"I gave them away," he finally whispered and stared blankly past her.

She leaned forward but said nothing. He caught her movement but was drifting away to that place where he could acknowledge the shame and punish himself yet again. He pushed himself away from the table and leaned forward, his elbows digging into his knees, his head bowed into cupped hands. He needed distance from Carla now. She couldn't possibly understand what he had done. No one could. No real father could do what he'd done.

"I gave them away," he repeated in a muffled tone. "I gave away my own kids. They don't even know me."

Sean drifted further away as he related the facts. He spoke as if in a trance as tears came and spilled to the concrete slab of the patio.

Sean hated Susan for suggesting he give up custody. Let her new husband adopt them? Ridiculous! He wouldn't consider it. Yet what choice did he have? Two days after she'd left, as he sat amidst the filth of his life trying desperately to survive—to save his career and to save his life—he'd retrieved the crumpled papers he'd thrown away and called his attorney, a woman Sean should have listened to. She'd tried to convince him he shouldn't do it, that he could find another way to make the payments for the house, the lawsuit, the State Bar claim, and for his very survival. But he knew he couldn't. He needed the money, needed help. He told himself he'd go back afterwards, after he got himself back together. He'd go back to court then and get his rights back, something his attorney said would be difficult. But he hadn't listened. He'd signed the papers, and he'd never gone back to court to fight to get his kids back.

"Have you seen them?" Carla's voice was a whisper.

Sean pushed himself up to a sitting position, leaned far back in the chair. His disgust with himself was palpable. He wiped tears from his cheek and turned his eyes to Carla. He expected to see her disgust but saw only concern.

"No," he answered hoarsely.

"Did..." she hesitated, afraid to ask more lest the questions cause greater harm. "Did you ... write?"

Sean nodded his head. "I don't think the kids ever got them. I never heard back." He hesitated as Carla continued to stare at him. "She won't even let them talk to their grandmother," Sean continued with a nod to the house. "It breaks her heart."

Sean looked away from her and leaned his head back against his chair.

Carla nodded slowly and leaned back herself. Her mind raced to find words, but she knew expressions of sympathy would do no good. They would fall hollowly as she could see clearly that Sean was far past such words. He'd long since convinced himself he was not worthy of sympathy. So Carla did what she always did. She searched for a solution, a way not to sympathize but rather to help Sean address the problem the way he had always addressed problems from the time of their youths: by confronting them directly and resolving them.

"Go to them now, Sean," she started. "You can find your kids on the net. They're adults now aren't they? We can find them, and you can talk to them, explain."

Sean looked at Carla, his eyes now streaked with red. He shook his head slowly, wondering why she didn't see how silly that suggestion was— not that he hadn't thought of it at times himself, but rather that she didn't see how ridiculous it was to think it would change anything.

"Don't you see?" he started, trying to be calm but speaking deliberately. "I abandoned my kids. I gave them away. To them, I did worse than die. I told them I didn't care, that they weren't important to me, that my own kids meant less to me than my career," he said and hesitated before nearly shouting "than my damn career!"

Carla started to respond, but Sean cut her off with a raised hand and a look that withered her.

"I don't have a right to contact them," he spat the words. "They don't care now, anyway. Why would they? They've got lives of their own, lives that someone else gave them, lives a real father gave them ..."

"You don't know th ..." Carla started.

"I know it!" he shouted. "I know I'd have nothing to do with a man claiming to be my father if he abandoned me during the most important part of my life. I wouldn't forgive the son-of-a-bitch. I know the last thing I'd want would be to hear from the guy." He shook his head coldly. "They don't want anything to do with me. Would you if you were them?" He finished with an accusatory glare.

Carla sat in silence, shocked by the vehemence in his voice and demeanor. She saw a hatred she never believed possible in him and was stunned by it. She knew the hatred wasn't meant for her, but she grew angry. She bit down hard to hold her tongue and considered his question even as she fought the urge to lash out at him for his blindness. It would do no good, she thought. It would only feed his self-pity. She slowed her breathing before she finally stood, took her untouched pie plate and fork in hand, and turned away from Sean. She walked away from the table. Sean's eyes followed her to the slider. There, she turned back to him.

"You know, Sean ..." she started, trying to breathe evenly.

"Wait." Sean said, again raising his hand and beginning to say something else.

"No!" Carla shouted and squared to him. "You wait, Sean Donovan. You asked me a question and I'm going to answer it. You asked me if I would have anything to do with a father who did to me what you say you did to your children." He tried to interrupt, but she silenced him with her own raised hand.

"My answer to you is yes. If I loved my father the way I know those kids loved you, I would be desperate for any word from him, anything that would show me that he still loved me. I would want to see him, to touch him, and to know that he wasn't dead. I might be angry, and I might want an explanation, but I would want to know my father again."

She glared at him. He sat in silence, surprised by her outburst.

"You've got to stop this, Sean," Carla started again. She had to get it all out now. "This life isn't about your fears and problems. Dammit, there are others who hurt and love and feel pain and passion. There are people out there who need you, people you can help if you'd stop worrying about yourself. There are actually people out there who might love you if you'd let them," she said as tears began to well in her eyes. She hesitated, again raising her hand and dropping her head to gain control of herself. Finally she looked up, steeled herself, and continued.

"For God's sake," she pleaded, "your kids are suffering this very minute, probably still wondering about you, and all you're doing here is worrying that they're angry at you because you abandoned them. Well ... if you did abandon them, undo it. Don't sit there and tell me it can't be done. Get up and do something about it."

A tear rolled down her cheek, and she swept it away quickly. She stood in silence for several seconds eyeing Sean before she turned abruptly and walked through the door. He stared after her, dumbstruck, as if for the first time in his memory a door he never knew existed had suddenly been thrust open before him.

She was right. He knew it the minute her torrent of angry words spilled from her mouth. He felt as if he'd been slapped and suddenly woken to a sharp pain. But this pain was different than that he'd suffered through at every waking moment for the past fifteen years. It was not the pain of self-pity he'd grown to believe was a part of his life. It was another pain, a pain of the need for urgency. It was like an overwhelming desire to act immediately, to stand up and move, to do what was suddenly necessary. He tried to resist the knowledge that came with the slap, but he couldn't. It washed over him like a wave, and it kept coming. With every internal argument that he was evil and worthy only of further punishment came another rush of understanding that it didn't matter what he was or what he felt. It mattered only that his children didn't deserve this any longer. They were the ones for whom thoughts, words, and passion had to be expended, not him. He realized in flashes of sudden understanding that it was his children who needed to know and who needed peace.

As the conflicting arguments raged in his brain, he stood suddenly. Where was she going? He needed to tell her he understood, that she was right, and that somehow her words had gotten through to him. He ran around the table to the open slider where he stopped and quickly viewed the kitchen, dining room, and living room. She was gone. His eyes moved to the front door, across the living room, past the narrow hall. The door was closed.

"Carla," he called but received no response.

Sean ran across the living room, yanked open the door and continued through the tiny exterior courtyard, past low lying jasmine to the walk that turned right for two concrete squares around an overgrown fern to the driveway. From there he saw her silhouetted against the street light. She stood at the driver door of her sedan, frantically pushing the unlock button on her key.

"Carla," he called again.

She glanced up quickly but immediately dropped her head and struggled more frantically with her key, desperate to gain access before she had to face Sean again.

Sean jogged across the driveway, past his own car to the sidewalk. There he stopped and called her name again.

She didn't raise her head as she continued to fumble with the keys and tried to speak.

"Please, Sean, no more tonight," she pleaded through soft sobs. She fumbled with the keys for another second before she finally dropped her hands to her side and gave up. She glanced toward him, sadness and resignation barely visible in the pale streetlight. "Please, I can't do this anymore," she said as she struggled to control her emotions.

He strode around the car and touched her lightly on the shoulder.

"Carla," he said softly. "You're right."

His hand slid slowly away as she stood in front of him, head still bowed, facing her car. When she finally turned slowly and lifted her tear stained face up to his, the street light caught the gleam of crystal blue in her eyes, and he reached for her tentatively.

"I'm so sorry, Carla," he said. "I know ..." but before he could finish she stepped into him, threw her arms around him and buried her face in his shoulder. He folded his arms around her, smelled the sweet scent of spring in her hair, and came alive with Carla's warmth against him. He stroked her soft hair gently until she slowly pulled her head away and raised her eyes to his. He bent to her and kissed her on full lips that opened hungrily to him.

TWENTY-EIGHT

SEAN WOKE SLOWLY THE next morning, sated and, dare he think it, happy for the first time in many years. He reflected languidly on the irony of the previous evening, one that started with the pain of utter hopelessness and ended with a realization of life and purpose beyond his own. It surprised him how it struck him so suddenly. He'd become so enamored of his own suffering that he'd closed off all roads upon which he might find a future, yet suddenly a road opened for him. It was thrust open by Carla's passion, by her tears, not for herself and the constant rebuke of his words, but out of caring, and finally, by her words that thundered past his defenses and bore into his soul, so desperate for the quenching surge of understanding that his life could mean something, but only if he committed to what he'd known his entire life: that life lived to love and give was the only life worth living at all.

Carla had come back into the house with him. They walked without words in a tight embrace to his bedroom and made love, not with the animal hunger with which they'd kissed under the streetlight, but with tenderness and giving. They undressed each other slowly, touching softly and stroking gently until they lay in a warm embrace that heated to a crescendo of ecstasy when he lost himself in her and she in him. They lay together afterwards, each dozing for a time until they woke and loved

212

again, this time with probing curiosity of the other's needs and passionate giving of all each had.

By the time Sean woke, Carla was gone. She'd slipped out quietly with a gentle kiss he only half remembered now, and he smiled at the memory the act conjured—a memory of his younger days when such play always ended before dawn, especially when it was down the hall from a parent's room.

Sean didn't know if he was in love. The thought didn't cross his mind. What did, however, in the still uncluttered moments of a new morning, was that he was alive and that there was hope in a world in which he had felt only defeat. He knew, as full consciousness came upon him, that the road ahead would not be easy. There would be doubts and insecurities, and he would stumble again toward the abyss of self-pity. For now, however, he saw hope. All he had to do was act, push forward with passion, find a way to help Mrs. Jackson, reconnect with his children, and ultimately find love again.

He yawned and stretched with a half smile still playing across his face when he was jarred to reality again by first the frantic vibration and then the tinny sounds of Zeppelin from his Razr on the nightstand next to the bed.

He reached for the phone but didn't flip it open until his eyes cleared sufficiently to see the name of the caller. It was from his office.

"Hello," he answered cheerily.

"Mr. Donovan?" said a frantic voice on the other end.

"Patty?"

"Mr. Donovan, it came Saturday," she said excitedly. "The envelope from Mr. Finnerty arrived on Saturday. I didn't see it until this morning, but it's here. I have his declaration and something else."

"Something else?" he asked absently, still stunned by the initial news.

"It looks like an agreement of some kind, Mr. Donovan. Like an old agreement signed by ... let's see here ... it looks like Willy ... yes sir, Willy ... Jackson, I think it says ... and ... oh it's real hard to figure out the other signature, but it looks like it could be something Finnerty."

Sean didn't say a word.

"Mr. Donovan, are you still there?"

213

"I'm here, Patty," he said, still in a state of incredulity. "Can you read the agreement?"

"Oh, yes, sir. It looks like it's written by the clearer hand ... Willy Jackson's probably."

"Go ahead and read it to me, please."

She did.

Emily Finnerty arrived at Mercy General Hospital on J Street in Sacramento just after 10:00 the night Morgan's car threw him to the shoulder along Highway 80. When she hadn't heard from him by dinnertime, she'd tried to raise him on his cell phone but got no response. By 8:00 and still no word, Emily was frantic. Morgan never stayed away without calling. He had always been good about that, considerate of her and the boys. She made her first phone call to the police a few minutes later but heard nothing until about 8:30 when someone from the Sacramento PD called her back and said Morgan Finnerty had been in an accident. The caller gave her the number of the California Highway Patrol and told her where her husband had been taken but had no other information to relate.

The CHP was immediately more forthcoming once she explained who she was.

Morgan was unconscious at the scene. When he'd been stabilized he was rushed to Mercy General. He'd suffered severe head trauma and was being treated at the intensive care unit. Emily called her parents and asked them to meet her. She left the boys in a neighbor's care and rushed to the hospital in a fog of concern and tears.

Emily clung to her parents, Claude and Jan Mason, after their arrival only minutes after her own. The nurses said the doctor would be out to see her as soon as they were out of surgery, which they had been performing for almost three hours. Other than that they gave her nothing, and she broke down. It wasn't until almost 11:00 that Doctor Samuel Bannerjee, a dark-skinned, good looking man with a thick Indian accent finally approached her.

"Your husband's surgery went well," he smiled noncommittally and bowed slightly. "His head injury ... it was most worrisome upon his arrival."

"Can I see him?" Emily asked anxiously, her eyes rimmed with red.

The doctor shook his head slowly.

"Not yet, I'm afraid. He broke an arm, which is being set, and my colleagues are checking for other injuries. It would be best to wait for a while. We will let you know when you can see him." He raised his eyebrows and bowed slightly again as if to ask if that would be okay.

"Is he conscious?" asked Claude Mason.

The doctor's face screwed up into a grimace. "Oh, I'm sorry, sir, he is not conscious. I apologize for not telling you sooner. He fell into a coma. We have been working continuously since then. It was necessary that we open his skull." He stopped as Emily's mouth dropped open and she sagged against her mother.

"Please, Mrs. Finnerty," he reached for her with one hand and motioned to a chair. "Please sit over here. I will explain."

Emily staggered with her parents to the seats where Doctor Bannerjee pulled a chair around to face them.

"Your husband was thrown from a car, Mrs. Finnerty." He dropped his voice to describe the head injury. "His skull was broken. We were forced to go in immediately to relieve pressure on his brain. You see, a portion of the skull had embedded itself into the brain ..."

Emily swooned against her father. The doctor called for a nurse to bring water and a sedative. Emily refused the sedative and demanded that the doctor continue.

"We extracted the bone and repaired the skull. We don't know the full extent of the damages until our testing is complete, but we are satisfied there is no further damage being done at this time."

The Masons held back their rebuke of the doctor for the clinical and seemingly heartless way in which he delivered the news to the patient's wife, their daughter. They clenched their teeth, held onto Emily, and listened intently.

"What is your prognosis?" asked Claude.

"We have none yet, sir. Again, we continue to test and will not have further information for some time yet." Again the doctor bowed slightly, this time without a smile.

Further word did not come until early in the morning. Emily had long since sent her parents to be with her sons and accepted an empty bed in the hospital to sleep until she heard some word. The good news was that they had indeed gotten all bone fragments out of Morgan's brain. All other body breaks and bruises were repaired. The bad news was that Morgan was still in a coma. Only time would tell when, or if, he would wake.

Emily cried with the news but pulled herself together with the assistance of a wonderful old nurse who told her she had to be strong when she sat with her husband. He would feel her. It was better for him if she was strong, encouraging him with that strength to come back to her.

It wasn't until the evening after the accident that one of the nurses, while checking Morgan's vitals, brought Emily her husband's backpack.

"This should have been given to you sooner, Mrs. Finnerty. I'm sorry about that. I think it was important to your husband because one of the paramedics told our duty nurse the strap was wrapped around his arm when they arrived. They said it looked like the pack had tangled itself around his arm when he flew out of the car. They cut the strap before putting him into the ambulance." She shrugged as Emily looked at her uncomprehendingly. "It doesn't feel like there's much in it," the nurse concluded and extended the pack toward Emily again.

Emily, dazed from long hours sitting with Morgan, holding his hand and speaking soft, encouraging words to him, stared at the backpack, not sure what she should do. Finally, as the nurse bent to lay it on the floor next to Emily, she reached for it, nodded to the nurse, and hugged the pack close to her breast.

"Thank you," she mumbled softly before she turned again and directed her troubled gaze back to her husband.

She sat for several minutes hugging the pack and staring at Morgan. Her thoughts were muddled as she wondered how and why something like this could have happened even as she struggled with the concept that it did happen. Her husband was in a coma from which he might never wake, yet she prayed it was only a brief sleep, one during which he would regain his strength, fight off the injuries, and come back to her and the boys.

When she finally loosened her grip of the pack, she glanced down at the worn nylon, fingered the cut at the shoulder strap, and absently unzipped the main compartment. It was, as the nurse suggested, almost empty. The only thing Emily saw was the manila envelope, a couple pens, and some blank sheets of paper. She pulled out the envelope, noticed it was addressed to "Sean Donovan, Esq." in Torrance, and remembered that it was for Mr. Donovan that Morgan left home the previous afternoon and did not come back. She held tightly to the envelope, a part of her arguing that it was Donovan's fault that this happened but knowing that was not the case. Still, she wondered what could possibly have been so important that Morgan was adamant about getting it out to Donovan that day.

Emily wondered if she should look inside but realized immediately she was not interested. She simply didn't have the energy or the interest to see what it was. All she cared about was Morgan, and it was clear the envelope was important to him. She sealed it and resolved to mail it as soon as she could, because that's what her husband would have wanted.

She mailed it the next morning.

As Patty finished reading the handwritten agreement, Sean couldn't help but smile at the irony of his life. He dared not assume his luck had changed and suddenly his life would be different simply because he had seen the light and made love to Carla Anderson. His smile broadened with the thought that if that's all it took, he could get used to the latter. He knew well this good fortune was just another of life's little vagaries. Rather than look at it as some cosmic change meant for him, he would view it for what it was: the conscientious act of a man he'd only the day before believed was a flake.

Sean instructed Patty to prepare a declaration for his signature. It would state that Morgan Finnerty's signed declaration, the original of which was attached, had indeed arrived in the mail over the weekend. It would further state that the attached copy of an agreement, the original of which was held safely in Sean's files, was clear evidence of an agreement between the adjoining property owners for the use of the Jackson property and the payment of taxes by the Finnertys for such use. Although Morgan Finnerty was unavailable to sign a declaration attesting to the legitimacy of the agreement because he was lying unconscious in a hospital in Sacramento, Sean declared that Morgan sent the original agreement to him in direct response to Sean's request that he search his grandfather's records for just such an agreement. Although, again, not the best evidence, Sean was convinced it would win the day on the motion.

Patty e-mailed the declaration to Sean for his signature. He signed it, faxed it back to her for filing, and then called Mercy General Hospital in Sacramento.

"How is Morgan doing?" Sean asked when he was put through to Morgan's room and Emily picked up.

"He came out of the coma early this morning, Sean." She was jubilant, although he could hear a quaver in her voice. "Thank you so much for calling."

"Is he there? Can he talk?"

"No, he's having some tests done, but he's in good spirits … it's almost like nothing happened." Emily's voice cracked in a half sob of joy mixed with fear.

"I'm so happy to hear that, Emily. Please let him know I called. I'm thinking about him."

"I will," she hesitated for a moment. "Did you get the envelope?"

"Yes, it came in over the weekend. I was surprised. I heard about the accident yesterday. I didn't think he'd been able to send it out."

"I sent it," she said softly. "I found it in his backpack addressed to you. I knew it was important."

Sean didn't say anything. It was hard for him to fathom this beautiful woman's commitment and seemingly clear thinking in the face of such devastating injuries to her husband.

"Was it worth it, Sean?" she asked.

He hesitated and shook his head slowly.

"It's not worth Morgan's life, Emily," he said softly. "I thank God he's going to be okay. ... Please tell him it makes Mrs. Jackson's case, will you?" he said and then hesitated for a second before closing softly with, "Thank you."

TWENTY-NINE

"WHY AM I HERE again, Richard?" Carlos Perez demanded acidly. It was late Friday morning. Carlos sat imperially in one of Wolf's leather chairs, his elbows propped on the arm rests and his hands cupped together at the finger tips just below his chin. He eyed his attorney curiously.

Perez's man-mountain stood grim-faced two strides behind and to the right of his boss. In the chair next to Carlos sat Guillermo "Billy" Perez, Carlos's younger brother. His most distinguishing characteristics were a thick black mustache that consumed his upper lip and a bristle of short-cropped black hair atop his square head. He was wide-eyed and anxious.

To Billy's left, sitting on Wolf's couch in front of legal pads and files splayed on the coffee table, were Matt Dunne and Wolf's Spanish speaking junior partner, Frank Gutierrez.

"As I mentioned over the phone, Carlos," Wolf started with his usual air of control. "Donovan has found what looks like an agreement between Mrs. Jackson's husband and Boner Finnerty." He stared unflinchingly into Perez's eyes.

Wolf had rarely been intimidated in the man's presence despite Perez's history and Wolf's intimate knowledge of his capabilities. Perez was head of the largest and most powerful Mexican crime family in Southern California. There was little doubt he was a man with whom no one trifled. That knowledge was widely held even before Wolf first pursued Perez's business. As a result, the firm's management committee hadn't been excited about representing Perez. But Wolf assured his partners he could handle him and his multi-million dollar a year business and he did it well for eight years, a time during which all parties had grown rich.

"I heard what you said on the phone, Richard," Perez responded icily.

Wolf's eyes widened for an instant, surprised at the tone. The thought crossed his mind that perhaps he should be careful. It was a thought he'd had on only a few occasions, but it struck him with more force this instant. He shook his head, leaned forward in his chair, laid his forearms atop his desk, and adopted a conciliatory posture.

"Yes, I'm sorry, Carlos, of course you heard that. The problem is that the agreement seems to indicate the Finnertys' use of the Jackson property all these years was with express permission, and part of the deal appears to be that the Finnertys were to pay property taxes. Make no mistake, we're still going to fight this thing. There are a lot of questions as to the legitimacy of the agreement, particularly since it's attested to only by the attorney."

"What are you talking about, Richard? What the hell does that mean?" Perez dropped his hands to the armrests, pushed himself up firmly in his seat, and glared across the desk at Wolf.

Wolf nodded and bit down hard to gather himself. He needed to make this clear. No bullshit. When he'd received Donovan's initial response to the motion, he set his team to work creating objections to the unsigned Finnerty declaration and to Donovan's plea for the court's indulgence. The argument was that the unsigned declaration wasn't evidence and that Donovan should be shown no leniency; he had plenty of time to gather his evidence and submit it properly. Furthermore, even if Finnerty had signed the declaration, the testimony failed because it was based upon hearsay, and there was no evidence of any written agreement, something required in matters relating to real estate.

By the time the alleged Jackson/Finnerty agreement was faxed to Wolf's office Tuesday morning accompanied by Donovan's supplemental declaration, Wolf's team had completed their objections to the original opposition. The fax sent them back to work.

The basic position regarding Donovan's supplemental documentation was that Donovan was not a viable witness. Without a declaration from the witness who supposedly found the alleged agreement, there was no way for Donovan to establish a chain of custody and therefore no way to establish by credible testimony that the alleged agreement was anything other than a forgery.

Wolf intended to explain all of this to Perez when he invited his client to the office. He would explain the plan and how it was still possible to win the motion. He realized, however, that Perez wasn't interested in explanations of tactics. He moved immediately to the bottom line.

"They're going to win the motion," he said and watched Perez's eyes widen. "I don't know where he found this agreement or if it's even real, and I certainly don't think they'll be able to make it stand under my cross examination at trial. Unfortunately, however, for the motion, the judge is most likely to give them the benefit of the doubt. It's a harsh motion we're making, and judges aren't willing to grant them unless there's no question as to the probable outcome in court. The possibility of a real agreement creates a question."

"Where did the agreement come from?" asked Perez.

"Donovan's declaration says it came from Morgan Finnerty," Wolf responded and followed Perez's look at Billy, who fidgeted anxiously, glancing furtively between Wolf and his brother. When he started to say something, the older Perez raised a hand, shutting him off with the gesture. Carlos then turned back to Wolf.

"What happens next?" he asked without emotion.

"We file our papers and prepare for the hearing in the middle of the month."

Perez glared at Wolf.

"What happens with the property, counselor?" he demanded.

Wolf nodded slowly, pensively.

"This is a hit, Carlos; not a direct loss, because nothing other than costs associated with the lawsuit has been expended, but rather a strategic loss. The real issue is that if they win at trial, we lose the chance to steal a valuable piece of property, maybe the most valuable of all the properties we've pursued because of its proximity to the Silver Lode. It is the best piece outside the valley. I think we should take another shot at buying Mrs. Jackson out. She's represented by counsel who should see ..."

"This is that Donovan guy, right?" Perez interrupted.

Wolf nodded.

"This is the same guy who told you his client wouldn't accept any money for the property when the case was a loser?" Again Wolf nodded. "What the hell makes you think he'll talk differently when he suddenly has a winner?"

"He knows the cost of litigation, Carlos. He knows we'll bury him in discovery and motions if the case doesn't settle, and he knows anything can happen in trial. There's no certainty. I know Donovan. He's a practical guy."

"Yeah," said Perez, "but he hates you. A man who's been backstabbed sometimes don't act so practical," Perez finished with sarcasm.

"That's true, but that's not the Donovan I know. He'll put his hatred aside and do what's right for his client. He can claim victory at the motion stage, get his vengeance there, and still advise her to accept a big payday for a property she'll never use."

"What kind of numbers are we talking here?" asked Perez as he again glanced at Billy, who still fidgeted next to him.

"We'll work up the numbers after we give it some more thought," Wolf said as he motioned to Dunne and Gutierrez. "I'd guess we're looking north of thirty million, though."

Perez grinned and shook his head slowly.

"You're pretty damn certain of yourself here, Mr. Counselor. Any problems with the main case we should be talking about?" he asked.

Wolf shook his head.

"Nothing we need to worry about. The trial is less than a month and a half away. We're in as good a position as we've ever been, better because we walk in with a mandate from the Supreme Court." Wolf shook his head and smiled. "We don't have any problems."

Carlos nodded as a malevolent smirk passed across his face.

"This is your ball game, Counselor. Let me know how you want to go," he said as he pushed himself up to his feet and turned away from Wolf.

Wolf stood to follow. Perez turned back to him. "Don't let me down, my friend."

Wolf stopped in his tracks as Perez eyed him, the smirk still playing across his face. "We can find our way out, Richard. You and your associates," he made a head motion toward Dunne and Gutierrez, "better get to work here." He turned and walked deliberately out the office door with his man-mountain and brother in tow.

Richard Wolf's anger at Matthew Dunne had not abated. He was still fuming over the young attorney's mistake in Mrs. Jackson's deposition. But for that mistake, the chances Sean Donovan would have even spoken to Morgan Finnerty and pressed him for an agreement were remote. As it had been in their past together, Donovan still had that unique ability to see an opening, even in the simplest of statements, and run to that opening with all the strength of his intelligence. While attorneys were taught to parse through every sentence, not for grammatical error, but to understand the substance of every word, there were few attorneys in Wolf's experience who were as capable as S. Michael Donovan. Matt Dunne's mistake was one that should never have been made by an attorney of Dunne's experience, yet to most attorneys reading it, it would not have seemed so grave. To S. Michael Donovan it turned out to be the key to a case that should never have existed.

After Perez's departure, Wolf dismissed his associates, and his thoughts turned to one matter he neglected to relate to Carlos Perez: Curtis Golden had been served with a subpoena. His deposition was set in a conference room at McCormack, Stein & Wolf one week hence.

Wolf couldn't understand how Curtis was served so quickly. The service occurred on the Monday after the hearing in San Francisco. It was probable Curtis hadn't lain low, as he'd promised his father. Wolf could tell, even over the telephone, that Curtis wasn't sold on the idea and only agreed to go along with it in order to save his aging father some anxiety. Whatever the reason, Curtis's deposition was set. There was no way to avoid it. The only option was to prepare him for his testimony. If he handled that well, there was no reason for concern, and Wolf's failure to inform Perez of the deposition would be of no moment.

However, there was that one fear, the fear that one slip by Curtis could open a door through which their opposition might see light. Since that opposition now included S. Michael Donovan, there was no certainty. Richard Wolf would not allow Matthew Dunne to sit as protection for Curtis at the deposition. He would not permit any of the other litigation partners in the firm to do so. Dunne, after all, was one of his best, and he had already shown his weakness. No, Wolf would appoint the only attorney he knew would be able to contend with Donovan. Wolf would take on the responsibility himself. He would sit next to Curtis Golden during the deposition.

THIRTY

ONE WEEK LATER, CURTIS Golden sat alone in Richard Wolf's office. The deposition was to start at 9:00 a.m., in about fifteen minutes. He'd arrived at Wolf's office nearly an hour earlier for last minute reminders about the general stance to take when answering deposition questions: answer the specific question, don't elaborate unless pressed to do so, don't offer any information unless specifically asked for, wait and make sure you thoroughly understand the question before you answer, ask for the question to be repeated or clarified if you don't understand it, answer with a simple "yes" or "no" if that's all that's necessary to answer the question, never try to explain your answer, don't be intimidated into talking to alleviate silences.

Curtis, like most executives in businesses of high visibility, had been deposed before and understood the rules. He also understood that depositions were part of the war that was litigation. Although a deposition's purpose was to discover information that could lead to the establishment of a case by the deposing attorney, the reality was that it was often used as a tactic to intimidate, exhaust, and sometimes anger a witness. Curtis wasn't worried about any of these things because this deposition was going to be relatively short by order of the court. As far as Curtis knew, the deposition as a tool of the opposition didn't seem to concern Richard Wolf or his father. They both understood Curtis could handle himself through the procedure, particularly with Wolf sitting next to him to object to any questions that might pose a problem. That's why the whole "lying in the weeds" plan his father and Wolf had concocted flummoxed him. What did they have to worry about if they knew he could handle himself during the questioning?

Atticus was enraged when he heard Curtis was served just three days after the ex parte hearing.

"God dammit!" he shouted. "They got you leaving your house for lunch? You were supposed to hide away for a few weeks till it got too close to trial for them to do the deposition. What happened?"

"You know me, Dad. I couldn't do it. That's not me," Curtis answered, pleading with sadness in his eyes, the tone of his voice, and a shrug that he hoped would remind his father that it wasn't in his nature to be deceitful.

The muscles in Atticus's jaw twitched as he glared through red-rimmed eyes at his son. Curtis looked directly at Atticus. He wouldn't turn his head in shame even though he could clearly see the impact his failure was having on his father. He knew he hadn't done anything wrong by being honest, yet he was concerned for his father's health.

"Dad, please don't do this to yourself. There's nothing they can ask me that we haven't considered. We've done it right; every judge we've come before said so. Heck, even the Sierra Club was impressed with the analysis and the mitigation we offered in the EIR. I can hand ..."

"Curtis!" Atticus exploded. "Don't you see it's about the goddam shell Anderson found? Don't you see what that could do to our plans?"

"No, Dad. I don't," he answered, puzzled by his father's concern. "The EIR mitigates for all flora and fauna in the valley. It won't be a problem. We've covered it all."

Atticus eyed his son, never one to be intimidated by his father's anger, even when he was a boy. He'd always stood up for what he believed was right, always fought for it. He was so much like Atticus in that way. Perhaps that's why Atticus felt about him the way he did.

The old man spread his arms out over his desk, took a couple deep breaths, and spoke again, more calmly now.

"We haven't mitigated for a condor son. If it's a condor, they'll send us back to the EIR. We'll be stuck in this mess for another ten years... or more," Atticus said as he struck his desk top with an open palm. He then stared at his son again. "I can't take that at this stage. Do you understand that?"

A quizzical look covered Curtis's face.

"Condor?" he asked in surprise. "Buck never said anything about a condor. He showed me the shell and wondered what it could be. Did we hear it was a condor shell somewhere?"

Atticus didn't respond. He'd forgotten it wasn't Curtis who'd mentioned the shell could be a condor shell. He'd heard it first from his attorney. How Wolf learned of it wasn't clear. What was clear was that if it was a condor shell, the impact on the environmental community would be so great that mitigation would be impossible. No live birth of a California condor in the wild had occurred in decades. If the shell belonged to a condor hatchling, there was a chance the entire valley would be shut off to human activity forever.

When Atticus didn't answer, Curtis spoke again.

"Buck believed it was from a big bird, Dad, that's all. He never said condor to me. He thought it might be an eagle or some other bird of prey."

"I know, Curtis. You're right, of course," Atticus said, trying to backtrack lest he taint his son's testimony. "I don't know how I came up with the condor. I'm just concerned, that's all. Forget I mentioned it."

Atticus hesitated as weariness descended upon him. His face was wan, and he looked old and frail to Curtis.

"Be careful, son," Atticus continued with a sigh. "That's all I ask. Listen to Richard; follow his lead. Don't say something that will drag this thing on any longer. We need this to end, now."

When the office door opened, Curtis glanced up to see Richard Wolf gesturing for him to come along.

"Ready, Curtis?" Wolf said as he clapped the young man lightly on the shoulder and escorted him out of the office.

Curtis nodded gravely and pulled away from Wolf's touch.

THIRTY-ONE

SPORADIC BLASTS OF COLD air had been warning the denizens of Southern California to brace for the coming storm. The freak condition that hurtled out of the north came with a fury not seen in the southland in decades. Although it was rare to see rain anytime before Christmas, it was unheard of to get snow in early October. But both struck hard Friday. The sky opened about three o'clock in the morning and dumped torrents on the usually parched land before the world was awake. By the time Sean left Visalia at 5:00 a.m., the frigid north wind was howling and turning the rain into icy pellets of snow above the 2500-foot level. Under normal circumstances, even with traffic, he would have been able to make the trip to Richard Wolf's office for the deposition in under three hours. These weren't normal circumstances.

The Grapevine was a mess—first because of the icy roads making them slick, dangerous, and slow, and then because of the snow itself. It raced to the earth, swirling and blowing in icy gusts once it got there. By the time he reached Frazier Park at an elevation of just over 4100 feet, the entire landscape was covered in snow, traffic was stopped, and Sean knew he wouldn't make it to the deposition. Even though he could clearly see the horrific road conditions before him, he listened intently to whatever radio reception he could get for word that there might be some hope of getting through. While never in October, it wasn't unusual for the Grapevine to occasionally be closed due to snow. Typically early traffic in such circumstances was escorted through the pass into the Los Angeles valley, but once the road was shut down, all traffic was turned back down the hill.

Sean peered through the labored rhythm of his windshield wipers as they struggled unsuccessfully to keep the glass clear. He could barely make out the police and emergency vehicles that sat only three car lengths ahead of him with red lights flashing a sickly glow through the mist of cloud and snow reminding him that he shouldn't have even been in this situation. He should have gone back to Torrance last night. The trip from his apartment would have been dangerous because of the rain, but it wouldn't have been impossible. He shook his head and dropped it against his knuckles at the top of the steering wheel.

"Dammit," he thought. "Now what?" His cell phone sat without service next to him, not that it would make much difference yet since no one would be at Richard Wolf's office until at least 8:00 and he had no clue what the cell numbers for Andrew Harper and Pete Luckman were. What he did know is that the Sierra Club attorneys needed him at the deposition, and he wasn't going to make it. Of course, he was assuming they would make it there themselves. If they'd made the same bonehead mistake he'd made and didn't show up, Sean had no doubt Richard Wolf would cancel the event and send the court reporter home after a "reasonable" fifteen-minute wait. In that event, any chance of getting the younger Golden's deposition would disappear, even if they were able to serve him again. Wolf would make a motion for protective order to prevent the deposition after he and his client, at great expense to his client he would add, had been stood up without even so much as a call.

He picked his head up and craned to catch a glimpse of Harper's light blue Prius somewhere in the mass of vehicles forming behind him or somewhere in front, but he saw nothing. He hoped they had listened to the previous evening's forecast and made the trip down before the storm hit, although his rational mind kept trying to convince him that was unlikely.

Sean glanced at his watch, which read forty-five minutes past seven. There was still a chance to get there if the emergency vehicles would escort some of the cars through. Then he heard the traffic report on L.A.'s KNX 1070 and knew there was no chance.

"We just received word that the Grapevine has been closed to traffic in both directions. CHP roadblocks have been erected at the 5/99 junction to the north and at the 126 to the south. The CHP will be directing traffic to the west and east for those who still need to travel today. Our best advice is to avoid the roads completely if you can. Stay home. Call in sick. It's a mess out there."

Sean's windows began to fog around the edges even though he had the heat on full blast. He wondered absently how long he'd be able to survive in his car without any cold weather clothing as he peered ahead again, hoping to see something that might provide hope.

The brittle knock on his side window came suddenly. He jerked up and leaned away from the shadowy figure standing at his door. Again the figure knocked. Sean rolled down his window slightly.

"You okay in there," the CHP officer shouted.

"Fine … I'm okay. What's going on?" Sean responded and shivered as the cold surged into the cabin.

"We're taking you through," the officer shouted again. He pointed ahead and said, "Keep a distance of about 15 feet between you and the car in front. Follow the snow removal vehicles. They're the tall ones with the red and yellow lights. Don't try to pass anyone." The officer peered through the crack, and Sean nodded.

"Thank God," he thought.

Sean's cell phone reception didn't return until an hour later. They made it to the bottom of the grade just past the Piru cutoff at Highway 126 where the CHP finally let the vehicles go on their own. Sean breathed a sigh of relief and was finally able to reach the receptionist at McCormack, Stein & Wolf at 8:45. He was still 45 minutes from the office, he said, and he wondered if Mr. Harper and Mr. Luckman had arrived yet for the deposition. They had.

Sean spoke to Harper, asking him to delay the start as long as he could, but if Wolf pressured him, start without him and Sean would get there as quickly as he could.

He jogged up to the reception desk at 9:40. He was quickly ushered into the conference room. He handed the court reporter his card and was then directed to a chair next to Pete Luckman, down the table from the court reporter and Andrew Harper, who was questioning Curtis as Sean stumbled into the room. Next to Curtis sat the impeccably dressed Richard Wolf, and next to him, Matthew Dunne.

"Hello, Michael," Wolf nodded somberly. "A little wet out there I guess."

Sean nodded and expressed his apologies to all in the room. He plopped into the leather chair next to Luckman with his note pad and file in front of him on the table. He then looked at Curtis and returned the smile the man was aiming at him.

"Nice to see you again, Curtis," Sean said as he pushed up out of his chair and reached across the table to shake his hand.

"Good to see you, too," Curtis nodded and took Sean's hand.

Wolf glanced back and forth between the two, sat forward, and said, "Can we get back to this now that Mr. Donovan has made his appearance?"

An awkward silence fell over the room before Harper finally spoke to Curtis again.

"Now, Mr. Golden, are you taking any medications that would make it difficult for you to testify today?" Harper asked.

"Good," thought Sean. "They're just getting started. He's still on the introductory material." Sean only half listened to the early questions and answers as they dealt primarily with Curtis's background and basic information about the Silver Lode project. It would take Harper some time to get to the hiking trip upon which Curtis and Buck had embarked together.

Sean stared at his notes and, despite a pad full of questions, realized yet again that neither he nor Harper knew exactly what they were going after. They'd spent the previous two weeks poring over files, notes, and notebooks compiled by Buck Anderson. They'd reviewed all files on the project and all correspondence between Buck and the Sierra Club. They'd gone through other files containing materials on Buck's travels and cases other than the Silver Lode on which he'd worked relating to the Sierra Nevada Mountains. They searched for any hint of what Buck had discovered, but they found nothing and finally acknowledged the deposition of Curtis Golden would be nothing more than a fishing expedition with no guideposts.

Sean's thoughts were continuously interrupted by Richard Wolf's objections to questions from Harper. Wolf was determined to keep Harper off rhythm while Harper gamely tried to stay the course and find some path of questions to follow.

Sean had spent almost the entire two weeks since he'd received word of the arrival of Morgan Finnerty's declaration, in Visalia. Between the intensity of the preparation for Curtis's deposition and the sudden incredible lightness he was feeling each time he and Carla were together, he'd only been back to Torrance once, and even that was just to check on his office, instruct his law clerk to prepare a response to Wolf's objections and rebuttal to the Jackson motion for Sean's review, and to pick up some clothes.

As morose and without hope as he had been only the day before this two week run, Sean couldn't believe how his life had changed. He even dared think that life hadn't passed him by and that there was hope for happiness out there yet. The only setback for him during that time was when Carla raised the issue of Sean's children. She'd suggested on a few occasions that he look them up and try to contact them. His initial responses were that he'd get to it as soon as he could until finally, exasperated, he said he wasn't ready yet. He needed time. It was clear that time wouldn't come until after the Curtis Golden deposition, and Carla backed off.

By Thursday evening, the night before the deposition, Sean and Andrew Harper had put together a line of questioning intended to draw out any information that might lead them to the discovery Buck had made. Unfortunately, information of this sort usually came out in a deposition when the deponent was loose tongued and unguarded in his testimony. There was little doubt Curtis would be well prepared to give the briefest of answers, and with Richard Wolf sitting next to him he would be well protected. So Sean sat with his mother drinking a glass of wine at the end of the day and quietly reflecting on the upcoming deposition.

"You're not out with Carla tonight, Sean," Mary said with a bit of surprise.

"She had something going with her father and a visiting aunt and uncle," Sean answered absently. He smiled and nodded at his mother's expectant gaze. "Everything's fine, Mom. She really had something else she had to do tonight."

Mary nodded and smiled back at him while she tended the meal of short ribs, boiled potatoes, and a salad she was making.

"Are you thinking about the case then?" she asked.

He nodded again.

"Yeah, tomorrow's depo is so important, but we haven't been able to find the break Buck uncovered. His notes didn't reflect anything helpful, yet these two guys from the Sierra Club believe he had something. They think he was killed for it."

Mary turned back to her work and said sadly, "Maybe they were right, Sean."

Sean threw her a quizzical look. "What do you mean, Mom? Did Buck ever say anything to you?"

She turned to him and nodded. "He did, son. Before he took his last trip." She hesitated and took a deep breath, the pain of her loss still apparent. "He said it would soon be over and all this silly talk about riches in Visalia would end. He felt bad for the people who desperately wanted that ski resort, but he believed he had to do what he was doing."

Sean was shocked at his mother's revelation. He'd spent two weeks immersed in the files and official documentation of the Silver Lode case, and he hadn't bothered to talk to the one person Buck Anderson may have actually confided in. He hadn't even taken the time to explain the case to the woman who, despite her coy protestations, was probably the old man's lover.

"Did he tell you what he was doing?" Sean asked as he held his breath in anticipation.

"No," she said slowly as she glanced up to the ceiling in thought. "He did say something about a bird ... that it would save this bird ... and that it would make some people very angry. I think he was concerned, Sean."

He stood and walked to the counter separating the kitchen from the dining room.

"Did he say what kind of bird it was? Did he tell you that?"

"He did son, but I've forgotten now," she said before she suddenly brightened. "I have some of his papers and things though ... and some letters. I know he mentioned it in a letter or card he sent me when he was out gallivanting."

Sean's eyes shot open. A wide grin spread across his face. Mary returned the grin and led her son to the back bedroom to a thick plastic file box in which was some notebooks, photos, letters, and postcards. She hesitated before handing the letters over, clearly concerned about giving her son absolute evidence of Buck's feelings for her and hers for him.

"Mom, I know you were in love with each other. Dad wouldn't have minded. He liked Buck. We all did. Please don't worry about me. I'm proud of the life you made and lived after Dad's death. I never told you that because I was lost in my own pain, but I mean it. You did great, Mom. And if you loved Buck and he loved you, that's even better."

Tears came to Mary's eyes as she stared at her son and clung to the file box. Slowly she extended her arms and handed it to him. "I hope it helps," she said quietly and turned away.

"Mom," Sean called. She turned as he placed the box on the ground. He stepped to her and took her in his arms. "Thanks."

Sean spent the rest of the evening reading and re-reading every piece of paper in the box and then re-reading relevant sections of his files and the EIR. He went on-line and read whatever he could find about the California condor and its life and growth since its near extinction. He ran off copies of Internet articles, read others, and finally packed up his materials for the next day. By the time he turned in, Mary was asleep. The next morning he left the house before she woke.

THIRTY-TWO

As ANDREW HARPER DRONED on and got nowhere with his questions of Curtis Golden, Sean searched for answers in his notes and the Internet materials he'd copied the previous evening.

From Buck's notes and letters Sean gleaned that he'd found some kind of shell that was of a California condor. Unfortunately, the lab to which Buck had taken the shell for analysis was vandalized, and the shell disappeared before Buck could retrieve it. Although the technician's computers and backups containing notes of the analysis also disappeared, the technician told Buck it was a condor shell and that the technician would testify to that fact if it were necessary. Sean was able to piece together further that Buck was convinced the vandalism was aimed at the destruction or theft of the shell and the report of the analysis because the results would cause some financial interests significant harm. That's the reason he chose to keep the find secret and apparently chose not to leave any notes or briefs of his thoughts at his office.

The problem for Sean was that this was all well and good, but he needed more. There was no specific evidence where the shell was found or if it even had anything to do with the Silver Lode Valley. Furthermore, even if Sean were to assume it was from the valley, what relevance did it have? It was clear, beyond any further question, that the EIR had considered a number of enumerated large birds in its analysis of environmental impacts

236

and had provided adequate mitigation for all of them. The Supreme Court confirmed as much when it sent the case back to the trial court with a ruling that the EIR was sufficient. In addition, a catchall for other large birds of prey that were missed in the specific enumeration was also included with mitigation measures that would cover every eventuality. So, what could Buck have been talking about?

As for the fact of a California condor, Sean clearly understood the bird was on the endangered list and was protected. He also understood the condor's captive breeding had resulted in the growth of the population from less than 30 birds in 1983 to now more than 200 of them plying the skies above the Los Padres National Forest, which ran north along the California coast from Ventura to Monterey. They were coming back, so what the hell was the problem?

These were Sean's thoughts when he was reviewing Buck's letters and the articles from the Internet, and they were his thoughts up until just a few moments before Richard Wolf tried to end the deposition. Sean looked up quizzically and closed his eyes briefly to capture a thought—something Morgan Finnerty had told him. Morgan said he'd seen what he believed was a condor flying above Beverly Jackson's property. He'd seen the large bird on more than one occasion, in fact. Sean glanced down quickly at his notes and began shuffling through them as Wolf suddenly interrupted Harper's monotonous questioning.

"Look, Mr. Harper, we waited here for over a half hour for all of your team to join us," he started sarcastically with a quick glance at Sean. "We've now been here another two hours hearing questions that have raised nothing new. You've asked Mr. Golden about his hike with Mr. Anderson in every conceivable way, and you've gotten consistent, unwavering answers. They hiked and camped together, enjoyed the beautiful valley, and talked about nature the way environmentally conscious people do. If you don't have anything more than what you've been asking, I'm going to put an end to this, and we're all going to go back to something important."

"This is our deposition, Mr. Wolf. Judge Marks gave us the right to take this deposition. We tell you when it is over." Harper was uncharacteristically harsh, undoubtedly put off by the numerous interruptions of his questioning already made by Wolf.

Wolf glared at Harper for only a second.

"As you know, Mr. Harper, Judge Marks's order was clear that your questioning was to be limited. I have already permitted you leeway in that regard, and I am now growing very thin on patience. I'm telling you right now, if you don't get to some point where you're not wasting our time with the same questions, I will end this deposition, and I will seek sanctions against you and your client for wasting our valuable time."

Harper glanced quickly at Pete Luckman and then at Sean as if to ask for help. He hadn't been able to get anything of substance from Curtis Golden. In fact, not even a hint of an opening had presented itself. The reality was that Curtis was bright and controlled. It was clear he'd been well coached, and despite Harper's numerous attempts to get him talking, Curtis just answered the questions simply. Harper was desperate as he eyed his cohorts because he could clearly see the end of their case and of any opportunity to save the Silver Lode. Sean sat forward as Harper turned back and began to fumble frantically through his notes.

"Gentlemen, why don't we take a five minute break to gather ourselves. It's getting a little testy in here, and I could use a bathroom break." Sean smiled at both of them as Harper glared at Wolf. Wolf simply smiled smugly.

"A break would be good, Michael, but I want to be clear that I'm not going to let this continue if your boy here doesn't come up with something more."

Sean stood up quickly as the usually contained Andrew Harper appeared ready to launch himself across the table at Wolf. "Andrew!" Sean said firmly, using his given name for the first time in their relationship. "Let's take a break." He turned to Wolf and said, "We'll take no more than ten minutes of your time after the break."

Wolf nodded and thought that maybe S. Michael Donovan could still be reasoned with just as he had told Carlos Perez he could.

"Five minutes!" Matthew Dunne stated firmly so that everyone understood the break would be brief.

———————

In the hall outside the offices, Sean spoke softly to a fuming Harper and Luckman.

"Let me take it from here guys. I think I found something," he said as the two looked at him expectantly. "It's complicated to explain in a short time, but I think I've got it."

What Sean suddenly "got" came to him in the moments before Wolf's interruption. It came in a rush of sudden understanding. Although Morgan Finnerty's revelation of his condor sightings had little effect on Sean when he'd first heard it, the significance finally struck him as he sat in Wolf's conference room. If it was indeed a condor that Morgan had seen, it was flying over an area that was far outside its range. The articles Sean read indicated a condor's typical flying range was about one hundred miles. Beverly Jackson's property was nearly one hundred forty miles northeast of the Los Padres National Forest condor sanctuary into which the captive-bred birds had been released. While some expert hired by McCormack, Stein & Wolf could probably explain that anomaly, the next piece of the puzzle would not be so easy.

The piece came by way of yet another Internet article that described the find of a condor egg in Mexico. The egg was of a California condor in another area where the captive birds had been released into the wild. That was the first and only condor egg found in the wild since the near extinction of the massive bird. All previous eggs and births had occurred in the captive breeding program under the strict controls of the bird's saviors. Unfortunately, the Mexico egg didn't hatch. The chick died inside the shell, and the mother abandoned the egg. But it was the fact of the egg's existence that struck Sean.

Buck Anderson had found what he believed was a hatched egg in the wild. It wasn't clear that the find had taken place in the Silver Lode Valley because none of the notes and letters Buck left with Mary said that specifically. What was clear, however, was that Buck believed he had found something that would help the Sierra Club in its quest to stop the development of the valley. If it wasn't the eggshell, it was something else. It was reasonable for Sean to assume Buck found the shell in the valley, and it certainly gave Sean an avenue of questioning upon which to take Curtis Golden. If he was right in his assumption, Buck's find could prove monumental. It would be strong evidence of the only potential live birth of a California condor in the wild in decades.

"I'm Sean Donovan, Ms. Court Reporter. I'm co-counsel for the Sierra Club in this matter, and I'd like to ask the deponent a few questions if I may," Sean said as he sat in Andrew Harper's seat and nodded at Curtis Golden.

Curtis eyes seemed to light up. "So you're calling yourself Sean now?" he asked.

Sean nodded and smiled. "I am. It's the name I was given by my parents. I never liked Michael all that much anyway." He turned to the reporter. "May we go back on the record?" She nodded, turned on the recorder, and positioned her hands above the keyboard.

The following, except for the parentheticals inserted by this observer, is a transcript of the deposition responses of Curtis Golden to the questions of Sean Donovan:

> Q. Mr. Golden, you stated earlier that you hiked and camped with Buck Anderson in the Silver Lode Valley in the spring two years ago, is that correct?
>
> A. Tha ...
>
> Mr. Wolf: Objection. This has been asked and answered Micha ... Mr. Donovan ... and as I informed your colleague, Mr. Harper, I will not permit my client to sit through a barrage of repeat questions. We will end this matter if that is your intent.
>
> Mr. Donovan: I assure you I have no interest in covering ground already covered by Mr. Harper. I simply wish to lay a foundation for Mr. Golden of the context of the questions I intend to ask

him. As I told you before the break, I expect my questioning to take no more than ten minutes. I will now restate that provided there aren't too many interruptions.

Q. Do you need me to repeat the question, Mr. Golden?

A. No, I've got it. Yes, I was camping and hiking with Buck in the Silver Lode Valley two years ago this past spring. I believe it was in late May.

Q. You indicated that you didn't recall anything unusual occurring on the trip and that the conversations were generally about the flora, fauna, and beauty of the Valley?

Mr. Wolf: Objection. Again …

A. Yes.

Q. Did Buck find what he believed was an unusual egg fragment during your hike?

Mr. Wolf: Objection. (*Richard Wolf nearly leaped out of his seat to object. He placed a restraining hand on Curtis Golden's arm and squeezed a caution to stay quiet.*)

Mr. Donovan: What's the problem with that. Mr. Wolf?

Mr. Wolf: Mr. Golden can't possibly testify to the state of mind of Buck Anderson. He is not clairvoyant. He cannot read minds. I instruct him not to answer that question.

Mr. Donovan: Ah, you're right, Mr. Wolf. My mistake. Sorry.

Q. Did Buck show you something he referred to as an egg fragment or eggshell when you and he were in the Silver Lode Valley?

Mr. Wolf: Objection. This is irrelevant.

Q. You may answer the question, Mr. Golden.

A. (*Curtis glanced at a clearly flustered Richard Wolf, who could do nothing but nod his assent.*) Yes.

Q. How big was the shell fragment he showed you?

A. Well, it was more than a fragment actually. It looked to be about half the shell.

Q. Did he say to you what type of shell he thought it might be?

A. He said it was a big bird, an eagle or something bigger.

Q. Did he mention condor to you?

Mr. Wolf: Objec ...

A. No. *(He glanced sharply at Richard Wolf.)*

Q. Has anyone other than your attorney ever told you that the shell Buck Anderson showed you might be from a condor egg?

Mr. Wolf: Objection. The question asks for speculation, hearsay, and is irrelevant. I instruct him not to answer.

Mr. Donovan: Mr. Wolf, there is nothing speculative about this question. I will admit I am asking for hearsay, but you know as well as I do that I am entitled to ask and receive answers to such questions in a deposition as I am to seemingly irrelevant questions. I ask you to withdraw your instruction that he not answer the question. If you don't, we will end this deposition right now and take the matter before Judge Marks for his determination of whether Mr. Golden will answer the question.

(Richard Wolf's face reddened as he glared across the table at Sean. The only instruction he'd heard from Atticus Golden was that there be no further delays in the matter. He knew his objection was not proper just like most of the others he'd made during the day. The others had gone unchallenged, however, and he'd been able to keep Curtis's testimony under control. With Donovan, things were different. He couldn't challenge him here without violating the most important instruction his client had given him. He hoped his outburst alerted Curtis to the danger in the question and that he should be wary.)

Mr. Wolf: You may answer the question.

A. Yes. *(Richard Wolf turned to Curtis sharply and glared at him.)*

Q. Who told you that?

A. My father, Atticus Golden, said it might be a condor egg.

Q. Do you know if California condors are birds of prey, Mr. Golden?

Mr. Wolf: Objection. Mr. Golden is not an expert on condors or birds of prey. Any answer he would give to that question would be pure speculation on his part, and I instruct him not to answer.

Mr. Donovan: Fine. Mr. Golden, can you show me on this map of the Silver Lode Valley, which is marked exhibit 8 to this deposition, where it was that Buck found the shell?

A. Let's see ... Well, it's really hard to see on this map here. It's kind of in this general area, but I can't get more specific than that with this map.

Q. Do you know specifically where he found the shell?

A. Sure. I was with him.

Q. If you can't show me on the map, is there a better way of showing me where it was found?

A. Sure. (*Curtis smiled.*) The best way would be to go out there and take you to the exact spot.

Q. Okay. When can you go?

(*Wolf was concentrating hard on the line of questioning and practically jumped out of his seat yet again at the last question.*)

Mr. Wolf: Objection. That's way beyond the scope of this deposition, Mr. Donovan. I'm not letting him agree to go into the Silver Lode for this.

Mr. Donovan: Look, Richard, we've got enough here to convince Marks that a field trip to follow up on Buck Anderson's research and investigation is worthwhile. I figure it'll take a month for the motion to be heard, and since we'll be smack dab in the middle of winter by then, I suspect, for safety's sake, we won't actually be able to make the trip until next spring. That should put the trial off until next summer. Do you want that? If Mr. Golden agrees to go sometime before the end of the month, we can hold the existing trial date.

(Wolf was silent for several seconds. He glared flames at Sean as he crushed his back molars in a clench that sent quivers through his cheeks. Again, he was in a spot as a result of his client's very explicit instruction. He had to find a high ground. Slowly he calmed himself before he spoke again.)

Mr. Wolf: I will permit this field trip on one condition, Michael. Your client must agree on this record that it will neither seek more discovery nor request further delays in the trial. No matter what the result of the field trip, your client will proceed on the existing trial date without delay of any kind. Your client must also agree that if it or any of its members request any further delay for any reason including illness or death, its case will be forfeit and the court will be obligated to dismiss on summary motion by this office.

(Andrew Harper's leg struck Sean's below the table. Sean turned and eyed his co-counsel. He then leaned over to Harper's ear and said, "We have no choice here. Without the field trip, we have no case. None! We have to agree. It gives us the only chance of finding anything that can help our cause." Harper glanced at Luckman, who sat wide-eyed and bewildered. He turned back to Sean and nodded slowly.)

Mr. Donovan: The Sierra Club agrees to your conditions.

THIRTY-THREE

THE FREAK STORM TURNED out to be just that. It blew out of the north unexpectedly with considerable promise of turmoil and destruction and disappeared almost as quickly, leaving minimal damage in its wake. Just when some were blaming the "never before seen" weather condition on the catchall bad guy "global warming," the weather turned. Two days after the snow was cleared to the sides of mountain highways, normal October weather returned. Within a week after the Curtis Golden deposition, most evidence of the storm had disappeared. Except for the shaded north-facing mountain slopes of Southern California, which still bore evidence of the intense but short-lived snowfall and the occasional pockets of chill air that still worked their way into the southland, a visitor would never have guessed such a horrific storm had passed through. In those few areas where the snow lingered, it didn't stick as a dense foundation pack but rather as a thin, unstable sheet of snow crystals that would probably melt before the heavy fall of the real snow season began.

Plans for the trek into the Silver Lode commenced immediately after the deposition. Andrew Harper was shocked at the turn of events orchestrated by Sean. In one brief burst of contentious discourse, Sean was able to illicit stunning revelations that had pulled the Sierra Club's case off the edge of the precipice and given it at least a semblance of solid ground upon which to stand. None of Curtis Golden's words would constitute good evidence in any court, but they had clearly provided Harper with the information that had been so elusive since the moment Buck Anderson first mentioned he had something. For the first time, Harper knew what he was looking for. Now all he had to do was gather the evidence, assuming, of course, such evidence still existed. With only a month and a half until trial, Andrew Harper set to the task of planning the trip with great excitement.

Pete Luckman got the job of coordinating matters with Matthew Dunne, who was expectedly uncooperative. It took a dozen calls from Luckman before he was finally able to touch base with Dunne. Even though Dunne returned Luckman's earlier calls, he'd done so late in the evening or early in the morning, so it wasn't until almost a week after the deposition that they finally spoke. Dunne argued that with the recent storm it was probably too dangerous to make the trek, but his argument turned out to be specious given the new turn in the weather. In addition, Luckman countered that he had checked weather forecasts up through Halloween and learned that the calm, warm weather should hold through at least that time. Since that was still almost three weeks away, there shouldn't be any problem getting the trip in. To his credit, Luckman wouldn't let Dunne off the line until they had agreed upon firm alternative departure dates of either the following Thursday or the Thursday after that. The intent was to get into the valley by Thursday afternoon and spend at least two nights there before they returned. Dunne promised to get back to Luckman within a day. Surprisingly, he did so, stating that Curtis Golden, a Forest Service representative, and he, Matthew Dunne, would be able to make it on the later of the two dates.

The motion for summary judgment in the *Jackson* case was heard during the week after the deposition. Sean left the planning of the trip to Harper and Luckman and focused on the hearing, spending most of the week reviewing rebuttal papers and evidentiary objections from McCormack, Stein & Wolf and preparing for oral argument.

The fact that Visalia's Superior Court Judge Catherine Cassidy didn't issue a tentative ruling on Flow Corp.'s motion could have meant many things. Sean's concern was that despite the high he'd experienced when Patty informed him of the arrival of the Finnerty declaration, the judge simply hadn't bought the argument. Sean felt he'd presented evidence that, if believed by a trier of fact, would destroy Flow Corp's entire case. That's all he needed to do to defeat the motion, yet the judge seemed to want oral argument before she would make her ruling. Of course, the non-existence of a tentative ruling could also mean the judge's clerk simply hadn't gotten around to issuing it. Sean doubted that.

Sean eyed the judge after he and Dunne announced their appearances. She was a stern looking woman in her mid-forties who tended not to smile when she sat on the bench. Her demeanor had been brusque with the motions that preceded Flow Corp's. She stared down at the open file for several seconds before she finally raised her head.

"Counsel," she nodded at Dunne, "proceed with your argument, please."

Both Sean and Dunne were surprised. Typically a judge will have thoroughly reviewed the file, including the moving and opposition papers, and would start the hearing by directing counsel to limit their argument to specific issues. That was exactly what Judge Cassidy had done in all the preceding motions. She appeared to now be asking Dunne to make his entire argument.

Dunne did just that. He recited the facts and explained in concise, well-reasoned words why it was imperative that the judge grant the motion. In addition to the compelling legal reasons, he argued that the savings in both court time and expense would be enormous if the motion was granted because the case would then be complete, the matter would come off the docket, and the parties and the court could go on with their lives.

The judge stared at Dunne for several seconds after he finished. A slight smile, the first any of the attorneys in the courtroom had seen from her that morning, turned her features. She nodded once and then directed her gaze to Sean.

"Mr. Donovan," she said.

"Thank you, Your Honor." He glanced down at his notes trying to determine whether he should do as his opponent had done and simply restate the points and legal arguments from his papers. He looked back up at the judge quizzically for an instant and decided he didn't need to do that. He would cut through all of it and get to the point.

"Mr. Dunne and his client haven't changed position despite what I see as pretty compelling evidence that the major fact in this case is still at issue," Sean said. "We've given them Morgan Finnerty's declaration, which unequivocally confirms that the Jacksons granted the Finnertys permission to use their property. As a result, the use by the Finnertys and their successors could not possibly be hostile, a requirement that must be the very foundation of their case. This declaration clearly corroborates Mrs. Jackson's deposition testimony to Mr. Dunne that permission was given. In addition, we've provided them with a copy of an agreement—the original of which I have here in my file—establishing that the permission granted was indeed reduced to writing."

"Your Honor," Dunne interrupted. "May I respond to that?" He didn't wait for the judge's permission.

"That so-called agreement could very well have been a forgery. There is no evidence anywhere that it's real, and there is certainly no chain of custody established. In fact, the Defendant's only witness hasn't made any reference to the agreement or provided any testimony as to its authenticity in his declaration, yet he was the one who supposedly found the document," he said with emphasis and a hint of sarcasm as he glanced at Sean. "All we have is Mr. Donovan's declaration, and that is not evidence of anything."

"And how, Mr. Dunne, would you expect Mr. Donovan to have obtained Mr. Finnerty's authentication of the document while he was lying in a coma in a hospital?"

Dunne was taken aback by the judge's question.

"I … I don't know," he stumbled. "But Mr. Donovan's testimony is irrelevant, Your Honor. It has no probative value. He's the attorney, not a witness. It's his duty, as the attorney, to make sure his witness information is properly presented." His voice trailed off as he watched the judge's face grimace, and he finished with a meek, "isn't it?"

"Don't you think that's a bit harsh, Mr. Dunne?" the judge asked, and before he could answer, she continued. "Well I do. While I believe your firm had at least a colorable basis for the motion it made on behalf of your client, I believe that color disappeared once you had the Finnerty declaration corroborating Mrs. Jackson's deposition testimony."

"Your Honor, we ..." Dunne started but was cut off immediately as the judge raised her hand for his silence and glared at him.

"What I do know is that once you received a copy of the agreement with a declaration from a member of the bar, stating on his oath that the agreement came from the potential corroborating and chain-of-custody witness, and that the only reason this witness didn't sign a declaration authenticating it was because he was in the hospital recovering from an accident that occurred while he was in the process of getting his declaration and the agreement to Mr. Donovan, ... well that would lead me to believe my motion is pretty weak if I'm you."

As Dunne started to speak again, the judge again raised her hand.

"It's entirely possible that you will be able to prove in trial that Mr. Donovan lied to this court. While I doubt that will happen, if it does, I assure you disciplinary action against Mr. Donovan will be taken. However, given his declaration under penalty of perjury combined with the other evidence plainly laid out in Mr. Donovan's papers, I see no basis whatsoever for granting your motion and the harsh results it will engender. I therefore deny your motion. If you and your client do intend to pursue this matter further, I suggest you be wary of accusations you make, and I also suggest you make sure your facts justify wasting this court's time. Otherwise, I assure you this court will not hesitate to award substantial sanctions payable by your firm and your client."

She hesitated as she continued to glare at Dunne who, to his credit, knew not to say another word in protest.

"Thank you, Your Honor," he finally said meekly.

"You will give notice, Mr. Dunne?" the judge concluded.

"Yes, Your Honor, I will give notice."

"Thank you, gentlemen," the judge said as she closed the file, reached across the bench to hand it to her clerk, and then reached for the next file.

———

Richard Wolf didn't believe someone's luck could change. In reality, he had little tolerance for the entire concept of luck, either good or bad. He believed only in a man's ability to determine his fate by his actions and the actions of those around him. It had always been his conviction that if he were strong in the face of even the most difficult circumstance, he would find a way to solve it. All he had to do was focus, bring forth his considerable skills, and manage a situation to the point where it turned to his liking.

He sat deep in thought staring out his office window. He was slouched in his chair, his back to his magnificent onyx table, with his legs extended in front of him and his elbows propped up on the leather arms, his fingertips steepled at his lips.

It wasn't luck that brought Donovan his victory in the *Jackson* motion. Wolf knew when he sent Matthew Dunne to the hearing that it was a loser. He knew as soon as he'd learned about the supposed agreement between the Finnertys and the Jacksons. He'd told Carlos Perez as much. The problem was that he, Wolf, had made a mistake. He hadn't anticipated the involvement of an attorney of Donovan's once formidable capability. He'd taken the case for granted. Although he'd understood the mistake his protégé made in the deposition the minute he read the last few pages, he hadn't expected the old woman to come up with an attorney who knew how to deal with that mistake.

The loss of the motion was a setback. There was no question about that, and there was no question that had he taken the deposition instead of leaving it to Dunne they would not now be in this position. As a direct result of Dunne's mistake, he had been forced to call Donovan and have the conversation that just ended.

"Michael," he'd started, "do you mind if I still call you Michael? It's hard for me to get used to Sean."

"Michael's fine," Donovan said flatly.

"Look, Michael, that agreement was a good find. You nailed us with it." He bit his tongue at the compliment, but knew he had to give it if he was going to manage the conversation. Donovan said nothing. Wolf continued in a calm, conciliatory tone.

"I'm calling to let you know we would still like to buy the Jackson property. You and I both know what comes next: ridiculous costs of discovery, time commitments, and ultimately trial, which will require expert witness expenses as well as several weeks in court." His threat was clear: he would bury Donovan in paper, requests, and motions and make it impossible for him to handle any other cases, let alone the *Jackson* case, without expensive help. The threats fell on continued silence.

"I don't think anyone is interested in that," Wolf continued, "particularly since the court could go either way in this. I've talked with my clients and know they'd be willing to offer a substantial amount of money for the property just to avoid the aggravation of further litigation."

"Mrs. Jackson hasn't shown any interest in selling, Richard. I don't ..."

"You can talk to her, Michael." Wolf sounded desperate for a second but calmed himself as he continued. "This sum could set her and her family up for the rest of their lives. None of them would ever have to work again, and they wouldn't have to go through the aggravation of this litigation and the costs involved with no guarantee of any outcome. Her sons would ..."

"What kind of number are you talking about, Richard?" Sean interrupted.

"Several millions, Michael," Wolf brightened at the opening presented by his enemy.

"How many is several?"

Wolf hesitated for a second. He needed the number to be high enough to get Donovan's attention yet low enough to leave room for negotiation. This was where Wolf liked to be—setting the parameters of a negotiation he knew would go his way. There was no doubt in his mind that Donovan knew exactly what Flow Corp. had paid for the Finnerty property. Wolf also knew well that the Jackson property was worth more than a hundred million dollars once the Silver Lode project was approved, and that was as raw land. He and his team had already spoken to Visalia's city council members, contributed to their campaigns over the years, and knew, as a result of his contacts in the city, that the property would become the gateway to the Golden World Resort in the valley. The hotels and retail and residential structures that would be built would have finished values in excess of a billion dollars. Profits would be beyond comprehension.

"We're willing to pay her twenty-five million dollars, Michael," he finally said firmly. "All cash in sixty days, or if she wishes to put the proceeds into the New Year for tax purposes, we can move the closing to mid-January."

There was silence again on the other side. Wolf imagined Donovan picking himself up off the floor. There was no way he could have anticipated the first number would more than double the Finnerty number. Finally Sean spoke softly. The subtle tension that had been in his voice from the moment he picked up the phone was gone. There was no doubt he was surprised. Wolf had him, even if he came back with a larger number. He was certain a deal would be made.

"I'll take that to my client, Richard. I should be able to get back to you within the next day or so."

"Fine, Michael," Richard said calmly. "Get back to me anytime this week. I'll hold my dogs off till I hear from you."

"That's fine. I'll call you."

Wolf's current mood was not the result of that conversation with Donovan. In fact, the conversation was the one bright spot in his current thinking. He knew he'd get the property. The trick would be to hold off commitment until they were assured of the Golden World victory over the Sierra Club. Although victory itself was no longer at issue given the Supreme Court's stand, it was the additional hoops they would have to go through to confirm it that bothered him.

He was angry he'd not had the ability to tell Donovan to go screw himself during the Curtis Golden deposition. Had he not been hamstrung by his client's specific instruction that the trial was not to be delayed even one more day, he would have taken his chance on the motion before Judge Marks. He'd have argued it himself and let it be known that it was clearly unreasonable for the Sierra Club to request a visit to the valley on a mere hope this late in the game. He would have given himself a seventy-five percent chance of victory, and even if he'd lost the motion, it would just have put the trial off until next spring. But he couldn't take the chance. He had no choice. The field trip would take place in less than two weeks.

Wolf shook his head, stood up, and stretched his muscular frame. They'd find nothing on the trip—of that he was certain. Still, it bothered him because it should have been avoided.

THIRTY-FOUR

"DAMMIT, CURTIS," SAID SANDY Golden. "Couldn't you have just said no?"

Curtis's head was bowed. He glanced up at his brother and bit down hard on his back teeth.

"I couldn't lie," he responded tightly. He'd been hearing the same rant since the day of the deposition nearly two weeks earlier.

"Dad didn't say it was a condor shell, did he?" Sandy continued accusatorily. He received no response. "You should have just said no one ever told you it was a condor shell. That would not have been a lie."

Curtis knew if he had given the matter a little more thought, he would have been able to evade the question with the type of response Sandy was suggesting. He didn't see the need, however. He believed the Sierra Club had no case. They probably wouldn't find anything in the valley, but even if they did, the EIR had covered every possibility.

"Leave it alone, Sandy," said John Golden, the oldest brother. "It's done. We can't go back now. We'll have to make the most of this."

The brothers sat in silence at the large mahogany table in front of their father's desk. They awaited Atticus, who had stepped out to greet his attorney and escort him into the office. This had always been Atticus's way. He'd always made a point of meeting visitors in the lobby and walking with them, making small talk about the wonders of Golden World and watching

254

as the visitors invariably fell under the spell of the magic dust that wafted off the framed and sculpted creations that graced his halls.

"I'm worried about Dad," said Will Golden, the youngest brother. "He's pretty nervous about all this right now. I don't think his heart can take much more."

"No shit, Sherlock," fumed Sandy.

"Look, guys, let's hear what Wolf has to say," John said. "Then let's figure out how we're going to handle this."

Seconds later Atticus pushed open the office door with the same flourish he always did, as if he was pushing aside a curtain and revealing the prize beyond.

The brothers stood and shook hands with Wolf and Matt Dunne and then resumed their seats opposite each other. Atticus sat at the table next to Wolf rather than in his chair behind his desk. Dunne sat across from Wolf, next to Curtis, with his note pad at the ready.

"Where are we, Richard?" asked John without preamble.

"Matt and Curtis leave in three days, unless the weather changes and we cancel."

"Can we do that?" Will asked.

"No!" Atticus stated firmly. "No, we can't. If we cancel, they'll make another motion, and the goddamn trial will be continued again. We've got to go through with this."

Wolf nodded his agreement around the table.

"This is their last shot. Even if they find something new, they won't have the time to do anything with it. Whatever testing they'd need would take too long and wouldn't give them anything, certainly nothing to justify a finding contrary to the Supreme Court's ruling."

Atticus glared at Wolf as the attorney spoke. His face grew red, and he could feel himself growing faint.

"They won't find anything, Richard," he growled.

"No, Atticus," Wolf said and looked directly at his client. "There's nothing to find."

Curtis eyed his father. He loved the old man more than he could describe. What kid wouldn't love a dad who made magic, one who everyone in the world loved, one who taught them all how to dream and dreamed right along with them? How he now rued his deposition testimony, when he could have done exactly as Sandy suggested instead of creating a new mess. He could have danced around the question with answers that weren't lies but also didn't give anything away. He should never have suggested that the best way to show where the shell had been found was to take them out there. It never crossed his mind that anyone would take him up on it. When Donovan did, he'd been taken by surprise and responded too quickly. He screwed up and knew it. It wouldn't have bothered him so much if he hadn't seen the impact it was having on Atticus.

Curtis was concerned. Like his brothers, he knew Atticus's health couldn't take more surprises, particularly if they had a chance of shattering his greatest dream. He couldn't let anything happen to Atticus because of him. He had to protect his dad. He had to make it right.

As the meeting ended, Atticus's last words echoed in his mind. "They won't find anything, will they?"

And Wolf's response as he stared at Curtis confirmed the point.

"They won't find anything.

Sean responded to Flow Corp.'s offer to purchase the Jackson property the day after it was made. He'd completed marathon discussions with Mrs. Jackson and her sons late into the night. He'd explained the legal and expense issues involved in the litigation and then reminded them again of his conflict in the matter because of his involvement in the Sierra Club's attempt to prevent Golden World's plans for the Silver Lode Valley. He explained that if the Sierra Club lost its case and Golden World was permitted to build its resort, their property could be worth considerably more than the amount offered, but if the Sierra Club won, the likelihood was that the property would be worth considerably less. Sean thought the family's biggest difficulty with the offer was going to be that they really had no interest in selling. He was wrong, however, as he quickly realized once the numbers were given.

"Damn, Sean," Horace Jackson said, "why don't you just back away from that case and let them build that ol' resort?"

Sean was silent as he tried to come up with an explanation. He had committed to the case, and the Sierra Club was his client the same way Beverly Jackson was. But he didn't need to explain. Horace laughed to break the silence.

"I'm kiddin', buddy. We all understood the conflict, and we know you're doin' what you gotta do. We're happy you stayed on Mom's case and helped her get this far."

The conversation continued with all members of the family throwing in their opinions until they finally came to a conclusion. It was based in large part on the fact that none of them wanted Beverly Jackson to go through the anxiety of the trial process, but also on the reality that the case was not a slam-dunk, and even if Golden World won its case, there was no assurance the Jackson property would skyrocket in value. That was a risk only entrepreneurs should take. Sean ended the discussions after a unanimous vote. It was with the result of that vote that he called Richard Wolf the next day.

Sean presented Wolf with a counter-offer of fifty-five million dollars. After the usual show of shock on Wolf's part and continued haggling on both sides, they settled on a number, which was never the major issue anyway. It was the terms that ultimately gave Wolf his anxiety.

Sean demanded that the settlement agreement be prepared, fully executed, and entered into the court record as a judgment enforceable against Flow Corp. and its shareholders. A further condition was that half the price would be put up with the court in cash and the other half in an irrevocable letter of credit written by a major bank, all payable in January without condition. The final kicker was that all had to be done before Sean left for the Silver Lode.

Wolf's response was silence. Sean had no doubt Wolf's plan was to drag out the documentation until he was sure of the result in the Sierra Club case. He tried to create a payment schedule that was contingent on the outcome. Sean would have none of it. If Wolf's client wanted the property, it would be on the stated terms or the Jacksons would take their chances in the litigation. The terms were non-negotiable. Wolf backed off and negotiated only price.

The final number was forty-two million dollars, payable on Sean's terms.

THRITY-FIVE

ALTHOUGH THE WEATHER CALMED, it wasn't exactly what forecasters predicted. Rains buffeted the southland intermittently during the two weeks after Curtis Golden's deposition. In the higher reaches, shafts of icy northern air conjured new layers of snow atop the unstable crystals that still clung to shaded slopes. Golden World's legal team suggested the weather made the Silver Lode trip too dangerous, and that since it would be fruitless anyway, perhaps it would be better if they cancelled it. Although Andrew Harper considered the suggestion because of his own weather fears and his growing doubts about the trip's efficacy, he held steady. He realized, yet again, the trip provided the only chance the Sierra Club still had in the case.

The night before his departure, Sean sat with Carla and his mother on Mary's back patio. The rains stopped before noon, leaving behind a clear night and scrubbed-clean scent in the chill autumn air. They sipped wine and talked about the coming excursion.

"I'll be honest with you, son," said Mary. "I'm not excited about you going off into the snow and all. Our family never enjoyed the snow much. It's very cold, you know."

Sean laughed. "Thanks for that, Mom. If there's one thing I know about snow, it's cold."

"You don't have to go, Sean," Carla said. "You know that. Andy and Pete can handle it."

Sean smiled and nodded. "I know, but I guess I'm feeling like I have to see this through. I'm not sure what it is, just that I'm connected to this case, like it's really mine. I need to do it."

"What do you hope to find?" asked Mary.

"I don't know. I'm hoping we'll see what Buck saw—a shell, a cave, or tree with a nest, something that confirms his belief that wild condors live above that valley. Hell," he said as he leaned forward and looked across the table at his mother, "I guess I'm hoping to see one of those birds. That's really the only thing that'll change the way the case is moving. I don't think a new shell fragment alone will help."

Silence fell awkwardly over the trio as Sean sipped his wine and followed the gazes of his companions into the black night. Something was amiss, and he could feel it—just as he suddenly realized he'd been feeling it all evening. Conversation, even through dinner, was stilted and awkward. He looked at his mother, who continued to stare beyond the back wall. She was in deep thought, something Sean had caught her at several times during the evening. He turned to Carla. She dropped her head, avoiding his eyes to focus on something on the table before her. "Am I missing something here, you two? What's going on?" he asked.

Mary took a deep breath, turned slowly, and eyed her son with sudden resolve. Sean was taken aback. Concern covered his face.

"I spoke to Johnny," she said firmly. "This morning. He returned my call," she looked directly into Sean's eyes, daring him to respond.

Sean's look was of bewilderment. Johnny? *Johnny who*, he wondered, and an instant later he knew. The bewilderment became incredulity. He glanced at Carla, who also eyed him resolutely.

Sean had asked Carla to back off on pushing him about his children, saying he needed time to get his mind right, to work through what he would say, and, although it wasn't said, to push through the fear that gripped him. Carla honored his request and stopped pestering him, but she didn't end her efforts to locate the children.

Carla knew Mary was broken-hearted about the loss of her grandchildren. Mary told her as much. When Carla explained that Sean intended to contact them she was overjoyed, but when he said he needed time, Mary's hopes crumbled. She could take no more delay. She asked Carla how such contact could be made, and Carla showed her the way. In fact, not only did she show her via the Internet, she went online and found John Donovan Abrams. Mary made a call, stumbling over her words to an answering machine and ending with a sigh and a "you're old grandma loves you, Johnny." Two days later, just before noon, he returned the call.

"How ... What.·." Sean had no clue how to respond. A jumble of conflicting thoughts raced through his mind: I wanted to contact my son ... how did you find ... why did you do this ... I'm not ready ... I ... Finally, all he could ask was, "How is he?"

Mary smiled and spewed.

"He's wonderful Sean ... so grown up. He sounds like a man, with a fine strong voice like yours, son. He's in school—law school—like you— somewhere in the east. He comes out this way to see his sister. Marie lives here ..."

"Wait, Mom ... please," Sean interrupted. "How did you find him?"

Mary turned to Carla.

"Carla helped me," she said softly. "She used the computer ... showed me, but you know I don't understand it so well. I don't have the patience I guess. But Carla found my grandson, Sean, and I spoke to him after all these years."

Sean turned to Carla, whose eyes hadn't left him. She wasn't sure what his reaction would be. The relationship they'd developed over the last weeks had been one of growing trust and commitment, one in which they had grown confident in their daily contacts and in the matters they discussed. Only one topic was taken off the table, and it was that one topic that was now front and center. Carla at first felt she might be betraying some trust, yet she knew Sean would be hard-pressed to ever make the contact because of his years of self-recrimination. To overcome the self-loathing such recrimination engendered could take more years. Carla decided it couldn't wait. No matter what the effect on their relationship, if the ice was not broken with his children now, time would slip further away, and it would never be broken. She justified her actions by attributing them to her desire to help Mary. But she was really meddling, and perhaps it was somewhere she should never have gone. Although her eyes didn't waver as Sean's rested on hers, her heart quaked, and she awaited his response.

"You found him," he said softly. It was not a question but a simple statement, which betrayed a hint of relief.

"I did," she said flatly, softly, and nodded. "And Marie, too. They spoke to each other. Johnny called your mother."

Sean glanced across at Mary, dropped his head, and said quietly, "Thank you."

Carla smiled and turned to Mary, who returned her own tear-filled smile.

"Thank you, Carla," Sean said again, this time with sincere conviction. "Are they okay?"

Carla nodded.

"They're grand, Sean," Mary said, beaming through her tears.

The rest of the evening was spent discussing every second of the conversation between Mary and Johnny. He was in his last year of law school at Harvard, and Marie had just started a master's program in nursing at the University of San Francisco, just a short hop up the road, according to Mary. Johnny was planning to visit his sister in the city by the bay soon. Mary invited him and Marie to come visit her. Johnny had agreed to discuss it with his sister and get back to Mary.

"Will he talk…?" Sean stammered when he finally had the nerve to start the question.

"He asked after you, son," Mary said before he finished. She didn't give Sean the entire truth, which was that Johnny was hesitant about his father. He'd mentioned that his sister cried a lot when their father never contacted them. Mary's defenses were immediately roused. She wanted to explain what happened but resisted the impulse. She moved to other matters quickly, knowing a telephone conversation was not the medium through which to resolve such things. She didn't reveal that part of the conversation to Sean.

"We can call him in the morning," Mary said hopefully.

Sean nodded, a wary smile playing across his face.

"I think it'll be best to call when I return," he said softly as he looked off into the distance, lost in his own fears and wonder at the contact. "We'll need time to talk."

THIRTY-SIX

THE ONLY IMPROVED ROADWAY near the Silver Lode Valley is an old route built during the Civil War by a crusty old wilderness builder named John Burkett. The Union army hired Burkett to design and route the road from Visalia, over the Sierra Nevadas, to Fort Independence in the Owens River Valley. It was needed to supply troops stationed at Independence to stop iron ore shipments out of the Cosos Mountains to the Confederacy. Even after years of reconstruction, rerouting, and improvement, the Burkett road never traversed the Silver Lode. With no direct access, visitors to the valley were rare. It therefore became a haunt for intrepid helicopter skiers and wilderness adventurers rather than casual visitors.

The Golden family made several heli-ski trips into the Silver Lode in Atticus's younger years. He fell in love with the valley, and his plan to build the greatest ski resort in Southern California was hatched. When real planning started, his engineers and planners journeyed to the valley via helicopter. Although Atticus offered to build a modern all-weather road into the valley in exchange for prompt approval of his plans, the bureaucratic morass through which he would have had to fight for such construction rivaled that for the project itself, and the offer died.

The Sierra Club/ Forest Service litigants considered taking a helicopter in, but Curtis Golden was firm that the place to which they were going was not reasonably accessible by air. The only natural landing place was deep in the valley, and horses would have to be transported in to get to their ultimate destination anyway. The only reasonable means of access was via horseback along the Little Kern River through Sentinels Gap, the very means and route he and Buck Anderson had used more than two years earlier.

Sean, Andrew Harper, and a Sierra Club ornithologist named Wilton Froman left the parking lot in front of Anderson's office just after dawn Thursday morning. Froman was a slight man who spoke very little and gave no indication that he was anything other than a pocket-protector-sporting egghead whose affinity happened to be for birds rather than engineering or research science. While Froman's expertise was a potential benefit on this trip, Sean wondered why the Sierra Club couldn't find someone with a little personality.

Harper rented a four-wheel-drive Jeep, which the three loaded with packs engorged with clothing and equipment chosen by consultants at Visalia's REI store. Although Sean made no bones about the fact he was not a camper, hiker, or wilderness man of any kind, he was surprised that neither Harper nor Froman appeared to have any more experience in such matters than he. They represented the best known environmental organization in the world on matters dealing specifically with the wilderness, and neither of them had a clue what to bring along. He chuckled as they boarded the Jeep for the drive to their rendezvous point on the Little Kern.

Harper drove two hours over the modern-day iteration of John Burkett's road to their cutoff—a gravel-packed, rutted dirt road on which they bounced for a half hour before reaching a dreary clearing, the gate to which sported a battered sign that read "Logan's Stables." At the center of the clearing sat a small, bleached grey, ramshackle wood structure that served as the business office for the stables. A rusted, mold-stained double-wide trailer accompanied by two smaller, similarly stained trailers sat atop a slight rise behind the office and served as living quarters for the proprietors and workers of the establishment. Some distance beyond the office along a soggy mud track was a large, weather-beaten barn with attached stables surrounded by unkempt corrals and a dilapidated riding arena.

The weather was blustery and unwelcoming the entire drive but seemed even worse as Sean and his companions exited the Jeep. A steel grey blanket of mist fell across the clearing and stretched to the forest of dark shapes that ringed it, some showing only their skeletal remains while the evergreens loomed black and foreboding in their distance. Rain, which fell intermittently, making the already soggy footing treacherous, and a chill wind that cut shivers to the bone completed the gothic tableau. Some distance down that soggy track, Curtis Golden spoke casually with a leather-faced man wearing a thick silver ponytail that fell below the back rim of a well-worn straw hat. Matthew Dunne was nowhere to be seen.

Sean stretched the stiffness of the drive out of his bones and joined his companions in lugging their overloaded packs to the office's sagging porch, where they dumped them unceremoniously. Two idly lolling stable hands smirked smugly at their efforts, offering no assistance. Sean could feel the pain already starting in his lower back. What the hell had he gotten himself into?

"Deke … Willy … git off your asses and lend a hand to these folks," shouted a smiling, weathered woman who emerged from the office with papers in hand. "Mornin', boys," she said cheerily to Sean, Harper, and Froman. She stepped lightly down the steps, extended a strong, coarse handshake around the circle, and gave them each a form and pen. "Just go ahead and fill these out and we'll git you goin.'"

The woman's name was Bitty, presumably because of her tiny stature. She wouldn't have made five feet but for the heels on her cowboy boots, but it was the wiry, almost gaunt frame that really attested to her size. No matter what the reason for the name, it was clear this woman, who might have been attractive once, had more energy and good spirits than any woman of any size ever had. She swirled about them making sure they had everything they would need, first opening their packs and extracting the un-necessaries, and then directing Deke and Willy to take the considerably lighter packs and "load-up Samson," a bulky, ornery old mule of considerable strength, stamina, and stubbornness.

While the two hands struggled with Samson, Bitty escorted Sean and the others toward the leather-faced man, who walked with Curtis

Golden up the dirt track. That's when they first saw Matthew Dunne. As Sean approached Curtis with outstretched hand, he heard Dunne yelling. Glancing over his shoulder, he saw him bolt down the steps of the office toward them.

"Hold it, Donovan," Dunne shouted. "I don't want you talking to my client outside my presence."

Sean dropped his hand and turned to face Dunne. He grinned at the young attorney's frantic approach over the slick mud and puddles.

"Mr. Donovan, as Mr. Golden's attorney, I hereby demand that you avoid all contact with my client unless I am involved in such contact."

"Mr. Dunne," Sean said with exaggerated respect as he extended his hand to the attorney. "Nice to see you. Do you mind if I shake your client's hand?"

"There's no need for that, Sean," said Curtis as he came up behind him. Sean turned and the two shook hands. Sean smiled warmly, but, surprisingly, Curtis's usual warmth wasn't apparent. He seemed preoccupied.

Dunne frowned and started to protest, but Curtis turned away and again directed his attention to his leather-faced companion. The man was the owner of what he referred to as "this ranch." He looked to be in his mid-forties, like his wife Bitty, and he called himself Carter Logan. He took Sean's hand with a firm grip, and then he took the hands of the others following introductions by Curtis. The last person he shook hands with was the attorney for the U.S. Forest Service, a young man named Jeff Wuller. Of all the travelers except Logan and Curtis, it was Wuller who looked the most like a wilderness explorer. He was tall, athletically thin, and wore his jeans and flannel shirt as if he was born to them. Thick black facial hair completed his ensemble. Perhaps he should have been the one representing the Sierra Club instead of the city slicker trio of Harper, Froman, and Donovan.

They gathered tightly around Logan, and he proceeded to explain what they could expect on their journey. His voice was a deep guttural rasp but carried with it an authority and confidence that was reassuring.

"I'll be takin' you fellas through the pass and into the valley today. Usually, it would take about four hours to git through and over to Golden

Two." He spoke of one of the three old cabins in the valley that the Golden World team had refurbished to provide comfort and safety for overnight stays in the Silver Lode. He glanced up at the charcoal sky and then around him at the wet conditions. "I figure it'll take maybe two hours extra today, especially if the Little Kern is runnin' as high and fast as she has been. We'll be to the cabin before sundown, though."

He stroked his scraggly chin with his calloused right hand as he turned and pointed down the mud track he and Curtis had just traveled.

"We'll be headin' down this way and pickin' up the Little Kern just beyond that there tree line. We'll follow her most of the mornin' and into the afternoon afore we start the climb to the Sentinels. I'd ask you all to stay close to the pack. Don't go wanderin'. It can be dangerous out there, 'specially with the weather. Keep the PLB's Bitty gave you on you at all times." He referred to the Personal Locater Beacons with which each traveler had been outfitted. They hung in leather holsters at each man's belt. "You get lost, that'll be the only way we'll find you."

Logan took a deep breath and turned back to the tree line. Although the grey cast was dark, there was no evidence of the heavy black clouds that would portend a coming storm. In fact, in the far distance, thin shafts of sunburst cut through the cloud cover.

"There's snow in the valley. It's been heavy at times, so it'll be pretty thick in some places. Bitty here," he pointed at his continuously smiling wife, "she'll be monitorin' the weather for us from down here and stay in touch with me on the SAT phone." He held up the bulky hand-held device. "We been checkin' forecasts since we heard you was comin' up. It appears we'll be okay. There ain't no major storm expected through here for maybe two weeks."

He turned back and squared with his charges. He glared at them from piercing blue eyes. "I'll be honest with you, fellas. I'd rather not be takin' you up there now. No matter what the forecasts say, they tend to turn out wrong, and I'd hate to have you out in the open if these are wrong. For now, the weather ain't bad, but it ain't the best travellin' weather neither, and it would be best not to take this trip. Curtis here tells me how important it is for you, so I'm goin' along with it. But if I hear from Bitty that things are lookin' dicey, I'm turnin' us all back… and no arguin' the point. If we're on the other side and I get such news, I'll instruct you to stay in at Golden Two. In that case, it would be real good if you folks got to like each other, 'cuz the quarters will be cozy."

Logan's eyes roamed the circle of nodding, sullen-faced men.

"Any questions?" he asked.

When no one raised a hand, he smiled broadly. For the first time he exhibited the thrill he experienced when he embarked on such a trek.

"Mount up!" he shouted.

THIRTY-SEVEN

IT HAD BEEN YEARS since Sean was last on horseback. It was on a trip to Tahoe with Susan and the kids. He vaguely remembered the butt pain and weariness in his knees and thighs as he now lifted himself out of the saddle to relieve the pressure on his posterior. He expected those pains. What he didn't expect was the pain in his lower back, which now exacerbated the suddenly less subtle pains of age. Thankfully, the trek along the Little Kern was at a moderate pace because of numerous obstacles in the path and the continuous ascent. He didn't have to deal with the jouncing of a trot or canter more than a couple times.

They reached the Little Kern quickly and confirmed Logan's assertion that the river was running high and fast. The regular trail along the river's bank was submerged in places, and the troop was forced to adjust course further up the slope, around the water, and then back down to the trail. That wasn't overly difficult until the river took them into a steep canyon strewn on both sides with rock and thick, impenetrable vegetation that made the slopes impossible to climb. When the trail was submerged inside the canyon, they were forced to dismount and pull their steeds through ankle and sometimes knee deep frigid water that dragged at them along the river's southerly course. The physical strain of the trek wasn't their only discomfort, however. The dank chill and constant drip of wet overhead foliage together with the all-consuming grey took a psychic toll that none of the travelers had anticipated. To the inexperienced of the group, the question that reverberated was what anyone would see in such an adventure. Thankfully, just short of two hours inside the canyon, they found an opening in the thick vegetation. They turned into the opening, which was canopied similarly to the riverbank, but it was a welcome change of course that took them away from the fast, icy water.

The new path proved steep and treacherous, made more so by patches of snow that began to appear as they climbed higher. Whatever relief the riders felt at leaving the riverbank was undone quickly. Instead of apprehension that they might be washed away with the strong tide, each feared a misstep by his horse would send him tumbling down the rock and ice strewn slopes to his death. When they finally reached a small plateau, they breathed relief, albeit with difficulty as the air was considerably thinner at the plateau's eight thousand foot elevation.

The travelers stood about the plateau, stretching their backs and necks while gingerly rubbing life and warmth into their backsides. Some walked in exaggerated bowleg gaits to relieve the chafing between their thighs; none was interested in the sandwiches Bitty had packed for them. The increasing chill of the higher reaches forced them to don heavier jackets and rub their arms for life-giving warmth. Wilton Froman, clearly the least comfortable of the group, suggested to Harper that they abort the trip and head back down the mountain to Logan's. Harper considered the suggestion until he heard Carter Logan call out to all of them.

"There they are," Logan said, pointing through an opening between two large pines to a strange rock formation about two hundred yards up the slope. "The Sentinels."

The travelers gathered around Logan and followed his finger to a large gap in the rock. It appeared as a depthless black cut through thick granite, and although there was nothing unusual about that, there was something strange about the rock peaks that formed the gap and towered high above it: they were perfectly symmetrical.

Sean had never given any thought to nature's asymmetry, perhaps because the concepts of the "wild" and "nature" implied a haphazard structure, disorganization, and chaos. Yet he was witnessing perfect symmetry. The peaks were not only the same size and shape. They were mirror images of each other. Crevices, cuts, and protrusions in one matched perfectly their counterparts in the other. Each was bare of vegetation in exactly the same spots, and each bore snow patches in corresponding sizes and locations. They seemed unnatural in this pristine setting—more like massive, handcrafted columns than anything that had sprung from the earth.

"The hands of God created the Sentinels," Carter Logan said softly, reverently. "There's nothing like 'em anywhere."

Tiny shards of sunlight pierced the clouds like beams tracing a path up the slope to the gap. Snow runs sparkled like rivers of bright baubles beckoning the travelers even while the black gap whispered a message of foreboding. Logan turned to the others.

"This is Paiute country," he said solemnly. "The gap is the entryway to one of the most sacred places in Paiute tradition. Legend is that spirits guard Sentinels Gap from intruders. You'll feel a strange wind as we get close. It's them guard-spirits checkin' on you to make sure you're worthy. Most of the horses will handle it just fine." He glanced back at the horses huddled together grazing the sparse scrub on the plateau. "Some'll get skittish, though. Just stay calm. Me an' Curtis'll help you. Once we're through, it'll be okay."

As they remounted and started up the last rise, this one shallower but with considerably more snow and ice than what came before, the riders were wary, first because of Logan's cautioning words and then because of the balkiness of their rides. To a man, they sensed a difference, as if the horses knew what was to come and wanted no part of it. The higher they climbed, the greater became the force of the unusual wind that surged through the gap. It wasn't simply a cold wind borne of freezing temperatures, but rather a piercing force that sent shivers of fear through each of them.

Once Logan's black Palfrey reached level ground some twenty feet below the gap, it shied to the side, stepped forward again, and then shied again as if it had lost its equilibrium. Logan leaned low over its right withers, stroked the anxious beast, and spoke softly as the rest of the party gradually attained the same ground. The Palfrey's ears were cocked forward with its head held high, watching as its hooves shuffled skittishly on the frozen earth. It whickered, wanting to follow its master's commands yet somehow understanding this was not the place to do so.

The other horses snorted angrily behind Logan's. They pawed the ground nervously as riders tried to steady them, leaning over and soothing with hand strokes and soft words. But nothing the riders did could entice their horses to push on to the gap until Samson reached them.

The old mule was led by Curtis who stayed to the rear of the troop to contend with the animal. Samson had been uncooperative and cranky the entire trek, stopping suddenly here, moving off the path for some perceived delicacy there, and simply making life as difficult as possible for Curtis as he coaxed it along the trail. Once he reached the other horses below the gap, however, things changed. He stood awkwardly at the edge of the flat behind his stomping, skittish cousins, their larger bodies jouncing about the small space, crowding the mule ever closer to the edge.

Samson tried to avoid his brethren until he grew angry at the inconvenience they were causing him. The graying, knobby-kneed creature suddenly laid back his ears, extended his neck, and let out a loud, contemptuous bray. The horses staggered aside at the harsh, piercing sound, and Samson exploded past them with a speed not even Logan had ever seen. His sudden charge yanked his leading rein from Curtis's grasp, and he raced past him, up the final twenty feet and through the gap. Curtis's horse shied as the mule thundered past, and then he bolted through the throng of anxious horses after the mule. Suddenly the others took up the chase. They stampeded en masse after the mule. Within seconds, all except Matthew Dunne's powerful courser were attacking the gap with speed and liveliness borne of fear.

Dunne's horse spun around as the others ran past. It dodged and shied, its eyes wide and senseless until it finally reared up protectively on its hind legs and clawed the air with its forelegs. Dunne struggled to maintain his hold, gripping the reins, squeezing his knees tight to the saddle and leaning forward for balance. The beast came down suddenly and hit the ground, driving shock waves through Dunne's body. He was still aboard, but only for another instant. The horse came up on its forelegs and threw its hind legs out in mighty jabs that sent the attorney flying over its head. Dunne ducked and landed hard on his shoulder whence he rolled over snow, rock, and bush before he crashed to a stop against the trunk of a sturdy Douglas fir.

He looked up groggily to see his horse's hindquarters disappearing into the darkness of the gap, leaving him alone and in pain. He felt his arms and legs with probing hands to confirm nothing was broken. When he realized he was whole, he pushed himself up to his feet. He stretched and turned gingerly to work out the stiffness and pain. Finally he saw two figures emerge from the gap on foot. Curtis Golden and Sean Donovan were picking their way down the shallow slope to his aid.

THIRTY-EIGHT

THE GHOSTLY FINGERS GRIPPING their spines disappeared the moment they squeezed through Sentinels Gap to the narrow flat on the other side. The chill wind that struck them with so much horror was also gone, replaced suddenly by a warmer breeze that soothed them as surely as the former had shaken them. By the time Sean and Curtis trudged back through the gap with Matthew Dunne stumbling between them, the rest of the troop was standing awestruck at the edge of the shelf-like flat, staring over the magnificent valley of the Silver Lode.

The shelf, below the southern rim of the valley's bowl, was enclosed on three sides by enormous pines and rock formations. On the fourth it was open to a world of vivid color and majesty that stretched from the valley's floor some 1,500 feet below up to the sharp peaks that loomed above them. The slopes that fell off steeply from their stage were covered with a heavy blanket of thick, pristine powder while the other slopes carried more sporadic snow masses, heavier on the western slopes and lighter to the east and north. Black oaks and their deciduous cousins grew in thick groves slightly up from the valley floor and, despite the early snow, still clung to the last of their autumn leaves, creating a canopy of gold, red, and orange that gave way to the dark greens of pines and firs further up the slopes. Overhead, cloud breaks revealed darkening patches of clear sky that lay in stark contrast to the dreary grey through which the riders had traveled the previous hours. But it was the cast of the setting sun below the cloud cover on the western horizon that gave the valley its surreal wonder.

The sun, not visible from their vantage, had dropped below the western peaks and cast its flaming glow onto the underside of the charcoal clouds. It bathed the cloud undercover in a yellow/orange wash that reflected off dark granite and returned in a mystic haze of purple that permeated the entire valley. To a man, the travelers were stunned. Nowhere had they seen anything like the natural beauty that confronted them. The kaleidoscope of color revealed new wonders with each passing second until it finally disappeared and all that remained was the last fading remnant of orange at the westernmost fringe of cloud.

They were transfixed until Carter Logan's voice pushed through their consciousness with a reverence for the wonder they all felt. "We've got to get on to the cabin, fellas," he said softly.

Not another word was spoken as they remounted, eyes still glued to the horizon until the last of the light disappeared.

Golden Two was another hour down a gently sloping trail to the west of Sentinels Gap. From the outside, the cabin looked much like the office at Logan's Stables: bleached grey wood slats torn, slivered, and worn by the Silver Lode's extreme weather. The first view of the dilapidated cabin in the moon's occasional glow gave little succor to the weary riders hoping for a comfortable place to rest their bodies. Once the horses were stabled and fed and the riders had all made their way into the cabin, however, it was clear they would have a good sleep.

The structure was small, with three rooms and a loft. The largest room sported a massive, stone, open-hearth fireplace and served as the meeting room, kitchen, and dining room. The other two rooms were good sized, each containing three bunk beds and a desk and chairs. There was one bathroom off each bedroom. Each was supplied with running recycled water for the toilets and well water for cleaning and drinking. The water was carried into the structure through annually re-insulated pipes. The recycled water came from a waste regenerating septic system that Golden

World was testing as the model for their ultimate development in the valley. The travelers, who were expecting the worst of sleeping conditions after their long hours in the saddle, were pleasantly surprised to find comfort.

There was little banter that night. The group ate a hearty stew prepared in advance by Bitty Logan and carried aboard old Samson. After dinner, the Sierra Club group retired to one of the two bedrooms together and the Golden/Forest Service group to the other. Carter Logan climbed the spiral staircase to the loft and made his bed there. Everyone was snoring loudly within minutes.

The next morning, they woke to the popping of Carter Logan's sizzling bacon and grease-soaked eggs. Outside, the air was brittle and grey with thick clouds once again. At the rough-hewn oak dining table the conversation was light with everyone in less than robust moods. Despite the rest they'd gotten, their bodies ached in places most didn't know existed, and none was looking forward to another day riding and hiking. Some spoke softly of the wondrous beauty they'd witnessed upon entering the Silver Lode, but the main conversation was the instructions for the day's expedition given by Logan and Curtis Golden. They again warned the others to stay close on the four-hour ride to a warming hut some two thousand feet above the cabin, whence they would hike to their destination.

Sean wondered at the reticent attitude Curtis Golden had adopted on the trip. Despite his handshake in the yard at Logan Stables, Curtis made little effort to engage any of the travelers. Sean's memory of Curtis was of an affable man with no stomach for duplicity or gamesmanship. He'd been friendly and forthcoming in his early years, and whenever there had been any legal matters discussed among the brothers and their attorneys when Sean was one of them, his was the voice of reason, leaning toward resolution rather than conflict. It was one of the characteristics Sean liked in Curtis. On this trip, however, he saw none of the old Curtis Golden.

Perhaps the man had hardened in the years since they'd last seen each other. Back then, they were both only a few years out of the idealism of school and were untainted by the real world of business and the greed it engendered. The real world was harsh, as Sean knew so well, and it had probably caught up with Curtis, too. But that explanation didn't sit well with Sean. He'd seen Curtis during the deposition, how he'd been so forthcoming and honest—the way Sean remembered him. He'd been friendly and helpful and not the least bit concerned about his testimony because of his belief that he and his family were honorable, truthful, and good. But something changed in Curtis in the weeks since.

Undoubtedly, this trip and the lawsuit were bothering him more than Sean first believed.

They didn't reach the warming hut until just before noon. This structure was of a less permanent nature than Golden Two and looked as if it had been placed at this location within the last few years. It was a single room structure with a black, pot-bellied stove in one corner and a large oak table and eight chairs in the center. There was floor space to throw down a half dozen sleeping bags comfortably and a few more if the need arose. Twenty feet east of the hut was a three-sided lean-to for the horses to feed and rest within some semblance of a shelter. Behind the structures loomed a rock slope laden with thick snow, sporadically spotted with widely separated, solitary pines.

Sean stood on the hut's front porch, leaning against a roof support, munching a turkey sandwich and gazing through a thin stand of pines into the snowy expanse that fell off to the valley. Grey clouds hung bloated overhead and blocked out all attempts by the sun to find its way through. To the far north, over a distant peak, enormous black clouds churned, not yet spilling over the peak but seemingly waiting for the call to arms when they would charge down the slopes and into the valley to dump their icy loads. The entire scene was of a barren rock terrain covered with snow and the occasional wayward tree, yet, even with the grey overcast and the threat of the distant clouds, the view was magical, especially to eyes that rarely saw much other than concrete and asphalt.

"Beautiful, isn't it?" asked Curtis Golden.

Sean turned slowly. Curtis was smiling, nodding into the distance. Sean was surprised but happy to see him smiling. He returned his gaze to the distance.

"Yeah ... beautiful," he said and then waxed philosophical. "We never see this. I guess we forget it's out here."

Curtis nodded slowly.

"You ready to take a hike?" he asked.

Sean smiled, nodded, and began to turn when something suddenly caught his eye. He squinted into the grey and picked up a speck in the distant sky. It appeared to be a large bird, gliding higher on widespread wings, barely visible at this distance.

"What's that?" he whispered to himself.

Curtis heard the question and followed Sean's gaze. He could see nothing and shook his head. "What are you looking at?" he asked.

Sean frowned, as the creature seemed to blend into the overcast. He continued to peer into the distance but couldn't pick it up again.

"I lost it in the backdrop. It looked like a big bird, though. I wonder what kind," he mused.

"Probably an eagle. They're all over the valley," Curtis said. "There's good game for them, even in snow."

"Yeah, maybe," Sean said absently without removing his eyes from the northern horizon. He wondered if it could be Morgan Finnerty's condor. "Where the hell's my ornithologist when I need him?" he said with a smile before he turned and followed Curtis into the hut.

The hike took only fifteen minutes. Although vegetation at this higher elevation was sparse, snowdrifts and uncompromising granite made the trail unsafe for horses. They were left behind at the lean-to. The trail took them on a slightly upward trajectory to a small flat tabletop that fell off sharply at its edge to rocks a hundred feet below. The face of the rock wall that dropped off from the flat was not completely vertical, but it was sheer enough to warrant the skills and equipment of a mountaineer to scale.

"I was looking out over the valley at this point," Curtis said as he stood at the cliff edge and motioned casually over the snow-basted bowl of the Silver Lode.

Although the view here, like the one that first struck them after they emerged through Sentinels Gap, was of wild, untamed magnificence, it was devoid of the color that made yesterday's scene mystical. They could see the same black oaks, pines, and firs working their way up the various snow-splashed slopes, but the colors were so subdued by the growing overcast as to almost disappear to black.

"How did discussion of the shell come up?" asked Sean casually.

"Objection!" grunted Matthew Dunne. "That question assumes there was a shell. No foundation has been laid, and I instruct my client not to answer the question."

They all looked at Dunne. Although the objection might have been legitimate in a formal court or deposition setting, they all understood he was being ridiculous. Unfazed, Dunne stood his ground.

"Look, Matt, let's cut the crap," Sean said, trying to control his anger. "We all know why we're up here. There's no need for this. We want to know where the shell was found, and everyone here knows what we're talking about without a foundation. Can you just let it be?"

Dunne eyed Sean with a smug smile. Sean understood Dunne's purpose was to warn Curtis to be careful. Curtis, meanwhile, stepped away from the edge and over to a large boulder some five feet away from the edge. It had a flat top that was sitting-distance above the ground.

"Buck was sitting here looking pretty intently at something, so I walked over to him. He showed me the shell."

"Can you describe it?" asked Harper.

"Mr. Harper … Mr. Donovan … all of you," Dunne started confidently as he eyed each of them. "I'm not going to let Mr. Golden answer any questions about the shell. Our purpose in coming up here was to show you where he and Buck were when they found it. That's it."

Harper glared at Dunne.

"Actually, Mr. Dunne, the purpose was to show us where they found the shell, not where they were when it was found. Would you like me to read you the language from the deposition?"

"That won't be necessary. I'm familiar with the language. Your statement is correct. Please, Mr. Golden, show these people where the shell was found, if you know," Dunne concluded.

Curtis, who had been standing calmly with his head bowed as the attorneys jousted, lifted his head slowly and looked squarely at Harper.

"Actually, I don't know exactly where Buck found the shell. All I know is that when I saw him sitting on the rock here," he motioned again to the rock stool, "he was examining the shell, and he showed it to me," he said.

Sean knew he was lying. Curtis didn't look at Sean when he spoke. He stared hard at Harper, purposely it seemed, to avoid eye contact with Sean. Sean tried another question that was within the now limited scope of the trip.

"Did Buck tell you where he found the shell?" he asked.

Dunne interrupted again, shaking his head vehemently.

"I'm not going to let him answer that one, Mr. Donovan. That's..." he started.

"Look, you son of a bitch," Sean started. "You've made your point. We understand where we can go with this, but we also understand the judge will give some leeway in getting us to the answers we came up here for. You make any more of these bullshit objections and we'll end this, go back down this hill, and see the judge. I can guarantee he'll allow my last one, and we'll sure as hell be coming back up here in the spring before the date for the continued trial."

Dunne stared at Sean. He wasn't cowed. He'd made his point. He was in control and could make sure his opponents would get as little information as possible. He turned to Curtis.

"Did Buck tell you where he found the shell?" he asked calmly.

Again, Curtis didn't look at Sean. He spoke to Dunne with a quick glance at Harper.

"I don't recall that he did ... No, he didn't," he said without conviction.

No one spoke for several seconds. Sean's heart sank. He realized the trip was now, officially, a wild goose chase just as Richard Wolf said it would be. The chances of finding another eggshell more than two years after the original find were nonexistent. He had no idea where they would look, and he was getting no assistance from Wilton Froman, the erstwhile ornithologist who stood to the side staring absently into the upper branches of a sickly looking pine. Sean turned and strode to Froman as Harper shrugged and started moving around the clearing in search of nothing in particular.

"Mr. Froman," Sean whispered to the birdman. "Can you help us here? Do you see anything that would indicate a wild condor might have nested here?" Sean waved his hand over the clearing.

"As I told the people at the Sierra Club, Mr. Donovan," he started in his tight, high-pitched nasal voice, "I am not an expert on condors. My knowledge of them is more general."

Sean lost contact with the man's voice at that moment even as Froman babbled on. Sean was stunned at the blunder of the trip without proper preparation, and a rush of concern over his failure struck him. His stomach lurched. He bit down hard to regain control.

"... caves, rather than the open spaces we see here," Froman finished with a nod as if to punctuate his last point.

Sean came back to himself at the mention of caves.

"What was that, Mr. Froman?" he asked. "What was your last statement about caves?"

Froman looked at him quizzically. "You mean about nesting in caves?"

Sean nodded.

"Something I do know about condors is that they typically nest in caves rather than open spaces like we see here. You see, many birds nest in trees, like that pine there." He pointed to a sickly, sparsely branched tree near the cliff edge. There were virtually no branches for the first six or seven feet of its height, and then sporadic stumps measuring anywhere from two to four feet in length protruded amidst other branches sporting the tree's namesake pine needles all the way to the top.

"You'll often find the nests of birds in such trees, but I would venture to guess they wouldn't hold a condor nest. They want something enclosed and already made up," he concluded.

"Of course," Sean thought as he turned back to Curtis and Dunne. They were conversing softly with their Forest Service cohort. Sean eyed the rock wall looming above him and saw immediately that it appeared solid, no cave-like openings anywhere on its face. He then strode past Dunne and Curtis to the edge of the clearing. He leaned over to view the rock face beneath them. The wind, which was ruffling the few trees atop the clearing, blew a gust that gave Sean a slight lift as it bounced off the granite face and burst up the wall. He backed off to stabilize his footing and then stretched out for another look.

"There has to be a cave somewhere here," he thought.

He saw nothing as he squinted to protect his eyes from the increasing force of the wind.

"Storm's comin," Carter Logan shouted from behind Sean.

He turned to see Logan pointing northward, his eyes wide. He followed Logan's gaze. The monstrous black clouds that had been lurking behind the northern peaks were finally pouring into the valley. They carried black curtains that fell to the valley floor and obliterated all over which they passed, and they came on powerful winds that were buffeting all before them.

"Let's get back to the hut," Logan shouted, suddenly frantic as the storm bore down on them with increasing speed and fury.

Sean's first instinct was to argue the point. He'd figured it out. He knew where Buck found the shell. They were rock climbing and found the nest somewhere down the side of this cliff. They'd found a cave during the climb. He was sure of it. It was conceivable that Curtis lied about where he and Buck discussed the shell and that they weren't even in the general vicinity of the find. But, despite Curtis's reticence and Matthew Dunne's clear attempts to obfuscate, Sean didn't believe it was all a lie. The shell was found somewhere in the area, which meant there was a nest nearby. He remembered reading condors tended to reuse nests, especially if they were in protected caves. He needed to find that cave, but it wouldn't be this day.

The wind began to howl as it picked up momentum, and suddenly all thought of staying out in the open disappeared.

"Move it, fellas," Logan shouted.

In seconds, everyone was running as Logan guided them over jagged granite through mounds of snow.

"This one's big," he shouted again.

THIRTY-NINE

WIND POUNDED THE WARMING hut for hours. The adventurers huddled with their respective teammates in the close quarters, heated uncomfortably by the black, iron, pot-bellied stove. There was little interaction between the sides because of Matthew Dunne's adamant strictures. The only activities besides listening to the thunderous storm and occasional dozing was reading, in the case of Wilton Froman who pored over a bird book, and card playing by Sean, Harper, Logan, and Wuller. Curtis sat quietly with his attorney, neither appearing interested in speaking.

By late afternoon, the wind abated, and the storm calmed. Everyone was beyond bored, most dozing awkwardly in sitting positions against whatever wall was available. The room stank of body odors and closed-in stuffiness. Sean stood, stretched his stiffening muscles, and made his way to the door, where he threw on his jacket and exited the hut.

Outside, snow fell straight down in a shimmering curtain of soft flakes. It was yet another wonder Sean had never witnessed. Even on the occasional family ski trips, he never saw such volume and the immediate effect of covering everything it touched with a whiteness as pure as crystal. He stepped to a wooden bench built into the hut's outside wall beneath the overhang, brushed off the snow, and sat down. The air was cold, biting into the lining of his nostrils. He withdrew a scarf from his pocket, wrapped it around his nose and mouth, and huddled there quietly, deep in thought.

His initial thoughts were of the plan to wait out the storm, delay their departure, and get back to find the cave. Whether it would contain any other shell fragments was academic. What he needed was to find it, and then he'd figure out what would come next. After a time in the calm of the cold air, his mind wandered—to Carla, to Johnny and Marie, and to his life—how he'd come to this place and where he would go from here, and surprisingly he was at peace. He wondered if the peace came from the complete silence that cocooned him or if he truly was on a path to the happiness he once believed he had. While lost in such thoughts, the snowfall slowed to occasional flakes, and the hut's door opened next to him. He glanced up to see Curtis Golden emerge, zippered up and looking down at Sean.

"You mind if I join you?" Curtis asked.

"Is your watchdog okay with that?" Sean asked, head-motioning into the cabin.

"He's snoring away," Curtis smiled. "He's a pain in the ass."

Sean nodded and slid over on the bench to make a space. Curtis sat and leaned his head back against the wall.

"What happened to you, Sean?" Curtis asked.

Sean looked at him, surprised at his boldness after such distance on the rest of the trip.

"You were Dad's favorite at the firm," Curtis continued. "He thought you were going to be a great attorney. He was disappointed when all that went down for you."

Sean nodded, his heart sinking at the memory of the pain and anger he'd experienced.

"It was tough, Curtis," he started and then, not feeling the need to explain anything, said, "but that's over now. I'm back at it and actually starting to enjoy my small practice."

Curtis nodded, seemed to want to say something more, but Sean interjected.

"How's your dad?" he asked.

Curtis hesitated, didn't look at Sean.

"This case is tough on him ... on all of us," he shook his head and leaned forward, propping his elbows on his knees. "You know me, Sean. This is my place," waving out to the snow and trees. "I love this. All we want to do is build something that others who love this can enjoy. The skiing and hiking are incredible here."

Sean didn't answer. He didn't want to get into the issues in the case.

Curtis dropped his head.

"If we don't get this thing resolved now, it'll kill him," Curtis mumbled. "His heart can't take any more."

Again Sean said nothing, as Curtis seemed intent on trying to unload some great weight. Sean listened and began to understand at least some of the brooding he'd witnessed on the trip. He would have thought the trip would be a thing of cheer for the very reason that this was Curtis's element. He lived for the outdoors and the wonders of nature and its beauty. He knew Curtis's motivations for the development were to share the Silver Lode with the world rather than for the money, but there was so much more involved, so many more considerations. But that discussion was not for now. That, unfortunately, was better left to the courtroom.

Curtis turned to him.

"Do you get out to the snow much?" he asked.

"No," Sean smiled. "It's damn cold!" He faked a shiver. "It's growing on me, though."

Curtis smiled.

"How about you? Are you still getting out a lot?" Sean asked.

"As often as I can. Business gets in the way, but I try to get out for a few ski trips during the winter and hiking trips the rest of the year."

"Are you still doing any rock climbing?"

Curtis turned and eyed Sean, who silently berated himself for the question outside Dunne's presence. Yet he had to know. Curtis's look was quizzical before he smiled and nodded.

"I am," he said. "There's some great rock climbing here." He turned away and stared into the white expanse.

"I think Carter's about to cook up some dinner for us," Curtis continued. "We should get inside."

"I'll catch up with you," Sean nodded.

When Curtis stepped back into the hut, Sean leaned back against the wall. His eyes roamed the clearing. The snowfall had stopped. Overhead, the clouds had thinned, and patches of a blackening sky pocked with stars and moon-glow lit the night.

"Amazing," Sean thought. "One minute we're in fear for our lives, and the next we're at peace in this winter wonderland." He smiled at the thought of the Christmas tune before he rose to follow Curtis. And then he saw it again.

It was just a glimpse, but he knew it was the bird. He scanned the sky urgently but saw nothing. Clouds scudded slowly across his canvas until the moon re-appeared. It hung full in the eastern sky behind wisps of cloud that slipped slowly past to give it open sky, if only for a moment, before it disappeared again behind another cloud. But it was in that moment that he saw it again.

The bird soared, on widespread wings, across the moon's face. It canted to the right, exposing its distinctive white under markings against the black of its powerful wings before it turned into a gliding descent toward Sean. Then, not fifty feet away, it turned sharply and disappeared to his left, toward the cliffs upon which they'd stood hours before. He was stunned. No matter how much he'd hoped for just such an occurrence, he didn't believe he would get it.

It's what Buck had found: the biggest bird anyone had ever seen.

What Sean didn't realize was that another pair of eyes had also seen the massive creature.

Sean waited until everyone was asleep. He'd placed his sleeping bag close to the door so he would have fewer bodies over which to step. He hadn't even dozed as he wrestled with whether he was insane to even consider the action he would take. But he had no choice.

Over a meal of bacon and potatoes, Carter Logan announced that they would be leaving the next day.

"Bitty said the big one's coming in tomorrow night. It looks to be a full-blown blizzard. We best be out of the valley before it hits. They're expecting the last wave of this one we saw today to kick up sometime tonight and end before noon. That's when we'll get moving. If we push hard, we'll get out of the Silver Lode before dark."

Andrew Harper protested the decision. He and Sean decided earlier that they needed to extend the trip if they were to have any chance of finding evidence that would help their case. If there was a wild condor in the valley and this was the place where Buck and Curtis had discussed the shell, there had to be a nest nearby. They suspected it was over the edge of the cliff, down the rock wall above which they'd stood. They had no idea how they'd get to it, but they needed to try. Although Harper was in favor of the extended stay and further search, his support was shaky. His fear of nature's vagaries had become more apparent as the trip proceeded, and it was clear his heart wasn't totally into his protest of Logan's order.

"You're my responsibility," Logan stated firmly. "We can't get caught up here in a blizzard. They last for weeks, and none of us is prepared. We leave as soon as it's clear tomorrow."

Sean hadn't told anyone about the massive bird. He'd intended to discuss it with Harper and Froman so they could work on a plan for the next day. But that idea was dashed at dinner. There was no arguing with Carter Logan. There would be no plan for the next day other than to get out of the Silver Lode as quickly as possible. As they prepared for sleep, Sean thought about talking to Harper, but it was clear Harper had given up. He was prepared to leave, and, like the rest of the Sierra Club hierarchy, he was prepared to give up on the case. There was no way he could enlist Harper's aid in what he was planning.

———

Sean slipped his arms into his jacket and sat up. He listened to the snores, grunts, and flatulence of his companions until he was satisfied all were asleep. With a flashlight tucked into his pocket, he lifted his boots and stood slowly. No one moved. Without a sound, he opened the door and slipped out quickly, before the frigid air could overrun the room.

Against the far wall, eyes that had been watching Sean forced their body up and after him.

As he emerged from the hut, intermittent shafts of the moon's glow provided Sean a guiding light to the path they'd traversed earlier. Clouds from the north were quickening on a rising wind to snuff out the light, but at least in the early going only smaller cloud clusters ran intermittently across its face. When light disappeared, the flashlight paved his way. When he finally stood in the clearing breathing relief that he hadn't gotten lost, the moon-glow was gone completely, and the wind blew with renewed ferocity. He was frozen in place in the pitch black, the only light now being the funnel from his flashlight. He should turn back, he thought. This is stupid. People die in weather ... and then the moon shown again. He glanced up and saw the cloud break—not a large one, but enough, he hoped, to take a look.

He stepped gingerly to the pine tree at the edge of the cliff. He gripped a long thin branch that fell from a point some eight feet above the ground to his waist. He leaned out into the wind and shone his flashlight over the side.

He saw them immediately. His stomach lurched with shock and excitement. He almost swooned but held on to the branch and stared.

Perched on a ledge thirty feet down were two creatures illuminated by the soft white of the moon and then by the beam of Sean's hand torch. The heads of both creatures swiveled up at the touch of Sean's light. Black eyes stared at him from wrinkled bald heads. After several seconds, one of the heads swiveled back. The creature spread its massive wings and pushed off into the wind that crashed against the rock. It lifted the bird toward Sean.

Sean pulled back, reached into his pocket, and withdrew a camera. He prayed the light would hold, and suddenly the creature was in front of him. On wings that measured twelve feet from tip to tip, the creature rose before him in a wide circle that brought it closer as he aimed his camera.

So immersed was he in the majesty of the prehistoric creature that his brain didn't register the footsteps that rushed up from behind. By the time it did, it was only for an instant, and it was too late. He turned as a tickle of fear scuttled up his spine. Something's coming. He turned sharply but caught only a glimpse before he felt the force of a mighty shove that sent him flailing over the cliff. He clawed air, desperately seeking purchase, and his eyes bugged out when he saw there was nothing to grab. He fell, flipped, tried to scream, and knew in an instant of absolute clarity that his next breath would be his last.

FORTY

THE FREAK STORM THAT had stranded motorists on the Grapevine nearly three weeks earlier had unusual effects on the slopes of the Silver Lode. Because the snow from that storm was relatively light and of short duration, that which stuck to the slopes during subsequent warming and freezing formed a thin layer of base that turned to snow crystals. These crystals were never intended to hold together, but rather they became a sugary, grainy powder upon which the recent storms dumped large, heavy loads. In the vernacular of the U.S. Forest Service Avalanche Center, these conditions created a precarious snowpack. It was as if a brick had been placed on a steep slope atop a thin layer of corn flakes; it would slide with any sudden jolt or wind.

When Curtis Golden stepped out of the warming hut before dawn the next morning, he was shaken. He walked alone in the swirling wind, away from the hut in the direction of the flat where he and Buck had discussed the eggshell two years before. He castigated himself for the evil he had done, and to what end? He tried to convince himself his efforts were for his father. He knew Atticus couldn't take it. It had to end, and it had to end now. There could be no more delays. Any delays would kill the old man. Curtis couldn't be the cause of that. Yet, he couldn't believe he'd sacrificed his soul, even if it was to save his father.

The ground beneath Curtis shook with a sudden jolt. It was as if some great crack had suddenly opened in the earth. It came from deep inside the rock at his feet, and it unbalanced him for a second. He glanced down and then up the steep slope above him. He saw the break immediately. It ran across the top of the snowpack, a squiggly cut along its entire length, spewing snow dust up into the bracing wind. An instant later it started its descent. Curtis's eyes opened wide. How could he have missed the signs? He turned, frantic to find safety, but realized he had nowhere to go. He could not outrun it even if a safe place was near. He flipped the switch on the PBL at his waist and turned back to face it, a wave of cascading snow that took him without resistance, thundered down the slope, and over the cliff.

Inside the warming hut, the roar was deafening. Logan understood immediately.

"Avalanche!" he shouted into the satellite phone to his wife. "We're going to need some help here, babe. She's coming down!"

Everyone in the hut gawked wide-eyed at the guide, who leapt to his feet and stared at the back wall of the hut. He knew it would hit there.

"Under the table!" he shouted. "Get under the damn table—brace yourselves and hold it steady!"

They jumped at his command, terror written on their faces.

The enormous weight of the snow struck the back wall with a force that sheered the structure off its foundation, drove its front line into the earth and rock beyond, and crushed it onto the massive oak table beneath which they cowered.

The rumbling rage of the snow's mad charge over the cliff continued for seconds that seemed like an eternity before a deep silence suddenly fell.

Outside the crushed structure, the avalanche left a wide swath of thick snow through which sharp rocks, massive boulders, and skeletal limbs—the detritus of its deadly slide—protruded. Just beyond the swath's eastern line, the lean-to stood untouched, while the stabled, wild-eyed horses stomped and pawed the ground frantically. Only Samson stood outside the structure, slightly up the slope, far out of reach of the deadly slide.

From her satellite radio at the ranch, Bitty was frantic trying to reach Carter. She'd called in the avalanche immediately after her husband's plea and then started trying to raise him again, but she had no luck.

Rangers based out of the Arrow Gulch Ranger Station mobilized as soon as Bitty called. Her information was concise and specific. Carter Logan had taken a group of six men into the Silver Lode; only one was a seasoned backcountry adventurer. They stayed at Golden Two one night and were hiking and exploring around the West Bench Warming Hut when the first part of the storm struck earlier in the day. Bitty's information was that all except two of the party were in or around the hut when the mountain came down. She had no information about the two missing members of the group. They all carried PBL's.

"God dammit, Carter, talk to me. Are you there?" she shouted into the mouthpiece, frustrated and tear-streaked as she imagined her husband crushed under the horrific weight.

She waited for a response and then tried again … and again … to no avail. She dropped her head, said a silent prayer, and gritted her teeth in determination as she raised her head to try for the hundredth time. He had to be alive. It couldn't end this way. Carter knew how …

Static and a crack announced his return.

"Bitty … Bitty," he said, sounding breathless and strained. "I'm here, babe."

"Carter, are you okay?" She stood and stared at the console as if she'd be able to see her husband's face, a wary grin of relief spreading across her own.

"I'm here!" he hesitated. "Damn … I'm okay. Looks like we're all okay … some injuries, but okay …"

Bitty was thrilled.

"… help coming?" Carter asked.

"They're on their way, honey. You hold tight. Search and Rescue's coming. Are you all still in the cabin?"

"It's cramped … hut collapsed … we're here, under the table. Goddam oak … strong shit …" he mumbled.

Bitty's smile broadened.

"I'll call it in Carter … I'll be right back."

Bitty switched to the emergency frequency, immediately got dispatch, and relayed the information that a group was still in the hut. They had gotten under an oak table as the hut collapsed around them. The dispatcher said a helicopter was already in the air and on its way. Bitty gave her Carter's number so the rescue team could communicate with him directly.

"They're on their way, Carter," she said. "They'll call you. If you don't hear from 'em in a minute, call me back. Stay safe," she begged.

"We're good. See you shortly, babe."

Bitty signed off to open the line.

───────────

Backcountry rangers in the Sierra Nevada's were a motley crew of part-time adventurers who offered their services for a pittance because that was the life they loved. They were former engineers, teachers, photographers, writers, ski instructors, winter guides, academics, military veterans, pacifists, and others who weren't official rangers with the uniforms of the National Park Service but were devoted to the life of the wilderness. They were "temps" —seasonal hires who were often more permanent than the full-time park service employees. For the most part, they were long-time veterans of the wilderness, and despite the look of misfits, they were the finest wilderness search and rescue professionals in the world.

As soon as the rangers obtained Carter's number, they made contact with him and held it the entire flight to the West Bench Warming Hut. Bitty was able to listen in on the call the entire time. Twenty minutes after they first spoke to Carter, their helicopter was hovering above the clearing in which the warming hut once stood. All that was left of the hut was two feet of roof that poked out of the debris path and tilted and twisted awkwardly. Unable to put down near the hut because of the wind and the unstable snow pack, the copter winched down four rescuers and equipment at the hut and then maneuvered toward the flat rock about a quarter mile west of it. It was able to land there, and two other rescuers joined the first group.

It took only an hour to open up an air path to those trapped inside the crumpled hut but another five hours to get them out and onto the chopper. By then the wind had picked up and was whipping snow off the rocks in stinging gusts. Overhead clouds churned and forced a decision upon the rescuers.

"Who's left?" shouted Dave Guildenstern above the wind. He was tall and angular with a heavy dark beard and thick hair that joined his goggles to cover all other features. He was the leader of the squad.

"Curtis Golden and Sean Donovan," shouted Carter Logan as he cradled a broken arm, now stabilized in a sling. "They were gone when we woke this morning."

Guildenstern nodded gravely. He glanced up into the blackening sky and then back to the broken and infirm travelers in the chopper. Except for Logan's arm, most of the injuries were simple scrapes and contusions, although one had suffered a broken leg and possibly a broken rib and a third was contending with a serious wound in his lower back. Guildenstern shook his head knowing he had no choice but to get the five he currently had to safety before the storm struck with its full force. He considered leaving two of his people behind to search for the two missing hikers, but another glance at the black clouds rushing in from the north convinced him otherwise. The storm promised to be deadly. He couldn't subject any of them to the risk.

"We've got to get you out of here," he shouted at Logan as he took Carter's good arm and assisted him onto the chopper. "We'll have to come back when this clears to get the animals and the others."

There was no objection.

The copter was like a pendulum swinging out of control in the buffeting wind as it lifted off the shelf. Brushing tree tops and nearly scraping treacherous rock faces, the pilot was finally airborne and able to fight off the storm's pockets of wind sheer to climb up out of the Silver Lode to relative safety west of the range.

FORTY-ONE

"THEY LEFT HIM UP there?" Atticus shouted with incredulity. "They left Curtis?"

John Golden nodded into the phone, grim faced, scared for his father, but determined.

"I've got our rescue guys loading up now, Dad. We'll find him," John said. "As soon as we can get the information from the rangers our guys will be in the air."

It was just before midnight. The rangers had gotten the survivors to a hospital in Sacramento by early evening, but it wasn't until eleven o'clock that Bitty was able to talk to John Golden at the number given by Curtis as his emergency contact. He immediately called his brothers to get them over to Atticus's house. He then called his father.

Atticus stood in stunned silence, his heart thumping too fast and lightheadedness coming upon him. He gripped the telephone table with his left hand and teetered for a moment before he plopped down into the chair next to the table.

"Dad," John called anxiously. "Dad … are you okay?" He wanted to tell his dad in person but had too much to do to get his rescue crew moving. He'd hoped Will and Sandy would be there when he placed the call, but they hadn't arrived yet.

When Atticus didn't respond, John became frantic.

"Dad! Talk to me!"

"I'm here, son," Atticus finally mumbled. He rested his forehead in his free hand and tried to gain control. "Why are they waiting?"

At that moment, Will and Sandy stepped into the room. Atticus didn't look up. The boys moved to their father, Sandy sitting in a chair across from him and Will standing next to him, a reassuring hand placed on his slumped shoulder.

"There's a storm raging up there, Dad," John said. "The rangers won't give us the coordinates of the slide. We don't know where it happened."

Atticus lifted his blood-shot eyes and drawn face to Sandy. His son nodded encouragement as Atticus struggled to remember the itinerary. He turned to his youngest.

"Where were they going, Will?" he asked.

Will glanced at Sandy for assistance as his mind raced to recall the plan he and his brothers had agreed upon.

"I think they're at the West Bench Warming Hut," he said and nodded to Sandy for confirmation. Sandy nodded.

"The West Bench Warming Hut?" Atticus asked into the telephone.

"It could be," John responded hesitantly. "They were supposed to be there the second night." He paused for a moment. "That's got to be it."

"Get them up there, son," Atticus said flatly. "Bring Curtis home."

"We will, Dad. Is Sandy there?"

Atticus nodded. "Right here." He handed the phone to Sandy and turned to Will, threw an arm around his son.

"John, we're here. Are you sending them up?" Sandy asked.

"Yeah. Is Dad okay?" Sandy nodded and grunted a yes. "Stay with him. I'll keep you posted." Sandy nodded again with a look of firm conviction despite the crack he heard in his older brother's voice.

"We'll be here," he said.

Carla held Mary as they anxiously awaited word. Mary called just after midnight, frantic with the shocking news. Carla drove to her house in a fog of contradictory thoughts. They'd find him, wouldn't they? They were with a guide who knew the area, and Sean assured them it was safe. Sean couldn't be dead. Surely he was somewhere safe. They'd find him—they had to. And then the doubts: how could anyone survive an avalanche? How could anyone survive the frigid storm that was pounding the mountains? People survived such things. She'd read about them. But it had always been when rescue workers were immediately on the scene. Why weren't they back up there?

It wasn't until nearly four hours after she first hugged Mary that they received any word. By then the tears had dried, but their eyes were streaked blood-shot and drooping with worry and lack of sleep. Coffee percolated in the kitchen, and they sat in silence wringing their hands and assuring each other that Sean was alright. They'd tried to contact the rangers but received only minimal news: they're going up again since the storm seems to be letting up; the storm's bad, but we've got men on the ground; we're following a PBL; we'll call you when we have news.

The phone's bell tone was shrill to their caffeine-addled senses. They both jumped. Mary answered.

"We haven't found your son yet, Mrs. Donovan, but I wanted to let you know two things: first that the storm is letting up. It's making it easier to search. We have a dozen searchers on the ground. The second thing is that we've located a second beacon. We weren't seeing it in the beginning, but we now have a lock on it. One of them is Sean's."

"Does that mean he's alive?" Mary asked anxiously, daring to have hope.

The caller hesitated.

"We don't know ... It tells us the beacon was activated, and we can follow the signal and find him. We can't tell anything else right now," she said, the tone of her voice dropping from hope to sadness. "I'm sorry I can't give you more, Mrs. Donovan ... We'll find him."

———————

Richard Wolf didn't hear about the disaster until 8:30 the next morning. Vanessa informed him upon his arrival that Bitty Logan called saying an avalanche struck the previous morning and that Matt was apparently recovering in a hospital in Sacramento. He instructed Vanessa to get Matt's room.

"How you doing, Matt?" Wolf asked, concern touching his tone.

"Good, Richard. I'm okay," Dunne responded.

"Are you okay to talk?"

"Sure," Dunne's voice sounded tired.

"What happened up there?"

"The mountain came down on us. I've never heard anything like it," he stammered. "The sound was deafening—like the earth was breaking open under us."

Wolf listened, trying to be patient.

"Was anyone hurt?" he asked.

"A broken arm for our guide, and one of the others broke something, too. I ... I got stabbed through the lower back ... It just missed my liver and spleen ... I got thirty stitches."

"Are you okay," Wolf asked rather than getting to the real question. "What did the doctors say?"

"I'll be okay. Thanks," Dunne said, happy his mentor was interested in his welfare.

There was silence for several seconds before Wolf again spoke.

"Did they find anything?"

Dunne didn't understand for a moment, and then he smiled.

"No," he grimaced through a shot of pain.

Wolf smiled.

"Richard ... they're gone," Dunne said softly.

"What's that? Who's gone?"

"Donovan ... and Curtis."

"What do you mean?"

"They're dead. Both of them," he said hesitantly. "They were out in the open during the avalanche. They've been buried for more than twenty-four hours. The rangers are searching, but they haven't found the bodies yet."

Wolf stared hard at the telephone. He couldn't believe what he was hearing. He understood the effect the loss of Curtis would have on Atticus. He also knew he would be able to deal with the old man. He'd be able to convince him to soldier on in the memory of his son who gave his life for the most spectacular ski development the world would ever know. Although he didn't know exactly what impact Donovan's death would have, he believed it was one about which he would not have to worry.

A smile spread slowly across his face.

"You get back to us quickly, Matt. You've done well," he said to the appreciative young man on the other end of the line.

FORTY-TWO

THE FALL CRUSHED HIS stomach and lungs, forcing his last air out in a gust of panic and wide-eyed dread before he lost consciousness. He lay in a heap of bruises, breaks, and blood, teetering precariously at the edge of the stone perch where only seconds before he'd seen the condors.

When he went over the cliff, the surging storm's powerful wind buoyed him before it smashed him against the cliff's granite face. Its lift and violent force slowed his descent, his body skidding and scraping along the jagged rock to the condors' perch. He bounced in an agonizing crush, flipped, and came to rest at the edge. He teetered at that edge, one wind gust from another fall, this one to his death a hundred feet below.

Sean woke to wind-whipped ice crystals against his exposed face and a strange pressure at his left arm. It felt like something poking him, something firm and sharp through the thickness of his jacket. He was on his stomach, his head covered by his hood and his face turned away from the poking pressure into the ferocious wind. His right arm dangled over the side, his left was splayed out behind him. Pain drummed his brain as he tried to find focus. Understanding came slowly.

The only parts of him that moved were his eyes, which grew wide, despite the pelting snow and ice, as he realized where he lay and that he was not dead. He breathed in quick gasps, belabored by pains in his torso, and he closed his eyes to calm himself, somehow knowing calm was necessary for him to survive.

It was a sudden pull and a tearing pain that finally forced him to lift and turn his head. The movement jarred him as blood surged in waves of agony to his battered limbs, but the sight that confronted him made him forget the pain. The creature pulled back, stunned at Sean's movement, its wings spread cautiously as if ready for escape, yet its head cocked down eyeing him closely.

"A condor," he thought through the cobwebs he was struggling to clear.

He laid his head down again, this time with his right cheek pressed against icy stone. "Don't move. Don't scare it away. This is evidence," he thought in his fractured state.

The fact he had no means of preserving the evidence because his camera lay at the bottom of the gorge didn't strike him; all he knew was he shouldn't scare it away ... until his next thought struck him. He realized the painful pull and tear he'd felt seconds before was from this bird. The creature tore at his jacket to get at the flesh inside. It had torn through with its sharp beak and gashed his flesh, which, he knew without looking, bled tantalizingly.

The bird slowly pulled its wings back into itself. It dipped its bald head to stare at Sean's now exposed face, and it took a short hop toward him. The bile rose in him with a vision of himself being consumed by the creature, and he started to retch in a spasm of disgust and fear. The movement sent the condor back again, and when Sean suddenly pushed himself away from the edge, the bird jumped, ran with wings opening, and pushed off into the swirling blackness.

Sean rose gingerly. Pain and weakness in both arms restricted his movement, but it was from his side that the most excruciating pain came. It stabbed him, and he screamed into the howling wind. He maneuvered himself to relieve the pressure of the broken rib. Finally, he sat back against the rock wall and drew deeply of the frigid air to squelch the tears and nausea of pain. The cold bit at him but slowly cleared his mind, and he opened his eyes again, squinting to protect them from the storm.

He wondered how long he'd been lying there, but only for a second as he recognized the numbness of the bitter cold spreading up his battered frame. He glanced skyward, saw only darkness, and then felt warmth—the numbing warmth of his body freezing, he thought. Or was it real, from some magical source in the midst of a blizzard? It seemed to be coming from his left. He turned, grimacing with the stab of pain from his rib, but understanding as long as he still felt something, he was not frozen.

Next to him was an opening, just short of three feet high, and wide enough for his body to access. He couldn't tell how deep the opening was but it struck him it was at least deep enough to hold the nest from which the condor had emerged.

He rolled carefully to his left side, flinching spastically until he could find comfort by stretching his right side. He pulled himself to the opening, peered inside at the pitch-black void, and was struck with the sulfuric odor of the warmth he had indeed been feeling. He pushed himself up onto his hands and knees, careful with his side, and crawled inside until he saw the first glow of light. Immediately inside the tiny cave, his hands felt tree branches, leaves and feathers strewn about the stone floor. To the left across hard packed earth he saw a faint orange glow squeezing through a fissure in the wall.

He crawled to the fissure, put his face up close. The stench was horrific, but the warmth sent shivers up his spine and throbbing pain to his freezing extremities. Soon, the life-giving warmth of a magma pool encased in the mountain enveloped him. He closed his eyes, turned away from the stench, and screamed with the motion as a convulsion of pain took him into oblivion again.

He woke before dawn, crumpled within the cave's warmth, awakened by the purposeful rustle of feathers and grunts of challenge inside the cave. He lay on his side and dared not move lest the agony that put him out hours before return. But as images of himself as the main course at a feral feast ran through his mind, he jerked up suddenly. The creature turned and scampered from the cave while Sean grimaced and clutched his side. He pushed himself up slowly into a sitting position.

He couldn't see outside the cave, so he couldn't tell if the bird had flown. He was back and to the side of the cave's opening, out of its direct line, but he hadn't heard the frantic unfurling of wings, and he hoped it was just outside. He listened intently until he heard grunts over the wind. It sounded like more than one bird communicating how best to deal with their intruder.

Sean leaned his head back, pain continuing to pierce his body. He gritted his teeth and squeezed his hand into a fist to grab his jacket at his ribs. He felt something hard in the pocket within. The pain subsided slowly, and as it did, he thought about the object his hand held through the fabric.

He realized with a surge of sudden hope that it was his cell phone.

He unzipped gingerly, reached inside the pocket, and withdrew the device. He'd brought it along in hopes of communicating with Carla, but it hadn't worked in the circle of the mountains. He'd made sure it still had a charge at Golden Two with the hope, despite Carter Logan's assurances otherwise, that as they ascended the slope to the warming hut he would be able to pick up a signal. He'd had no luck, so he'd shut it down to preserve its battery.

Sean flipped open the phone and pushed the start button. Instantly, the Razr's light bathed his narrow confines in its dull white glow. He waited impatiently for the phone to go through its startup routine and then was met by the flash of "no signal." He closed his eyes in frustration and flipped the phone shut. How could he get word to someone? Fear nipped at him as the faint hope he'd felt only moments before disappeared. They'd never know—at least not until it was too late for him. His mind moved toward uncontrollable fear of the dizzying impossibilities of his situation until he closed his eyes and tried to take hold of himself again. He did so only when his thoughts turned to dark anger at the one who had put him in this predicament.

Sean knew who did it. He'd seen him. He'd turned just in time to see the face of the man who pushed him. As he recreated the scene in his mind, he wondered how he'd known, how he'd followed Sean without Sean noticing, and how he could bring himself to do what he had. How could a man who was once undoubtedly so steeped in idealism step to the edge of evil and then cross the line to commit murder for a cause he probably didn't even fully believe in? Was it concern for someone else, or was it something more? Was it something dark inside the man, an evil that lurked there all the time? Was it an evil that lurked in every man? Was it an evil that lurked in Sean and only needed the anger he now felt to cut it loose?

The enormous orange/red head of a giant condor pushed through the cave opening followed by a body that dwarfed that of the one who'd been poking Sean the previous evening. From behind the bird, the faint grey light of a rising sun through heavy overcast filtered into the cave, and the sound of the wind's fury grew muffled behind the bird's feathered body.

Sean's head rolled to his left shoulder along the back wall. He eyed the massive creature just four feet away from him. Although he understood condors were not predators—that they were scavengers who feasted only on carrion, and that they were timid creatures in proximity to the living—fear again ran down his spine. The close quarters with his path to freedom blocked by a monstrously ugly creature that stared menacingly at him spawned a tide of claustrophobia that Sean fought with clenched teeth, eyes, and fists. The bird did not advance. It simply stood there, unmoving, staring through the dim light. Sean began to breathe easier. He stared back at the bird, making no sudden moves, and then understanding suddenly that Buck Anderson had indeed been murdered.

Buck had found this very cave. He'd found the empty shell in the very nest over which Sean crawled the evening before. Buck had known they were condors but couldn't prove it without the lab tests that proved it beyond doubt. But he'd wanted more, something that would be irrefutable to a finder of fact, something that could be held so the truth would be known without doubt rather than simply believed on the faith of his testimony. Buck came back to get that evidence, but he'd been killed before he could deliver it. He hadn't just died. He'd been murdered so the knowledge he'd acquired would never be revealed. Buck found the evidence to save the Silver Lode, but he died before he was able to reveal it.

Sean leaned back and closed his eyes to lament his predicament. He'd seen what Buck saw, and, like Buck, he would die with the knowledge and no one would ever be the wiser for it.

When he heard the bird ruffle its feathers, he looked at it again. The massive creature appeared to have stepped closer. He would have liked to have a camera. That way, if his remains ever were found, picked clean by his host and its family, some evidence would exist. But he had no camera. He'd lost it in the fall, and it now lay at the bottom of the gorge.

Then he remembered the cell phone.

It was gripped tightly in his right hand on his lap. The phone had a camera. Patty had showed him once how to use it. Did he remember?

He flipped the phone open, again releasing its wan light. The condor jumped, its wings flared out, and it crouched, waiting to make its next move. Sean held steady until its wings again came back to the body and it rose out of its crouch. He dipped his head to view the phone's open face and saw the "camera" designation at the lower left corner of its screen. He pushed the button with his thumb and then lifted it until he could see the bird's shadowed shape on the screen. He centered it and pushed the "capture" button. A flash caught the bird in full color, and its wings spread instantly in the cramped quarters. Sean depressed the button again and another flash sent the bird scurrying out of the cave.

Sean levered himself with pulling hands and pushing feet from his seated position to a point in line with the cave opening. He saw three birds, the other two much smaller than the first. They eyed the interior with their backs to the steel grey world of winter and wind-whipped snow. Sean lifted the phone again and snapped a photo and then another before the birds looked up as the earth and rock beneath Sean suddenly trembled.

As one, the birds pushed off from their perch and disappeared. Sean gripped the ground on either side and waited in silence. There was nothing for several seconds, and then, without warning, came the roar. He covered his ears and looked frantically to his right expecting to see molten rock spewing into his cavern. But there was no lava, only the crushing roar, which shook his cave as by the pounding of heavy machinery. And then suddenly a cascade of snow and ice came down in front of him, across the face of the cave. It tumbled over itself desperate to reach the gorge's floor, piling up outside his cave, a mass that covered its face and left him trapped.

———

From the first shake of the earth until silence again reigned only seconds elapsed, yet the fear that gripped Sean in a world in which he had no control made it forever. His body quaked with panic that the cave would fall in on him, that it would crush him beneath the weight of the entire mountain. His head ached from the strain, and his side was merciless as he waited for his end, an end he almost wished for as doubt that he would ever escape this place overwhelmed him. But the end didn't come.

Hours passed, hours during which he listened and waited; yet nothing happened. His confinement was solitary behind the ice wall, the only light coming from the orange glow from the fissure in the cave and the occasional white from the phone he opened to remind himself he was alive. He dared not approach the ice wall lest one touch destabilize the fabric of the mountain's support and complete the task the murderer had started the night before.

Outside, the storm raged. It was silent for a time after the avalanche, but the wind picked up gradually. And now, from beyond the wall of ice that entombed him, he could hear its fury.

Sean talked to himself, trying to maintain sanity and fight off the despair that nipped at him. He dared not move for fear of the pain that lanced through him at each motion. Although he was grateful for the warmth of his sanctuary, he wondered why he still lived in a place where no relief could come and from where his wounds and the elements would prevent his escape.

It wasn't until the drumbeat in his head and the rumble of his stomach reminded him of his hunger and thirst that he resolved he had to do something. He couldn't sit there and wait to die. It would be better to finish the murderer's task and crash through the ice wall than to die of starvation and deprivation in this icy tomb.

He gritted his teeth, rolled to his knees, and started to crawl toward the ice wall. The first forward motion of arm and knee shook something loose from a fold of his open jacket, and it clattered to the floor of the cave.

He looked down but saw nothing until he again opened his cell phone and noticed his PLB lying at his right knee. Shock at the find was immediately supplanted by hope. He reached for the device, kneeled back on his heels, and pulled it to his face and the dim light from the phone. He tried to remember what Bitty had said about its use.

"It's made of some unbreakable polymer," she'd said, "so it won't break even it you fall on it. You gotta remember to activate it though. Try to be somewhere out in the open so's the signal can get up to the satellites. You undo the antennae like this." She grabbed the flat stainless steel antennae wrapped around the device's edge, slipped it off, and extended it to its full length. "And then you push the buttons. It'll send a signal that'll locate you within a hundred yards. Stay alert for rescue once you activate it."

As simple as that, Sean thought. He did exactly that, expecting some light to appear on the face of the device, but none did. Had he broken it after all with the fall ... or was it the cave? Did he need to get out of the cave so the satellite could pick it up?

He maneuvered the antennae and pressed the button again, keeping his face close to the cell-phone sized device, but nothing changed. No light appeared, and doubts again rose in him. He bit down hard and tried to focus his thoughts on the PLB lest he lose hope so soon after he had once again found it.

"I need to get outside," he thought. He lifted his eyes and stared at the shimmering wall of ice. Casting aside all remaining fear in favor of the realization that he had no other choice, he gripped his side and kneed over the condor's nest to the ice wall. He struck it once with an open palm and then again with a fist, both to no avail. It was solid, like rock, and would require force greater than his hands to open it. He pressed his hands against the ice's surface and dropped his head between them, steeling himself against the new panic, and then he noticed the moisture.

Rivulets of water ran down the inside of the ice wall. The cave's heat was starting the process that would eventually free him. All he had to do was wait it out and the wall would melt away. The thought that the outside cold could keep him entombed for months didn't cross his mind for the moment as he realized he also had his source of water while he waited.

FORTY-THREE

THEY FOUND CURTIS'S BODY the day after the avalanche. It was crushed beneath tons of snow and rock at the base of the cliff. There was no attempt at revival as the stiffly frozen corpse was broken and twisted beyond any hope of life. Golden World's rescue team took control of the body, reverently loading it onto a stretcher to winch it up into the Golden World helicopter. The team flew off despite the rangers' request for assistance in locating the last of the missing.

"We've got to get Curtis back to his daddy," said a well-muscled former special ops officer who commanded Golden's six-man team. "We'll come on back if we can."

David Guildenstern, the rangers' leader, knew they wouldn't be back. As he watched the chopper disappear into the snow flurries, he wasn't hopeful. The weather was dicey and getting worse again. The reality was that they needed every able hand to find Sean Donovan before it turned and the blizzard conditions they all expected struck. It was coming fast.

"David, we've got him somewhere around here," shouted June Gleeson, Guildenstern's second in command.

Guildenstern nodded and eyed the massive mound of snow upon which the others were still digging after the removal of Curtis Golden's body. He wasn't looking forward to what he expected to find of Donovan, but he was Search and Rescue, and this was the unfortunate part of his job. They'd already had the jubilation of victory with the quick rescue of yesterday's group and the removal earlier in the day of the animals. Unfortunately, only the dead remained.

"Let's keep at it," he said resignedly and turned to join the rest of his team.

"David, wait," Gleeson said, her eyes still glued to the portable GPS device to which Donovan's signal was relayed from the main station. "The signal doesn't look like it's coming from here."

Guildenstern turned. He strode to Gleeson and looked over her shoulder.

"Golden's beacon was showing up here." She pointed to a spot in the lower right corner of the screen. Donovan's was off a small fraction on her screen. She'd just called into the station, where they confirmed that the two beacons were not coming from the same place. It was hard to know exactly where it was, but it didn't look like it was under the mound on which they were working.

A quizzical look crossed Guildenstern's face. He turned to survey the remains of the avalanche. It stretched far up the gorge to the north. It was definitely possible that Donovan had gotten separated from Curtis and gone over further up.

"They think he's inside the mountain," Gleeson said.

"What do you mean?" Guildenstern asked.

"Somewhere up there," she pointed up the wall where block-sheets of ice clung in thick patches.

Guildenstern nodded slowly. "There're caves up there," he mumbled thoughtfully.

———

Sean's mind was playing games on him. He'd satisfied himself for a time with the knowledge that the ice wall would melt away. In the interim, he had plenty of water, and although he had no food, he convinced himself he could make it for a week without it. Surely by then the ice would be gone, he'd step outside, reactivate the beacon, and his rescue could come.

His positive thinking was short lived. He'd slept and woken two times since discovering the melt of the ice wall. He'd stayed close to the wall with his PLB in hand, and he'd rested, hoping it would strengthen him for whatever effort would be needed when rescue came. But rescue didn't come. Although a rational mind would have argued the ice wall hadn't melted yet, he hadn't stepped outside and reactivated the beacon, and he wasn't in the open where the beacon could be detected, the only thing his mind said was that he was trapped, the ice wall wasn't melting fast enough, it would take months, and he would starve. He had to help it along. He struck the wall, used small tree branches to scrape away slivers of ice, and took off his belt to use the metal clasp for gouging. And he shouted in frustration and fear. He even stuck one of the nest branches through the fissure toward the magma pool somewhere beyond in the hope it would ignite so he could apply direct flame to the ice. None of it worked. He plopped down again in excruciating pain and utter despair, and he did the only thing he could think to bring him peace as he awaited his death: he prayed.

Later, his mind toyed with him again. He heard the thump of blade against air and believed a helicopter had come to his rescue. He shouted until he was hoarse, and he pounded on the ice until he bled; yet no one came, and then he no longer heard the thump.

Now, he heard something new. It wasn't a thumping like a helicopter; it was more like a knocking, a heavy, uneven pounding. It was irregular and unsteady, but it was consistent. He listened intently. He glared at the wall. The sound continued to an unsteady rhythm for several seconds until he heard the voice. Could it be? Did he hear someone shouting his name?

"In here," he shouted back. The knocking stopped. "I'm in here," he shouted louder from a hoarse throat. The knocking started again, this time with more urgency, as if there was more than one seeking access.

"Sean Donovan," he could hear it faintly. "Step back away from the ice," the voice commanded.

Sean kneed backwards, all the while clutching his aching side.

The knocking grew louder until finally a pinprick hole appeared, and then one the size of a fist, and finally Sean saw a face. It was a bearded face of a young man he had never seen before. It was the face of his savior.

FORTY-FOUR

IT HADN'T OCCURRED TO Sean that the others in his party were in jeopardy. They were searching for him—all except the one who put him over the side. He hadn't connected the dots of the storm, the avalanche, and the Search and Rescue team that had braved it all to find him. He remembered, vaguely, asking about the others on the chopper flight out of the Silver Lode, but the only memory that stuck was that they had made it out and he'd been relieved. The thought that one of his group might have died didn't cross his mind. It wasn't until his two broken ribs were stabilized and wrapped, the condor's puncture wound cleaned and bound, and the mild frostbite in two toes dealt with that he'd spoken about the ordeal. It was then that he learned the truth.

Carla, Mary, and his sister Shannon were at his bedside, their faces streaked with tears the morning after his rescue. They'd come up the previous evening, after they'd gotten word from the rangers. They weren't permitted to see Sean, as it was late when they arrived and he was heavily sedated. They spent the night in a Sacramento hotel and were back at the hospital early.

After spending over an hour assuring a distraught Mary that he was fine and then promising he would never scare his "old ma" like that again, Sean was tired. He smiled weakly, and Shannon suggested she and Mary step out for a cup of coffee. Carla, who had stood in the background, occasionally catching Sean's eye over his mother's shoulder, stepped up to Sean and took his hand when the other two left. She smiled, but the lines of worry were still on her face. Thoughts of anger and fear ran through her mind, and she considered adding to Mary's words chastising Sean for taking risks better suited for others, but she said nothing. She looked into his blue eyes and didn't see the disheveled hair and haggard edges of the man. All she saw was the man she loved, and was relieved he was alive.

"You okay?" he asked.

Her smile broadened. She nodded as tears filled her eyes and threatened to spill over. She wiped them away with her free hand.

"Are you?" she asked.

"I'm good." He glanced at himself from his propped position and chuckled. "I was losing it in that cave," he shook his head without looking at her. "I didn't think I was getting out of there." He looked up and saw a tear escape the well in her beautiful eyes. The smile left his face. "They saved my life."

Carla wiped her cheek and felt the mild tug on her hand. Without thought she leaned into Sean, and they embraced. He held tight, smelled the fresh fragrance in her hair. He closed his eyes in thanks that he was alive and able to hold her. She could feel his strength and was suddenly at peace in the comfort of the two of them.

When they parted, she pulled up a chair, sat eye level to him, and clutched his hand. She wasn't sure if she should talk or just sit silently and let him rest.

"I saw Buck's condors," he said. He smiled at the look of surprise on her face. "I was in a nest, Carla. That's how I survived. I went over the cliff and landed on their perch outside the nest. It was a nest of wild condors. The one where Buck found the shell."

Carla shook her head, surprised at the news.

"Do the others know?" she asked. "They're saying the trip was a waste. There's a lot of anger at the Sierra Club, Sean."

"I've got pictures. My phone." He glanced around the room, saw nothing, and concern covered his face. "My phone, Carla. Where is it? I got pictures. Buck's condors are on it."

"Your mom has it. It was in the bag of belongings they gave your mom. I saw it," she said, and he calmed. "It's safe," she said, and hesitated.

"Did the others see them?" she asked.

He shook his head.

"No ... well ... One of them did," he said, and she looked at him quizzically expecting him to continue. But he said nothing about the man who pushed him over the side. He wasn't ready for that yet. He needed to think it through when he was alone. He needed to understand completely and then determine his action.

"I think Curtis knows they were there. He wasn't giving us the whole story, but I'm pretty sure he knows. When he sees the pictures, he'll come ar ..."

He saw the look on Carla's face turn from surprise and interest to sudden sadness.

"What's the matter?" he asked.

"Curtis Golden didn't make it."

"What do you mean?"

"The avalanche took him, Sean. He's dead."

Sean's devastation at the loss of a former friend turned to anger when he was alone again. Although it was possible Curtis didn't know about the condors, Sean knew he was hiding something. But he didn't blame Curtis for what happened. He understood the man's concern for his father, the turmoil created by that concern, and the lies he was telling. Curtis was a good, honorable man. Sean believed firmly the pictures he took would have set Curtis straight. They were irrefutable evidence to a man of Curtis's character, and he would have stood tall as he always had. He would have come back to his senses the way a good man always came back after making a mistake of which he was ashamed. Sean knew he'd be ashamed. He knew it the moment Curtis came out to talk to him in front of the warming hut. He knew it when Curtis smiled at him and told him rock climbing was excellent here. He'd told him subtly that Buck had found the shell where only rock climbers could. Sean wasn't angry with Curtis. He was sad for the loss. He was angry with another, for without that other the loss of such a good man would never have occurred.

Sean knew instinctively that Richard Wolf was behind all of it. It was he who had brought about Curtis's death just it was he who was behind Matthew Dunne's attempt to kill him. He couldn't bring himself to believe Richard instructed Dunne to do it, no matter what he felt about his former friend. Dunne's action was his reaction to circumstances that were beyond him in furtherance of what he believed his mentor wanted. The young man guessed what Sean was planning when he'd followed him out to the cliff. When the massive bird rose like a phoenix out of the gorge's abyss and hung before Sean for the photograph that might destroy their case, the young man reacted. Sean was convinced of that. It didn't justify his action, and Sean had no intention of letting it rest. What he really wanted was that the whole truth come out, however, for he knew it was Richard Wolf's doing.

Wolf's mindless support of his clients' positions combined with his intense will to win at any cost had been stamped into Matthew Dunne. There were no excuses for failure; there never were. In Wolf's book, you either won or you were a failure. The pressure that came from such an approach would be crushing, particularly to a young attorney trying to make his way. Dunne was Wolf's star protégé, no doubt a status earned through zealous, almost vicious, disregard of opponents to the point, perhaps, of doing anything to attain victory … even committing murder.

Sean found it hard to believe that Richard Wolf had crossed the line to complicity in murder, yet the facts rang loud of the possibility. There was no longer any doubt that Buck Anderson was murdered, and the probability that the deaths of the two graduate students who'd found his body and the explosion at the coroner's lab were accidents was unlikely. When Sean added Morgan Finnerty's "accident" and his own ordeal to the mix, the evidence was overwhelming. But Sean knew Richard. He'd turned on Sean and shown his true colors so many years ago, yet even that was a far cry from murder. Or was it?

FORTY-FIVE

ON FRIDAY, RICHARD WOLF wore black. It was another of his two thousand dollar suits, and it fell elegantly over his muscled frame. He wore black because he had a funeral to attend. The favorite son of his beloved client died and was being buried this day in a ceremony that would be covered by the press of the world. Atticus Golden and news surrounding his company commanded that kind of attention, and Richard Wolf was the attorney who stood tall on behalf of the man and his company.

The cause of Curtis's death was the talk of blogs, pundits, and journalists the entire week. Although no one was able to obtain a quote from Atticus or his other sons, Atticus's attorney commanded center stage. He'd spoken about Curtis's valor in leading an expedition into the untamed Silver Lode all because the Sierra Club couldn't see reason, because the club wouldn't acknowledge it was wrong. The Golden project was environmentally sound, yet the Sierra Club, that bastion of self-righteous fanatics interested only in stopping things and never in creating something beneficial, simply refused to see it. And now a wonderful man was dead, but his legacy would live on through the development of the valley he loved even unto death—the valley he wished only to share with the rest of the world.

Wolf couldn't have asked for better press. At a time when jobs were scarce in the Golden State and across the country, his message rang a clarion call: stand with us all you who value the environment and jobs. The public responded loudly with support from around the world. Of course, Wolf would never have wished for the death of such a fine man. The reality, however, was that it could be the lightning rod that settled the matter once and for all. Not even the news that S. Michael Donovan survived his ordeal could diminish the sense of fate and destiny Wolf felt about the project. Even if Donovan had witnessed anything in the valley, who would want to believe him, a disgraced attorney, in the face of the tragedy that had befallen the Goldens?

Wolf's face expressed his sorrow as he pulled into the parking lot of St. Mary Magdalene Catholic Church in Camarillo. He liked Curtis and wished it hadn't gone the way it had. But he was gone, and Richard Wolf would have to stand strong in this moment of despair for the Golden family.

A large crowd gathered early, many to bid farewell to the well-liked Curtis, and others to gawk from behind security ropes and guards at the elite of business and entertainment who'd come to pay their respects to Atticus and his family. When Wolf marched through the throng, he walked with his head high. He heard the whispers of those who recognized him from the media interviews, and although he longed to turn to them and acknowledge them, he knew it would be unseemly. He walked alone, resplendent in his dress and position in the Golden circle.

Inside the church, Wolf sat in a reserved spot in a pew in the fourth row behind three rows of immediate family. Atticus sat with his boys in a separate place cordoned off to the side by a velvet-braided cord and two beefy guards. The old man was slouched over, face drawn and pale with eyes rimmed red and vacant. He barely looked up during the ceremony.

Each brother spoke eloquently and lovingly of their departed brother as did various nieces and nephews. They spoke of a compassionate, loving man who would never have hurt any creature on God's earth and whose purpose in life was to share God's wonders with all. There were few dry eyes in the church, even among the usually cynical press, and the send off proved to be a loving tribute that touched all who attended.

A crowd of nearly two thousand, including uninvited guests outside the church, filed past the closed coffin at the end of the ceremony to touch it lovingly or simply to stand and pray for the repose of Curtis's soul or for the strength of his family. Richard Wolf followed the family to a side room, where they waited together to take the casket to the cemetery.

"I'm so sorry for your loss," Wolf said softly to Atticus, who rose with the help of John and Will as he approached. Wolf bent forward and took the suddenly frail old man in a hug and held him close.

"I killed my son," Atticus croaked in a broken, inconsolable voice into Wolf's ear. Wolf's eyes widened in shock as he pulled away and shook his head.

"No, Atticus," he said softly, yet urgently. "It wasn't," he started and then caught John Golden's stern look of warning. He stopped and glanced at Will, who eyed him sadly and shook his head to warn Wolf to say no more. Wolf nodded.

"He was a great man, Atticus. We're going to miss him," Wolf concluded as Atticus nodded slowly and then slouched back into his seat with the help of his sons.

Wolf accompanied the family to the cemetery and then to Atticus's Camarillo ranch for a wake that included two hundred family members and close friends. He smartly made the decision not to approach Atticus again but rather to make himself compassionately visible to the sons and other members of the circle. As the day drew to a close, sadness and understanding smiles continued to move across Wolf's face, and although he didn't let on, two things began to play badly in his mind.

The first was Atticus's shocking admission of fault. Wolf's belief when he'd first heard it was that the statement was the knee jerk reaction of a grieving father. It was something with which he would have to contend over the weeks before trial. Wolf was sure he could get Atticus back on track. After all, this was his lifelong dream, and he was predisposed to continue the fight, especially after his son died for it. So Wolf went about his business, shaking hands and offering condolences until evening approached and he received the phone call that made him wonder.

"Richard, Liz here," came the tight, terse salutation from Liz Harris, the no nonsense junior partner from Wolf's office.

"Liz … what is it?" Wolf asked sharply as he walked away from the crowd.

"Matt's been arrested," she said.

Wolf stopped dead in his tracks. He stared at the ground, dumbstruck, mouth agape and in silence for several seconds.

"Richard, are you there?" Liz asked.

"What the hell are you talking about?" Wolf demanded.

"I flew up this afternoon to bring Matt home, as we'd discussed," she said efficiently. "Matt signed the release, and the nurse was wheeling him out in the wheelchair when three Sacramento police officers approached. They arrested him for the attempted murder of Sean Donovan."

FORTY-SIX

RICHARD WOLF UNDERSTOOD DAMAGE control. He'd been doing it his entire career. That was his job for God's sake. This one was different though.

"I pushed him, Richard," Matthew Dunne sobbed. Propriety and respect for Wolf's office were long gone.

Wolf sent criminal attorneys up to Sacramento immediately after he'd received the call from Liz Harris. They'd been able to have the bail hearing Saturday morning, and bail was set at one million dollars over the vehement objection of the Sacramento District Attorney, who felt there should be no bail in a case where the defendant had the means and will to flee. The judge didn't buy the argument, as the firm vouched for Dunne and put up the bail. Dunne was home by Saturday evening and in Wolf's office early Sunday morning. Every day since then, the two had met with each meeting ending in seeming understanding, only to find that the next day the distraught young attorney returned to his office.

Earlier in the week, Wolf responded to Dunne's assertion, pointedly stating, "You didn't push him, Matt. You weren't even out there, were you? You were in your sleeping bag. ... The only one missing that morning other than Donovan was Curtis Golden, right?"

Dunne nodded as he raised his tortured eyes to Wolf.

"There's no evidence other than Donovan's fleeting glimpse that you pushed him. How could he know for sure in one quick glance, particularly when everyone's clothing looked similar and whoever it was that pushed him was wearing goggles and a beanie by his own admission."

Again Dunne nodded, understanding coming slowly but surely. He didn't smile at the understanding but rather looked less lost. Clarity seemed to come and then a resolve that his mentor was correct. He hadn't pushed Donovan. Someone else had if indeed he'd been pushed at all. The son-of-a-bitch was only blaming him to garner some of the sympathy that had come to the Forest Service's case as a result of Curtis's death.

And then the next day he'd be back in tears because he knew the truth. He'd done it because Donovan had seen the condors. Dunne was in the doorway when he'd seen it the first time as clear as day as it glided right at them before it veered off, inviting them to follow. Dunne knew Donovan would. That's why he waited up and followed him. He didn't know what he'd do if Donovan saw the bird again. It came to him suddenly; in a flash as soon as the monstrous creature crested the cliff and hung on wind currents for Donovan to snap his shots. Dunne felt powerless as his enemy fired away, gaining the evidence that would undo the firm's work of the past twelve years. He'd reacted. It was without thought, but he was committed the minute he stepped out of the shadows and ran at Donovan. Although his mind was a fog for days after, the awful reality of the evil he'd done descended upon him and tore at his sanity as his mind cleared.

Now, after an entire week of coddling his protégé, Richard Wolf wasn't sure how much more he could take.

"We've been through this enough, Matthew," he said sternly. "You've got to man up here and see the big picture. You pushed him, but his proof is for shit. If you don't stand up and be smart about this, you're going to hurt a whole lot more than yourself. Do you get that?" Wolf demanded.

Dunne nodded, wiped away the tears. His eyes were bloodshot with lower lids sagging. He had aged ten years in the last week.

"He's got no proof other than his word. For you, my friend, you did what you had to do for your client. You know you're on the right side. If those sons-of-bitches bring back anything, all it does is further delay a foregone conclusion, but," he emphasized this with a finger in front of Dunne's nose as he bent down closer to his face, "it also kills your client. They would have murdered Uncle Atti."

Dunne's look was quizzical.

"Don't kid yourself, Matt. They fabricate a case for the sole purpose of delay while knowing as sure as we're here together that the old man dies. Is that anything less than murder: an intentionally wrongful act that kills another man? If anything, Matt, you saved Atticus's life. Your act was in the defense of your client's life."

Dunne nodded slowly. He understood. If he hadn't done what he did, Atticus would have died. He had no choice.

"You okay now, Matt?" Wolf asked as he eyed the young attorney closely.

Dunne nodded again and wiped an arm across his eyes.

"The trial's in less than two weeks. I need you for it. Can you give it to me?"

Dunne looked up at Wolf, who was leaning back against his desk smiling encouragingly like a father to a son. He bit down hard with resolution and nodded firmly. He could handle this. It's what attorneys did for their clients. They stepped up at difficult times. When others would back off, give up, let it go, attorneys made the tough choices, and it was through those choices that they won the day for their clients. He'd saved Atticus's life. He knew it all along … He now understood it so clearly.

"I'm okay this time, Richard. You're right," he said.

Wolf stood and extended his hand to help Matt to his feet. After Matt rose, Wolf put a strong hand on the young man's shoulder and stared him in the eye.

"You get to your work now, son," he said for the first time in his life to anyone. "You're a great attorney. Your client and your firm need you more than ever now. Can you handle it?"

"Yes," Dunne said firmly. "I can do this."

Wolf escorted Dunne to the door, instructing him on the way with the large volume of special motions he still needed completed for the trial. Wolf's purpose was to now push aside the concerns by getting the young man's mind elsewhere. Maybe that would help him deal with the conscience, although Richard Wolf wasn't so sure.

Monday morning at 10:00, Carlos Perez sat in Wolf's office. His brother Billy and his man-mountain bodyguard again accompanied him.

They'd been speaking for just under a half hour, generally about the case and more specifically about Matthew Dunne—how the young man had been so traumatized by the events in the Silver Lode and his arrest, but that he appeared to be under control, although one never knew for sure in such matters. Silence followed for several seconds with Perez and Wolf eyeing each other in silent communication. Finally, Perez moved to the final issue.

"Is this the end of it, Richard?" he asked as he sat imperially across from Wolf. As before, Billy sat in the seat next to him and his bodyguard stood, cymbal sized hands gripped in front of him, behind his boss.

Wolf nodded slowly.

"They can't ask for any more continuances, and we've got the Supreme Court," he said, nodding more assertively this time. "This is it, Carlos."

Perez eyed Wolf sharply. A deadly smirk curled the corners of his mouth.

"This is the end for me and my friends, Richard … no matter how the trial goes," his voice dripped with exaggerated subtlety.

Wolf didn't care for the tone or the message the tone implied.

"We've got just as much vested in this as you and your friends, Carlos," Wolf said with some frustration mixed with a hint of anger that Perez would dare to threaten him.

Perez pulled himself forward in his seat and stood up slowly. He glared into Wolf's eyes as he smoothed the front of his coat. He stepped to the desk and raised a hand, index finger extended.

"I don't give a fuck what you and your firm have in this goddamn case," he snarled and jabbed his finger onto the desk. "I'm telling you that this has gone on far too long now, and my friends are getting nervous. More important, Mr. Counselor, I'm getting nervous. My friends and I don't like to get nervous. When we do, bad things happen to the people who make us so."

He jabbed the air at Wolf. A chill shot through the attorney.

"Don't you give me or my boys any attitude. I'm telling you and your fucking firm that this ends now, Counselor, or there will be some unhappy spouses at your firm's Christmas party this year!" He glared at Wolf.

Wolf struggled to maintain composure, but he wasn't sure how to do so. Threats had been made against him and his firm in the past, but they had always been more distant: an opponent's angry client, a mob of NIMBYs bent on stopping a real estate development, the occasional disgruntled client. Never, though, had a threat of extreme bodily harm been made by a client of Perez's stature nor by one who had the unequivocal ability to carry it out. Wolf raised his hands in supplication.

"It's okay, Carlos," he said soothingly. "They have nothing new that can change the Supreme Court's ruling. It ends with this trial. I guarantee that."

Perez continued to glare at him for several seconds, and Wolf stared back, not flinching despite the fear that coursed through him. Perez finally smiled, stood straight, and ran his hands down the front of his coat again. He nodded curtly.

"Good … that's what I needed to hear," he said. He raised his hands to the sides in a brief shrug and said, "And now, we go. We leave you to your case."

He turned and was followed immediately by his companions. Wolf did not stand.

Wolf's comment that they had nothing that would change the trial outcome was accurate. Sean would have acknowledged as much if he'd been pressed on the issue.

The EIR was solid despite attacks all the way up to the highest court in the land. The U.S. Supreme Court had spoken loudly. The painstakingly analyzed and crafted EIR addressed all potential environmental impacts adequately. Unless compelling new evidence could be presented at trial, the proceeding would be short, and the result would be in favor of the

Forest Service's grant of final approval of Golden World's development in the Silver Lode Valley.

The Sierra Club had been drawing at straws for nearly a year and a half. Their final hope had been that Buck Anderson's discovery could be established with expert testimony to be of such environmental importance that any impact on it by the development would be so great it could not be mitigated. The discovery of wild condors nesting, hatching new chicks, and thriving in the valley might have been one of those discoveries if only they had sufficient evidence and testimony to establish the environmental importance.

Sean, like Buck, knew the condors were wild. The problem was his photographs couldn't confirm that. None of his shots had images of the tops of the wings, which would have shown that tags bearing numbers of their release were missing. Had he gotten any such shots, the opposition would have argued the tags had come off and the creatures were nothing more than captive condors that flew beyond their natural habitat. No matter the argument, however, such shots would have cried out for further investigation; no court would have been able to ignore them had they existed.

To compound their problems, there was no evidence the cave was a nest or that any condors had hatched inside it or anywhere else in the Silver Lode. Of course, a request for further study could have been made, but that would have required a continuance of the trial until after the winter storm season. Such a request by the Sierra Club was out of the question because of their deposition agreement.

Even the California condor experts consulted by Andrew Harper and Pete Luckman with Sean's photographs in hand could offer little hope. To a person, they were skeptical that the images were captured in the Silver Lode. The first response was that they had to be fakes or that the photos were taken elsewhere. It took a mighty effort to convince them the images were real and that they were taken in the Silver Lode—so far from the birds' natural habitat. Even with that, however, none could say without equivocation that the birds could not have flown from the Los Padres National Forest to the Silver Lode. Although beyond their normal range, it was not so far as to be impossible for their captive bred charges to have made the trip.

The tragic thing for Sean, Harper, and Luckman was that they knew they were right. They knew wild condors lived and bred in the Silver Lode, and they knew a development of the scope of Golden World's would destroy them. There was no amount of mitigation that could protect the birds from the cables, electricity, and pollution humans would bring even in the most eco-conscious development. The best evidence of that was in the captive program itself, where even those that were bred and nurtured in captivity found it almost impossible to survive in the habitat to which they were released because of man's intrusion. The remote, often inhospitable environs of the Silver Lode were perfect for the birds, but only if they were left in their natural state.

They struggled with their evidence and spent long hours trying to find the opening that would give the birds a chance at survival.

FORTY-SEVEN

SUNDAY AFTERNOON RICHARD WOLF awaited pickup for his flight to San Francisco. The trial was on Wednesday. He was going up early to instruct Jeff Wuller, the Forest Service's attorney, in final trial preparation and in what he could expect from Judge Tom Marks, Wolf's old law school friend. Although Wolf was more than confident in the Forest Service's case, two matters weighed heavy on him as he prepared for departure.

The first was Matthew Dunne. The young attorney's mood had changed since their discussion in Wolf's office. He'd immersed himself in trial prep, and his work was again of the highest quality. The problem was that Wolf didn't trust him. He tried to convince himself Dunne would be okay, but he knew he wouldn't be. He was fine while immersed in the intense work that took his mind off his troubles, but Wolf couldn't bring himself to believe the young man would be able to stand up under the grueling pressure of a criminal prosecution. He wished he was wrong, but knew he wasn't. The issue, then, was how best to take care of it. He was confident he'd made the right decision.

The second matter was that of his client, Atticus Golden.

Wolf tried his best to give the family space in the weeks after Curtis's funeral. His clerks and attorneys worked with the Forest Service to prepare for what they all expected to be a very short trial. Testimony from someone from Golden World would not be necessary, but someone had to be present at counsel table with Wolf to show the commitment of the bereaved family. Even though there would be no jury, since both parties had waived the right, sympathy would be a factor, even with a judge of Marks's acumen. Wolf met with Atticus on Saturday to make appropriate arrangements.

The attorney was ushered into the office by Atticus's sons. Few words were exchanged on the walk through the magic dust of the halls, and when they entered, Atticus didn't turn to greet them. He sat with his back to his desk, slouched low in his seat, staring absently over his creation. When Will stepped up to his father and helped him swivel to face the others, Atticus didn't smile. He didn't greet any of them. He cupped his hands on the desk in front of him, and he stared at them for several seconds before he looked at Wolf.

"It's over, Richard," he said without emotion. "We're done with the Silver Lode."

Wolf's heart skipped, his stomach lurched, and his mouth dropped open. His shock would have been apparent to all in the room except no one looked at him. All eyes except Atticus's were downcast.

"Atticus," he said slowly, searching for words. The old man stared through him. "Please don't do this, Atticus," he pleaded. "You've fought your whole life for this, and it's now within reach," he mumbled his mantra, but he knew it fell on deaf ears.

"It took my boy, Richard." Atticus's voice was barely audible.

"That's the reason to continue on," Wolf stepped in quickly. "Curtis loved the Silver Lode … more than anything else. He died tragically, but he died for the cause. It's his legacy that the project be completed … in his name … so that all can enjoy the wonders you and he have seen there for years. If you let this go, his death and the life he lived so well in the service of this world will have been for naught."

Atticus's glare turned to daggers.

"His life was everything," he growled. "It doesn't need this project to define it. Don't presume to tell me how to make my son's legacy."

"I'm sorry, Atticus," Wolf backpedaled quickly. "You know I loved Curtis, too. He was the best of men." Wolf searched for words that would soften his client and bring him back to the issue. "I don't mean to suggest his life is worthless without this. All I'm saying is that he loved it. He wanted this more than anything. He was so proud of you and the company and what this project would mean for everyone."

He was going to continue but recognized he'd struck a chord. Atticus's face softened, and he dropped his eyes again. Across the table John and Sandy sat up sharply when they noticed their father's softening.

"It's done, Richard," John said. "We're moving on."

Wolf turned on John, vicious anger about to spew across the table, but he caught himself.

"All I'm asking, John, is that none of us makes a knee-jerk reaction here. We've spent too long getting to Wednesday's trial. We're that close to approval. All I ask is that you don't make the decision yet. The Forest Service is the defendant in the case, we aren't. Let's move forward with the case for which we've prepared for years and then you can decide. Please don't make a decision today that all of us could later regret. A victory Wednesday gives you the leverage to make any decision you choose, even to sell the approved project if you see fit." He hesitated then to let his words sink in. "It's good business."

When Wolf left Golden World's offices, he was in a daze, stunned by the day's shocking revelation. He'd been able to save matters with the Goldens, at least for the trial. But he saw the real support was gone. Curtis's death had thrust open the door John and Sandy were searching for, he thought cynically. They didn't waste any time running through it. They'd continue to resist the project, and Atticus, who was completely wasted away in his grief, was an easy target of their efforts. Clearly an assignment of Golden World's rights to another developer was a possibility after the trial, but that created all kinds of issues, not the least of which was the delay and anxiety it might cause for certain other clients of Richard Wolf.

But, Wolf was a survivor. For now, they would join him at the trial. There would be time to figure out the next step when that was won. Now, Wolf had a plane to catch.

———

As Richard Wolf flew to San Francisco with Liz Harris Sunday evening, Matthew Dunne stayed behind. His initial reaction was disappointment since he was Richard's second chair. He understood the lead counsel in the case was Jeff Wuller, the Forest Service attorney, and that Richard and his assistant were there, not as the main litigants but as representatives of the Real Party In Interest. Still, it took another explanation from Richard to put his mind at ease.

"Matt, you're my man … you know that. You're the best I've got. I'd love to have you join us, but I need you here. Even if we forget the ordeal you've been through, I need someone I can count on here for emergency work out of the office. I don't need you sitting around doing flunky work for me up north. Liz will handle that."

Matt nodded his understanding and maintained a firm upper lip. Richard knew best, and he was honored Richard put such responsibility on him at the home office. He'd be happy to take care of that for his mentor. The problem was he was still disappointed. It would have been better to share the victory in the courtroom.

He left the office at nine o'clock Sunday evening. He'd worked late as usual this day to finish a few items he'd e-mailed to Richard while he was airborne. He also organized himself for the work he'd be doing the rest of the week so he'd be available to assist Richard up north. Who knows, Richard might even call and ask him to drop everything and join him there. That's what Dunne hoped. As for his psyche, as long as he focused on work, he was able to avoid a fall back into the deep void of conscience and remember his act was not just appropriate but necessary for his client's welfare.

Dunne noticed a vehicle behind him as he exited the parking structure of the Century City office, but he paid it little mind. When he turned right onto Wilshire Blvd., he didn't notice that the vehicle turned right behind him. Dunne pushed the satellite radio button to the heavy metal channel and moved into mild traffic toward his home on the west side.

The night was clear after a light rain the day before, and the air was warm enough for him to put his window down and crank up the sound. He immersed himself in the mind-numbing din of music and the waves of air, mercifully purging his mind of all other thought until he glanced casually to his left, out the open window, and noticed that the passenger of the car coming even with his was staring at him. The passenger's window came down slowly, and a moment of recognition struck Dunne. He smiled at the black mustached face of Billy Perez, but in that instant he noticed a slender cylinder jutting out of Billy's chest, just below his grinning face.

The recognition wasn't immediate, but it was quick enough to cause Dunne to jerk his wheel to the right just as the cylinder exploded in flame and a cacophony of staccato bursts that ripped through the cabin of his car. Bullets tore into his flesh, mixing geysers of blood with the flying glass, broken parts, and ripped leather of his vehicle as it swerved out of its lane, up a curb, and into the trunk of an old oak. Screeches of brakes and swerving tires followed the crash, and the car carrying Billy Perez, with license plate missing, sped off into the night.

FORTY-EIGHT

THERE IS LITTLE EVIDENCE that Mark Twain said, "The coldest winter I ever spent was a summer in San Francisco."

Although the statement fits Twain's sense of pithy overstatement in the name of humor, it is doubtful he spoke those words. Whether his or those of another sage, however, the words reflect an absolute: the great city is cold. Even during the summer, folks partake of the city's wonders only with jackets or sweaters on or over their arms in anticipation of the ultimate need. As a typical year moves into winter, going without some well-insulated garment is unthinkable.

Wednesday morning, the temperature outside the Federal Courthouse on Golden Gate Avenue was frigid. Wind cut exposed flesh like a knife, and even wool suits didn't do much to protect those making their way along the street. The sterile, straight exterior lines of the building's architecture invited no thought of the city's storied past; in fact, it lent only chill to those who approached it. Yet a crowd was gathered as the litigants approached the building for the trial that had been so long in coming.

Some onlookers came to gawk at the faces they'd seen on talk shows since the death of Curtis Golden. Others came either to support or to oppose Golden World, many bearing signs screaming their predilections. But the biggest contingent of onlookers was from the press. As with Curtis's funeral and everything else Golden World touched, this event was news.

Uncle Atti worked tirelessly for years for this day. The development would bring jobs to the beleaguered state; it would bring new dreams to all of Southern California; and it would all be done in the name of his beloved son, Curtis. That's how Richard Wolf played it as one of those talk show faces.

Atticus flew up the night before with Will. They stayed away from the press, leaving that chore to their attorney. Now, as Atticus sat at counsel table next to his attorney's chair, Wolf remained outside the courtroom. Will sat in the first row, behind his father, next to the seat where Liz Harris would sit during the proceeding. On the other side of Wolf's chair sat Jeff Wuller, the bearded Forest Service attorney. He kept glancing over his shoulder, hoping Wolf would enter the courtroom before Judge Marks came to the bench.

Wuller hadn't liked Wolf at any time during their association. His predecessor in the case warned him about the man, yet he'd bit his tongue numerous times during their brief association because the Silver Lode development was so important to his superiors, and Wolf was the person who represented the company that could make it a reality. In addition, Wuller had to admit Wolf was good. He understood the issues, the players, and the judge better than anyone with whom he had ever worked. As a result, Wuller swallowed his pride, accepted Wolf's suggestions, and was even grateful for his assistance. He just wished the man were more accessible, particularly now, when he had something he needed to discuss.

Sean approached Judge Marks's courtroom down a wide hall with Andrew Harper and Pete Luckman each pulling portable handcarts stacked with boxes on either side of him. The trio slowed as they reached the crowd gathered around Richard Wolf and his partner, Liz Harris. Both wore large smiles, and Wolf fielded questions with long dissertations on the tragedy of Curtis's death and the great wonder of the project his father was going to build in his name. Sean tried to push through the packed bodies to the courtroom's entry.

"Ladies and gentlemen, here he is now," Wolf said and pointed to Sean and his companions. Wolf wedged through reporters, who turned with his movement and stepped up to Sean. "This is Sean Michael Donovan," he said with dramatic flourish, "co-counsel for the Sierra Club. Mr. Donovan used to be a member of our firm many years ago. Go ahead and look that up. You'll see. He's gone over to the other side." He laughed, and others joined him. "I think we'll show him the error of his ways today, though. Maybe you'd like to ask him some questions."

Microphones rammed into Sean's face, and jumbles of words that included "chances," "why," "Curtis's death," and others geared to create sound bites and controversies were shouted.

Sean frowned uncomfortably, raised a hand in supplication, and tried to smile.

"Sorry, folks, Richard's much better at this than I am. He's the news here, not me," he said and pushed into Harper to get into the courtroom.

The air inside the courtroom hung heavy in stark contrast to that outside the building. It was stuffy and warm from the crush of reporters and onlookers who'd been able to get seats. The modern color and décor of the room provided some respite from the stuffiness, and lighting on the other side of the bar, where the counsel tables sat, was cool and comforting. Judge Marks's bailiff was a large, powerfully built man with a severe crew cut but a soft, low voice and affable nature that seemed contradictory in a man his size.

"I'll take your cards gentlemen," he said as Sean and his companions stepped through the swinging doors at the bar. "I'll get 'em to the clerk. You fellas can get yourselves organized here." After they handed their cards, he said, "You're all here for the Sierra Club?" They nodded, and he turned and walked to the clerk's desk.

Sean nodded at Jeff Wuller, who smiled his recognition before resuming his search for Richard Wolf. Sean's look moved to Atticus, who did not look up. He slouched, staring blankly ahead. Behind him, his youngest son eyed Sean. Sean nodded and smiled sadly.

"Thanks for the card," Will mouthed softly, referring to the sympathy card Sean sent for the family's loss of one of the good guys. Will nodded at his father and mouthed, "He appreciated it."

Sean nodded and touched his open hand to his heart. Will acknowledged the gesture with another nod.

Sean's eyes moved to the gallery. Every seat was spoken for as reporters either sat or stood in front of seats talking softly. Some lucky members of the public had been able to sneak in, and they clung to their seats as if they held great value. Far back on the side behind the defense table sat Carlos Perez. Sean caught his stare between bodies and finally got a clear view as a reporter stepped aside. He eyed Sean unemotionally, simply staring, as if he was in a contest daring Sean to blink first. Next to him sat his man-mountain who barely fit into the chair, and on the other side was a younger man with a thick mustache who bore a resemblance to Perez. Sean nodded. Perez smiled and returned the nod.

At the back on his side of the courtroom Sean spotted Carla and his mother. They smiled when they caught his eye, and Carla gave him a thumbs-up of encouragement. Sean could see someone sitting next to his mother but couldn't make out who it was because of the milling bodies. "Another spectator," he thought before the back door opened and Wolf blew into the room like a strong wind followed by his entourage. Jeff Wuller jumped up to meet Wolf when Judge Marks's bailiff's voice boomed the judge's entry.

"Be seated and come to order," he said. "The United States District Court for the Northern District of California is now in session. The Honorable Thomas J. Marks, Judge, presiding."

The judge lumbered into the room. He eyed Richard Wolf as he stepped through the gate resplendent in his navy suit and took his seat. His eyes next moved to Sean, who was seated, looking up at him. Marks nodded and gave Sean a half smile, which Sean returned.

"He's put on some weight," was Sean's initial thought. He hadn't seen his old friend in a good fifteen years, maybe longer. He'd grayed at the temples and back of his head and probably would have done the same on top except that what thinning hair he had the last time they met was now gone completely. He wore rimless eyeglasses that slid slightly down his sturdy nose, and his complexion was florid, particularly with the extra weight. Sean dropped his head and smiled at a fleeting memory of a drunken law school golf tournament he and Marks had attended.

"Good morning, ladies and gentlemen," the judge said in a voice that still carried the moderately-high pitch of his law school years but now bore the unmistakable timbre of authority.

Counsel uttered their "good mornings" in unison.

Marks dropped his eyes to his hands, flat in front of him on the bench, and appeared to be deep in thought for several seconds. Finally, he raised his head.

"Gentlemen," he started, "I considered recusing myself from this proceeding when I learned that Mr. Donovan had joined the plaintiff's team. As some of you may know, Mr. Donovan and I were in the same law school class together, and we were friends. When this matter was handed to me and I saw Mr. Wolf's name as the representative of the Real Party in Interest, I considered recusal at that time as well, because Mr. Wolf and I had also been in the same law school class. I did not step away from the case in the early going because Mr. Wolf did not represent one of the name parties in the case."

He eyed all counsel and their clients slowly.

"I have determined that I can be fair hearing this matter and that I will not be influenced by my relationship with either of the two attorneys. However, I will leave the decision to you. If there is any concern on anyone's part, I will step aside and hand the matter over to one of my colleagues. It is your choice," he extended his arms to the attorneys.

Richard Wolf stood immediately.

"Defendant and Real Party in Interest have no objection to His Honor hearing this matter."

The judge looked from Wolf to Jeff Wuller, who stood as Wolf was finishing.

"It appears the Forest Service might have a different opinion, Mr. Wolf," he said.

Wolf turned and glared at Wuller, who stood for several seconds thinking, not knowing which way to go before he finally turned to the judge and shrugged. "The defendant has no objection, Your Honor."

Marks turned to the other table. Harper and Sean had their heads together, considering the judge's request. When the conversation ended, Harper continued to stare at Sean even as he, Harper, stood up. Sean nodded. Harper looked at the judge.

"Plaintiff has no objection, Your Honor," he said.

"Good ... Thank you, gentlemen. Let's get started then," said Marks.

FORTY-NINE

SEAN AND HARPER WHISPERED a quick conversation about the
opportunity presented to them by Judge Marks while Wolf and Wuller
were responding to his question. They considered whether the judge's
recusal would continue the case without their having to request it. If no
other judge was available to hear it, or if a new judge would need time to
get an understanding of the case, they might be able to get a long delay that
would give them the time they needed to continue their investigation. Sean
glanced past Harper to Wolf and noted concern on his former partner's
face. Clearly, Wolf was still of a mind that any delay was out of the question.
Although their choice seemed obvious on its face, Harper and Sean had
other concerns that took the choice away, among them the possibility that
such a choice might be considered their request for a continuance. They
made the only choice they could.

"State your appearances, gentlemen, and let the court know if you are
ready to proceed."

Andrew Harper stood first. He stood slowly, staring at Jeff Wuller as he
did so. Sean also looked at Wuller, whose elbows were propped up on the
table in front of him with his head cupped face down, in his hands. Sean
and Harper glanced at each other; Sean nodded.

"Thank you, Your Honor," Harper started. "I'm Andrew Harper. I'm
here today with Sean Donovan and Pete Luckman. We are co-counsel for

the Sierra Club of California, plaintiff in this matter. Plaintiff is ready to proceed to trial."

"Thank you, Mr. Harper," Marks said and then looked over at Wuller, who still had his head in his hands.

Harper and Sean stared at Wuller. They held their breaths.

They were as ready as they could possibly be given that their only witnesses were going to be Sean and two experts. They knew they'd get objections from Wolf and Wuller on a number of grounds and that their only hope of getting any of Sean's photographs into evidence and thereby having anything for the experts to discuss would be in the hands of the judge. Although it was not unheard of to have a party's counsel testify as a percipient witness, it was unusual, and they hoped Marks would allow it even if it resulted in an appeal. But they also had one other hope, and that's why they stared at Wuller.

"Counsel?" asked the judge.

Wolf glanced at Wuller quizzically and nudged him. Wuller shot him a sidelong glance before he stood up.

"I'm sorry, Your Honor," he started. "I'm Jeffrey Wuller." He spoke firmly as if he had resolved something as he sat head-in-hand. Wolf eyed the judge as Wuller spoke, and his own face carried a smug smile as he waited his turn to put his appearance into the record. Wuller continued. "I am the attorney for the United States Forest Service, Defendant in the case at bench." He glanced at Wolf, who started to stand.

"Your Honor, although the defense had hoped to proceed with its case today, we must ask this court for a continuance of this proceeding."

"WHAT?" shouted Wolf, leaping to his feet. A murmur arose from the gallery. Sean and Harper turned to each other with broad grins spreading across their faces.

"What are you talking about?" Wolf demanded. He glared at Wuller before he turned to the bench. "Your Honor, we don't want a continuance. We don't need a continuance. Defendant and the Real Party in Interest are ready to proceed." He pushed in front of Wuller, muscling him into his chair.

The audience murmur grew. Reporters stood; cameramen snapped photos. Judge Marks grabbed his gavel, pounded it, and shouted above the growing din.

"Order! I want order in this room right now," he pounded again. "I'll clear this courtroom if I do not have order immediately."

The judge glared into the gallery, which quickly came to order despite the tension ready to burst.

"Don't make me pound this damn gavel again. I swear to you I'll throw you all in jail."

He looked at his bailiff and motioned him to move to the defendant's table where he directed his attention. Wuller was sitting in his chair, pushed back behind Richard Wolf, who stood in Wuller's place facing the judge, bent forward for battle, his fists clenched and jammed into the top of the table in front of him.

"Mr. Wolf, step aside so Mr. Wuller can give us a damn good reason why he's asking for a continuance. I must be very clear here that I am not inclined to grant a continuance in a case that has been sitting around this courthouse for well over a decade. Mr. Wuller?"

Wolf bit down hard, gathered himself, and turned to Wuller. He glared hate at him before stepping aside. Wuller stared challengingly at Wolf, who finally sat down. Wuller stood to address the judge. Silence fell over the courtroom.

"Forgive our table's outburst, Your Honor," he glanced at Wolf with disgust on his face. "I represent the people of the United States of America in this matter, Your Honor. My superiors at the Department of Agriculture received word late yesterday that the U.S. Congress and the President of the United States have requested this matter be continued so that the development of the Silver Lode Valley can be taken up in Congressional hearings as part of their consideration of the Omnibus Wilderness Act." Murmurs of incredulity broke the silence and crescendoed throughout the courtroom. Reporters scrambled over one another to get outside to make their calls. Judge Marks pounded his gavel, and Wuller raised his voice. "The Forest Service does not wish to take up this court's time if the future of this property is to be decided by the executive and legislative branches of this country's government," he closed with a shout.

Wolf was red with rage. He sprang at Wuller, grabbed his arm, and jerked him around to face him.

"You son of a bitch," he shouted amidst the growing cacophony. He raised his arm and balled fist. Wuller flinched and raised his hands in defense. "What do you think you're doing?" Wolf shouted and swung.

His strike was caught in mid flight by the burly bailiff.

Wolf struggled to free himself. The bailiff held tight to the arm with his other squeezed around Wolf's mid-section.

"You best back off, Mr. Wolf," he whispered menacingly in Wolf's ear as the attorney struggled against the man's bulk and strength. "You calm down now, or I'll be forced to get rough with you."

Wuller glared at Wolf. Judge Marks stood, pounded his gavel, and shouted for order. Bailiffs and security from other courtrooms charged into the room.

At the plaintiff's table Sean stood slowly in front of his chair. He took in the burbling chaos with a smile of deep satisfaction. He faced the bench, said nothing. He glanced to the ceiling, closed his eyes, and stood quietly, lost in the peace and calm of a great moment.

Senator Walker Krebs, senior senator from California, was passionate about his country's environment. He sponsored the Omnibus Wilderness Act that had wended its way through both federal houses for years. Its purpose was to provide large swathes of the country's untamed land the protection of the Wilderness designation, the highest environmental protection in the country. Krebs had always been a fan of Buck Anderson and listened with great interest to the environmentalist's pleas to include the Silver Lode in the bill. But, as Buck well knew, there was never sufficient evidence to justify its inclusion, particularly when the impacts of development could be mitigated according to the numerous studies done of the issues.

The Sierra Club's attack on the Silver Lode project had resulted in years of such studies. The constant scrutiny, appeals, and resulting changes in plans were something in which the Club could take pride, for without their efforts, the project would be underway, and the devastating harm the mitigations were intended to alleviate would be in process. Hundreds of pages in the EIR, contributed to by thousands of commentators and every conceivable agency, considered and provided mitigation for every impact ... at least that's what most believed after the Supreme Court's ruling. But Buck had additional information.

He'd kept the senator apprised of his efforts without giving him any specific information—only that the valley had to be saved because no amount of mitigation could protect the sensitive habitat he believed he'd discovered. Krebs, of course, welcomed Buck's efforts. He had long believed the Silver Lode was a national treasure that should be preserved in its natural state, but he never had the evidence to make his case to Congress.

The Sierra Club's case had run out of steam. After years of battle there were no more arguments. Yet there wasn't one among the members who didn't believe losing the Silver Lode would be a devastating blow to the disappearing natural environment of Southern California. Buck Anderson provided them one last hope.

As Sean worked with Harper and Luckman after his return from the Silver Lode, he understood well that his case in court was weak. It wasn't because they were wrong, for being wrong would have made a decision to back off very easy. It was only because their proof was weak. Sean knew Buck was right. He believed the Golden project would destroy one of the most magnificent natural wonders of California, and with it would go the only habitat in which the nearly extinct California condor actually bred and lived wild. It was this sincere conviction that helped Sean see the new path.

Senator Krebs took Carla's call immediately because of his long relationship with her uncle. When Carla introduced Sean on the telephone, Krebs was skeptical until Sean explained how he'd come across the evidence Buck had promised the senator.

"I was in the cave with them, Senator. They were wild," he said.

"I appreciate the ordeal you suffered, Mr. Donovan, but, if I understand you correctly, you have no evidence other than your word and some suspect photographs that they were wild. Is that true?"

"Yes," Sean said and sucked in a deep breath. "I know that won't prove anything, Senator. Not even the testimony from our experts can establish for certain from the photos that the birds I saw were wild."

"Then what do you think I can ..." started the senator.

"Please, Senator, hear me out," Sean interrupted, and Krebs hesitated. "The experts can testify right now, from the photos, that the bird I photographed in the cave is the largest they have ever seen. They can testify that although they don't know for sure it's not one of the Fish and Wildlife Service's captive bred birds, they do know none of those captive birds was anywhere near the size this one appeared to be at any time during their monitoring. They will state unequivocally that the photos, while not great, certainly open the door for more investigation and analysis. Senator," Sean didn't hesitate to let the senator get a word in, "this could be the most significant event in the long struggle to save this creature from extinction. To have a wild pair breeding in the wild is monumental."

Sean waited with baited breath while Krebs was silent for several seconds. Finally he spoke resignedly.

"Mr. Donovan, I must again say that I appreciate your efforts. However, this bill has been years in the making and will be coming up for a final vote in the Senate in less than a month. I don't think I can ask my colleagues to give me more time, especially when some of them are so close to the fence to begin with."

Sean was thunderstruck. He believed his plea would be welcomed with zeal from a senator known for his environmental passion, that it would require Sean and his experts to meet with Krebs and his colleagues, that, in the end, it would work the way it was supposed to, with the Silver Lode being included in the act. But the senator hadn't bought it.

"Mr. Donovan," Krebs started softly, "I'm sorry I can't help with this. If I had any real position that I could take to my colleagues, I would, but ..."

"Senator," Sean interrupted again, frantic that the call not end with a denial. "Senator, please ... you do have a position. It's the same one, sir, that you waited for before Buck's death. I saw the evidence Buck was going to bring you. I was in the nest in which Buck found the hatched shell. I crawled over the nest, was trapped with it. I'm not Buck Anderson, Senator. I could never *be a man of such staunch conviction and charisma that he could turn even the most hardened anti-environmentalists around, but I'm all that remains of Buck's hopes, hopes that you held firmly, to save the last magnificent wilderness area in Southern California. Buck was killed for those hopes, Senator. We can't let his death be the death of the Silver Lode and the wild California condor. If we had the time, we could still save it."*

After another long silence, the senator said, "Can you and your experts come up to Sacramento and show me what you've got?"

For the week and a half before the trial, Sean, his Sierra Club cohorts, and their condor experts met with Senator Krebs and several of his committee members with their evidence. On the day before the trial, Krebs gave them the word.

"I see what you have here, gentlemen. I believe Buck was right and that you, Mr. Donovan, have brought us the information Buck originally discovered. I don't know if it's too late, but I'll do my best to get this matter before the full Senate as soon as possible. As for your trial tomorrow, unfortunately, I don't know what I can do. I have my legal team looking into the matter, but I don't know. All I can tell you is that I will try."

By the time they left for the courtroom, they still hadn't heard from Senator Krebs.

Sean breathed calmly as order slowly returned to the courtroom. He opened his eyes and took in the judge standing behind the bench, looking sternly over the assemblage. To Sean's left, past Harper and Wuller, Richard Wolf, red-faced and enraged, was held down in his chair by the bailiff's powerful paw. And beyond the bailiff sat Atticus Golden. His blue eyes, whitening now with the age he'd held at bay for so many years, were fixed on Sean. A sad smile turned his lips. He nodded. Sean turned to the bench.

"Your Honor, Plaintiff has no objection to the defense's request for continuance. We only request that it be long enough for our country's legislature to conduct their hearings before we are forced to come back and take up any more of this court's time."

Marks continued to stand, his chair pushed back against the wall behind the bench.

"Defendant's motion for continuance is granted," he pounded his gavel, and the murmur started again. "This matter will be continued for one year!" he shouted, slammed the gavel again, and looked at the bailiffs and guards in the courtroom. "Now clear this courtroom," he commanded and stormed away from the bench, into his chambers.

FIFTY

BY THE TIME THE courtroom was clear of spectators and the press, the enormity of Richard Wolf's defeat had sunk in. He sat alone, Atticus now in the front row of the gallery, sitting quietly with his son while Liz Harris stood at the clerk's desk with Jeff Wuller, Harper, and Luckman looking at the calendar, finalizing the technicalities of the continuance. Sean sat alone, too, but for him it was in savoring victory he had not experienced in many years. The aura of calm and peace was pure and so complete that he wanted nothing but to sit in its wash.

And so he did until Harper and Luckman approached him with wide grins on their faces. They squeezed and patted Sean's shoulder before they started gathering their things to leave the courtroom. Sean finally leaned forward, took a deep breath, and gathered his own notes into his briefcase. Jeff Wuller stepped to their table, shook hands, and eyed the three. He nodded slowly.

"I'm glad it's working out this way. That place was magnificent," he said. "Congratulations." He then pushed through the gates with his briefcase in hand and left.

Liz Harris had completed packing Richard Wolf's materials and was helping him to his feet. Wolf stood unevenly, slack jawed and ashen faced, and seemed to need the support of his partner. They staggered past the plaintiff's table and the gallery without a word or glance to opposing counsel or his own clients.

The Sierra Club counsel came next, and despite rules against communicating with opposing clients, Sean stepped up to Atticus, who stood slowly with his son's assistance. The old man extended his hand to Sean.

"We should have had you on our side, Mr. Donovan." Atticus's voice belied his frail appearance. It was still strong, and his eyes peered into Sean's.

"Thank you, Atticus. I appreciate that," he said as he clung to the old man's hand. "I just want to tell you again how sorry I am about Curtis. He was one of the best men I ever knew."

Atticus dropped his head in thanks and then looked back up at Sean and smiled.

From behind Sean, Judge Marks's bailiff spoke softly again as quiet reigned in the courtroom.

"Mr. Golden," he said. "Judge Marks asks if you and your son would like to leave the courtroom the back way." He pointed to the door behind the bench that led to the judges' chambers and a back hall and elevator out of the building. "You could avoid the press this way."

Atticus and Will nodded appreciatively. They looked again at Sean, smiled, nodded, and followed the bailiff.

Richard Wolf emerged from the courtroom to the crush of press. Uncharacteristically, he did not smile for photographers, nor did he respond to the inane questions he had always been able to turn into pithy sound bites. Richard Wolf was numb. His entire countenance expressed it. He leaned heavily against Liz Harris, who staggered under his weight as she coaxed him along. Security personnel and U.S. marshals tried desperately to clear a path for them, but nothing could stop the photographs, microphones, and raucous flood of questions.

At one point, a large arm reached out of the crowd, grabbed Wolf's arm, and lifted Wolf's weight from Liz Harris. She turned sharply to see

Carlos Perez's man-mountain holding onto Wolf, pulling him toward Carlos. Security guards jumped to Wolf's aid, but a quick daggered look from Carlos to Liz Harris made her wave them off. Carlos stepped past the press of bodies and stood inches from Wolf. The crowd fell silent as all craned their necks to see what was happening. Even the emergence of Sean Donovan and the Sierra Club attorneys didn't change the focus of the crowd, now glued so intensely to the unfolding drama. Carlos leaned in close with his mouth only an inch below Wolf's ear.

"You messed up, Counselor," he rasped in a deadly monotone. "My friends and I are not happy."

Wolf seemed to come to as his client's words ran through his consciousness. He pulled his head away, stared down at Perez, and then tried to pull out of the bodyguard's grasp, but Esteban held tight.

"You don't pull away from me, Counselor. You and your firm are mine," Perez hissed.

Wolf pulled back again, this time exerting some of his own strength, and a marshal next to him saw his discomfort. He stepped between Perez and Wolf and glared at Perez's mountain. They stood transfixed for several seconds before Perez finally nodded to Esteban to release his grip on Wolf. Perez smiled at the marshal. He looked past the marshal's arm to Wolf again.

"I'll see you soon. Keep your eyes open," he said as a wide, malevolent grin spread across his face.

Wolf turned away, now under his own strength. Gone was the shock of the devastating loss, replaced now by the animal need for self-preservation. He pushed past Liz Harris, leaving her staring after him, shocked at his rudeness and loss of control.

Far down the hall, a tall man with a nondescript dark suit led a contingent of six uniformed federal marshals through the security path of press and onlookers toward Judge Marks's courtroom. Wolf marched brusquely toward the contingent, his senses frantic for escape, until he noticed the man in the suit slowing down, glancing at a piece of paper, and then looking up again at him.

"Richard Wolf?" the man asked.

Wolf stopped, glanced around, and then looked back at the man.

"Are you Richard Wolf?" asked the man again.

Wolf nodded slowly, hesitantly.

"Would you come with us please?"

"What for?" he asked. "What is this?"

"You're under arrest, Mr. Wolf." Wolf staggered, stepped back. The man stepped toward him. "You're under arrest for conspiracy in the murder of Buck Anderson and in the attempted murders of Morgan Finnerty and Matthew Dunne."

His briefcase slipped from his fingers. He staggered again, started to babble something, and then fell. The man in the suit grabbed him before he hit the ground. He helped Wolf down, motioned one of the marshal's to help, and then stood with the other marshals at his heels.

Back down the line of onlookers, Carlos Perez pushed into the wall. The man in the suit eyed Perez's man-mountain, who could not blend into any crowd. The on-lookers parted as the man stopped in front of Perez's position.

"Carlos Perez," he said firmly. "You and Guillermo 'Billy' Perez," he pointed at Billy standing to his brother's right, pushing into those next to him, "are under arrest for the attempted murder of Morgan Finnerty and Matthew Dunne."

Perez glanced around wild-eyed as one of the marshals reached for him. He threw off the marshal's arm, turned, but was hemmed in. Esteban reached for the offending marshal, grabbed an arm, and twisted as he leapt in front of his boss to make space. People from the crowd were thrown to the ground as the man burst forward and raised his arm to strike anyone within his reach. Two well-muscled marshals jumped at the charging hulk and swung clubs that landed heavily on his shoulder and stomach, bending the big man as he began to flail indiscriminately at his attackers, throwing them both to the ground. When he grabbed at the man with the suit, he stopped short as the muzzle of a Taurus PT945 was rammed into his forehead and the other marshals drew their revolvers. Within seconds, all three men were handcuffed and being marched up the hall passed a reviving Richard Wolf.

"Tu Muerta!" spat a crazed Carlos Perez over his shoulder at Wolf. "You're dead, you son of a bitch. All of you in that firm!" he shouted, and the marshal escorting him jammed an elbow into the proud man's midsection, causing him to fold over in a gust of lost air and dizziness that caused him to black out. The men accompanying him carried him to the elevator.

Sean watched the marshals lift Wolf to his feet. When he was steady, they pulled his hands behind his back and cuffed him. Wolf looked up slowly through suddenly blood-shot, sagging eyes. His face bore no expression, all wit and strength gone. The perfectly coifed, immaculately dressed attorney was disheveled and completely beaten. He glanced about the hall until his eyes found Sean's.

"What did you do, Richard?" Sean whispered to himself sadly. He stared at his former friend, and a cloud of melancholy cast a shadow over him. He shivered at how easily this once promising attorney had been duped by his own sense of worth to take such an evil turn. To throw away all the good he could have done for something even now he knew Wolf couldn't define.

Wolf stared vacantly at Sean, as if he looked at him but didn't see. The marshals turned him then and escorted him back up the hall. Reporters and onlookers followed in quick succession. Soon the only ones left in the hall were the Sierra Club attorneys, Sean, and, standing some ten feet away against a wall, a quartet that included Mary Donovan, Carla Anderson, and a young man and woman.

Sean's gaze landed on them. He smiled as he saw Carla smiling and then grinning broadly when their eyes met. Sean stepped toward them and wondered for a moment who the two young people were. The boy looked to be in his mid-twenties and the girl slightly younger. And then he stopped, stunned. He could see himself, a younger version with a darker caste and better looking, staring at him. Next to his younger self he saw his former wife, but even prettier because she was lighter of hue with the auburn tint of the Irish in her hair and the jade green of Egypt in her eyes.

"Johnny?" he stammered.

The young man took a step forward; the girl clung to his arm.

"Marie?" Sean said, his hands slack at his sides, his legs heavy and immobile.

Tears came to the girl's eyes as she released the young man's arm, and he took another step toward Sean. He reached out his hand.

"Dad," he said with a strong voice.

Sean mustered the strength to extend his hand. The young man took it firmly, and a surge of warmth ran up Sean's arm. "Is that you, son?" he asked, and, as the boy nodded, tears overflowed Sean's eyes as he pulled the boy to him. He wrapped him in a monstrous hug that the boy did not return until his sister joined them.

"Daddy," she cried and ran into the embrace of Sean's now extended arm.

He held them both with Marie's arms gripping him tightly and finally Johnny's wrapping around Sean and his sister. Behind the kids Mary and Carla stepped forward, tears streaming. They, too, joined the embrace.

EPILOGUE

MATTHEW DUNNE DIDN'T DIE in the barrage of bullets that tore his car apart. Billy Perez's aim, born of arrogance, was horrific. When Dunne woke in the hospital, just before midnight, he was in a mood for conversation. Police officers milling about the emergency room received an earful. It didn't take much for federal prosecutors, once they were called, to arrange for Dunne to turn state's evidence against Richard Wolf and the Perez brothers. The shock of his former mentor's betrayal was short-lived when he realized he wasn't out of the woods until he was hidden away somewhere safe. The story he told was beyond the mother lode as far as prosecutors were concerned. Not only had he overheard Wolf's instructions regarding the assassination of Buck Anderson; he'd actually been a part of the discussion, a silent part, of course, but a part nevertheless. And that was only the beginning. For a simple agreement to grant him full immunity, Matthew Dunne, protégé of Richard Wolf, gave prosecutors everything.

The partners at the internationally acclaimed law firm of McCormack, Stein & Wolf abandoned their former head partner as soon as it was clear there was merit to the charges brought against him. The firm might have survived the fallout from the criminal prosecution and lifetime incarceration in a slew of federal penitentiaries but for one small problem. In addition to being the lead partner, Richard Wolf was in charge of investments of the firm's savings and retirement accounts. The partners ended up being the ultimate owners of a lot of greatly overpriced real estate in and around the city of Visalia once the United States Congress completed its studies of the Silver Lode Valley and included the area in its Omnibus Wilderness Act for signature by the President less than one year after Richard Wolf's arrest. To compound matters for Wolf's former firm, the Jackson family collected on the irrevocable letter of credit for the sale of their property, and it was the firm that stood behind that letter, especially after the assets of Carlos Perez and his family were confiscated in conjunction with drug raids precipitated by Matthew Dunne's information. McCormack, Stein & Wolf, together with each of its partners, was wiped out financially. The associates ran for the hills; the firm disappeared.

As for Sean, he found a new life. Make no mistake—he had much explaining to do to his children. There was much healing to be done, and that would take time. But for Sean Michael Donovan, time meant nothing anymore. He had as much of that as was necessary to share the gift of happiness he now knew with those he loved.

ACKNOWLEDGEMENTS

SOME BELIEVE NOVEL WRITING is cosmic inspiration spewed on paper. The truth is that hard work, intense drive, grueling research, and heart-wrenching struggle are far more important than inspiration. A novelist must have vast knowledge or, more likely, do extensive research of the places, events, people, and settings experienced in his novel even if such elements are entirely fictional. Such knowledge and research is essential to breathing life into the story. The most difficult of story elements are the characters. It is not simply a matter of describing physical, emotional, spiritual and psychological characteristics that bring the players to life. The author must live in each character's head to ensure the actions and words that come from that character are real. The task is akin to our childhood daydreaming when we all believed the world was fantasy and fairytale, and we became the characters about whom we dreamed. The main difference is that we now know the real world, and the process of separating ourselves from that world to live in the mind of our fictional characters is painstaking. I am amazed at the ability of modern writers like Robert McCammon, Larry McMurtry, Scott Turow, Dean Koontz, and Joe Abercrombie who create living, breathing characters to whom all of us can relate. I thank them and other great writers for the many hours of wonderful characters, places, times, and events to which they have introduced me. I hope someday my abilities will approach theirs.

I wish to thank the Sierra Club Legal Defense Fund for its terrific 1990 coffee table book titled Wild By Law. The Fund's work in saving some of this country's most magnificent places was part of the inspiration for this book. The rest came from my years as a lawyer and as a student of the people I have had the great pleasure to know.

I would also like to thank Julie Doughty for her reading and magnificent editorial advice on the book; Scott, Debi, Cathy, Mark, and the people at About Books, Inc. for helping bring this work to print; and Marika and Elaine at PR by the Book for helping inform the world this book exists.

The Third Term

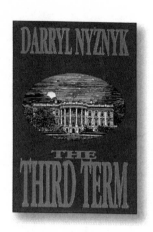

... *masterful plot of terror, faith, deception, and conviction. Readers will be drawn immediately into a carefully and splendidly crafted vortex of memorable characters and unpredictable events.*

MIDWEST BOOK REVIEW

Keep your eye on Darryl Nyznyk. ... He is on a par with the best – already better than Grisham, Forsyth, and Harris.

JOHN ANTHONY MILLER,
PHANTOM BOOKSHOP

Mary's Son

Winner of the Mom's Choice Gold Award for Fiction and Inspiration

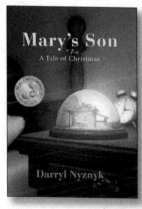

... a wonderful and poignant story ... an inspiring read that reinvents the real Christmas story and crowns it with a modern twist.

LAUREN SMITH, EZINE BOOK REVIEW

Aimed at readers of any age, it's a book for all seasons.

ROGER ZOTTI, RESIDENT BOOK REVIEW

"... a timely, inspirational novel" that has the *"hallmarks of a new Christmas classic."*

CARL ANDERSON, SUPREME KNIGHT
OF THE KNIGHTS OF COLUMBUS

Made in the USA
San Bernardino, CA
06 July 2020

75039620R00222